Clawthorn

By Keith A Pearson

CW00468094

For more information about the author and to receive updates on his new releases, visit...

www.keithapearson.co.uk

Author's Note

Clawthorn is the third instalment of a series. You'll appreciate (and understand) the story to a greater degree if you've read the first two novels in the series: *Who Sent Clement?* and *Wrong'un*. Both novels are available from Amazon in ebook and paperback format.

If you've already read both, welcome to Clement's next adventure...

1.

My legs are cold and the polyester skirt too tight around the waist. I should have followed my instincts and worn the navy-blue trouser suit. Fuck funeral etiquette.

The organist concludes the service with a stirring rendition of *Amazing Grace* as the pallbearers lift the coffin and edge their way down the aisle of the packed village church.

Contained in the polished walnut casket is my old friend and colleague, Eric Birtles. Actually, it isn't Eric, but an already decomposing mass of flesh and bone. According to the priest, Eric's soul is already heading off to some wonderland in the clouds. I kind of hope he's right but suspect he isn't.

The pews at the front clear one by one as the mourners shuffle down the aisle. There are a few faces I recognise but most of the congregation are strangers.

As the pallbearers pass my pew, I look to the floor and start counting to sixty in my head. Once that minute has passed I dare to look up; just in time to catch sight of a few stragglers at the end of the sniffling conga as they head into the vestibule. The church falls silent.

I'm not keen on either people or religion; ergo, I'm no fan of funerals, and this one isn't over yet.

Wearily, I get to my feet and traipse outside.

Unsurprising for November but fitting for the day, the sky is a sombre shade of grey. The mourners are already five deep around the grave and that suits me. I can stand on the periphery and disappear the second this farce is over.

I shuffle close enough to afford myself a reasonable view of Eric's forever home and watch on as the casket is lowered into the grave. The priest then continues with a quote from *Corinthians,* apparently.

"Behold, I show you a mystery: We shall not all sleep; but we shall all be changed."

Rather than listen to a priest going through the motions, I let my mind drift towards memories of Eric, and happier times.

I left Manchester University in 1993 armed with a first-class degree in English. Determined to forge a career as a journalist, I cut my teeth working for a provincial newspaper in a sleepy market town. Six long years passed before I accepted I was never going to win a Pulitzer Prize reporting on village fetes and charity fundraising events. I then managed to land a job at a national but I was so far down the food chain I could have proven the identity of Jack the Ripper and nobody would have taken me seriously.

Then, Eric joined the team and took me under his wing.

Thirty-one years my senior, he was already an established hack and a winner of countless awards -- I learnt so much from the man. Eric treated journalism like archaeology, and believed the truth had to be slowly and meticulously unearthed. We were partners in crime for seven years before the paper closed its doors and we went our separate ways. Eric retired and I secured the best job I could find, which wasn't a particularly good job but it paid the bills.

"We therefore commit his body to the ground."

I return to reality. The priest bends down, grabs a handful of soil, and scatters it into the open grave.

"We come from dust; we return to dust."

Beginning with Eric's widow, the mourners then take turns throwing soil into the hole — when you think about it, a ridiculous gesture.

With no great finale, the funeral comes to an end. Slowly, the crowd disperses as thoughts turn to the wake, and the drowning of sorrows no doubt. This is my cue to exit.

I manage a dozen steps across the damp grass before a voice calls out. "Good Lord. Emma Hogan, as I live and breathe."

It's a voice I recognise but I'd rather ignore. Unfortunately, I'm too close to pretend I didn't hear.

I turn around and feign a smile. "Oh, hi, Alex."

It must be nine or ten years since I last saw my former colleague, Alex Palmer. He hasn't aged well.

He waddles over and pecks me on the cheek.

"You're looking well, Emma. How's life treating you?"

"Not bad, thanks. You?"

"I'm in fine fettle, thank you."

An awkward silence ensues as Alex searches for a conversation starter, and I search for an appropriate excuse to leave.

He wins the race with a moronically obvious statement.

"Terrible, wasn't it — what happened to poor Eric?"

Is there a non-terrible way to die? Drowning in a fishing lake wouldn't have been my choice but if you want to put a positive spin on it, at least Eric died doing what he loved. I think he'd have chosen that way.

I try to look grave. "Truly awful."

Alex shakes his head before moving the conversation along. "Are you going to the wake? It'd be lovely to catch-up."

No, Alex. It really wouldn't.

"Ah, I'd love to but I've got a prior engagement back in London."

"You still live and work in town?"

"Yep, for my sins."

I check my watch and Alex takes the hint. He plucks a business card from his pocket and hands it over.

"Give me a call and we'll have that catch up."

"Will do. Good seeing you, Alex."

Both lies slip effortlessly from my lips.

I scurry away just as the clouds decide to emit a fine drizzle.

By the time I make it back to the overcrowded car park, my hope of making an early escape is already scuppered. Rather than join the queue of cars waiting to exit, I sit in silence as the view beyond the windscreen blurs into a series of obscure shapes. If there really is a God, he couldn't have chosen a shittier afternoon to send Eric on his way.

Long minutes pass by as the gloomy weather and occasion suck at my soul. Before I know it, and without being conscious of any specific trigger, I feel a tear roll down my cheek. It's quickly followed by another, and another.

A crushing realisation sweeps over me — Eric is gone. The man who was more of a father to me than Dennis Hogan ever was — the despicable excuse for a father I've never met, or ever want to meet.

I choke back my tears and search the glove box for a tissue. Grief is a wicked emotion, and I've suffered enough of it over recent years to know how it plays. It lurks in the dark corners of your mind, and just when you think it might have finally left, it resurfaces at the most unlikely moments. Eventually, you accept it will never leave, and although the sharp edges dull, it still taints every subconscious thought for months, for years.

Pull yourself together, woman.

I take a moment to heed my own instructions. The rain stops and the last of the cars clears the exit. Time to head home.

The inbound journey through the Surrey countryside was fraught, due to my tardy departure from London. Now, I can take my time and appreciate the rural scenery. Although I hated the job, the time I spent working for the provincial newspaper offered a welcome change from living in London. When I left, I promised one day I'd escape the concrete and the crowds and see out my days in some rural idyll. The reason Eric is now buried in the village of Alford is he retired here, and I can see why.

For now, though, I have a career of sorts which keeps me tied to

8

our capital.

As I pootle through the country lanes, my thoughts turn to Alex Palmer. He was never a handsome man but the years have added pounds and stripped hair. I wonder what he thought of me. Have I changed that much? My hair is short and butter-blonde, which helps to conceal the grey, and I've managed to maintain a relatively slender frame due to good genes on my mother's side, rather than through diet or exercise. My face, however, is certainly showing the years; probably because I like a drink and the occasional cigarette. Some might call it 'lived-in'.

Notwithstanding how either of us have physically fared, seeing Alex is a reminder that time is marching on at an alarming rate. And with every passing year, that time seems to gather pace. I did go through a stage of telling myself I hadn't even reached the midway point of my life, but after my forty-sixth birthday I had to concede living to ninety-two might be a stretch.

I acknowledge I'm depressing myself and switch the radio on.

The sat nav informs me I need to take the next turning on the right. I comply, and turn into another narrow lane with no clear line of sight due to the meandering tarmac and high hedgerows. I'd rather avoid a head-on collision with a tractor so keep my speed low. The lane snakes left, and then right, before a long stretch of clear road allows me to up my speed.

The hedgerows peter out affording me a view of the surrounding fields and leafless trees. I'm sure the view is glorious in the summer but under a doleful sky it feels grim and foreboding.

I catch the slightest flash of blue light in the corner of my eye. It comes and goes in a blink.

Dabbing the brake pedal, I glance at the wing mirror. That glance becomes a prolonged stare once I identify the source of the blue light — three police cars parked on an open patch of ground next to a scattering of single-storey buildings.

As any good journalist will tell you: one police car is probably nothing but two or more, particularly if their lights are still strobing, and there might just be something worthy of reporting. In this case, three police cars are too much of a temptation.

I find a suitably wide stretch of verge and pull over.

A familiar feeling arrives as I step out of the car. Eric used to call it 'the buzz'; a sudden rush of adrenalin as your journalistic sixth-sense piques. He told me it was the only thing he missed after he retired, and why he took up fishing. Apparently, it requires the same saintly levels of patience before you finally experience the thrill of a catch.

I trot back down the lane as the buzz builds.

As I reach the open patch of land, I notice a sign almost buried in weeds: *Kenton Stables*. That answers one question. The reason why three police cars have been summoned to a rural stable yard remains unanswered, and my curious nature doesn't do unanswered.

A uniformed police officer arrives on the scene.

"Can I help you, madam?"

He's young, and therefore inexperienced — just the kind of police officer I like.

"I was just wondering what was going on."

"There's been an incident."

The word 'incident' is like cat nip to a journalist.

"Oh. What kind of incident?"

"I'm afraid I can't say, Ms ...?"

"Hogan, and it's Miss. I was supposed to be meeting a friend here. We always go riding on a Tuesday afternoon."

He eyes me up and down. "Is that your usual riding attire?"

"No, silly," I giggle like an air-head. "I've just been to a meeting. My friend is bringing a change of clothes."

"What car does she drive?"

Shit.

"Oh, I've never been good with makes of car. It's a white saloon."

I follow the officer's eyes as he scans the car park. Besides the police cars there are two other vehicles; neither of which matches my description.

"Looks like she's not here," he says flatly. "And I'm afraid the stables will be closed for the rest of the day."

"Right."

"Have a good afternoon, Miss Hogan."

His pleasantry is my cue to leave. I may have underestimated the young officer but I'm not ready to give up just yet.

"Nobody's been hurt have they, officer?"

"As I've already said, I'm not at liberty to divulge any information."

The answer to my question pulls into the car park; in the form of an ambulance.

For a moment, the officer appears torn between dealing with a nosey bystander and more pressing duties. He splits the difference and asks me to leave before striding off towards the ambulance.

I watch on as he gesticulates at the paramedics. This is my chance.

There are two wooden structures some twenty yards ahead of me; most likely stable blocks. A path runs between the structures and I can see several other police officers milling around which suggests it's the focal point of whatever incident they're investigating. I'll get short shrift if I head that way so my best option is to skirt the far boundary of the right-hand stable block. From there, I can remain hidden while watching the action unfold.

I risk another glance at the still-occupied young officer and make a dash towards the corner of the car park. The perimeter boundary is provided by a thicket of brambles which virtually abuts the stable block. However, there appears just enough space between the thorny barricade and the stable-block wall for me to squeeze through.

Another glance towards the police officer and he's now leading the paramedics wherever they need to be. Even the slightest turn of his head and he'll spot me. That threat proves the final push and I squeeze myself through the narrow opening, pressing my back against the damp wooden panels to avoid the wall of thorns.

I'm five foot six, but the thicket is at least seven feet high while the stable-block wall is higher still. As I shuffle sideways, I can only thank my lucky stars I don't suffer from claustrophobia. I do, however, suffer from wearing inappropriate footwear, and the cold mulch reaches my ankles. The sixty-quid shoes become another in a long line of sacrifices I've made for this career.

Whatever this incident is, it better be worth it.

Inch by inch, I edge closer to daylight. Not for the first time in my life I question what the hell I'm doing, but true to form, I press on in pursuit of answers.

Finally, I reach the end where I can peer around the corner; safely protected from view by the stable-block wall and surrounding undergrowth.

I recoil after taking my first peek.

Whatever is going on, it's happening in one of the stalls barely twenty feet from my vantage point. If anything, I'm too close and I need to be cautious. I squat down so I'm not directly in the line of sight and peek around the corner again. My timing is spot-on as the paramedics lead out an elderly man, and a woman who appears to have Down's syndrome. Before I can extract my phone and take a photo, they turn their backs on me and shuffle away. The waiting ambulance could be their destination but as they're both walking, rather than occupying a stretcher, I can only assume they're not the reason three police cars and half-a-dozen officers are in attendance.

As the couple disappear from view, I scan the wider area. A paddock, hemmed in by railed fencing, occupies most of the immediate view. Maybe sixty yards away a police officer is talking to a man in a navy-blue coat. I can't see the man's face but he appears animated as the officer scribbles notes.

I return my attention to the officers stood by the stable block and their lack of urgency suggests whatever brought them here is now over. Am I simply witnessing an over-reaction by the local police? There doesn't appear to be anything untoward going on, so why the cordon tape?

My attention is then pulled back to the scene as a man bursts through the stable door and marches across the open space towards the paddock. If his huge frame wasn't distinctive enough, he also happens to be dressed like an extra from *The Sweeney*, complete with bell-bottom jeans and a denim waistcoat. Hot on his heels, and at least a foot shorter, is a woman with sharp features and a somewhat pissed-off expression.

The two of them head towards the police officer still taking notes from the man in the navy-blue coat.

Words are exchanged and the conversation appears heated — perhaps I haven't missed the action after all. I pull my phone from my jacket pocket and, using the camera app, zoom in as close as the lens will allow.

Just as the camera finds focus, the man in the navy-blue coat turns to his left. I finally get to see his face.

"Holy shit," I gasp.

The man in question is William Huxley. *The* William Huxley.

2.

Eight hours ago, I wouldn't have recognised William Huxley if I passed him in the street — just another faceless backbench politician. However, after a damning front page revelation in a national newspaper this morning, I suspect Mr Huxley's days of anonymity are behind him.

The revelation was as scandalous as it gets, centring on an allegation from Huxley's half-sister that she'd indulged in an incestuous relationship with the Tory politician — one of those rare stories that can make a career, and I read it with envious eyes.

As of this afternoon, when I left London, nobody in the press had managed to track down William Huxley, let alone secure a comment from him. By some miraculous fluke, I've found him in the middle of nowhere, and seemingly in more hot water. Not that I believe in such things, but it's almost as if Eric has bestowed this rare opportunity as a parting gift.

The buzz reaches new heights as I watch on and snap several photos of William Huxley.

Judging by the way the uniformed officer has stepped back from the discussion, and her plain, functional attire, I'd wager the stern-looking woman is a detective. Her initial focus was on the big man but Huxley quickly intervened and the two of them are now embroiled in an animated discussion. The politician then reaches into his pocket and holds something up. Whatever it is, it provokes a deep scowl from the woman. She spits a few more words before spinning on her heels and heading back towards the car park.

Huxley and the big man then turn and lean against the railed fence. They talk for a few minutes before the big man storms away. As Huxley watches him leave, his face adopts a dejected expression — understandable, considering the day he's having. It sounds callous but, if I'm able to forge a headline story from whatever is going on here, his day, indeed his week, is likely to get much worse.

However, I need a lot more answers than I currently possess before I can think of front page exclusives.

More activity at the stable pulls my attention away from Huxley. The feisty detective has returned, alongside a thin, white-haired man in civilian attire. Carrying a bulky briefcase, I'm fairly certain he's a crime scene examiner.

The pair wait as an officer leads a chestnut-coloured horse out of the stable. Assuming the horse isn't a suspect, and they're not whisking it off for interview, I'd guess it needs to be re-homed while the crime scene examiner does his thing.

With the stable vacant, the duo enter.

Whatever is at the centre of this incident, that stable clearly contains the answers I need. Somehow, I need to know what's going on in there but the two policemen stood outside make access a near-impossibility. I could settle on revealing William Huxley's whereabouts, and that'll earn plenty of column inches tomorrow, but it's akin to being offered a free meal in a Michelin-starred restaurant and leaving after the starter.

Think, Emma. Think.

The damp wood I'm leant against offers a possibility — the adjacent stable.

If I can get in there, I might be able to hear what's being said. And if Eric is still delivering miracles from the afterlife, I might even be able to find a crack in the dividing wall and see what's going on.

Turning my attention to the stable-block wall, I'm encouraged to see the six-inch wooden slats have suffered from prolonged exposure to the soggy environment. On closer inspection, one slat in particular, nearest the damp ground, has warped to such an extent I should be able to force my fingertips behind it. I crouch down and do exactly that; ruining a perfectly good set of French tips in the process.

The sodden wood feels almost sponge-like to the touch, and should come away easily enough. I brace myself and tug. The slat departs its home with minimal resistance. With the bottom slat removed, it's easy enough to slide three further slats out of the frame so I'm left with a two-foot high gap I can crawl through.

Before I make my move, best to check on proceedings outside the stable to ensure my actions haven't caught anyone's attention.

I take another peek around the corner.

The two officers are still at their post, and William Huxley is deep in conversation with the same frail-looking man escorted away by the paramedics earlier. I take a couple of quick photos, just in case the man is in some way connected to whatever is going on here.

Now satisfied my crime has gone undetected, I return to the gap, and the realisation I'll have to kneel in the mulchy ground to gain access. No sense in thinking about it; I drop to my knees and poke my head through the gap.

Despite kneeling in mud and decomposing plant matter, I couldn't be more pleased.

The dividing wall between the two stalls doesn't reach the ceiling and I can clearly hear voices from the mystery stall. Better still, that same wall has a fist-sized hole in it which will allow me to see what's going on, and possibly take a few photos if I'm careful.

Barely daring to breathe, I carefully squeeze through the gap and crawl on my hands and knees across the floor of the empty stall. It would be a stretch to say it's a pleasant experience but the cold and the damp and the discomfort are a price worth paying for the thrill. My much-younger, millennial colleagues rely upon social media or the wider Internet for research, but give me proper, old school investigative journalism any day. It's why I fell in love with the job and I'm too old to change my ways; even if those ways involve bending the law from time to time.

I reach the hole and take a moment to let my adrenalin levels ease. I sense I've stumbled across something big here and if I'm caught now, it would be galling.

As I wait, a woman speaks.

"Can I leave you to it, Bruce?"

"Sure."

The female voice seems to perfectly fit the woman I saw outside, and I presume Bruce is the crime scene examiner. It appears my luck has run out and there won't be any conversation to eavesdrop. Any evidence will now have to be seen rather than heard.

I shuffle nearer to the hole and take a tentative peek.

My efforts are initially rewarded with the view of an upturned bucket and a pungent waft of horse piss — they won't be holding the presses for either revelation. I'm just about to shuffle a few inches to the right, in order to change the field of view, when Bruce suddenly coughs. I almost soil myself — he can't be any more than a few feet away from the dividing wall.

Pausing to let my heart rate settle, I assess my options. If Bruce is stood up, I can gaze through the hole with little chance of being spotted. However, if he squats down for any reason, he'll be at the same level as my vantage point and likely to notice my beady-green eye watching him at work.

It's an all-or-nothing punt: I look through the hole and hope, or sit here and wait until I know for sure he's moved further away from the dividing wall. The problem with the latter option is I could be discovered at any moment. If the detective insists on a thorough search of the grounds for any reason, I'm toast.

Time is not on my side.

Taking care not to make even the slightest sound, I crawl a few feet to the right so I can view the rear section of the stable. Once I'm in position, I turn and peer through the hole.

I'm rewarded with a sight I wish I could immediately unsee — the motionless upper body of a woman lying on the floor. Her head is mercifully turned the other way so I can't see her face, but what I can see is a knife protruding from her blood-soaked pullover.

Two involuntary reactions occur almost simultaneously. Firstly, my stomach spins a full revolution threatening to deposit my lunch on the stable floor. Secondly, I omit a noise somewhere between a shriek and a gasp.

The first reaction goes unnoticed. The second does not.

A shadow appears. It's accompanied by another cough but this time it emanates somewhere above my head.

Still reeling from the shock, I look up. My gaze is met by the face of a clearly agitated crime scene examiner.

"Officers," Bruce yells. "Here, quick."

Shitty, shit, shit.

I scrabble back across the floor and throw myself towards the gap I entered only minutes earlier. I know my chances of escape are slim but if I'm held by the police, I'll have zero chance of writing anything before tonight's deadline; and my still-spinning stomach is a reminder there's a lot worth writing about.

After an unceremonious exit through the gap, I edge my way back along the stable-block wall as quickly as I can. Almost as if they're trying to assist in my apprehension, the thorny bushes grab at my jacket all the way.

I reach the car park and skirt the perimeter in the hope I won't be noticed. It doesn't work.

"Oi! Stop right there!"

I wasn't even aware I was being followed, but I turn to find two police officers only twenty feet behind me. The game is up.

Coming to a stop, I raise my hands in surrender.

"Okay, okay," I sigh.

The first officer approaches — the same young officer I spoke to earlier.

"You again," he snaps. "I thought I told you to leave."

I've not been blessed with many talents but an ability to think on my feet is fortunately one of them.

"I know, but I needed to check on my horse. He's not been well."

As his middle-aged colleague draws up beside him, the young officer looks me up and down.

"If that's the case, why do you look like you've been crawling through a bog, and why were you spying on my colleague?"

Before I can answer, the sour-faced female detective arrives on the scene.

"Detective Sergeant Banner," she announces, holding up her warrant card. "And you are?"

Seeing her up close is like looking in a mirror. She must be more or less the same age as me, and has that same hardened exterior born from years of working in a similarly misogynistic work environment.

"Emma Hogan."

"Right, Ms Hogan. What are you doing here?"

I repeat my lie.

"She arrived just before the ambulance, Sarge," the young officer confirms.

"And you wanted to see your sick horse?"

"Yep."

Our eyes lock and we both instinctively know what the other is thinking.

"Cut the crap, Miss Hogan. Unless you fancy a few hours stewing in the cells, tell me what you're really doing here."

If Sergeant Banner really is like me, and can detect bullshit at a dozen paces, I know there's no point in keeping up the feeble pretence.

"I'm press."

"There's a surprise," she scoffs. "Who tipped you off?"

"Nobody. I was at a friend's funeral in Alford and just happened to pass by. I saw the police cars and thought I'd check out what was going on."

"Nothing is going on."

"Nothing? I'd hardly call a dead woman with a knife in her chest *nothing.*"

"An unfortunate accident," she shrugs. "There's nothing here likely to interest the press so I suggest you sod off before I nick you."

"For what?"

"Criminal damage, for starters."

She then turns to the young officer. "Check her ID and escort Miss Hogan off the plot."

"Yes, Sarge."

As she's about to turn and walk away, I grasp the final opportunity to ask a question.

"William Huxley. How is he involved?"

"You'll have to ask him."

Sergeant Banner then marches away, leaving me to her uniformed subordinates.

Once I've proven my identity, the two officers lead me all the way back to my car. With a stern warning not to get on the wrong side of Sergeant Banner, they wait at the roadside until I pull away. I cover a few hundred yards of tarmac and check my mirror to ensure they've returned to the stables.

I pull over and switch the engine off.

Grabbing a notepad from the glove box, I scribble down all the salient facts from my brief visit to Kenton Stables while they're still fresh in my mind. Admittedly, the facts are thin and unanswered questions plentiful. What was William Huxley doing there; particularly considering this morning's revelation? Who was the poor woman lying dead on the stable floor? Who were the two men with Huxley — the frail man and the big guy in denim? And where does a woman with Down's syndrome fit in with all of it?

As dusk arrives, I continue to sit and stare at the notepad, trying to see a picture from the limited amount of jigsaw pieces.

I smack the steering wheel in frustration.

If I'm to submit a story before tonight's deadline, it'll be riddled with conjecture and supposition. It'll be a story, but not the story I want to write. Sure, I'll get some credit, but if I cast it into the public domain now, every reporter in the country will be on it tomorrow and I'll lose the chance to complete the picture.

I need more time, and the identity of the dead woman would go some way to joining the dots. Time to push my luck.

After a laborious six-point turn in the narrow lane, I drive back towards the stables. Slowing to a crawl as I approach the car park, I aim my phone and press the record button to capture the scene. Besides the police vehicles, there are two other cars parked up: an Audi 4x4 and a Ford Fiesta that appears to have seen better days.

With their number plates captured, I continue down the lane and re-set the sat nav to take me home another way.

I now have something to go on and, coupled with an additional twenty-four hours for research, this story will be worth reading — I'd stake my career on it.

3.

My journey back to Kilburn was horrendous — pelting rain and mile after mile of crawling traffic.

However, I used the two hours wisely by formulating a plan of sorts.

The minute I arrived home, I put my plan straight into action with an email to Stuart Bond; a detective in the Metropolitan Police.

I met Stuart at a drinks party two years ago — the attraction was immediate and mutual. We met for coffee, twice, before we slept together. The sex was the better side of average, and for a few months I thought I'd met someone I could potentially spend the rest of my days with.

Turned out Stuart was married, with three kids. Wanker.

Once I'd got over the realisation all men really are bastards, I ended our relationship. I did threaten to tell his wife about our affair but the satisfaction would have been brief and hollow. I had a better idea — to make Stuart my bitch. So, whenever I need information only the police are privy to, I send him an email and attach the same selfie photo of us, naked in bed together. It's a reminder that fucking the wrong woman has consequences.

It's now seven in the morning and Stuart probably won't see my email for an hour or two. Last night's research determined William Huxley doesn't drive, so the two cars parked up at the stables have four potential owners: the frail old man, the big guy in denim, the corpse, and the woman with Down's syndrome.

I'm hoping Stuart comes back with a woman's name as the registered keeper of one of those vehicles. If he does, it shouldn't be too difficult to establish if that keeper is the corpse or the woman with Down's syndrome. My money would be on the former as only a small percentage of people with Down's syndrome possess a driving licence. Once I know the dead woman's identity I'll have something to work with.

After coffee, toast, and a ten-minute shower, I'm ready to leave for the office.

Gone are the days when journalists flocked en masse to Fleet Street. Once Rupert Murdoch moved his assets to Wapping in the mid-eighties, the decline set in and every national newspaper eventually left. The once famous home of world journalism is now just a byword. It still rankles I never got the chance to work there.

I leave the flat and immediately wish I'd worn a warmer coat. My motivation to get to the office is stronger than my hatred of the cold so I dig my hands deep into my pockets and begin the five minute walk to Kilburn Park tube station.

The offices of The Daily Standard are located in Belgravia; a twenty minute Tube journey to Hyde Park Corner followed by a half-mile walk. All told, my commute takes less than forty minutes. It would be quicker to drive but the office doesn't have parking and a staff reporter doesn't earn anywhere near enough to pay the exorbitant parking charges in one of London's most affluent areas, let alone the central-London congestion charge on a daily basis.

I arrive just after eight and head for my cubicle via the coffee machine. A few of my colleagues are already at their desks but there's still a quiet hush over the open-plan newsroom. It won't last. In an hour's time, it'll be thrumming with noise as calls are made and received, and fingers incessantly tap at keyboards.

I log-in to my computer and check the email inbox. Nothing from Stuart yet but that doesn't stop me from initiating the second part of my plan. That involves a quick chat with the chief editor, Damon Smith. I call his extension.

"Yep," he answers on the third ring.

"It's Emma. Have you got five minutes?"

"What's the magic word?"

Prick?

"Please."

"I'll give you three."

He hangs up.

Damon is two years my junior and half the journalist — he knows it, I know it, and it's the likely cause we dislike one another so intently. The only reason I still have a job is because one or two suits in the boardroom still appreciate my style. They won't be here forever, though, and once I lose their support, Damon will almost certainly find a way to terminate my employment.

I head over to his office, knock the door, and enter without waiting for permission.

He doesn't look up from his computer screen. If you stripped away his repugnant personality, Damon might actually be considered an attractive man, although he's too clean cut for my taste.

There's precious little point in wasting time on pleasantries so I get straight to the point.

"I stumbled across a potential story yesterday … a big one."

"And?"

"I need to borrow a couple of interns today to help with research."

He looks up and the glint in his brown eyes is obvious. Savouring the moment, he sits back in his chair and runs a hand through his mop of dark hair. It's always the same old routine — nothing comes easy where Damon is concerned.

"Research on what, exactly?"

I need to be wary. Although I can't prove it, I'm certain Damon has previously leaked my leads to his favoured reporters. On at least half-a-dozen occasions, I've worked on stories only to find one of my younger, and usually prettier, colleagues has already had a similar story accepted for the next edition.

"It's about a politician, and the unexplained death of a woman in Surrey."

"I need more than that."

"I'll tell you more when I know there's something to tell."

"In which case you're on your own."

"Don't be difficult, Damon. If I miss this opportunity, we all lose out."

"Tell me who the politician is."

As Huxley's incest story is already yesterday's news, time is of the essence. My story needs to be in tomorrow's edition or we'll have missed the boat. I guess there's no harm in giving him a name — it's useless without knowing what happened at Kenton Stables.

"William Huxley."

Damon ponders my revelation for a moment before reaching down beside his chair.

"Are we talking about the same William Huxley who was exposed by one of our competitors yesterday?"

"The very same," I reply, perhaps a little smugly.

He slaps a newspaper on his desk.

"Take a look at the front page," he orders.

Confused, I reach for the paper and unfold it. The front page is dominated by just four words: *William Huxley: an Apology.*

"The whole incest allegation was a crock of shit," Damon confirms. "And their editor has already been forced to resign."

Front page apologies are as rare as they are humiliating. Typically, a retraction or apology would be buried a dozen pages in, and restricted to a few column inches. Clearly the paper has royally fucked up.

"Bad luck for them," I shrug. "But what I'm working on has nothing to do with this."

"But it involves Huxley?"

"Yes."

"Drop it."

I toss the paper on the desk. "I don't want to drop it, and just because those idiots screwed up, doesn't mean I will."

"It's not open to debate. Huxley is off limits, and that's not just my order. I received an email from legal about twenty minutes ago."

"This is bullshit," I snap. "Huxley was up to something yesterday and I've got photographic evidence."

"Don't care," he says dismissively. "His lawyer is baying for blood which makes William Huxley tabloid kryptonite at the moment. A six-figure lawsuit would bankrupt us, so whatever you think you've got on him, we can't print it."

"But ..."

"Close the door on your way out."

He returns his attention to the computer monitor so misses the glare I deliver before slamming the door.

I return to my cubicle to stew. For several minutes I contemplate returning to Damon's office and resigning but it would give him far more satisfaction than I'm willing to sacrifice. Besides, I have a mortgage to pay and living in London is bloody expensive — I need this job.

Once I've calmed down, I have to swallow the same conclusion I always have to swallow after a row with Damon: my options are limited. In an ideal world I'd go freelance and write what the hell I want. Most of my contemporaries work that way, but the steady income that comes with being a staff reporter is my safety net. And living as a singleton, I don't have the benefit of a partner contributing to the mortgage payments and other bills.

Pragmatism wins the day and I try to get on with other work but William Huxley remains an itch I can't scratch. In the end I torment myself by looking at the photos I captured yesterday, hoping to find even the tiniest thread of hope should I decide to go over Damon's head.

Nothing comes of it.

An hour into my day and just to rub salt in my wounds, an email arrives from Stuart. For a split second I consider deleting it, unread, but I'm a slave to my own curiosity. As my mouse hovers over the email, I kind of hope he's refused my demand for information, or confirmed neither vehicle is registered to a female owner.

I open the email.

A few lines of text dash my hopes and stoke resentment when I learn the decade-old Ford Fiesta belongs to one Amy Jones — a high likelihood she's the dead woman. Of perhaps less interest is the Audi belongs to a Kenneth Davies, who might be the frail old man or the big guy in denim — no way of telling.

The revelation, combined with what I already know, does little to scratch my itch.

People die in accidents all the time but rarely do people accidentally stab themselves in the chest. Add that to Huxley's presence on the same day he was front page news, and it's enough

32

fuel for a conspiracy bonfire. There is a story here — I just know it.

Another email arrives, from Damon.

True to form, the email is a warning. Any further investigation into William Huxley will be considered gross misconduct, with immediate dismissal the stick. To enforce the seriousness of Damon's threat, he's copied the email to both the paper's legal department and the entire board of directors.

It now comes down to a simple question: what is more important — my journalistic integrity, or paying a mortgage? It's not a question I have to ponder too long. Unless the bank is willing to take integrity as a payment, I have no choice other than to forget what happened at Kenton Stables.

I'm not sure I believe it, but as Eric once told me: some stories are best left untold.

SIX MONTHS LATER...

4.

Kilburn was always considered a bit of a shithole; it certainly was when I bought my flat back in the late nineties.

It's now a shithole with overpriced property and too many coffee shops.

The two-bedroom flat I call home was a bargain because, at the time, it was located above a kebab shop. A year later, the food hygiene branch of the local council condemned the place and shut it down. The premises then became a pizzeria, but that only lasted eighteen months before they went out of business. Unsurprisingly, I now live above a coffee shop called The Jolly Barista. The smell of freshly ground coffee wafting through my bedroom window is preferable to that of doner kebabs or burnt pizza, for sure.

I have to settle for a mug of instant as I lie in bed and wait for the caffeine to deal with my tiredness.

Necking the dregs, I check the time on my phone: seven-thirty. I need to leave for work by eight, but my motivation levels are at an all-time low.

It's not unusual to suffer post-Christmas blues, but to still be suffering those blues in April is unprecedented. Perhaps I'm going through a particularly bleak mid-life crisis, or God-forbid, the menopause has decided to pitch-up ahead of schedule. I don't know why life feels so empty right now but whatever the cause, I'm struggling to shake it off.

My job isn't helping — that much is certain.

Damon has continued to be an arsehole and opportunities to write anything worthwhile have been few and far between. As much as I'd love to blame Damon, I do fear it's the industry as a whole rather than the editorial policy at The Daily Standard. Our profession is changing, and not for the better. The world now wants its news fast and dirty. Fake news is rampant and too many vacuous non-stories, which wouldn't have made it to the editorial slush-pile ten years ago, are now hitting the front page. But the bills still need to be paid, so I write not for the love, but the money — more whore than journalist.

I get up and go through the same old routine, with the same low expectations of another uneventful day ahead. Operating on auto-pilot, I manage to shower, feed myself, and consume another cup of coffee. A reluctant glance in the hallway mirror and I'm ready to leave the flat.

After completing the tedious journey to work, I arrive at the office and head straight to the coffee machine. Brown sludge acquired, I slope over to my desk and check my email inbox. Time appears to stand still as I sift through the pointless and the painstaking. As I thump the delete button for the umpteenth time one of my colleagues pitches up.

"Good morning, Emma."

I look up to find Gini Varma loitering with intent. Short, with the deepest brown eyes, lustrous black hair, and an ever-present smile,

I've always thought Gini's happy-go-lucky character would be better-suited to a nursery than a newsroom.

"It's definitely a morning," I mumble in reply.

"Sounds like someone hasn't had enough coffee yet," she chuckles.

Gini is a sweet girl and one of the few younger staff members I can tolerate. Unlike most of her contemporaries, she has a good work ethic and doesn't live in a bubble of self-entitlement. In the time we've worked together, she's matured into a bloody-good journalist and despite her puppy-like demeanour, Gini possesses the tenacity of a terrier. When she bites on a story, there's no letting go.

"No amount of coffee will make this morning better," I reply.

"Anything I can help you with?"

"No, you're alright, but thanks for asking. Anyway, did you want something?"

Her deep brown eyes flick left and right. "It's, um, Damon. He wants to see you in his office."

"Great. Do you know what he wants?"

"He didn't say."

"Right, thanks."

Gini departs and I finish my coffee before reluctantly heading to Damon's office.

I arrive to find the door open and stride straight in.

"You wanted to see me?"

"I've got a job for you."

He hands me a single piece of paper which turns out to be a brief sheet for an interview. I quickly scan it.

"Seriously, Damon?" I groan. "You've got to be kidding."

He glares up at me. "Do I look like I'm kidding?"

"But why me?"

It's a pertinent question. The Daily Standard has been granted an exclusive interview with some talentless bimbo from a reality show, and I'm the unfortunate sap who has to conduct said interview.

"I don't know a thing about Stacey Stanwell," I add.

"Precisely. I want a proper in-depth interview about her new role, and that lot out there will be too starstruck to ask the right questions."

He waves his hand towards the newsroom.

"Her new role?"

"She's secured a leading role in a movie; due out next month."

"Oh, for fucks sake, Damon. This isn't news."

"The news is what I say it is. Miss Stanwell has a huge following on social media and an exclusive will attract a ton of visitors to our website."

Why am I not surprised? Everything we write these days is aimed at getting more clicks to our website so the advertising department can justify their existence.

"Wouldn't this be better suited to Gini?"

"Gini is working on something else."

"So you thought you'd dump it on me?"

"Last time I checked we pay you a salary each month. That means I get to decide what you write, and if you don't like it you know where the door is."

It's a tired old line but one Damon knows I can't ignore. It seems I will be interviewing Stacey Stanwell after all.

"Oh, and one other thing," he adds. "No half measures. If this interview doesn't blow me away, I'll see to it you spend the rest of your career writing horoscopes. Clear?"

"Clear," I huff.

Instructions received, I return to my cubicle and sulk. I know it's childish but I feel better for it.

It takes a lot of caffeine, and a Danish pastry, to lighten my mood. No matter how much I complain, this kind of crap is now my job, so I've no choice but to suck it up until something better comes along.

I grab the brief sheet and call Stacey Stanwell's personal assistant. A taut-voiced woman answers with her name: Trina Smith.

"Hi. This is Emma Hogan from The Daily Standard."

"Who?"

"Emma Hogan. My editor, Damon Smith, asked me to get in touch to arrange the interview with Stacey."

"Okay, yes. Bear with me."

I hear the repeated clicks of a mouse as Trina presumably checks Stacey's schedule.

"How does July sixteenth work for you?"

"As in three months from now? I thought this interview was to promote her movie debut next month."

"Is it? Oh, um, bear with me."

More clicks of the mouse.

"I don't suppose you could do one o'clock this afternoon?"

The only thing less appealing would be a sudden bout of thrush.

"Don't you have anything available later in the week?"

"I'm afraid not. The only reason Stacey has a spot free this afternoon is because her nail technician has gone into labour."

Knowing her type it comes as a surprise Stacey hasn't insisted on a fresh set of acrylics between contractions.

"Fine. One o'clock today then."

Trina asks for my email address so she can send over a list of subjects I'm not allowed to discuss. It'll go straight into my junk folder: unread.

I end the call and rearrange my schedule for the day. With Damon's warning still fresh in my mind, I suppose I'd better conduct some cursory research into Miss Stanwell's career.

I open a web browser and search for the channel on which *Chelsea Lives* — the show which propelled Stacey Stanwell into the public spotlight — is apparently aired. With my headphones in, I then sit through the first hour-long episode. As best as I can tell, the show centres on a group of spoilt, two-dimensional brats living the high life courtesy of generous allowances from wealthy parents. I should be shocked at their ability to over-dramatise every minor hurdle in life but I've met too many similar characters over the years to know the 'stars' probably aren't faking it.

As the closing credits finally roll, my opinion of Stacey Stanwell has not improved. In the hope I might find some strain of credibility, I google her name but the results are almost all about her role in *Chelsea Lives*. It appears her reality show fame is all she has achieved, and is all she's likely to achieve despite her efforts to forge a career as an actress.

I click through to her sketchy Wikipedia entry, and scribble down some notes along with a dozen questions which shouldn't prove too challenging.

Research complete, I return to the original work I had planned in the hope it'll keep my mind from the impending horror of meeting Stacey Stanwell in a few hours.

It kind of does, until Gini finds out about the interview.

She approaches my cubicle like a kid on Christmas morning.

"I hear you're interviewing Stacey Stanwell," she squeals. "Can I ask a favour?"

"You want to take my place? Done."

"I wish. No, can you get me Stacey's autograph?"

"Seriously, Gini? Don't ask me to do that."

"Pretty please. I'll buy pastries for the rest of the week."

"Fine," I sigh. "But you do realise I now hate you."

She claps her hands together and mouths a thank you before skipping away to share her news.

As ridiculous as her enthusiasm is, it's infectious, and I can't help but smile. That smile soon withers as I think back to the last time I felt anything close to the same excitement. There's nothing worthy in my personal life; that's for sure. As for work; it would be that afternoon at Kenton Stables. Six months on and the itch remains.

A week after I was ordered to leave William Huxley alone, he suddenly resigned from Parliament and moved to the Isle of Wight where he is in the process of setting up a holiday retreat for disadvantaged kids. Some might say a noble act but I suspect there's more to it. I did establish the owner of the Audi. Kenneth Davies was the frail old man but he inconveniently died soon after, shutting down that avenue of enquiry. The big guy in denim was impossible to trace without a name.

With no other leads and William Huxley himself off limits, I've come to accept I must wait for the next career-changing story to land in my lap.

That won't be today.

Twelve o'clock comes around and I start gathering my things together.

After traipsing back to Hyde Park Corner tube station, I then experience the briefest of journeys to South Kensington — the nearest Tube station to Chelsea.

Emerging onto the street, I check Stacey Stanwell's address on my phone and set off on the ten-minute walk — a cloud of apathy follows all the way.

Lined both sides with tall, brick and render townhouses, Sydney

Street is not the kind of place a pleb like me could ever afford to live. I wander along while casting an envious eye towards the multi-million pound homes.

After covering a hundred yards of pavement, I finally reach my destination. Stacey's home is across the road from a suitably well-appointed church, although I suspect the convenient location wasn't a deciding factor when Stacey Stanwell, or more likely her parents, decided to purchase the townhouse. Something tells me Stacey prefers worshipping in the aisles of Harvey Nichols.

I ring the doorbell and wait.

Rather than a housemaid or Trina Smith opening the door, I'm slightly taken aback when Stacey Stanwell greets me in person.

"You must be Emma," she chirps. "Please, come in."

I take a second to conclude my first impressions. She is shorter than I imagined and, although it pains me to say it, prettier. Despite her physical perfection, she's under-dressed in a pair of jogging pants and a baggy sweatshirt — clearly not dressed to impress. Her dark hair is tied back into a ponytail and her face shows no obvious signs of makeup.

My first impression isn't what I expected.

I follow her through the hallway to a surprisingly modest kitchen at the rear of the house, with patio doors leading onto a small but beautifully landscaped garden.

"Can I get you something to drink?" she asks, offering me a chair at a distressed oak table.

"Water would be great, thanks."

"Still or sparkling?"

"I'm easy."

She smiles and crosses the kitchen to the fridge. Although she's only said a dozen words, the tone of her voice is noticeably different from the one I heard on screen earlier. That voice, although patently from a privileged background, had a whiney, fatuous lilt to it.

"Have you come far?" she calls over, while inspecting the interior of the fridge.

"Belgravia."

Stacey returns with two bottles of sparkling water and takes a seat opposite me.

"So, you drew the short straw then?" she says with a wry smile.

"Sorry?"

"Interviewing the empty-headed reality star."

"I, um, don't like to judge."

My flushing cheeks provide a different answer.

"Don't worry — I'm used to it. I'm guessing you googled my name, for research?"

"Of course."

"And I bet you didn't find anything about my first-class degree in history?"

Either I've grossly underestimated Stacey Stanwell, or she's one hell of a bullshitter.

"Err ... can't say I did."

"You can blame my previous agent for that. Did you know you can request to have all manner of personal information removed from Google's search results?"

"I seem to remember a case about some Spanish guy going to court a few years ago."

"The 'right to be forgotten' ruling," she states, casually. "It was based on the EU's 1995 Data Protection Directive."

Clearly, and ashamedly, Stacey Stanwell also possesses a better grasp of contemporary law than I do.

"Anyway," she continues. "My previous agent didn't want any information available online that might undermine my working persona. That's why he's now my previous agent."

"Your working persona?"

"Did you really think I'm as superficial as the character you see on TV?"

Her question is delivered with a grin rather than the sneer I might have expected.

"For what it's worth, you were pretty convincing. I can see why you want to break into acting."

"That's another preconception. I have acted before so I'm not looking to break into acting; more reboot my career."

It dawns on me I've already got more material than I expected but haven't made a single note.

"Is it okay to record our chat? I've got the feeling it'll be a little more in-depth than I envisaged."

Without waiting for an answer, I position my phone in the centre of the table and activate the recording app.

"I don't mind talking about anything, but please keep in mind the list of off-topic subjects Trina sent you. There are certain things I don't want reported."

"No problem."

I probably should have read that email. Too late now.

"So, Stacey. Tell me a bit more about your earlier career."

"I've been acting since I was a young child but put my career on ice when I was eleven, due to ill health. I fully recovered, thank God, and decided to concentrate on my studies rather than acting. It wasn't until after I left university I was offered the chance to appear in *Chelsea Lives*. It was a decision I made when my head wasn't ... let's just say I wasn't in a good place."

"You regret taking that role?"

"Life is too short for regrets but it wasn't the wisest decision, career-wise."

"What kind of work did you do as a child?"

"All sorts. Everything from commercials to soap operas, plus a bit of theatre. Oh, and I've got credits in two feature films."

"No wonder you sacked your agent. Fancy having every reference to that work removed from Google."

"Oh, no," she replies dismissively. "You can still find all the references to my earlier work if you search my *actual* name."

"Your actual name?"

"Stacey Stanwell is a pseudonym created for *Chelsea Lives*. My real name is Stacey Nithercott."

Her surname is unusual and I've only ever heard it once before.

"Isn't there a theatre director called Lance Nithercott?"

"My father."

Whilst Lance Nithercott isn't exactly a household name, on account he's a fiercely private man, he is well-known within the theatre world. Suddenly, this isn't quite such a waste of my time.

"Oh, Lance Nithercott is your father?" I confirm, trying to appear nonplussed at her newsworthy revelation.

Stacey's shoulders slump. "Was," she sighs. "He passed away."

Learning of Lance Nithercott's demise is mildly shocking; not least because I don't recall it being mentioned anywhere in the press. It seems his desire to shun the limelight continued even in death.

"I'm so sorry, Stacey."

"Yep, everyone is sorry," she replies flatly, making no effort to hide her bitterness.

I'm minded of some advice Eric once imparted: *empathy is the best hammer for breaking down walls*. It proved sage, and I've used it many times over the years to unlock a guarded interviewee.

"I never had a father myself. Well, not really."

My confession is met with an inquisitive glance.

"He walked out on us a few months after I was born," I add. "And I haven't seen or heard from him since."

My statement isn't strictly true. Dennis Hogan didn't walk out on us — he was convicted of raping and murdering a prostitute, and sentenced to life in prison. Still, as far as I'm concerned he is dead, so my empathy isn't without some foundation.

"I guess that puts my situation into perspective," Stacey says, sympathetically. "My dad was an amazing man, and a loving father, so I guess I should be grateful for the time we had."

"Do you mind if I ask what happened to your dad? Was he ill?

Stacey takes a long sip of water before answering.

"Depends on your definition of ill. He started drinking heavily a few years back. Over time, the drink took a hold of him and he started missing rehearsals and even the occasional performance. Eventually, the job offers dried up so he had more time to drink and it became a vicious circle."

I resist the urge to offer a sympathetic apology and, instead, ratchet up the empathy.

"I had an uncle who went the same way. Liver disease."

"I'm sorry to hear that, but my dad didn't die of natural causes. He fell from a motorway bridge."

"Oh, how awful for you."

There's a brief pause before she responds.

"Actually, that's not strictly true. My father *jumped* from a motorway bridge."

Her admission summons a feeling I've missed, and the buzz makes a welcome return.

5.

I'm caught speechless for a second; somewhere between the shock of Stacey's revelation and the joy of unearthing a real story at last.

"Your father committed suicide?"

"That's what it says on the coroner's report."

Losing someone you love is bad enough, but I can't imagine how awful it must be, knowing you might have prevented it.

I reach across the table and squeeze Stacey's hand.

"Life can be cruel sometimes. I honestly admire the way you've come through it, Stacey."

"What choice is there?"

"Granted."

She pulls her hand away and, in a heartbeat, her demeanour changes.

"You know none of what I've told you about my previous career, or my father, can't be included in the interview?"

"What?" I gasp. "Why not?"

"The list of off-limit subjects Trina sent you. I did say, Emma."

"But surely you want to use this to your advantage? It'll make compelling reading and, to be honest, help your credibility no end."

"I don't care. I will not have my father's memory sullied through any association with Stacey Stanwell or *Chelsea Lives*. He was one of the greatest theatre directors of his generation and that's how I want him remembered — not as the father of a reality TV star or a suicidal alcoholic who threw himself off a motorway bridge."

"But ..."

"Sorry. It's not up for debate."

I sit back in my chair. "Why tell me then?"

"I don't know. The wounds are still raw, I guess, and you have a certain maternal way about you."

It appears my empathetic approach has opened the door to a great story but Stacey won't let me in. In any other situation I might be tempted to write what the hell I want but this girl has been through enough. For all her privilege, life has dealt her the cruellest of blows and I kind of understand her reasons for wanting to keep the Nithercott name out of the papers.

"Fair enough," I sigh. "I'll stick to the new film."

"I have your word on that?"

"You do."

Her smile returns.

We spend the next thirty minutes discussing her new film and I'm left with an interview unworthy of the name. To cap it off, I then have to suffer the ignominy of asking Stacey for her autograph. The depths I'm prepared to plumb for free carbs.

As Stacey waves a goodbye from the front door, I try to ignore the now-familiar feeling of loss. Another front-page story has slipped through my fingers, albeit for different reasons this time. The net result is the same, though, and it feels like another step in the descent towards journalistic obscurity. I have to face facts: there is every chance I'll spend the remaining years of my career churning out this kind of mindless guff.

By the time I reach South Kensington tube station, my mood has shifted from self-pity to anger. This isn't what I worked so hard for. I kicked and I scraped and I gouged my way up the career ladder, only now to find myself slowly slipping back down towards the bottom, and through no fault of my own.

There is a solution, I know.

I could sell my flat and, after paying off the remaining mortgage, buy a place out in the sticks. I could work freelance and split my days between the garden centre and writing what I want to write.

So, why haven't I already done that? The answer, I know, is hope.

Moving to the middle of nowhere appeals on one level, but it terrifies me on another. I would be consigning myself to the life of a spinster; just counting the long and lonely days with half-a-dozen cats for company. London, for all its faults, is home. It's also home to eight million other people and I haven't quite given up hope that amongst them is a man I can share the rest of my days with.

He is, however, proving as elusive as the next front-page story.

I have given myself an arbitrary deadline to make a decision. Once I hit fifty, if Mr Right hasn't walked into my life, or my career hasn't advanced, I'll make the move regardless. For now, I'll have to continue tolerating Damon, and the meals for one, and the speed-dating nights, and the inevitable disappointment.

Probably best not to dwell.

I arrive at my cubicle having shaken off the worst of my malaise — I am nothing if not resilient.

Plugging a pair of headphones into my phone, I tap an icon to replay Stacey's interview. I hate hearing my own voice and try to block it out while scribbling notes. For a professional journalist, there is nothing more galling than throwing away the wheat and keeping the chaff, but that's precisely what I do. Not only does my finished interview have to pass Damon's inspection, but Stacey also wants to see a copy before it goes to print, or screen as is more likely.

I invest a couple of hours writing a piece I'm not proud of, but is fit for purpose. Reading it back, I don't even recognise my own writing style. Just as Stacey Nithercott gave up a credible acting career and became a reality TV star, I've given up being a credible journalist to become a writer of pulp.

I'm not sure which one of us is worse off.

I attach a copy of the finished interview and email both Damon and Stacey. A reply is returned from the former within minutes: *it'll do.*

Basking in Damon's high praise, I pack up my things. I'm just about to leave when Gini comes bounding over.

"How was it?" she coos.

It's not the question she wants to ask. I delve a hand into my jacket pocket.

"Here," I smile, handing over a scrap of paper.

"Oh, my God," she shrieks. "It's made out to me."

"Obviously. Not for one moment did I want her to think I wanted her autograph."

To my surprise, Gini then throws her arms around me. "Thank you, Em."

I struggle to deal with affection of any kind let alone a hug from a colleague. A psychiatrist would probably put it down to a lack of paternal love as a child, but I reckon it's because I'm not what you might call a people person.

I escape Gini's embrace. "Never call me Em, ever."

"You don't like being called Em?" she grins.

"No."

"You should hear what they call you in the advertising department."

"I can imagine."

I'm then invited to join Gini and a dozen pre-pubescent staff members in the pub. I politely decline — not because it's a Monday, but because I'd rather skewer my left tit than spend another minute listening to their juvenile drivel.

"Another time."

I escape before her pleading breaks my will.

With the clocks having shifted forward last week, the novelty of leaving work to daylight still lingers. Give it a few months and I'll be longing for the cold, dark nights again. London is a killer when the mercury rises, and any trip on the Tube is like descending into the bowels of hell. Add the city's pollution into the mix, and it's an inescapable cocktail of unpleasantness.

I take a slow stroll back to the Tube station.

By the time I emerge from Kilburn station, dusk is getting its act together and I'm met with a street bathed in muted shadows. There was a time I used to take a cab from the station to my flat; such was my paranoia about being mugged. These days, it's not such a concern as the muggers have moved online where the work is easier and the rewards greater.

On the way home I have no choice but to pass The Three Horseshoes; it lures me in all too frequently, and tonight I can't resist.

Up until a few years ago, I used to drink in The George & Dragon — a proper, spit-and-sawdust community pub, full of characters. Sadly, it went the same way as so many pubs, and closed down due to spiralling costs and diminishing income. Shortly afterwards, I wrote an article about the demise of community pubs but Damon refused to publish it, on the grounds it wouldn't resonate with our target demographic. Whoever they are, I hope they choke on their craft beer.

The Three Horseshoes is a chain pub — a plastic recreation of what a proper pub should be, minus the characters. Both the staff and the customers seem to change on an almost nightly basis so it feels more like a train station than a community hub. There are only a handful of regulars, and I'm one of them.

I order a large glass of Merlot and retreat to a quiet table in the corner.

There was a time I couldn't bear drinking alone but I concluded it's slightly less depressing than necking wine in an empty flat. Now, it feels like second nature and I embrace the solitude. Occasionally I might be joined by one of the few regulars who can still afford to pay five quid for a pint. Some of them I welcome, others not so much. Tonight, none of the faces are familiar.

I take a moment to check Twitter and find a notification. I have a new follower — Alex Palmer; my former colleague and fellow attendee at Eric's funeral. Curiosity gets the better of me and I click on his profile. If the number of followers on a social media platform is any measure of success in life, Alex is considerably more successful than I am. I note he's swapped careers and now works for a telecoms company. A dull career for a dull man.

Out of politeness, I follow him back but mute his tweets. I had no interest in anything Alex had to say when we worked in the same field.

I switch attention to my diary and scan the next few months: many meetings, two weddings with associated hen nights, a christening, and not a lot else.

Tossing my phone on the table, I puff a long sigh. Christ, I need to sort my life out.

It's at times like this I think back to the various relationships I've enjoyed, endured, and ultimately lost over the years. Could I have done more, been more? Could I have compromised? People do, don't they? I know too many couples who settle for less-than-ideal because the fear of being on their own is too much. Better to have someone than no one. I don't buy that; never have.

Perhaps I need to reassess my position.

I look across the bar at a group of middle-aged men. They're all dressed smartly enough, and three of them still have enough hair to style — kind of. Statistically, four of them will be married and experience tells me two would be willing to cheat on their wife. Not with me, though — been there, done that — never again.

One of them says something which prompts a raucous cheer from the others. Laddish behaviour and deeply unattractive; not that any of them are physically attractive anyway. Could I live my life with any of them? Perhaps I'd be willing to sacrifice the looks as I'm not exactly in the first flush of youth myself, but they're just so ... achingly ordinary. I'd bet every one of them is content with their position in life and happy to coast through the next two or three decades. Beers with the lads during the week, dinner with friends at the weekend, golfing in the Algarve during the summer, and maybe a week's skiing in Verbier, early spring.

No, fuck that.

I'm already compromising my principles enough at work and I don't think I could stomach doing it at home as well.

One of the men looks over and our eyes meet. He smiles, and I die a little inside.

Time to go home.

6.

A microwave lasagne, followed by a two-hour documentary about the Cold War, plus half a packet of chocolate digestives. Just enough to keep my mind occupied before an early night.

My morning begins with a crushing sense of déjà vu. It isn't déjà vu.

Walk, Tube, walk.

Coffee, desk, coffee.

The only variance this morning was the pervert on the Tube who 'accidentally' brushed my backside with his hand on multiple occasions. I won't put up with that shit and called him out on his antics in front of our fellow commuters. The stinking old tosspot fled the carriage before I finished my verbal assault.

Settled into my cubicle, where I'm far less likely to be molested, I scour my inbox and spot a reply from Stacey Stanwell. I open it up, expecting the worst, but her feedback on my interview is positive. She's also gracious enough to apologise for not allowing me to report the wheat. She signs off with the promise of an exclusive one day; when she's ready to publish her autobiography. I won't hold my breath.

I send her an equally gracious reply. Best never to burn bridges in this business.

My diary confirms I have a day of abject tedium ahead of me. Two phone interviews with witnesses to a z-list soap star meeting his alleged drug dealer, followed by a staff meeting and an afternoon of chasing up quotes from sources who don't want to talk to me.

On the upside, Gini arrives with a Danish pastry.

"How was the pub?" I ask out of politeness. I'd rather she left me alone to get better acquainted with the pastry.

"It was a blast. You should have come."

I sense a detailed summary of who did what, and how hilarious it was, is about to follow. Thankfully, the ringing phone on my desk saves me.

"Sorry, Gini. Better get this."

I grab the receiver a little too enthusiastically.

"Emma Hogan."

"Ahh, at last," a cut-glass male voice booms. "You're a hard woman to track down, Miss Hogan."

"Am I?"

"Yes. I've had to be quite the detective to find you."

He's very well spoken for a stalker.

"And who exactly are you?"

"My apologies. My name is Miles DuPont and I work for a firm of estate agents in Chiswick."

"Right."

"I'm calling about the flat in Mulberry Court."

I scour my mind in the hope of making a connection. Nothing comes, but it wouldn't be the first time I've received a call regarding a lead on a long-forgotten story.

"You might have to refresh my memory, Mr DuPont."

"Please, call me Miles."

"Okay, you'll still need to refresh my memory, Miles."

"It's a bit awkward, really."

"What is?"

"The flat, or more specifically, the chattels."

"Chattels?"

"Yes."

I look up at Gini and roll my eyes. She gets the message and heads back to her desk.

"Sorry, Miles, but I don't have the first clue what you're talking about."

"Oh dear, I feared as much. Whilst I don't wish to cause any embarrassment, we can't let this go on much longer."

"Let what go on any longer?"

"The chattels, and their removal."

I've never met Miles DuPont so it's quite hard imagining his face, but I try. I then imagine slapping it, repeatedly.

"Listen, Miles," I sigh. "I don't know anything about a flat in Mulberry Court, or any chattels. You've obviously got your wires crossed."

"Oh dear. That is a possibility, although there was a picture of you in the sitting room and it looks remarkably similar to that on The Daily Standard website – hence my assumption."

My imagined slapping edges towards punching.

"A picture of me in what sitting room?"

"The sitting room in Mr Hogan's flat, at Mulberry Court."

"Mr Hogan?"

"Dennis Hogan? I assume he's related to you?"

The line falls silent. Even the mere mention of my father's name stirs a pot of simmering resentment.

"Listen to me," I growl. "Whatever issue you have with my sorry excuse for a father, I suggest you speak to him about it."

"That's not exactly practical, which is why I called you."

The final strand of patience snaps. "Let me make this clear for you — Dennis Hogan is nothing to me, so if you're looking for someone who gives a shit, you've called the wrong woman."

"But, you do realise ..."

"Did I not make myself clear?"

"Miss Hogan," he barks, clearly losing his cool. "Your father is dead."

Silence returns.

"Sorry ... what?" I blurt.

"Forgive me," Miles replies, his calm tone returning. "That was insensitive. I assumed the police would have told you. I feel awful now."

Miles might well feel awful, but I'm struggling to decipher my feelings. There is shock, for sure, and that might explain why none of the usual suspects are present.

"Are you okay, Miss Hogan?"

"I'm fine."

"Are you happy to continue the conversation or should I call back?"

"I said I'm fine, or I will be when you explain the reason you're calling me."

"Yes, of course. Your father let a flat from us back in January. Five weeks ago we received a call from the police asking if we had a spare key. Apparently Mr Hogan's milk delivery had been stacking up on his doorstep and his neighbours became concerned, bearing in mind his age. I'm sorry to say that the police found your father's body."

It's strange how the human mind works as my first thoughts turn to my status — I am now officially an orphan. It's an odd word, and one I'd usually associate with impoverished children from Dickensian novels. I lost my mother when I was just nineteen and, now both my parents are dead, I suppose it's now a label I can attach to myself.

"Okay, understood," I reply without a trace of emotion in my voice. "And what exactly is the problem with the flat?"

"Your father's chattels. They need to be removed from the flat so we can re-let it."

"By chattels you mean his possessions?"

"Precisely. The flat was let fully furnished so it's just his clothes and a dozen boxes of other items. We didn't want to remove anything without at least making some effort to contact Mr Hogan's next of kin."

"Hence the call?"

"Indeed."

"But how did you establish I was his next of kin?"

"Ah, yes," he chirps. "We found three scrapbooks containing hundreds of old newspaper reports; stories going back twenty years or so. It was one of my colleagues who noticed you were the credited reporter on every one of those clippings, and that's how we tracked you down. I assumed the police would have made the same connection, but clearly not."

For a moment I'm taken aback by the revelation my father kept a scrapbook of my old reports. As for the police, knowing how many people die in this city every day and how stretched police resources are, it doesn't surprise me I wasn't informed.

"I appreciate you calling, Miles, but dispose of everything as you see fit."

"Well, yes, we could, but someone will have to pay for that service."

"What? Just take it out of the deposit."

"I'm afraid we can't do that. Against our advice, the landlord struck a deal with your father whereby he agreed to pay the entire tenancy up front in lieu of a deposit."

"Just do what you like. It's not my problem."

"It kind of is, as you've confirmed you're his next of kin. Unless you collect his possessions, I'm afraid we'll have to bill you for their removal."

In that single sentence, and with his true motive for calling revealed, Miles has validated my already low opinion of estate agents.

"How much?" I snap.

"Oh, only two or three hundred pounds."

"No bloody way. I'd rather come over and dump his crap in the bin myself."

"Can you do that today as we do have a number of interested tenants lined up for viewings?"

"Are you kidding me? I can't just drop everything at a moment's notice."

"When can you come?"

"I don't know. Next week maybe."

"Too late I'm afraid. We really need the flat cleared within the next day or two."

Seething, I open my diary and check my schedule for tomorrow morning. There's nothing I can't postpone.

"Fine," I snarl through gritted teeth. "I'll come over tomorrow at nine."

"Excellent, and once again, I'm sorry for your loss, Miss Hogan."

"Yeah, right. Email me the details."

I spit my email address and slam the receiver down before I say something I'll regret, or not.

As I struggle to quell the anger, my mind swings between the two men responsible: Miles DuPont and Dennis Hogan. DuPont might be a complete arsehole but our paths would never have crossed if it wasn't for my father. Even in death, that man continues to spike my hackles.

Despite the all-encompassing anger, another emotion joins the fray — one I would not have expected — disappointment. Perhaps a tiny part of me still hoped that one day I might receive an explanation why my father did what he did. My time to have children has passed but even so, I can't imagine how anyone could commit such a terrible crime, knowing they had a wife and new-born daughter at home. What kind of man could do that?

It's a question I've asked, and answered a thousand times — a deplorable shit of a man.

Growing up a curious child, I obviously asked Mum why I didn't have a father. She told me he was a bad man, and we were better-off without him. When I got older, I asked the same question; many, many times, as I recall. One day, not long after I'd turned sixteen, she finally relented and sat me down for a conversation I'm sure she didn't want to have. Mum confirmed Dennis Hogan was sent to prison when I was just four months old, and the reason why. Even as a sixteen year-old, I had enough awareness to tell how much resentment and pain Mum still harboured, and coupled with the damning truth about Dennis Hogan, I promised myself from that moment onwards I would never let that man back into our lives.

What I didn't realise is that in the intervening years since my mother passed away, I would gradually inherit all her pain and resentment. Knowing your father raped and murdered another woman is near-on impossible to forget, or come to terms with. I've managed neither.

I head to the coffee machine; silently chiding myself all the way. Haven't I wasted enough emotion on that man over the years?

No more. Dennis Hogan might now be dead but my father died a long, long time ago.

Despite my best efforts to focus on work, the call from Miles DuPont has poked at scars still to heal. While I can put my father to one side, my mind continually drifts back to my childhood and, inevitably, to my mother — the other woman he wronged.

Susie Hogan was more than my mother. She was my best friend, and my hero. After Dennis Hogan was sent to prison, and our family home repossessed, the council moved us to a sink estate in Haringey, and there she brought me up single-handedly. I don't remember having much, but I knew I was loved; and if it hadn't been for that love, and her unwavering support, I dread to think how my life might have turned out.

We both thankfully escaped the estate in Haringey. I went off to university and Mum eventually found herself a decent man and re-married.

It breaks my heart she only had twelve happy years with Ian.

I was planning her sixtieth birthday when it happened. A car mounted the pavement early one evening and struck her at forty miles an hour — she didn't stand a chance. The driver, pissed out of his tiny mind, served a little under three years for stealing my mother's life.

I've lost count how many times I've prayed that fucker meets an equally horrible end. Of course, nobody ever listened and he now lives in a nice little semi in suburbia, together with his wife and kids. And they say crime doesn't pay.

Perhaps it's the residue of my earlier telephone conversation but sorrow and anger continue to jostle for position. It's early days but the life of an orphan isn't much fun. Neither, come to think of it, is that of this journalist, and my day comes to an end in the same way every work day ends — a frenetic scurry to get stories to the relevant editor followed by a collective sigh of relief.

Much of what will appear in print tomorrow won't be news but opinions presented as news. The same people will buy their copy of The Daily Standard and pore over our work, content the narrative fits their own world view. The paper will end up in the bin by which point we'll be readying fresh pulp for the following day. The cycle will continue and nothing will change because nobody wants it to change.

When I finally leave the office, it feels like my head is ready to explode; if my heart doesn't get there first.

I need a drink.

7.

The journey from Kilburn to my dead-father's flat in Chiswick is a stark reminder why I avoid driving in London's morning rush hour. Six miles of hell played out to a soundtrack of blazing horns and sweary cyclists. Being stuck in traffic is bad enough but as I'm essentially being blackmailed into making the journey, I enthusiastically participate in the honking and the swearing.

Trying to grasp some positivity at least the sun is making an effort as it burns through the early morning haze.

I trundle along Chiswick High Road and consult the sat nav — not far to go. The range of shops I pass don't perhaps reflect the affluence of the residents. I expected more artisan bakeries but, still, they're definitely a step up from the retail options in Kilburn.

I'm ordered to take the next right and finally escape the crawl. A left turn at the junction and fifty yards before another right turn. That turn leads me into a tree-lined avenue in which Mulberry Court is apparently situated. The sat nav counts down the yards until I pull up to the kerb.

Despite the twee name, in my head I'd pictured Mulberry Court as a grim block of flats with all the architectural charm of a sanatorium. I certainly wasn't expecting to find a grand Edwardian house behind wrought-iron security gates.

A white Mercedes pulls up behind me and a suited man gets out. Everything about him screams estate agent. He walks up to the side of my car as I lower the window.

"Miss Hogan?"

I recognise the voice, and the face is eminently more slappable than I imagined — thin, weasely, and capped with slick black hair.

"Yep," I nod, before opening the door.

Miles DuPont then has the temerity to shake my hand and thank me for turning up. Like I had a choice.

"What I'll do is let you in and leave you to it. Just call me when you're done."

Cold comfort but at least I won't have to put up with his smug face longer than is absolutely necessary.

"Fine."

"Shall we?"

He aims a small box at the gates which then slowly swing open. I follow him through the gates and across an expanse of cobbles towards the equally expansive front door.

"Your father's flat is on the ground floor."

I half nod, half shrug.

As Miles fiddles with a bunch of keys, I take the opportunity to appraise Mulberry Court. They clearly spared no expense when the house was converted into flats. From the ornate arches above the windows to the antique-brass door furniture, everything looks like it was lovingly restored to retain the originality of the building. The only obvious exceptions are the security cameras on the gate and by the front door.

"What's the rent on a place like this?"

More a question I was asking myself but it escapes my mouth.

"Three thousand a month."

"Christ. Why so expensive?"

"Location primarily, plus the size and quality of the accommodation. Also, as you'll see, the developer spent a fortune on security and that added piece of mind comes at a price. Unfortunately, areas such as these offer rich pickings for burglars, so the developer ensured Mulberry Court had all the latest deterrents."

He opens the door and steps into a hallway with an exquisitely tiled floor and high ceilings. Pangs of envy arrive when I compare it to the featureless box I call home.

Another key is selected and the door to flat one opened. Immediately, a shrill beeping sound escapes.

"Bear with me while I deactivate the alarm."

The beeping ceases, and I'm invited across the threshold onto a polished wooden floor which extends about twenty feet.

"One of my colleagues gathered all your father's possessions together and put them in the master bedroom."

I follow Miles as he leads me into a bedroom bigger than my entire flat.

"This place is stunning," I coo.

"It is quite lovely. I'm sure your father was very happy here."

I ignore his insincere words of comfort.

"Everything is there," he says, pointing to a dozen boxes stacked in the bay window. "Apart from his clothes in the wardrobe."

I turn around, expecting to see a wardrobe. I find a chaise longue and an oak tallboy.

"In the dressing room," he adds, pointing to a door.

"Right."

"I'll leave you to it then. I don't wish to hurry you but I do have a gentleman arriving in thirty minutes and he's been desperate to view the flat for a few days."

"Why make him wait?"

"Company policy. If anything were to go missing from your father's possessions, we'd be liable."

"You should have let him view the flat — he might have nicked everything and saved me a job."

Ignoring my barbed suggestion, he hands me a business card and confirms he'll leave the gate open whilst I load the car. I watch him slither away and conclude he's the polar opposite of what I consider an attractive man.

The front door slams shut and the ensuing silence is absolute; probably due to triple-glazed reproduction windows. Beyond the silence, there's a faint scent lingering in the still air — cologne perhaps? If it is, it's not the same pungent, sickly-sweet cologne worn by Miles DuPont but a woodier, more masculine scent — the kind an older guy might wear.

It is, I conclude, the scent of my father — a man I never knew, yet I can almost feel his presence.

In an effort to distract myself from a sudden and unexpected cold shudder, I get on with the job in hand and approach the stack of boxes in the bay window. I remove the lid of the top box and I'm met with a waft of the same woody, masculine scent; only stronger. The box is full of clothes, presumably removed from the tallboy. I extract the top garment; a deep-red, lambs-wool sweater which has a quality feel to it. There's a similar one underneath, only black, and another beneath that in a shade of forest green. I check the labels and all three sweaters are sized medium but different brands: Ralph Lauren, Hugo Boss, and Giorgio Armani.

Clearly my father had expensive taste and, coupled with the eye-watering rent he paid for the flat, an income to fund it. That conclusion fuels my hatred.

I used to counter the pain of my father's absence by imagining he was suffering a dreadful life. I pictured him working some menial job where the hours were cruel and the pay low. I had visions of a grotty bedsit with damp walls where he'd endure restless nights atop a piss-stained mattress. I wanted him to suffer in the same way my mother and I suffered.

I never imagined this: wealth, comfort, luxury.

The pain brings me back. I realise I've been biting my bottom lip so hard I can taste the metallic tang of blood.

However Dennis Hogan died, I hope it was long and painful. I hope it hurt so much he sobbed into his pillow like I used to when the kids on the estate taunted me about my charity shop clothes and

72

home-cut hairstyle. And when he knew his time was up, I hope he felt the same cold weight of loneliness I endured. If there is any comfort to be gained, it's knowing karma might have fucked him good and proper at the end.

I put the lid back on the box and swallow the lump in my throat.

This is closure, girl. He's gone for good.

Two at a time, I carry the boxes to the car. With the back seats folded flat, all twelve fit with a little room to spare. I head into the dressing room and open each of the four fitted wardrobes; three of which are thankfully empty.

The one wardrobe I have to clear houses a dozen suits hanging from the rail, and at the bottom, as many pairs of shoes. I pick up a pair of highly-polished black leather brogues. Like the pullovers, they have a feel of quality about them — probably hand-made I'd guess. I check one of the suit jackets and it comes as no surprise to find a label for Huntsman — a renowned Saville Row tailor.

I take a step back and appraise the find. The contents of this one wardrobe alone must have cost close to thirty grand, and whilst I'm happy to make the odd donation to a charity shop, not on this occasion — Dennis Hogan owes me. If I recall correctly, there's a shop in Maida Vale which purchases quality, second-hand clothes and I reckon they'd pay at least a grand for this haul. That would easily fund a week in the sun which would go some way to banishing my blues.

Perhaps it was worth the trip, despite the pot of resentment receiving another thorough stir.

Carrying four pairs at a time, I transfer the shoes from the wardrobe to the front seat of my car. I then return and remove four of the suits which I lay carefully on top of the boxes. Two more trips and the job is done. I text Miles DuPont before slamming the boot lid shut.

If the traffic is kinder on the return journey, I should be home by ten thirty and back at work before Damon gets suspicious. The one perk of this job is you typically spend a lot of time out of the office so a few skived hours aren't likely to be noticed.

The same white Mercedes speeds down the road and pulls up behind me. It feels appropriately rude for me to drive off without saying goodbye: so I do. Sometimes, the most childish of gestures bring the most satisfaction.

The traffic is indeed kind, and I make it home within half-an-hour. I toy with the idea of leaving everything in the car and dealing with it tonight, but in this neighbourhood I wouldn't risk leaving a half-eaten sandwich on view, let alone a stash of expensive clothes.

I drape the first clutch of suits over my arm while reaching up to close the boot lid. As I stretch, something is dislodged from one of the jacket pockets and falls to the floor. I squat down and pick up a passport-sized notebook, bound in dark-blue leather. Plain on one side, there's a single word embossed in gold leaf on the other —
Clawthorn.

The word is meaningless, and the notebook could therefore

contain anything from poetry to train timetables for all I know, or currently care. I toss it into the boot.

The twelve journeys up and down the stairs are a painful reminder just how unfit I am — maybe I should invest some of my windfall in a gym membership. I did join a gym five years ago, but after three months of non-attendance, I decided it probably wasn't for me. Cancelling my membership proved more stressful and acrimonious than any divorce. On second thoughts, I think I'll stick to the holiday.

I lock the car and, still panting, head off to the Tube station.

Once I regain my breath, the walk in tepid sunshine proves a boon to my mood. There are many things I can't control but I can avoid slipping any further into the current malaise which has blighted my year thus far. The trouble with life is it's easier to count your curses rather than your blessings, and this self-pitying episode doesn't sit well. If I don't get a handle on it, there's only one way I'm heading.

By the time I reach the station, I've pulled myself together sufficiently to make a promise: I'm not going to let Dennis Hogan, or Damon, or any other tosser drag me down. As I descend the stairs I wish I had my headphones with me so I could listen to Gloria Gaynor's *I Will Survive*, or *Respect* by Aretha Franklin. I make do by playing them in my head as I stride purposefully across the ticket hall.

As I walk I reach into my handbag for an Oyster Card which is rarely where I left it. After much rummaging, I finally locate it. Just as I look up to regain my bearings a tall figure walks directly across my line of sight towards the ticket barrier.

"Holy shit," I inadvertently blurt.

Heart pounding, my brain catches up and processes the memory — it's the big guy from Kenton Stables.

Today just got a hell of a lot more interesting.

8.

The buzz returns.

I was warned not to contact William Huxley but nobody said anything about contacting other witnesses to what happened that afternoon in Surrey. The big guy, whoever he is, was slap bang in the middle of events. I have a one-time opportunity to follow the only remaining lead.

I watch him for a few seconds to be sure I'm not mistaken. The same huge frame and broad strides, and he's even wearing the same bell-bottom jeans and denim waistcoat, although the pullover he wore that day has been replaced by a black t-shirt. The only other difference is a battered rucksack slung over his shoulder.

It's definitely the same man and I definitely need to know who he is.

I scurry towards the ticket barrier as the big guy passes through. By the time I reach that barrier and slap my Oyster Card on the reader, he's already at the top of the escalator which leads down to the Piccadilly Line.

I step forward but the gate doesn't open. I turn around and tap the reader with my Oyster Card again. My effort is met with a red light.

"You okay there, Miss?"

An attendant approaches from the opposite side.

"No, I'm not. The bloody reader doesn't recognise my Oyster

Card."

"We've been having problems with that gate. Try the next one along."

I frown at the attendant, and consider asking why the hell the gate is still open, but time is not on my side. I slide along to the next gate and pass through with no problem.

Reaching the top of the escalator, I just catch sight of the big guy stepping off at the bottom. Desperate not to lose him, I have to barge past several tourists stood side by side, breaking escalator etiquette. I reach the bottom but the big guy has disappeared from view. Assuming he's taking the Piccadilly Line, there's only one way he could have gone. Adrenalin pumping, I set off in that direction.

I finally reach the end of the tunnel and cuss under my breath. To my right there's a stationary train waiting at the eastbound platform; the doors are currently open but they could close any second. Is the big guy on board, or is he waiting on the westbound platform to my left?

Heads or tails?

With no thought to the reason why, I dart to my right and just evade the closing carriage doors.

I scan the faces of my fellow passengers as the train pulls away. If the big guy is on board he's not in this carriage. With about a dozen stops before the train terminates, my best tactic will be to peer out of the open doors at every station and hope I spot him — that's assuming he's even on the train. If he isn't, I'm on a wild goose chase all the way to Cockfosters.

We reach Green Park.

I stand on my tiptoes and peer up and down the platform as passengers scurry to and from the carriages. Fortunately, my foe is big enough I'm sure he'll be easy to spot if he's amongst them. There's no sign of him.

The tactic is repeated at Piccadilly but this time I do spot him exiting the next carriage down.

I leap from the train and, keeping a safe distance behind, follow the big guy as he makes his way towards the Bakerloo line.

I've followed people before and it was Eric who taught me there's a right way and a wrong way. The trick is to tell yourself you're heading the same place as the person you're following, and to focus on something ahead of them in case they suddenly turn around. If you get caught and they make eye contact, you might get away with it the first time but the second time will raise suspicion.

Undetected, I follow him all the way to the southbound Bakerloo platform where he turns to the right and leans up against the wall. I turn left and stand behind an American couple arguing over a map.

The train arrives a minute later and I hold back to confirm which carriage he enters. I then dart across the platform and hop into the next carriage along.

We set off and pass through Charing Cross and Embankment. The big guy remains on the train.

The next stop is Waterloo; always chaotic as it's the access point to the busiest railway station in the country.

The doors open and a swarm of passengers fill the platform. Even on my tiptoes, and craning my neck, I can't see beyond the melee. Then some kind soul disembarking bumps into me from behind. I never was any good at ballet and my lack of balance is telling. Stumbling out of the carriage, I just manage to avoid a confused pensioner trying to embark.

As I regain my balance and turn around, the carriage doors close. All I can do is watch on as the train pulls away.

"Shit."

Like a lost meerkat, I frantically turn my head in every direction and scour the faces around me. As I'm simultaneously swept along in the crowd, it quickly becomes apparent I'm wasting my time with so many bodies blocking the view.

I want to scream. I fucking had him and, just as quickly, I've lost him.

I've waited six months to feel it again, but I can already sense the buzz fading away. I know the void will feel particularly empty this time.

With frustration ebbing towards resignation, there's little else I can do other than go with the flow and follow the mass stampede towards the platform exit. I'm late enough for work as it is and the only option is to take a cab. The fifteen minute journey should be just enough time to conduct a post-mortem on my lost opportunity.

I finally break through the bottleneck at the exit.

Two sets of escalators later and I arrive on the cavernous main concourse of Waterloo railway station; no place for those with a fear of open spaces or crowds.

I wander towards the exit where the black cabs congregate but I don't reach my destination. As I pass a group of boisterous teenagers, I catch a passing glimpse of denim in my periphery. My head snaps to the right, just in time to catch the big guy striding towards a platform entrance, only twenty yards away.

"Gotcha."

A couple of the teenagers stare at the odd woman talking to herself.

Ignoring their sniggers, I turn my attention back to the big guy as he passes through the ticket barrier. The digital sign above the platform entrance confirms the destination and departure time — four minutes.

It is at this point any sensible individual would concede defeat and head home — perhaps some questions really are destined to remain unanswered. However, my curiosity has always taken a front seat over sensibility.

A quick dash to the nearest machine where I purchase a return ticket for the same train. With only a minute to spare I slide through the barrier and make my way to the first carriage.

The train terminates in a suburban commuter town — just under an hour away. As I flop down on one of the few remaining seats, several thoughts occur: firstly, I really need the loo, and secondly, I haven't given any consideration to how I approach the big guy, or indeed if I even should approach him.

One of the many, many anecdotes Eric relayed to me over the years now feels relevant.

Back in the early nineties, Eric heard rumours about a politician who was allegedly taking bribes in return for asking specific questions in Parliament. Weeks of surveillance followed as Eric tried to unearth a lead. Then, one evening, he struck gold as the politician met with a man at a bar in Soho, and the two men surreptitiously exchanged envelopes beneath the table. Although Eric didn't know it at the time, it would transpire the man was a lobbyist by the name of Gavin Whittaker.

Eric then followed Whittaker across London but lost his nerve and broke cover too soon. He approached Whittaker just as he was about to hail a cab in Mayfair and, ignoring Eric's questions, the lobbyist simply hopped into a cab and fled. In hindsight, Eric admitted he should have established Whittaker's identity before pouncing, and that mistake killed his one and only lead.

A few months later, one of the national papers broke the 'cash for questions' scandal — a massive scoop at the time. Eric was gutted.

Sitting here now, I could be on the verge of unearthing another scandal, and I can't afford to waste such a monumental stroke of luck. William Huxley has escaped the truth once but I'm sure as hell not going to let it happen again. If my luck holds, I can follow the big guy, and hopefully establish who he is. On first impressions alone, he looks the very embodiment of trouble, and that in itself begs the question: why was such a man involved with a Tory politician?

A series of beeps break my thoughts as the doors close. The train pulls away.

I give it a few minutes and head to the loo. 'Disgusting' just about covers the experience.

With an empty bladder I work my way through the second carriage. It's quite an art trying to look for someone without making it obvious you're looking for someone; not aided by the swaying motion of the train.

I clear two more carriages but there's no sign of the big guy. He's not in carriages four or five, either.

By the time I clear the first class carriage, I'm starting to doubt myself. I did see him, didn't I? And if he went through the ticket barrier, where else could he have gone?

I enter carriage seven with more apprehension than I anticipated.

Then, I spot it — a battered Chelsea boot at the end of a denim-clad leg, stretched into the aisle. It takes a real effort not to punch the air in celebration.

I take a seat close enough to keep an eye on him but not so close he's likely to spot me; particularly as our seats are both facing forward. All I have to do is sit and wait.

The adrenalin dissipates with every passing station as the big guy remains planted in his seat. It has to be said: waiting and watching is tedious. I take to staring out of the window as the scene beyond transitions from industrial buildings to suburban housing, and then to green fields and woodland. I pull out my phone to check how far we are from London but the signal is too sketchy.

We stop at the penultimate station before the train terminates, and the big guy doesn't move. I now know where he's heading, and in eight minutes time I'll be able to get off this bloody train and continue the pursuit.

The buzz resurfaces.

The eight minutes drag but eventually the train slows to a stop. I know very little about the town I'm about to visit, which suggests there isn't a great deal worth knowing. That might be about to change.

The big guy gets to his feet and stretches. This is as close as I've been to him and while I could tell he was big, at this distance he looks positively enormous. Enormous and … something else. I can't put my finger on it but there's a gravity to the man which seems to extend beyond his physical size. Whatever it is, I can't deny it isn't intimidating. I need to be careful.

The doors open and he stoops out of the carriage. I wait a few seconds before I follow.

The station is small with only two platforms and one exit. There are just enough passengers milling around that I don't stand out; my charcoal-grey overcoat and black trousers adding to my anonymity. Cautiously, I make my way through the barrier and ticket office.

I reach the station forecourt and pause a moment, pretending to check my phone. The big guy is already striding away, but now I no longer have the same crowd cover as in London, I need to keep my distance to avoid detection. Twenty yards should do it.

Counting down those yards, I step off the kerb and follow.

Within a minute I spot a sign for the town centre, and the big guy crosses the road in the direction of the sign. It looks likely that's where he's heading. Hopefully there will be more people to hide amongst.

My guess proves right as we turn into a pedestrianised street lined with shops. It's interesting to watch the reaction of the locals as many stare up at the big guy as he passes. In fairness, he does himself no favours with the whole double denim vibe. He ignores most of the locals but occasionally returns a glare. It's enough to quickly shift every set of eyes in the opposite direction.

He reaches the end of the pedestrianised street and takes a right turn. I scamper up to the corner and check he's a safe distance away before I follow. The sight doesn't fill me with confidence as the street in question is narrow, and virtually deserted as far as I can see. Best I stay on the opposite pavement.

My fitness gets another test as the big guy's strides become more purposeful. He passes a row of empty shops, and suddenly slows his pace while staring up at the weathered sign above the last of those shops: Baxter's Books.

I find cover in the sheltered doorway of a building opposite and watch on as the big guy ambles up the alleyway to the right of the former bookshop. Clearly he's not here for the retail experience and, with little else around, I reckon the alley is his final destination. I'd wager it gives access to a flat above one of the shops.

A smile creeps across my face — it looks like I've succeeded where Eric failed. All I need to do is check the alleyway and I'll have the big guy's address. From that I'll be able to source a name, and then use my influence over Stuart to check if that name has a criminal record.

I wait a minute to be on the safe side and then cross the street.

Remaining cautious, I poke my head around the corner and check the alleyway is clear. As I hoped, there's no sign of the big guy.

I cover the entire length of the alleyway and there's no sign of a door either. To add to my concern, the flank wall of the bookshop eventually gives way to an eight foot high security fence, presumably erected to stop squatters taking up residency in the empty shops. Clearly not the big guy's destination.

Bugger.

I scan the area to my right but there's just a car park for the office building adjacent to the bookshop, and not much else.

Another scream builds. How the hell did I lose him? I was so close.

All I can do now is retrace my steps and double-check I didn't miss anything. Worst case scenario, I'll have to check the electoral roll for every property within a hundred yards, and hope Stuart doesn't call my bluff when I present him with a list of names. It's a damn sight more legwork, and guesswork, than I hoped for.

I turn around, and I'm greeted with a sight startling enough to summon a gasp — the big guy stood just feet away.

He glares down at me. "Alright, doll."

9.

My mind explodes into activity but my body is frozen. The big guy presents a large and impenetrable barrier between my position and the alleyway.

I am in so much shit right now.

"I ... ugh."

Words fail.

"Why are you following me?" he asks.

His voice perfectly matches his appearance: hefty and rough.

He takes two steps forward; keeping his almost unnaturally blue eyes locked on mine.

You don't survive life on an inner-London housing estate, or indeed this job, by being a shrinking violet. However, this guy is on a whole different scale of intimidating.

"Back off," I gulp. "Or I'll scream."

"Don't much give a shit. By the time the Old Bill arrive, you'd have told me why you're following me, and I'll be gone."

Another step.

"So, what's it gonna be? Easy way or the hard way?"

Maintaining eye contact, I slip a hand into my pocket in search of the phone I pray is there. It isn't.

I wait for him to take another step but he suddenly freezes.

As I scan my surroundings for a possible means of escape, the big guy remains rooted to the spot, motionless like a showroom dummy.

Seconds pass and I wonder if he's maybe suffering a seizure, such is his lack of movement and vacant expression.

Then, as quickly as his trance arrived, it passes.

He eyes me up and down. "What's your name?"

"Emma."

My reply appears to have a positive effect as his expression eases from fucking terrifying to just scary.

"Look, I ain't gonna hurt you. I just wanna know why you're following me."

Is there any sense in lying to him? I'll throw him a bone and see if he bites.

"William Huxley."

"What about him?"

"I was there; that afternoon at the stables."

He shrugs his shoulders. "So?"

"I just want to know what happened."

"Why?"

"I'm a reporter."

"Should have guessed. Which rag?"

"The Daily Standard."

"Don't read it myself. The sports section is pony."

"I'll pass on your feedback."

The merest hint of a smile passes his lips. It slips away just as quickly.

"Listen, doll, Bill Huxley is a decent bloke so if you're digging for dirt, you're looking in the wrong place."

"And I'm supposed to take your word for that, Mr ...?"

"Call me Clement."

At last, I have a name, if that actually is his name.

"And yeah, you should take my word for it," he continues. "Unless you wanna waste your time, or piss me off."

Pissing him off doesn't seem sensible, but why should I take his word for anything? I need answers, and they'll only come by pushing my luck.

"I don't suppose you fancy a quick drink, Clement?"

"No offence, but you're a bit on the old side."

I scramble for a suitable response. "I beg your pardon?"

"Just saying. You must be knocking fifty."

Fear walks off and indignation arrives.

"I'm forty-six, you cheeky bastard."

"I was close."

My turn to glare. "And don't flatter yourself — have you looked in a mirror lately?"

He smiles again, revealing a row of nicotine-stained teeth.

"Go on then. I'll have a pint if you're buying."

"I'm not asking you on a date," I snap. "It's just a drink."

"Yeah, yeah."

I roll my eyes. The dynamic has shifted and although I don't feel quite so intimidated, I need to remain wary.

"There's a pub by the station. Shall we go there?"

"If you like."

I nod towards the alleyway. "No offence, but I'd rather walk behind you. I don't like surprises."

"Suit yourself."

He turns and lumbers back down the alleyway. I wait until he reaches the end before following; keeping my eyes on him all the time. He appears fairly nonplussed by my cautious behaviour.

I emerge onto the pavement unscathed. Saying that, I now have to make conversation as we walk back through the town centre.

"Do you mind me asking: how did you know I was following you?"

"Because you're shit at it."

"Oh."

"You know when a train goes through a tunnel, the windows turn into mirrors, right?"

"Um."

"And shop windows do a similar job."

"Guess I need to go back to detective school."

"Yeah, you do."

If Eric was still alive, I'd kill him for omitting such obvious advice.

"I don't suppose there's any harm in asking if you live around here?"

"Nah. Too dull for my liking."

"Are you visiting someone then?"

"Nope."

"Here for work?"

He glares down at me. "You're a nosey mare, ain't you."

"I'm a journalist. It's my job to be nosey."

"Guess so."

"So, why are you here?"

We turn the corner, and as I'm about to give up on an answer he finally delivers one.

"I was looking for something."

"Did you find it?"

"Nah, but I found something else."

"Care to elaborate?"

He shakes his head and strides on at a pace — perhaps hoping I'll be too breathless to ask any more questions. It's a strategy that works and I'm almost perspiring by the time we reach the pub.

Clement, to my surprise, holds the door open before following me through to the bar.

"What can I get you?" I ask him.

"Pint."

I order a pint of lager and a glass of wine. I've got a feeling this day might be a write off as far as the office is concerned. I make a mental note to text Damon with an excuse I'm yet to concoct.

Clement has already found a table by the door and made himself comfortable. There's no further chivalry as I teeter towards the table with our drinks.

"Cheers," he says, finally relieving me of the pint glass.

"Yeah, you're welcome."

He either doesn't pick up on my sarcastic tone, or chooses to ignore it. I take a seat opposite.

"Do you mind if I record our conversation?"

"I do, so no."

"Oh, fair enough."

There's no sense in skirting the reason we're here so I get straight to the point.

"Can you tell me anything about what happened that day at the stables?"

"Some bird died," he replies in a low voice. "Nothing else to say."

"How did she die?"

"Accidentally."

"I saw her. She had a knife sticking out of her chest."

"And I'm telling you, it was an accident."

His defence is delivered forcibly but not aggressively. I don't know him well enough to tell if he's lying but there's no point asking the same question over and over again.

"Okay, I'll take your word for that but why was William Huxley even there?"

"Bad luck," he shrugs. "But he did nothing wrong. You're gonna have to take my word on that."

When someone is lying they find it hard to maintain eye contact but Clement has no such problem. Seated so close, I get the full impact of those eyes and they're completely at odds with the rest of his face — like two brilliant sapphires sunk into the leather of a battered satchel.

"Listen, doll. I know you've got a job to do, but Bill is one of the good guys. You need to drop this."

I have no intention of dropping anything just yet. It's time to switch strategy and use the technique which has successfully brought other sources to heel — empathy.

"Tell me, Clement, where are you from?"

"North of the river, same as you."

His answer takes me by surprise. "How did you know I'm from North London?"

"You've had an education?"

"I went to university, yes."

"Working-class roots?"

"Err, yes."

"Thought as much. I reckon you've been trying to bury the accent most of your life."

Clearly there is a brain behind the brawn, and a perceptive one at that. Back in the days, when I actually gave a shit about what people thought of me, my council estate accent felt like a stigma. I purposely hung around with well-spoken students at college and Uni in the hope I'd eventually pick up the tone of middle-England. It kind of worked, or so I thought.

"Alright, smartarse — you got me. I live in Kilburn but grew up in Haringey."

"You can take the girl out of London, eh?"

"Yeah, yeah. Anyway, what about you — what's your story?"

"Long … and complicated."

"I'm not in a hurry."

He takes a gulp of lager before answering. "Another time."

That avenue closed, I change tack. "Can I ask: what does a man like you do for a living?"

"This and that."

"Suitably vague."

"My life is suitably vague."

"So I'm discovering. I'm guessing you're not a nine-to-five kind of guy, though?"

"Nope."

His hands say as much; like gnarly bunches of bananas with too many scars to count.

"Some kind of security work?"

"Of sorts."

"For bands, you know, when they're on the road?"

"What makes you say that?"

"Your outfit for one. And it's been a while since I've seen such impressive sideburns. Let me guess: you handle security for one of those old rocks bands like The Who or Led Zeppelin?"

Rather than answer, he looks around the bar, while taking another swig from his glass.

"Am I even warm?" I press.

"I'm a fixer," he finally relents. "Amongst other things."

"Oh, interesting. And what kind of things do you fix?"

"Problems."

"And did William Huxley have a problem he needed fixing?"

It's a risky move but it feels an appropriate moment to make it.

"You really need to let it go."

"Tried. Can't."

He suddenly sits forward and rests his elbows on the table, our faces only three feet apart.

"You believe in fate?" he asks.

"Not really."

"Neither did I, but I'll tell you something for nothing — I reckon there's a reason you followed me today and it ain't because of Bill Huxley."

"Eh? Yes it was."

"That's what you think, but I'd wager a few bob it's for another reason. You just don't know it yet."

Has he just delivered the mother of all cheesy chat-up lines? Maybe he does have a thing for older women after all; although he's barking up the wrong tree with this older woman.

"Right," I scoff. "I think I'll rely on my own judgement over fate, thank you very much."

He replies with raised eyebrows before necking the final half of his pint.

"We'll see. Anyway, I'm off."

"Wait ... what? But ..."

He gets to his feet and slings the rucksack over his shoulder.

"Gotta get back, doll. Places to go and people to see."

"Back where?"

"London."

"So have I. Can we continue our conversation on the train?"

"Sit with me if you want but I need some shut-eye. I'm working tonight."

Before I can even stand up, he's already half way to the door. I empty my glass and scuttle after him.

I continue that scuttle all the way to the platform.

"Thanks for waiting," I pant.

"The train is due any minute. Didn't wanna miss it."

Proving his point, a train approaches in the distance.

A minute later, we're seated opposite one another in an overly warm carriage with Clement seemingly settled in for the journey back to London.

"Before you nod off, can I ask you one final question?"

"Make it quick."

"The thing you came here looking for — was it in that bookshop?"

"Dunno. Maybe."

"What was it?"

"That's two questions."

"Come on, Clement."

He lets out a long sigh. "A book, if you must know."

"You came all the way here for a book? Have you heard of Amazon?"

"I'm not a total idiot. It's a river somewhere in South America."

"Ha ha ... very funny."

He doesn't share the joke and stares out of the window, stony faced.

"What kind of book was it?"

"A bible," he mumbles.

"You don't strike me as the religious type."

"Yeah, well, that's me — full of surprises."

He then sits back in his seat and shuts his eyes. Conversation over, I guess.

I've never been able to sleep on any form of transport so, after texting Damon to say I'm chasing an unexpected lead, all I can do is stare out of the window and listen to Clement's heavy breathing.

As much as I don't want to, I can't help but stare at my travel companion. It would be true to say he's an odd one and, as offensively blunt as he is, it's strangely refreshing. What isn't so refreshing is his complete refusal to discuss William Huxley. It's also perplexing why a clearly working-class man is prepared to defend a wealthy, former Conservative politician. Unless, of course, he is telling the truth and there's no story to be told.

I have a horrible feeling my itch will never be properly scratched.

With nothing better to do, and before the signal dies again, I check for emails on my phone and quickly wish I hadn't. In amongst the usual dross is an email from Damon with yet another brief for an interview with a z-lister. This time it's the wife of a Premier League footballer I've never heard of, and relates to the launch of her own fashion label.

How the fuck does this kind of tripe constitute news? Did I miss the meeting where proper investigative journalism was struck from the job description and replaced with making the unimportant important? And who the hell wants to read it anyway? Not me, for sure, and I certainly don't want to write it.

As much as it kills me, I invest half-an-hour, and much patience due to the sketchy mobile signal, researching the former model, Madison Marsh. At least I'll be able to tell Damon I've done something constructive with my day if he asks.

"What's up, doll? You've got a face like a slapped arse."

I look up from my phone to find Clement has woken from his slumber.

"Are you always so charming?"

"Always. So, what's up?"

"Nothing really. Just work stuff."

He then looks at me — the wrong side of a socially acceptable glance. The carriage feels a degree or two warmer.

"Must be interesting, your job?"

"It was, once. Not so much these days."

"Is that why you've got your knickers in a twist about Bill

Huxley?"

"A bit. Good stories are hard to come by."

He appears to ponder my answer before gazing out of the window again. Seconds pass before he changes the course of our conversation.

"What's your surname?"

"Why do you want to know?"

"Same reason you followed me — curiosity."

"It's Hogan."

"That's a Paddy name, ain't it?"

"It's an Irish name," I frown. "If that's what you mean."

"So, your family are Paddies?"

"Will you stop using that word."

"Why?"

"Because it's derogatory."

"No it ain't. I had a Irish mate, Shaun, and we always called him Paddy. He didn't mind."

"He probably did, Clement, but I'd guess he was too scared of you to say anything."

"Doubt it. He was a tough bastard."

"Was?"

"He just upped sticks and went back home one day. Said he wanted to join the IRA."

I shake my head. "Shut up."

"What have I said?" he replies indignantly.

"Enough with the Irish stereotypes. Next you'll be telling me your mate loved a drop of Guinness, and potatoes for breakfast."

"Funny you say that ..."

"Stop."

"Alright. I was only making conversation."

An uncomfortable silence descends. Too uncomfortable.

"To answer your question, I have Irish family on my father's side. I never met my paternal grandparents but they were from Cork and came over just after the war."

"What was your old man's name?"

"Dennis. Dennis Hogan."

"Right."

Clement then shuts his eyes again choosing sleep over conversation for the remaining fifteen minutes of our journey.

He comes around just as the train edges into Waterloo.

"Sleep well?"

"Yeah, ta."

He then gets up and stretches his orangutan-like arms before grabbing the rucksack. The train squeals to a halt and the doors open.

"Cheers for the pint, doll. I'll be seeing you."

"Wait. Can I get your ..."

He's already out the door before I finish my sentence. That's twice he's walked away from me — twice more than I'd typically accept from anyone. However, something about Clement has got under my skin. He is intriguing, in a car crash kind of way.

I get up and hurry after him, but the platform is packed and the queue for the two functioning ticket machines bottlenecked. By the time I force my way onto the station concourse, he's nowhere to be seen.

"Yeah. See ya, Clement," I mumble under my breath. Without his full name or any way of contacting him, I'm not so sure I will.

Nothing else to do but trundle down to the Tube station.

I could go back to the office but I'm not in the mood. And if I'm in trouble for not turning up, I might as well go the whole hog and skip the entire day. I suppose I could head home and deal with the stack of clothes I left lying on my bed. At least I'll have something to show for my day; not to mention I'd rather not have a dead man's clothes hanging around any longer than necessary.

Decision made, I make my way to the Jubilee Line.

In an effort to boost my spirits, I spend the entire journey home thinking about where I might escape to, once I've sold the clothes. Morocco or Greece should be pleasantly warm this time of year, or maybe Malta.

I turn the corner into my road still undecided.

The building in which my flat is located is a red-brick Victorian end-of-terrace. With the coffee shop taking up the entire ground floor, the entrance to my flat and parking space are accessed at the back of the building via a scrubby patch of tarmac the estate agent tried selling as a courtyard garden. In reality, it's a litter-strewn area where the coffee shop staff congregate for a smoke and the bins are stored.

As usual, the search for a door key involves a prolonged rummage in my handbag. One day I'll get around to clearing out the unnecessary crap I carry around all day. I locate the key just as I reach the door.

I look up, and stop dead.

I'm not going to need the key after all.

10

Half an inch ajar maybe — enough I might not have noticed.

Did I close it this morning?

I try to play back the scene when I left earlier but the whole episode with Clement has consigned prior memories to the deepest recesses of my mind.

Conscious my home might now be a crime scene, I push the door open with my foot and listen for any sound of movement at the top of the stairs. I count a minute in my head but all I can hear is traffic on the road out front.

"Hello," I call up the stairs.

Seconds pass and there's no response; not that I'd expect a burglar to appear at the top of the stairs and return a polite reply. I would, however, expect them to be spooked and make a swift exit. Unless they're prepared to jump out of a first floor window, this is the only way out.

Do I go in or call the police?

I call up the stairs again. The same silence echoes back.

If I have been burgled, the perpetrators appear to have left. Perhaps it would be better to establish the facts before calling the police. I can't imagine they'll be too pleased if I simply forgot to shut the front door properly.

After a few seconds thought, I conclude it's far more likely I'm a victim of nothing more than my own paranoia. I take a breath and march up the stairs.

The lounge looks exactly as I left it — untidy. Same with the kitchen. The spare bedroom houses a desk and a lumpy sofa bed, but no intruders. Finally, I check my bedroom.

I don't own much in the way of jewellery and what I do own is of limited value. Still, seeing my jewellery box on the dresser in the same state I left it, brings a sigh of relief. I scan the rest of the room and nothing appears out of place. In truth, the only items in the flat worth stealing are Dennis Hogan's suits, and they're still piled on the bed as I left them this morning ... I think.

Conscious of their potential value, I'm almost certain I carefully laid them out on the bed to avoid creasing them too much. Now, though, they look almost as if they've been thrown on the bed. There's something else, too — the pile of boxes I neatly stacked up against the wardrobe. Three columns of four boxes? I'm sure I stacked four columns of three boxes.

Taking a seat on the edge of the bed, concern begins to mount. Is my memory going? You hear stories all the time of people my age, and even younger, developing early onset dementia. And while it's not common, it does happen as I know too well. My maternal grandmother, Irene, was diagnosed in her mid-fifties and never made it to her fifty-eighth birthday.

Perhaps I'm being ridiculous — it's more likely just stress. There would surely be other symptoms if there really was cause for concern. People forget things all the time, and I was in a hurry this morning. Maybe I'm just remembering how I *thought* I left everything, rather than the scene left by an unfit, middle-aged woman rushing around and stressing about being late for work.

Christ, I need that holiday.

Satisfied I've not been burgled, and I'm probably not losing my marbles, I pull out my phone and search for the second-hand clothes store.

A quick call confirms they're definitely interested in purchasing any and all quality clothing, so I tell them I'll pop in with my haul shortly.

Apart from the suits and the shoes, I need to check if there are other clothes stashed in the boxes besides the pullovers I found. It's a task which doesn't hold much appeal but if it helps fund a few poolside cocktails, I suppose it'll be worth the effort.

I start with a quick trip to the kitchen and return with a dozen carrier bags to separate the items of value from those which will end up either in a charity shop or the bin. I then discard the lid of the first box, which happens to be the same box I've already checked. All three sweaters go into one bag, along with a couple of equally expensive shirts. The rest is just underwear, vests, and socks, which I bag up for the bin — nobody wants second-hand pants.

I open the lid of the next box and immediately drop it. Staring up at me, and cased in a silver frame, is a picture of my own face; or at least a slightly younger version of my face. I recognise the photo as it's one I used for a profile picture on Facebook a few years back —

and it isn't the only one.

By the time I empty the box, I'm left with a dozen framed photos of Emma Hogan; all of which have been pulled from my Facebook profile.

The find is unsettling.

Did Dennis Hogan display them just to torment himself, or was he some kind of fantasist trying to pretend he was a proud father?

It makes no sense.

The third box only adds more questions when I unearth the scrapbooks Miles DuPont referred to. In chronological order, each of them is stuffed with newspaper clippings of reports and articles I've written — going right the way back to my days working for the provincial newspaper. I take a closer look at the first scrapbook which appears to cover my early career and contains age-tarnished slips of paper printed with some of the first words I ever had published.

I sit on the bed and spend ten minutes reading long-forgotten articles penned by a naive, but fiercely ambitious, young reporter. It's an experience akin to reading old school reports and fills me with a mixture of nostalgic pride and perhaps a little sadness for selling out on that young reporter's dreams.

Soon enough, though, the reason I've being gifted the chance to reminisce becomes more of a pressing consideration. I've unearthed what would appear to be the possessions of a proud, loving, and supportive father — not terms you would ever use to describe Dennis

Hogan. Were the photos and scrapbooks his coping mechanism to ease a guilty conscience? I hope they didn't work and he carried the burden of guilt until he drew his last breath.

My angst rekindled, I work through the rest of the boxes but don't find much of interest or value. Part of me is relieved not to find any other items Dennis Hogan used to offset his guilt.

Once everything is bagged up, I stand back and assess my handiwork. It strikes me that my father shuffled off this mortal coil with very little to his name. Clearly he had money but owned very few material possessions. A pile of bags and boxes isn't much to show for a lifetime, and immeasurably less than what he could have possessed if he hadn't so abhorrently squandered the opportunity to be a proper husband and father.

I make another dozen trips up and down the stairs to load everything back into the car. I then double and triple check I've shut the front door before heading over to Maida Vale.

There's an old saying: one man's junk is another man's treasure. This is apparent when I step through the door of 'Loved Again'; the second-hand clothes shop.

I'm greeted by a tall, willowy woman who introduces herself as the proprietor, Penny. Rather than lug everything into the shop, Penny comes out to the car to inspect my wares.

"These are superb quality, and in exceptional condition," she coos, inspecting the suits. I think I'd like to play poker with Penny.

We then shift everything into the shop where I have to stand around like a spare part while each garment is individually appraised. That process takes forty minutes but eventually Penny is ready to make an offer.

"How does fourteen-hundred sound?"

It sounds far too much for a load of old clothes.

"Oh, I was really hoping for a bit more. It's for my father's headstone, you see."

Wherever my father is buried, and I don't much care, I'd rather dance on his grave than mark it with a granite tribute. Nevertheless, it's a useful bartering tool.

Penny taps away at a calculator. "I could push it to sixteen-hundred but that's my limit I'm afraid."

"Okay" I sigh. "That'll go some way I suppose."

If there is a hell, my ticket is already booked so I feel no guilt playing the part of a mourning daughter for financial gain.

Penny then counts out sixteen hundred pounds and we shake hands. I leave the shop with a handful of empty carrier bags and a purse stuffed with cash.

I throw the bags in the boot and resist the urge to scream with joy once I'm behind the wheel — just in case Penny is looking out of the window. The journey home is dominated with thoughts of sandy beaches and tight-buttocked waiters.

I pull into the parking bay and retrieve the carrier bags from the boot. Just as I'm about to slam it shut, I spot the notebook I abandoned earlier, lodged in the gap behind the wheel arch. I pick it up, intent on adding it to the rest of Dennis Hogan's possessions destined for the tip.

Relieved at finding the door to the flat firmly shut, I head back upstairs. A coffee is definitely in order so I head straight for the kitchen and toss the notebook on the side.

As I wait for the kettle to boil, I hide my wad of cash at the back of a drawer. If I am ever burgled, I trust the intruder won't look beyond the pile of old utility bills and other assorted crap I hide in the drawer when I can't be arsed to find a proper home for it.

I turn my attention back to the still-rumbling kettle and the notebook lying on the side. With nothing else better to do while I wait I pick it up and flick through the pages. The content isn't quite what I expected. Each page has what appears to be a hand-written surname at the top, and is divided into two columns. The left column is headed with the letter G and the right column the letter R, and both columns contain some kind of tally system — four vertical lines with a horizontal line struck through the middle to denote a total of five. Some of the pages have a tally of two or three; others have ten or eleven. Quite what the letters indicate is a mystery.

I flick through the whole notebook and there must be close to a hundred surnames listed across the pages. Perhaps Dennis Hogan was a bookie, and this was a way of keeping tabs on which punter owed him what. It's a possibility and might explain his income, but still a stab in the dark.

With my curiosity piqued, I turn my attention to the name

embossed on the front cover – Clawthorn. I can honestly say it's not a word I've ever heard before but it could simply be the name of a stationery company. I grab my phone and google it.

The results are limited and there's absolutely nothing relating to stationery. In fact, there's not a lot relating to anything beyond random user profiles and geeky gaming forums. Whatever Clawthorn is, or was, it appears obscure enough to have escaped Google's search indices.

I take a step towards the bin intent on adding the notebook to its contents. I don't quite make it – my curiosity won't allow an unanswered question to fester. As little as it matters, I kind of want to know what Clawthorn is, and maybe even what Dennis Hogan was keeping tally of.

I snap a photo of the front cover and three further photos of the inner pages, and post them on Twitter, asking my eight hundred followers if the name rings any bells.

Content the investigation requires no further effort on my part, I toss the notebook into my handbag. Caffeine is now my priority.

11.

"Yeah, babe. They're like totally amazing threads for the modern girl."

If Madison Marsh calls me 'babe' one more time, I'm going to hop in a cab, head to Essex, and punch her in the throat. I rang with the intention of booking an appointment with her PA, but now I'm embroiled in a mind-numbing conversation with the woman herself.

It's too early for this shit.

"It sounds amazing, Madison. So, when would you like me to pop over?"

"Oh my God," she gasps. "And there's this dress with a lace bodice. It's just so gorgeous — you've never seen anything like it in your life, babe."

"I can't wait to see it ... maybe next Thursday, or Friday?"

"What about Wednesday?"

If I could do Wednesday, I'd have said Wednesday, you dumb fuck.

"Unfortunately I'm stuck in meetings all day Wednesday. How about the following week?"

"That's totally cool, babe. Tuesday?"

"Great. Shall we say one o'clock?"

"Brilliant ... I'm so excited, babe, and I know you're just gonna love the clothes."

I end the call before she gets a second wind.

Madison Marsh is a prime example of what happens when stupid people get rich. Her husband, Danny Marsh, earns seven million quid a year. Seven million quid for kicking a football around — what is wrong with the world?

After their fairy-tale wedding last year, which reputedly cost six hundred grand, the young couple moved into a ten-bedroom McMansion in Essex. Clearly bored out of her tiny mind, Madison felt she needed a respectable job — rather than her prior job of being photographed with her tits constantly on show. So, she's now set up a clothing brand which is about to be launched on an unsuspecting public.

Given the choice, I think the public would prefer a chlamydia epidemic.

It would be fair to say my morning is not going well, and a far cry from the pleasurable evening I enjoyed yesterday; on the sofa in my pyjamas, browsing exotic holidays with a bottle of wine and a pizza for company — all courtesy of my unexpected inheritance.

Before I can make a decision on the destination of said holiday, I need to book some time off, and that means a conversation with Damon. With zero enthusiasm, I head to his office.

"Have you got a minute?" I ask, knocking on the already open door.

"Not really."

"Fine — thirty seconds will do. I want to book some leave."

He looks up. "Why?"

"Because I'm entitled to it."

"Right," he huffs. "You keep skipping out of the office like yesterday and you'll find yourself on permanent leave."

"I was chasing a lead on a story."

"You know the rules. Everyone attends the morning briefing without fail or excuse."

"Point taken. Now, can I book that leave?"

His face painted with disdain, he turns to the computer monitor.

"When?" he grunts.

"Next month."

"No can do."

"The month after?"

"There's nothing free until late July."

"I don't want to book anything during the school holidays. It'll cost double, and every resort will be full of screaming brats."

Disdain morphs to smug. "Not my problem. You should have booked earlier."

"Actually, thinking about it, I quite like the idea of going away in September. And didn't Gini just switch her leave from September to October?"

Fuck you, Damon.

"Fine, whatever. Now, get on with some work, will you."

I leave him with a smile.

I'm not happy about waiting until September but I don't want Damon to know that. It's still five months away but the wait is preferable to taking a break in the school holidays. A fortnight of daily smear tests would be preferable to that experience.

I head back to my cubicle; content to have won the battle if not the war.

With all the motivation of a politician in July, I slump down in my chair and stare at the monitor. I have plenty to do but little worth doing. Rather than actual work, I decide a browse through Twitter might rile me into action.

I click the icon in my bookmarks and the Twitter page opens up. I expected to see a few notifications about my post from yesterday but there's nothing — no comments, no retweets, and no likes. Either Clawthorn is as much a mystery to my followers as it is to me, or I've been summarily unfollowed by eight hundred people overnight. I click on my profile to check, and discover the tweet containing the photo of the notebook isn't even there.

I think back. I definitely compiled the tweet but did I actually post it? I can't remember but the evidence is clear to see, or not in this case. I grab my phone and tweet just the photo of the notebook cover, ensuring it's definitely on my timeline. If I can't take a holiday, I need to take up yoga or something — this stress is messing with my mind.

While I've got my photo album open the notorious shots taken at Kenton Stables last November scroll into view. Not much use for them now. I delete all but three: those featuring Clement. I think back to our conversation yesterday and what he said about fate.

A thought occurs.

Whilst I don't believe in fate, I do believe there's more to the big man than meets the eye, and an exposé about the life of an underworld fixer might be just the kind of story my career desperately needs.

There's only one minor glitch — I have no idea how to find him.

Just for the sheer hell of it, I type 'Clement' into Google and conduct an image search. If I scoured the results for a solid week I wouldn't reach the end. Why didn't I get his phone number, or at least his full name? I have nothing to go on ... or do I?

Tapping my pen on the desk I consider the ramifications.

Fuck it.

It takes five minutes to find what I'm looking for and, when I do, I'm taken aback by the name of the residence I'm about to call. I plan what I'm going to say and dial the number.

A distinctly middle-class voice chirps a greeting. "Good morning, Clement House."

"Mr Huxley?"

"Speaking."

"My name is Emma Hogan and I was hoping you might be able to help me."

"That depends," he replies suspiciously. "Who are you Ms Hogan?"

If I tell him I'm a journalist, this conversation will be over before its even started.

"I'm calling about a mutual friend."

"And who might that be?"

"Clement."

The line falls silent.

"Mr Huxley? Are you still there?"

"I'm here," he finally replies in a low voice.

"Did you hear what I said?"

"Yes."

"And?"

"You know Clement?" he asks, his tone guarded.

"I met him yesterday."

"Where?"

"To cut a long story short, we had a chat for a few hours but I lost him in the crowd at Waterloo Station."

"Is he ... okay?"

"I can't really answer that Mr Huxley. As I said, we didn't speak long enough for me to really get a measure of the man."

"Right. Forgive the blunt question but why are you calling me?"

"He told me he helped you with a problem. Is that correct?"

I let the question hang.

"He did."

Despite the gnawing temptation to ask about Kenton Stables, I can't risk saying anything which might put William Huxley on the defensive. I stick to my plan.

"Well, I also have a problem and I could really do with Clement's help."

"That may be so, but you haven't answered my question. Why are you calling me?"

"Because I have no idea how to find him."

"And you think I do?"

"That's what I'm hoping."

"I don't," he sighs. "But trust me, Ms Hogan — if you genuinely need his help, Clement will find you."

"Err, okay. Is there anything else you can tell me about him?"

"I think this conversation is over."

"Sorry?"

"If Clement offers you help, take it, and be grateful. Beyond that, I have nothing more to say."

"But ..."

"Good day, Ms Hogan."

He hangs up.

I sit back in my chair, perplexed. It's not the strangest telephone conversation I've had with a source but it's certainly up there. Huxley's tone throughout the call felt oddly familiar. In the past I've had to interview people who've witnessed all manner of tragic events from fatal road accidents to terrorist bombings, and they all spoke in the same shocked, subdued tone. With Huxley, though, there was something else — something I can't put my finger on.

Frustrated, I throw my pen across the desk. It seems I've wasted months fretting over the wrong lead, as it's now clear Clement is the one with a story to tell, not William Huxley.

My computer chimes the arrival of an email. I glance at the screen to see who's pestering me but don't recognise the sender's email address. The subject is a single word: Notebook.

I open the email ...

Dear Ms Hogan

My name is Allen Tamthy and I saw your post on Twitter regarding the notebook.

I must confess I have an ulterior motive in that I'm quite interested in purchasing the notebook from you; if you'd entertain selling it? I wish I could tell you something exciting about the name Clawthorn but it's actually just an old English card game. It was popular for a brief period in the seventeenth century but fell from favour in lieu of simpler games.

There was a brief resurgence in the popularity of Clawthorn in the early sixties and your notebook is actually an official score pad from that period. I'm an avid collector of Clawthorn memorabilia, hence my interest.

To cut to the chase, I'd be willing to pay £350 for it. If you're interested, I'm in London for a few days and willing to pay cash.

I look forward to hearing from you.

Regards, Allen Tamthy

Now the names and tally system make sense. Not only has my curiosity been sated, but it appears some sap is willing to pay good money for the notebook. I email Allen Tamthy back, telling him I'd be willing to do a deal at four hundred quid, and I can meet him after work.

Clearly keen, his reply arrives within a minute ...

I'm happy to pay £400. I'm in a meeting near Paddington most of the afternoon but I should be free by seven o'clock. There's a wine bar called Marco's on Spring Street where we could meet, if that's convenient for you?

I reply to confirm we have a deal, and I'll meet him at the wine bar at seven. Suddenly my day feels a little less shit.

Buoyed by another unexpected windfall, and because I've got so much work to catch up with from yesterday, I work like a beaver for the rest of the day. It's not work I'm proud of, but it's work nonetheless. I even stay at my desk until half-six — not because I'm committed, but because Paddington is halfway between work and home so I can head straight from the office to the meeting with Allen

Tamthy.

After a lazy stroll to Hyde Park Corner tube station, I hop on the Piccadilly Line and then the Bakerloo Line, arriving at Paddington with five minutes to spare. Low cloud and dusk combine to greet me as I emerge from the Tube. I check the map on my phone to confirm Marco's Wine Bar is just a few minutes' walk away.

Spring Street turns out to be no different from any other London backstreet, in that it consists of a mix of flats, shops, takeaways, and a pub. Without even seeing it, I know Marco's will be much more down-market than the wine bars around Belgravia and Chelsea.

As it transpires, it's so down-market it appears to have gone out of business — the lack of lights and bailiff's notice in the window offering conclusive proof of the fact. Clearly Allen Tamthy isn't a regular and probably isn't even aware our meeting place won't be serving chilled Prosecco this evening, or any evening.

Seeing as he's due in a minute or two I decide to wait rather than arrange an alternative venue. As the day's workload catches up with me, I lean against a brick pillar adjacent to the door and contemplate how I can spend Mr Tamthy's money.

A new handbag? A spa weekend? A phone upgrade ...

"Move an inch and you're dead, bitch."

Before I can even process the warning, let alone react, something sharp digs into my rib cage.

"Yeah, it's a knife," the voice confirms. "And I'll fucking use it if you don't do as you're told."

12

The only part of my body I dare move are my eyes. They widen, and flick left and right, but there's no potential saviour anywhere to be seen. I could scream but to what end? Panicking a man with a knife surely isn't a good idea. I should talk to him; try to calm the situation.

"Look, I don't ..."

His next move takes me by surprise as a hand grasps the collar of my coat and yanks hard. Within a split-second I've left the relative safety of the street and I'm stumbling backwards into the dark alleyway adjacent to the wine bar. Somehow, I move my feet quickly enough to maintain balance, until an outstretched leg proves an effective trip hazard.

I sprawl backwards landing hard on my backside. The pain is accompanied by the stench of damp, and stale piss.

Shock eventually gives way to fear, but that fear is tinged with a grim acceptance. All these years walking the streets of London — it was always a statistical probability I'd be the victim of a mugging one day. My luck has run out, it seems.

I look up at my assailant — a genuine streak of piss — tall, and rake thin. Despite his hooded top, there's no disguising his distinctive face: acne-scarred, sunken eyes, and an unkempt goatee beard. However, his tardy grooming is not my biggest issue. That would be the six-inch knife he's waving around.

The alley is narrow so there's no chance of scrambling to my feet and escaping his clutches. I just want to get this over with.

"What do you want?"

"Gimme your bag, and your phone."

His accent is one I've heard a thousand times — the accent of a disaffected, sink estate, youth. It's strangely reassuring but his youth and accent confirm the motive here is almost certainly financial; a drug habit to fund, no doubt. If he'd been older and more articulate, the motive might be decidedly more sinister.

I tug the strap over my head and hold up the handbag. Like a feral dog being offered a scrap of food, he cautiously reaches forward and snatches it away.

"Gimme your phone."

The cost of the phone is immaterial. What I'd rather avoid is the tedious inconvenience of setting-up a new one.

"Look, it's just a cheap Android model. It's not worth anything."

"Gimme the fuckin' phone!"

"Fine," I snap, reaching for my pocket.

I take my eyes off the youth for a second, and in that second a shadow suddenly swallows all but a few slivers of light from the street.

My head snaps up, and the source of the shadow now stands in the same patch of ground previously occupied by the youth. The youth himself is now pinned to the wall; held in place by an outstretched arm.

123

I clamber to my feet and double-check my eyes aren't deceiving me. They're not, and an involuntary gasp escapes.

"Clement!"

"Alright, doll."

The big man's demeanour is strangely relaxed, considering the circumstances, whereas the streak of piss is wide eyed and petrified. As deeply satisfying as it is to see him suffer, I can't imagine he'll last much longer with the big man's hand clamped around his throat.

"Youth of today," Clement tuts. "No respect."

"Um, you do realise he's suffocating?"

"He'll last a few seconds more. You okay?"

"I think so."

I grab my handbag from the floor as Clement turns back to the youth.

"You still hanging in there, sunshine?"

"I don't think he's in a position to answer."

"Fair point."

He releases his hold on the kid's throat and grabs a fistful of his hoodie. "I think you owe my friend an apology."

"Careful," I urge. "He's got a knife."

"*Had* a knife."

With his free hand, Clement delves into his pocket and pulls out the knife. He then turns back to the youth.

"Did nobody tell you not to fuck around with big boy's toys?"

It seems fear has robbed him of words and all he can do is shake his head.

"Shame."

Clement turns to me. "Step aside, doll."

I do as instructed and watch on as Clement grabs the youth's hoodie with both hands.

"See ya, dickhead."

He then hurls him down the alley with such force it's like watching an Olympic shot-putter throwing a grapefruit. Open mouthed, I watch in shock as the young man bounces across the litter-strewn ground.

My shock turns to relief as he then sits up and whimpers a few profanities.

"Christ, Clement. You could have killed him."

"If I wanted to kill him, he wouldn't be sat there with just a few cuts and bruises."

No doubt true.

"But, thank you," I puff. "I don't know what I'd have done if you hadn't shown up."

My gratitude prompts an obvious question. "But how did you ..."

"I followed you."

"Why?"

"Let's just say I had a feeling you might need help at some stage."

"A feeling? Do you follow many women on the off-chance they might be mugged?"

"Nah. This is a first."

"I don't know whether to be flattered or concerned."

"I'd stick a few quid on concerned."

I flash him a smile but it's not returned.

"What were you doing here?" he asks.

"I was supposed to be meeting a guy in the wine bar next door."

"The wine bar which isn't open?"

I nod.

"At what time?"

"Seven."

"And where is he?"

I check my phone. It's now ten past seven and there's no text message or email from Mr Tamthy. I poke my head out of the alley and look up and down the street but there's no one loitering around.

"He's either running late or a no-show."

Clement strides down the alley. Looming over the youth, he barks a question.

"What's your name, dickhead?"

The terrified youth stammers an answer. "Jaydon."

"Listen up, Jaydon — I'm gonna ask you a question, and if you bullshit me I'll tear you a new arsehole. Got it?"

Jaydon nods.

"Did you just randomly decide to mug my friend here?"

"Yeah."

"Wrong answer."

Clement reaches down — perhaps to deliver another throttling —

and the kid reacts by shuffling backwards on his buttocks. Unfortunately for him, there's nowhere to go.

"Alright, alright," he pleads. "Some geezer said she'd be here. He gave me a hundred quid and said I could have another hundred when I handed over her bag and phone, and I could keep any cash she had."

"What geezer?"

"Dunno his name. I was walking out the bookies on Napier Road and he called me over to his motor."

"How were you supposed to tell him when the job was done?"

"He said he'd call me in an hour."

"What did he look like?"

"I dunno, bruv. Like, ordinary."

"Ordinary?"

"Yeah, apart from his nose. It was well crooked."

"Was he old, young? Black, white?"

"White and … I dunno … old, and fat as fuck."

"How old?"

"Mate, I dunno. Could have been fifty, could have been seventy for all I know … I'd taken some ket so my head was mashed."

"What motor was he driving?"

"Didn't pay much attention … it was black, maybe a Merc or an Audi."

Clement squats down and clicks his fingers. "Gimme the hundred quid."

"What?"

"You heard. I won't ask again."

"I've already spent forty."

"Give it."

Jaydon mutters something unintelligible and digs a hand into his pocket, pulling out three twenty-pound notes which Clement quickly snatches away.

"Consider this payment for a life lesson: crime don't pay, unless you're any good at it, and you ain't, sunshine."

Clement throws the kid a parting glare before ambling back up the alley.

"Fancy a drink, doll? His round."

Nothing would be more welcome than a stiff drink, but not before I take my turn to glare at the kid.

"Not such a big man without your knife, are you? Stupid little prick."

Restoring some measure of dignity, I follow Clement out of the alley.

"Feel better for that?" he asks.

"A little."

"Good. There's a boozer just up the road."

I've never felt unsafe on the streets before and it infuriates me I now find myself walking as close to Clement as I can. That in itself is troubling; I'm putting my faith in a man I only met yesterday. Maybe it's delayed shock, but it's a safe haven I'll take for the moment.

"You know you were set up, doll?"

"Eh? How do you know that?"

"The kid was waiting for you. Muggers don't tend to hang around in alleyways hoping some bird just happens to stop by."

"Why would anyone set me up?"

"You tell me. You must piss off a lot of people in your job."

I think back over the last few months. It doesn't take long to establish I haven't written anything interesting, let alone capable, of pissing anyone off.

I'm still scouring my mind when we step through the door of a pub I'd usually try to avoid — the kind of shithole where football hooligans flock pre-match.

We head straight for the bar and Clement orders a pint.

"What you having, doll?"

"Brandy, neat. Make it a double."

He gives my order to the trashy barmaid. She flutters her false eyelashes in return but Clement's attention appears focused on her cleavage.

Drinks acquired, I follow him over to a table by the window.

"Is she your type?" I ask as we sit down opposite one another. "The barmaid?"

"Nah. She'd do for a night but she's all tits n' lips. Nothing upstairs."

"What a charming turn of phrase."

"You asked," he shrugs.

Ordinarily, the kind of casual chauvinism Clement just displayed would have me on my soap box. On this occasion, however, there are more immediate issues to debate.

"I've thought about what you said, Clement, and I can't think of anyone who'd set me up."

His eyebrows arch. "No one?"

"Honestly," I plea.

"Alright. Who was the geezer you were supposed to meet."

"Some anorak obsessed with old card games. We only swapped emails but he seemed harmless enough."

"He didn't show up, though."

"No."

"You got his number?"

"Err, no."

"How did he arrange to meet you then?"

"He emailed me. I presume he got my email address from my Twitter profile."

"But he didn't give you a phone number? Ain't that a bit odd?"

In hindsight, perhaps I let the chance to make a fast buck cloud my judgement.

"When you add it all together," Clement adds. "This definitely smells like a set-up."

I take a slow sip of brandy and let Clement's theory sink in. Being mugged is one thing, but knowing I was lured into a trap is deeply disturbing, particularly as I can't think of any motive.

"What was this bloke's name?" Clement asks.

"Allen Tamthy."

He sits back in his seat and stares into the space above my head, all the while stroking his ridiculous moustache. I wait patiently for a response but nothing comes.

"Am I boring you?"

"Eh?"

"You're miles away, Clement."

"I was thinking."

"About what?"

"That name. I'm sure I've heard it before but ... nah, it's gone."

"That happens at our age."

"What does?"

"Forgetting things. Someone can tell me their name and I'll forget it within ten seconds."

"Yeah, well, some of us have to think a lot further back."

"Don't make excuses. You can't be much younger than me, if at all."

"Dunno. I've lost track."

"Of your age?"

"Of my age, of my life."

"'Course you have," I scoff. "Some would call that getting old. Happens to the best of us, Clement."

The scowl he casts my way implies a change of subject might be prudent.

"Do you think I should go to the police?"

"If you reckon they'll do anything. Keep me out of it, though."

"Why?"

"Cos I said so. I don't trust 'em."

From what I saw of Clement's brief meeting with Sergeant Banner down in Surrey I suspect the feeling is mutual.

"I'll just say a random passer-by intervened."

"That works for me, but you know they'll do fuck all?"

"They're the police, Clement. They can't just choose to ignore a threat to my safety."

"You ain't had many dealings with the Old Bill, have you, doll?"

"Err, not really, no."

"You'll make a statement, fill out some forms, and they'll send you on your way."

"I doubt that's how they work."

"What do you reckon they'll do then?"

A few seconds thought undermines my rash defence. This is the same police force that came a distant second to a firm of estate agents when it came to locating my father's next of kin.

"I, err ..."

Realistically, what can they do? No direct threat has been made against me and I don't even know why, or if, this character, Allen Tamthy, set me up.

"Well?" Clement prods.

"Maybe it's just a coincidence. If someone really wanted to get at me, why send some junkie fuckwit to do it?"

"Cover."

"Not with you."

"Our little friend said some bloke approached him outside a bookies, and that he'd call him to collect your gear. That sounds like someone covering their tracks. Whoever that bloke was, he picked some random kid to turn you over because there's nothing connecting them."

"Hmmm ... that all sounds a bit too cloak and dagger to be plausible."

"Maybe, but either way the Old Bill won't be arsed to investigate."

"So, what can I do?"

"Be careful."

"Thanks for that pearl of wisdom. I feel so much safer now."

I finish the brandy and delve into my handbag in search of a stale packet of cigarettes I started two months ago. At times of high stress, a crafty smoke always calms my nerves. On this occasion, it has the reverse effect, as I can't find the packet amongst all the junk. I start removing individual items to make the task easier.

"What's that?" Clement asks.

"That's the notepad Allen Tamthy was supposed to buy. I guess it was too good to be true — that's four hundred quid I can kiss goodbye to."

He picks it up; inspecting it closely. "Shit, doll."

"What?"

Rather than answer immediately, he slowly flicks through the pages.

"Where did you get this?" he asks, his tone grave.

"It was in an old suit jacket belonging to my father."

With a degree of reverence, he carefully places the notebook on the table and continues to stare at it.

"What's so fascinating, Clement? It's just a score pad for some lame card game."

"No, it bleedin' ain't."

"What is it then?"

"A fuckload of trouble. If this is what I think it is, I know who it belongs to."

I can't imagine much worries Clement but something has clearly unsettled him.

"Spit it out then. Who does it belong to?"

"The Tallyman."

13.

I can't control the cynic in me, and a snort of laughter escapes. "The Tallyman?"

Clement nods, his expression still grave.

"Right," I scoff. "And would you say the Tallyman is like Batman, or more like Superman?"

"Nothing funny about Clawthorn, doll. Trust me on that."

"If it's not a card game, what is it then, smartarse?"

"You're gonna need another drink."

Much to my annoyance he gets up and marches over to the bar — I don't like cliff-hangers. I continue searching for the elusive packet of cigarettes to fill the time. He returns just as I unearth a beat-up packet of Silk Cut.

"Here," he says, handing me another brandy.

"Come on then. Don't keep me in suspense any longer — who is this mysterious Tallyman?"

Ignoring my sarcastic tone, he sits down and takes a long draw on his pint.

"Right, doll. First things first — you can't tell anyone you've got the Tallyman's notebook, and I mean anyone."

"Okay," I huff, rolling my eyes. "Just tell me what it is for Christ's sake."

"Clawthorn is a club started in the late fifties," he begins, his voice low. "Originally, it was for business folk, and they'd meet up to discuss whatever shit business folk talk about."

"Like a networking club?"

"Dunno what that is, but if you say so. Anyway, sometime in the late-sixties, they decided to move in a different direction and started by culling the members who weren't considered important enough, and adding new rules to keep the riff-raff out. I 'spose it was a bit like the Freemasons, but a damn sight harder to join. That's when they adopted a new motto: *favent, in gratiam*."

"Yeah, I'm not great with Latin."

"It means: *favour for a favour*."

"I'll take your word for that. Carry on."

"Basically, it became a place where the rich and powerful could swap favours. Rumour has it that members included cabinet ministers, heads of major banks, high-ranking police officers, newspaper bosses, High Court judges, and all manner of businessmen — anyone in a position of power and influence."

"That doesn't sound so scandalous. Why the secrecy?"

"They weren't doing each other's shopping, or lending the odd fiver, doll. These were men who had the power to get a court case dropped, or to crash a stock value, or to run a smear campaign in the papers. What kind of favours do you think they were doing for each other?"

"Are you saying the members were breaking the law?""

"Fuck breaking the law. If you were a member of the Clawthorn Club, the law didn't apply to you. It was as corrupt as it gets."

"And this infamous Tallyman character?"

"He was the top bloke, like a chairman, I suppose. He kept tabs on all the members to monitor their favours and make sure they were playing by the rules. The tally in the notebook shows how many favours were given and received."

I pick up the notebook and flick through the pages. The letters G and R at the top of each page do tie-in with Clement's claim.

"So, you're telling me that all the names listed in this are high-profile individuals who were members of a corrupt club? Individuals who've broken the law to give and receive favours?"

"That's about the strength of it."

"Does this Clawthorn Club still exist?"

"Dunno, and to be honest, doll, even if it does still exist there's no way you'd be able to find out."

"Why not?"

"It's not like a normal club — you won't find their address in the Yellow Pages, and all the members were sworn to secrecy."

"So how do you know so much about it?"

"I don't know that much, but I do know ... I *knew* certain people back in the day, and there were whispers about the Clawthorn Club all over the manor. Thing is, you hear the same whispers over and over again, there's usually somethin' in it."

From my own experience, I don't disagree. Some of my best reports were founded on the same snippet of gossip from different sources.

"No smoke without fire, eh?"

"Yeah, and there was a lot of smoke about the Clawthorn Club."

"When was this?"

"A long time ago."

"Can you be more specific?"

"I could, but it don't matter — not to you, anyway."

A twenty-five year career in journalism has made me a deeply sceptical woman. I couldn't do my job without checking and double-checking facts, so whilst Clement's claim is deliciously intriguing, it could be a fairy-tale for all I know.

"And you think I was mugged because this Allen Tamthy, or Tallyman, wanted his notebook back?"

"Yeah."

"Okay. Ignoring the question about why it was in my father's jacket pocket, why didn't Allen Tamthy just buy it from me as we agreed? Why send the kid to steal my bag and my phone?"

"You're the journalist, doll. You tell me."

Surely four hundred quid is a drop in the ocean compared to the information in the notebook; assuming it is as Clement claims. He could have met me, handed over the cash, and I'd have walked away none the wiser.

"It doesn't make sense."

"One thing don't: how did he even know you had it?"

"He said he saw my ... oh, fuck."

"What?"

138

"I posted photos of the notebook on Twitter."

He pulls a face as if I'd just replied in Norwegian.

"I have photos of the notebook on my phone, including the inner pages with the names. That's why Tamthy couldn't just buy the notebook from me — he needed my phone as well."

"Makes sense."

"It does, assuming any of this is actually true."

"You've got another explanation?"

"The absence of an alternative explanation doesn't mean your story is the truth. And another thing, if this Clawthorn Club is so secretive, why the hell would Allen Tamthy use his real name?"

"He didn't. Haven't you worked that out?"

"Err, worked what out?"

"I said I'd heard the name before, and there's a reason why it stuck in my head."

"Go on."

"Allen Tamthy ain't a real name — it's an anagram for 'The Tallyman'."

Rather than take Clement's word for it I rearrange the letters in my head.

"Oh my God. So it is."

"Believe me now?"

An involuntary smile creeps across my lips as the buzz awakens.

"If this whole Clawthorn Club tale is true, Clement, I could be sitting on the story of the century."

He almost chokes on a mouthful of lager. "Are you fucking kiddin' me?"

"What?"

"Did you not listen to a word I just said? Seriously, doll, you don't wanna get involved with this, unless you've got a death wish."

"You could help me. That's what you do isn't it — solve problems?"

"Yeah, and this one is easy to fix. You just drop it."

"But what about the notebook? If it is what you say it is, this Tamthy character will still want it back."

Clement sits back and scratches his head. Long seconds pass as I await an answer.

"He ain't gonna give up on it," he concedes. "Even if you tell him you've got rid of the notebook, I doubt he'd believe you — I wouldn't."

"So what can I do? I don't fancy spending the next few weeks waiting to be mugged again."

My answer comes in the way of more head scratching.

As Clement ponders, I think about turning what I've learnt into a story. I don't have to think long to conclude I'm woefully short of enough evidence to even hint at what I now know. Stories of this magnitude can take months, if not years, of investigation and research. I've barely scratched the surface of this supposedly corrupt club and facts are thin on the ground.

"You know something, Clement, they say attack is the best form of defence."

"They also say fools rush in. What's your point?"

"My point is, why should I sit around and do nothing? I don't want to be constantly looking over my shoulder while this Allen Tamthy character plans how to get his notepad back."

"And what do you suggest doing instead?"

"Going after him."

"And how are you gonna do that, doll?"

"Help me investigate the Clawthorn Club. If I can get some hard evidence about what went on there, the notebook won't matter, and neither will Allen Tamthy, whoever he is."

It's a plea made from the heart rather than the head. I'm putting a huge amount of faith in a man I barely know, chasing a story that might be nothing more than a figment of that man's vivid imagination. It's a risk I'm prepared to take; the potential rewards are just too great to ignore.

Clement stares at his pint closely examining the beads of condensation trickling down the cold glass.

"I've got money, Clement. I can pay you."

"It ain't about the money," he mumbles.

"What is it then?"

"I'm one bloke."

"Yeah, but I bet you're a resourceful bloke."

He glances up and our eyes lock for just a second or two before he returns his attention to the glass.

"Fine." I huff. "I'll do it on my own."

I grab the notebook and throw it into my handbag along with the pack of cigarettes. I then get to my feet, intent on leaving, when Clement reaches across the table and grabs my forearm.

"Two conditions," he sighs.

I look down at his hand. Any other man grabbing me like that would get a slap for their troubles but Clement's grip feels reassuring rather than threatening.

"Go on."

"Firstly, you never leave my sight."

"That could be awkward when it comes to the bathroom."

"This is serious, doll."

"Okay, but obviously I have to go to work."

"I'll see you there, and be waiting when you finish."

"I can live with that. And the second condition?"

"I need a phone — nothin' complicated. Just in case you need to get hold of me in an emergency.

"You don't own a mobile phone?"

"Never needed one."

"So how do people get hold of you?"

"They don't."

He releases his grip on my arm. I retake my seat.

"We can pick one up in the morning. There's a mobile phone shop near my flat."

He nods.

"So, we're doing this?"

"Looks that way."

"Brilliant."

Not quite the full buzz but I feel a flutter in my chest. Finally, something to get my teeth stuck into, although my partner's solemn expression suggests he doesn't share my enthusiasm.

"Are you absolutely sure you want to do this, Clement? You seem reluctant."

"Not a case of wanting to, doll — it's a case of having to."

"Nobody's forcing you."

"Ain't they?" he mutters, getting to his feet. "I need a smoke. You coming?"

I don't need asking twice. The residue shock and two brandies has left a savage craving for nicotine.

We cross the bar and step through a door, leading into a scaled-down version of a prison exercise yard.

"What a lovely beer garden," I comment. "The overflowing bucket of fag butts is a nice touch."

Clement ignores my sarcasm and plucks a cigarette packet from his breast pocket. I wrestle one from my battered pack as he offers me a light.

The first drag is sublime, and whilst I accept it's a terrible habit, I condone it by virtue I've cut down from ten a day to just four or five a month.

We stand and puff away in silence. With Clement seemingly

unwilling to engage, I'm forced to rekindle our conversation.

"We'll split any money, you know."

"Money?"

"A story like this could be worth a small fortune."

"I told you, doll, the money ain't important."

"Of course it is. We all need money, Clement."

"All I need is enough for booze, fags, and food."

"What about paying your mortgage?"

"I work my rent."

"Oh, you don't own your own place?"

"Nope. Never have, never will."

"That's a very short-term attitude. I'm going to assume you don't have a pension so what are you going to do for an income when you retire?"

"I retired a long time ago."

"Eh? You said you were a fixer — that's surely a full-time job, isn't it?"

"More of a ... what's the word ... vocation."

"And that's why you don't want paying?"

He takes a long drag on his cigarette before answering.

"Let's just say I have different life goals from most folk, and none of them require money."

"Okay, but if you change your mind, my offer stands. Where do we start then?"

"Why are you asking me? This is your gig."

Bluntly put, but not an unfair statement, considering I haven't given it any thought myself.

"I'm going for a piss," he adds. "You'd better think on, before someone else does."

He flicks his butt away and leaves me to do exactly that.

Now the buzz has left, all that remains is the stark realisation there are no tantalising clues or obvious leads to pursue. Beyond what Clement told me, I know the sum total of not much, and that's not exactly a solid foundation to build a story.

Clearly Allen Tamthy is a non-starter as I don't even know who he is. That just leaves the notebook itself as my only source of inspiration.

One question immediately comes to mind: how did it end up in Dennis Hogan's jacket pocket?

I think back to my days working with Eric, and what he'd do in this situation — this is just the kind of mystery he used to revel in but Eric had a highly analytical mind whereas I've always tended to go on gut feeling. On this occasion, my gut is telling me I might need to search for answers in a place I hoped never to revisit.

I stub out my cigarette and head back in.

Clement has returned from emptying his bladder and is seated at the table, topping it up again.

"Same again?"

"Go on then, doll."

"It's Emma, by the way."

"What is?"

"My name — I presumed you'd forgotten as you keep referring to me as 'doll'."

"Just my way. Does it bother you?"

Only a few weeks ago, I overheard a conversation between a female customer and the manager of my local supermarket. The customer was complaining the male checkout operator called her 'love' on at least two occasions — an affront to her feminist principles, apparently. I remember feeling so sorry for that poor checkout operator whose only crime was being friendly. My feelings for the customer extended to a simple conclusion: she was a pernicious twat.

I flash Clement a smile. "No, it doesn't bother me."

After a quick trip to the bar, I return to the table and a belated thought strikes me.

"When you said I'm not to leave your sight, Clement, what exactly did you mean by that?"

"Trust me — I don't wanna watch you taking a shit."

"Yeah, that's reassuring, but what about the rest of the time?"

"You got a sofa?"

"Err, yes."

"It's now mine, at least until this is over."

Perhaps I was a little too keen to secure Clement's assistance, and didn't take his first condition as a cue for him to move in.

"I'm not sure I'm entirely comfortable with that."

"And you reckon I am?"

"It's just ... I haven't lived with anyone for years, and the last guy I lived with I'd known slightly longer than twenty-four hours."

"It's your call, doll, but remember what happened in that alley earlier — next time it might be your bedroom, and it won't be some dopey kid waving a knife around."

As I think of a way to backtrack, my phone chimes with the arrival of a text message. Welcoming the chance to think of anything but sharing my home with Clement, I delve into my handbag.

The message is from a withheld number ...

Place the notepad on the table and leave. This is your last chance to walk away unscathed.

14.

Sometimes, people don't like what you write. Emails, letters, and messages on social media websites — whatever the medium, I've received just about every threat a warped imagination might conjure up. It comes with the job and I've long since accepted that.

This is different. This feels close, and unnervingly real.

I slowly turn my head and scan the bar. A run-down backstreet pub on a Thursday evening, and not one of the two-dozen patrons look out of place: wiry old men with nicotine-stained fingers, bald men with beer bellies and crude tattoos, and a couple of cackling harpies with bottle-blonde hair. Every one of them lost in their own depressing world.

I nudge the phone across the table so Clement can read the message. After a quick glance, he repeats my action and scans the bar.

"This is it, doll — a chance to walk away and forget all about Clawthorn."

I should be scared, but there is an altogether different emotion blocking fear's path.

"Do you like theme parks, Clement?"

His blank stare suggests not.

"I do. Put me on the tallest, fastest rollercoaster and I'm in my element."

"Not with you."

"That message was sent to scare me but it's had the opposite effect — it proves I'm on to something big, and that excites me."

"You're getting a cheap thrill from being threatened?"

"Not exactly. I'm getting a thrill because this is what I've been waiting for my whole career. This is a once-in-a-lifetime opportunity."

"And your lifetime could be cut short if you don't leave the bleedin' notebook on the table."

I could, and probably should, heed Clement's advice and walk away; just as Neil Armstrong should have listened to those who warned a trip to the moon was fraught with danger, and stayed home. Nobody achieves anything worthwhile without risk, and the greater the reward, the greater that risk.

I've received a threatening text message. I'm not about to be shot into space atop a tube of burning rocket fuel.

"I can't leave it, Clement. I just can't."

He shakes his head. "That sofa better be comfortable."

My concerns about sharing my home aren't quite so significant now. Whatever it takes, I'm all in.

"I can do better than a sofa. I've got a spare room with a sofa bed, and it's all yours."

I doubt the promise of a lumpy sofa bed is really his motive but with a resigned sigh and a frown, Clement appears to be in.

"Right, listen," he orders. "We do this, you listen to me and do as I say. Clear?"

149

"Clear."

"We're gonna get up and leave now. Once we're on the street, you stick to my side until we hail a cab. Got it?"

Clement appears to be revelling in his protector role and although it's quite endearing, I'm not sure it's necessary. No harm in humouring him, I guess.

"Understood."

He gets to his feet and nods to indicate I should follow. I do as I'm told.

Once we're back on the street, more scanning ensues as Clement checks for potential threats. Seemingly content with the risk level, he beckons me to walk by his side and we head in the direction of Paddington Station.

With London being home to more than twenty-thousand black cabs, finding a ride is rarely a problem. After waiting barely a minute, we're being whisked away by one of those black cabs.

There's little in the way of conversation as Clement stares out of the window while I wrestle with my consequences of my decision. They say it's better to look back and regret the things you did, rather than the things you didn't do. In this instance I hope I don't regret not leaving the notebook back in the pub.

"What do you think he'll do next?" I ask.

"Depends. Does he know where you live?"

"I don't think so ... wait ..."

"What?"

"When I came home yesterday, I found my front door ajar. I thought I'd just forgotten to close it, but now I think about it I've got a horrible feeling someone might have been rifling through my father's possessions."

"You live with your old man?"

"Christ, no. It's a long story but I'll give you the highlights."

Before I get the chance the cab pulls up on my street. I pay the driver while Clement gets out and surveys the neighbourhood.

"Do you think he'll send someone to my flat again?" I ask, joining him on the pavement.

"Dunno, but it'd be a risky move. You call the Old Bill and it'll shine a light on things he'd rather keep in the dark."

"So, what are his options?"

"I'd guess he'll find your soft spot and exploit it. You got any family local?"

"No."

"Friends?"

"Spread far and wide."

"We'll have to wait and see then, doll. What's for dinner?"

How he can even think about food is beyond me but at very least I owe him a decent meal.

"We'll order a takeaway. Come on."

We make our way around the back of the coffee shop and I'm relieved to find the door still securely locked. As I step inside another concern comes to the fore.

"You'll have to excuse the mess. I wasn't expecting guests."

"I'm not a fussy man. I'll lay my head anywhere."

I return an embarrassed smile and head up the stairs, with Clement's heavy boots thumping the treads close behind.

We reach the top and Clement insists on checking the rooms while I stand like a lemon on the landing. He only takes a few seconds to peer through each door, until he gets to my bedroom.

"Nice pants," he comments over his shoulder.

"Uh?"

"Hanging on the radiator. You should get yourself a clothes horse."

I switch the landing light off to hide my flushed cheeks.

"Erm, drink?"

"Yeah."

He closes the bedroom door and I just catch his smirk before I cringe my way to the kitchen. I then learn there's only so long you can stare into a near empty fridge.

"Wine okay?"

"I'd rather gargle my own piss. Got any beer?"

"Afraid not, but I've got spirits: vodka, whisky, and I think there's some tequila somewhere."

"I'll take a whisky. Straight, no ice."

I grab a wine glass and a tumbler from the cupboard as Clement leans up against the door frame — it's never looked smaller.

"Lived here long?" he asks.

"Long enough."

"I worked in Kilburn for a bit; a few streets away I think."

"Really? Where?"

"A club. Don't think it's there anymore."

"I didn't even know there was a club nearby. What was it called?"

"The Canary Club."

I pour our drinks and hand Clement his whisky.

"I trust it wasn't anything like the Clawthorn Club."

"Only if they had strippers."

"Nice. And what was your role there, dare I ask?"

"Owner had a problem with some mob intimidating the girls — a protection racket."

"Let me guess: you did it for the perks?"

"Not gonna lie to you."

As interesting as Clement's work history is, we have more pressing matters to attend to.

"Let's go through to the lounge."

He follows me back across the landing, and after a quick check to ensure I haven't left a threadbare thong on the radiator, I beckon him in.

"Grab a seat."

He casts a lazy gaze across the walls and furniture before lowering himself into the armchair. I kick my shoes off and flop down on the sofa.

"Not what I expected," he says.

"In what way?"

"Hardly any pictures, bare walls, no knickknacks … it's more like a bloke's pad."

It's a fair assessment. I've never considered it a home; to me, it's just somewhere to while away the lonely evenings and lay my head at night. It serves that purpose well enough.

"It takes more than one person to make a home, Clement."

"I'll drink to that," he replies, raising his glass.

I have to concede it's nice having someone to raise a toast with, even if that someone is a hulking stranger blessed with the social graces of a troglodyte.

"Come on then, doll — tell me the full story. And I'm starving so make it quick."

"I'll order dinner first. What do you fancy?"

"Chow mein."

"How adventurous. Do you want ketchup with that, or are you more of a brown sauce man?"

"Either, both. Don't give a shit."

I grab my phone and open the takeaway app. It only takes a few seconds to order-in a chow mein and my personal favourite: Szechuan chicken noodles.

"It'll be here in forty minutes," I remark, placing my phone down on the coffee table.

"Eh? You didn't speak to anyone."

"It's an app. I don't need to speak to anyone."

"You just prod that thing a few times and food turns up?"

"Pretty much."

"Fuck me. Maybe I do need one."

Dinner sorted, my guest quickly moves the subject on, and poses a question.

"I'm struggling with somethin'. How did Tamthy know we were in that boozer?"

"Perhaps he had someone watching us."

"I didn't see anyone suspicious."

"That excuse for a mugger could have followed us?"

"Only if he had a death wish."

"I've seen people do some pretty stupid things when they're desperate for money, Clement."

My phone chimes to signal the takeaway are processing my order. I know without looking at the screen — it's an app I use far too often.

As we wait for our food to arrive, I relay the diabolical tale of Dennis Hogan, and how the notebook ended up in my possession.

"You've never even met your old man?" Clement asks.

"Nope. Never have, and never will now. I've seen a photo of him, and that's about it."

"I'm sorry, doll."

Considering I'm a virtual stranger, Clement's apology carries more sincerity than I would have expected.

"Thanks, but it's no loss."

The doorbell rings and as I'm about to get up, Clement clambers out of his chair.

"Best I go," he says. "Just in case."

Before I can argue, he's already gone. I suspect his sudden show of gallantry is as close to sweet as Clement ever gets.

Any fears of the caller being someone other than the delivery driver prove unfounded as I hear the door open and close within seconds. The sound of Clement's boots clomping up the stairs soon follow. He appears in the doorway clutching a paper bag.

"Grubs up."

I get up and take the bag from him. "Sit down. I'll bring it through."

Once I've decanted our food onto plates, I return to the lounge and hand Clement his insipid-looking meal.

"Nice one."

I turn the TV on to mask the sound of Clement destroying his chow mein. Once half the plate is empty he pauses for a sip of whisky, and poses a question.

"Does Tamthy know what you do for a living?"

"He contacted me using my work email address so I presume so. Why do you ask?"

"Just trying to figure out what his next move will be."

"And why is my job relevant?"

"Threat level. If I were Tamthy, I'd be a damn sight more worried about a journalist having that notebook rather than say, a barmaid or a bus driver."

"But as far as Tamthy is concerned, I don't know what Clawthorn really is."

"But you tried to find out, didn't you, and that's my point. You're digging around and the lengths he's already gone to prove the notebook is more than just a score pad for a bleedin' card game."

I ponder Clement's conclusion as he forks another skip load of food into his mouth. I can't argue with much of what he said, and it's now clear the moment I posted those photos on Twitter, I unwittingly brought myself to the attention of Allen Tamthy.

"What do you suggest we do?"

"At the moment, Tamthy is a ghost. We need to know who he really is before we can deal with the bloke, and the names in that notebook are our best bet."

"And you think the members of Clawthorn are going to tell us anything? Seriously?"

"I've got a very persuasive interview technique, doll. People tend to get quite chatty within a few minutes."

"Do I want to know what's involved in that technique?"

"Nah, you don't."

"Thought not."

I shoot him a look of disapproval but it's wasted as he turns his attention back to the chow mein. It proves a short return.

"Cheers, doll," he remarks while stifling a burp. "Not bad."

What little appetite I had already sated, I drop my fork on the plate and place it on the coffee table.

"You finished?" he asks.

"I'm not very hungry."

"Do you mind?"

"Err ..."

Too late. I watch on as Clement makes light work of my Szechuan chicken noodles. If he'd actually bothered to savour the taste, he might have realised they have a kick.

"Flamin' Nora," he puffs, after the last mouthful is gone. "That was a bit spicy."

"That'll teach you. And congratulations."

"For what?"

"Being the only man on earth under the age of fifty to still use the term *Flamin' Nora*."

"Everyone says it."

"No, Clement — they really don't."

With no discernible response, I retrieve my handbag and extract the source of my troubles — one tatty, leather-bound notebook.

"I guess it's time to start our offence."

I flick through the first dozen pages and it becomes apparent finding anyone for Clement to interview might not be so easy.

"One minor problem with our plan," I note.

"What's that?"

"The pages only list surnames — no first names. Unless anyone in here has a highly unusual surname it's useless."

"Shit."

Clement flops back in his chair as I flick through more pages of all-too-common surnames: Grant, Williams, O'Connor, Evans, Patterson, and Harris. More pages, more surnames: Middleton, Turner, Hawkins, Lang, Watts, Saunders … and Nithercott.

"Oh, my God."

"What is it?"

"This name," I blurt, jabbing the page. "Nithercott."

"That's a possibility, doll. Can't be too many people with that name."

"It gets better. I interviewed a young woman earlier this week, and her name was Stacey Nithercott."

Clement returns a blank look.

"You might know her as Stacey Stanwell, from that TV programme, *Chelsea Lives*."

Still blank.

"Actually, forget that. I hadn't heard of her either."

"That's not what I'm confused about. You said she was young, and obviously a bird, but they don't allow women to join Clawthorn; least they didn't."

"I guess we can add blatant sexual discrimination to their list of crimes but I wasn't suggesting Stacey is a member."

"Who then?"

"Her father, Lance Nithercott. He was a prominent theatre director and well-known for forging the careers of some heavyweight acting talents. A role in one of his plays could literally make an actor's career."

"Why would another Clawthorn member want to do a bit of theatre?"

"They wouldn't, but imagine if they wanted to secure a plumb acting role for one of their kids, or their wife, or mistress even. Money can't buy that kind of opportunity but if you were asking a fellow member of the Clawthorn Club for a favour …"

"Ahh, gotcha. Sounds like this Nithercott fella is worth having a chat with."

"He might have been if he hadn't committed suicide a while back."

Clement rolls his eyes. "As a general rule, doll, dead men don't talk much."

"No, but Stacey might have picked up on something in the months before he died. It's got to be worth talking to her, don't you think?"

"Might not even be the same bloke but no harm I guess."

"It's the only name we've got," I reply, returning to the notebook. "But there's still a few dozen pages to check."

As it transpires, those few dozen pages fail to provide any further candidates.

I close the notebook and toss it back into my handbag. "I guess one name is better than nothing."

"It's a start."

"Well, this is it, Clement. I think we've established our first potential member of the Clawthorn Club."

"And you know what that means?"

I do — the point of no return. For an alcoholic it's that first tantalising sip of the day. For me, the buzz is my weakness, and as intoxicating as any liquor. I can't fight it.

"I have to do this, Clement. I know it's risky as hell, but I need ..."

"You need answers. I get it."

"Do you?"

He sits forward so I can't escape his gaze. "Not knowing is a curse. Trust me — I get it."

Eric's first rule of journalism springs to mind: *trust no one, believe nothing*. I'm not ready to place my complete trust in Clement, nor believe everything he tells me, but his eyes have an entrancing quality which would test anyone's resolve.

"As you said: Tamthy isn't going to let this go. I might as well give him a run for his money."

"I'd drink to that, doll, but my glass is empty."

He holds it out to prove his point.

"This is the twenty-first century, Clement. If you think I'm going to play the dutiful housewife role, you've got another thing coming."

"Different times, eh," he replies with a half-smile.

"Yes, very."

"But who's to say the old days weren't better?"

I get up and stack the dinner plates; completely undermining my previous point.

"Well, unless you've got a time machine, we'll never know. Personally speaking, though, I think we're better off without three-day working weeks, power cuts, and casual racism."

"No argument there, but if things are so great these days, why is everyone depressed? According to the papers it's a bleedin' epidemic."

"It's complicated."

"Exactly my point. Life wasn't so complicated back then, therefore, it was better."

"And you're an expert on modern history, are you?"

"You'd be surprised."

"Not much surprises me these days. Anyway, come with me and I'll show you the spare room, and how to pour your own whisky."

He clambers out of the armchair and stretches. Without the extra inches of my heels, I get a sense of how a Chihuahua must feel when stood next to a Rottweiler.

Clement follows me through to the spare bedroom, which also serves as a home office and an overflow for my wardrobe.

"It's more comfortable than it looks," I lie, pulling out the sofa bed.

"It'll do me."

"Don't you need anything? Toothbrush? Change of clothes?"

"Nah."

"Right. Well, I think we'll have that drink and then maybe an early night is in order. I've got a feeling tomorrow is going to be a long day."

I show him back to the kitchen to pour another whisky before I visit the bathroom.

My backside has barely touched the seat when the question arrives: *have you taken leave of your senses, woman?*

I leave the bathroom without an answer.

15.

One of us slept well and it wasn't me.

Both my mind and body endured a night of tossing and turning; haunted by the voice of David Attenborough in my head as he described the sounds emanating from the spare bedroom.

And as night falls, the thunderous roar of rutting wildebeest can be heard across the savanna.

The question I asked myself on the loo last night is more salient than ever as I wander, bleary-eyed, into the lounge.

"Fuck me. You look like shit, doll."

My guest has made himself at home, sprawled on the sofa in just a t-shirt, socks, and pants.

"So sweet of you to point that out, Clement. Perhaps it's because I only managed about two bloody hours sleep last night."

"You having second thoughts about this whole Clawthorn thing?"

"Only the part where I agreed to share my home with a man who's snoring registers on the Richter Scale."

"The what?"

"Never mind. Where are your jeans?"

"In the bedroom. They'll do for a few more days before they need a wash."

I glare down at him. "That wasn't why I asked. Can you put *that* away, please?"

"That?"

I nod towards the offending item.

"Shit," he snorts, tucking the errant bollock back into his Y-fronts. "I think the elastic has gone."

"So has my will to live. You want coffee?"

"Tea, please. Milk and three sugars."

"I'll make tea if you go put your jeans back on."

"Yeah, alright," he grins. "Don't want you getting too excited before breakfast."

"Fat chance."

Shaking my head, I plod through to the kitchen and put the kettle on. As I wait for it to boil, I pull my dressing gown tight to stave off a chill and attempt to bring some clarity to yesterday's chaos. A minute into that analysis and I can see how the term, *in the cold light of day,* was coined.

I try to dismiss the negativity; putting it down to a lack of sleep, and caffeine. As Eric always told me: *ignore the doubts and keep your eye on the prize*. In this instance the prize is a story with the potential to propel my career into the stratosphere. All I need to do is look beyond my doubts: Tamthy's threats, and living with Clement.

The second of my doubts wanders into the kitchen — with his jeans on, thankfully. I hand him a mug of tea.

"What's the plan, then?" he asks.

"The phone shop opens at eight-thirty so I'm going to drink my coffee, take a shower, and then we'll head straight there."

"And breakfast?"

"Help yourself to toast, or whatever else you can find."

"Think I'll wait."

"Fine. I'll call Stacey when I'm in the office and arrange to pop over there after work. Are you still insisting on being my escort?"

"That's the deal."

"I can't imagine Tamthy will try anything in broad daylight, but if you insist."

"I do. I'm gonna go watch TV while you're getting your shit together."

He disappears back out the door. I finish my coffee and head to the bathroom where a glance in the mirror confirms Clement's observation wasn't far from the depressing truth.

After I've showered, I wipe the mist from the mirror and attempt to fix the problem. There was a time I could leave home with nothing more than a touch of lip gloss. Nowadays, I have a regime which involves more restoration work than the ceiling of the Sistine Chapel. Getting old is shit, but I suppose it's preferable to the alternative.

I emerge fifteen minutes later and scour my wardrobe for one of my favourite work outfits; a dark red midi-length dress which accentuates the parts of my anatomy Mother Nature hasn't yet ravaged.

A glance in the mirror. Not exactly sassy, but I'm happier than I was half-an-hour ago. I head into the lounge.

Clement turns his head from the TV. "You scrub up well, doll."

"Gee, thanks," I reply with mock gratitude. "Go easy on the

compliments, eh — you'll make a girl blush."

"I'm guessing it takes more than a compliment to make you blush."

"You would be right. Shall we get going?"

He clambers to his feet and switches the TV off. "That was irritating the fuck out of me anyway."

"What were you watching?"

"The news."

"Anything exciting happening?"

"It's all political shit, doll. I don't understand half of it."

"That's more than most of us. Come on."

I slip my coat on and we head downstairs to the kind of bright and breezy morning which would be glorious if we weren't in Kilburn.

"Don't you own a jacket?" I ask Clement, as we walk along the street. "You must be freezing."

"Nah, don't feel the cold."

Considering he has the physique of a Grizzly Bear, I'm not altogether surprised.

We reach the phone shop and, upon entering, find the one sales assistant is already dealing with a customer. Conscious of time, I scour the displays looking for a suitable phone, unaided.

"Why are there so many?" Clement asks.

"Consumers like choice, I suppose."

He turns his attention to a display of the latest iPhones.

"Fuck me gently," he booms. "Thirteen hundred quid. You can buy a half-decent motor for that kind of money."

"Yeah, fortunately I don't think an iPhone is necessarily what you're looking for."

I leave Clement to stare bewildered at the overpriced Apple products and locate the section where drug dealers likely acquire their burner phones. The cheapest handset is only twenty quid and appears as basic as it gets, with rubberised keys in lieu of a touch screen.

"Clement, here," I beckon.

He ambles over and I show him the phone. "Will this do you?"

"Does it make calls?"

"Err, yes."

"Will it send food, like yours?"

"Probably not."

"Suppose it'll do."

Another young sales assistant appears and I confirm our order. Irritatingly, he makes repeated attempts to sell me a more expensive handset, but fails. As punishment for his chippy attitude, I insist the irksome young man shows Clement how to operate his new phone. I've seen bomb disposal engineers execute their duty with less trepidation.

With Clement embracing at least one facet of twenty-first century life, we leave the phone shop and head to the Underground station. Despite no further communication from Tamthy, Clement remains on high alert.

"Were you ever in the army?" I ask.

"I went to Aldershot, once, to watch a football match. Decent boozers but the ground was a right shithole."

"That's not quite what I asked."

"Do I look like I was ever in the army?"

"No, you look like the lead singer of Motörhead, but again, that wasn't what I asked."

"I weren't in the army."

"So where did you learn to do whatever it is you do?"

"School of Hard Knocks."

"That's reassuring. Can you be more specific?"

"All you need to know is I have a job to do, and I intend to finish it."

"About that — we never did get to the bottom of your motivation."

We reach the entrance to the Underground station and Clement stops.

"Ever heard that old saying about looking a gift horse in the mouth?"

"Yes."

"Then don't."

"Alright. I've got an inquisitive mind, that's all."

"Ain't that the truth," he huffs. "Come on."

He holds his arm out to shepherd me along. It's probably just the novelty factor but it is nice to feel someone has your back.

After an uneventful journey on the Tube, and an equally uneventful walk from the Hyde Park Corner station, we arrive at the steps of The Daily Standard office.

"Swanky," Clement comments, looking up at the four-storey, nineteenth-century building.

"It's not exactly Fleet Street, but I've worked in worse places."

"What time do you finish?"

"It varies. I'll call you when I know."

"Alright. Is there a cafe round here? I could murder a full English."

I'm about to remind him we're in Belgravia when one of my millennial colleagues bursts through the office doors.

"Good morning, Emma."

A recent graduate in feminist studies, Bridget is a junior reporter and self-appointed taker of offence.

"Morning, Bridget."

Despite willing her to walk straight past us, Bridget loiters next to me. Even by her standards, her attire today is particularly dour, not helped by her cropped hair and stern features.

"Anyway," I smile through gritted teeth. "I'll ring you later, Clement."

"Yeah, you said," he replies, missing my hint to leave.

"Clement," Bridget comments, looking up at him. "That's an unusual name. Where's it from?"

"Dunno, doll."

She frowns. "I beg your pardon?"

"Said, I dunno."

"You called me *doll*," she snaps. "Do I look like a doll to you?"

"You ain't no Barbie, that's for sure."

Bridget turns to me, clearly offended. I cover my mouth and feign a cough to hide a snort of laughter.

"Did you hear what he just said?" she huffs. "Tell your *friend* to apologise."

"Sorry, Bridget," I splutter. "He's a work in progress."

She returns her attention back to Clement. "Men like you disgust me."

"No offence, doll," he shrugs. "But you ain't exactly doing much for me either."

Bridget's face reddens but she seems unable to find the words to convey her rage.

Clement turns to me. "See ya later."

He then flashes a smile at Bridget. "You should try wearing a nice dress — might bag yourself a fella."

Fashion advice delivered, he strides away.

"I'd better get going, Bridget. I'll see you later."

I leave her stood on the steps, and chuckle all the way to my desk. Unfortunately, my merriment is cut short when Gini saunters over.

"Hey, Emma," she says with less enthusiasm than usual.

"Morning, Gini. You okay?"

I fear she's about to share details of a petty argument with her fiancé so I switch my attention to the computer screen.

"I'm fine, but I need to warn you — Damon is on the warpath."

"Is it because I missed the morning briefing?"

"I honestly don't know, but he was really annoyed you weren't here first thing."

"How annoyed?"

"You know I order-in cakes on a Friday, and Damon usually has a cream horn?"

"Erm, yeah."

"This morning he chose a custard tart. He only ever orders a custard tart if he's in a bad mood."

"Hmmm ... serious. Thanks for the heads-up."

I send Gini on her way with a reassuring smile and get on with checking my emails; specifically for anything from Allen Tamthy. Before I get a chance to start, my phone trills a tone to denote an incoming internal call.

I snatch the receiver up. "Emma Hogan."

"Get to my office. Now."

Damon ends the call before I can catch a breath. Gini was right — he does seem pissed off.

I get up and prepare what I'm going to say. My late father has been of absolutely no use to me throughout my life but his recent demise does make a handy excuse. There's nothing like news of a dead relative to take the sting out of a bollocking.

I head over to Damon's office and breeze straight in.

"Where's the fire?" I ask.

"Shut the door and sit down," he orders.

This is new. I've never been offered a seat before.

I comply, and make myself comfortable while Damon taps away at his keyboard. Ignoring me, he stares intently at the screen, pausing a couple of times to run a hand through his hair. My patience stretches until it finally snaps.

"I thought this was urgent."

"It is," he replies flatly, finally turning to face me.

"Well?"

"I'll cut to the chase. This is an official disciplinary meeting and, as such, you have the right to ask for a third-party to be present, such as a union rep, colleague ..."

"Whoa! Back up a minute, Damon. You're giving me an official warning because I was half-an-hour late?"

"If you let me finish ..."

"For the record," I interrupt. "I was late this morning because I just found out my father died."

Bombshell delivered, I sit back in my chair and await the look of shame and grovelling apology.

"I'm sorry to hear that," he continues. "But that has no relevancy to the reason for this meeting."

"Of course it does. I was late because I had to deal with the estate agent who let my father's flat."

Technically, I'm not lying about the reason — just the day it happened.

"This has nothing to do with your timekeeping."

"What then?"

He glances at the computer screen. "At 11:22am yesterday, our call logs show you rang a charity based in Sandown on the Isle of Wight. Correct?"

I had no idea our calls were being logged.

"Um, possibly."

"And one of the two directors of that charity is a certain William Huxley."

"Err ..."

Ohh shit.

"Now, correct me if I'm wrong, but didn't I send you an email six months ago, strictly forbidding any communication with William Huxley?"

"You might have done."

"I know I did, and I also know you read it because our IT guy checked the mail server."

He's got me bang to rights, and no amount of dead relatives are going to get me out of this hole.

"Alright," I sigh. "You got me, Damon. Give me a slap on the wrist and we can both get on with our day."

"There won't be any wrist slapping."

"Great. I'll be on my way then."

"You are suspended with immediate effect."

"I ... sorry?"

"And your employment contract will almost certainly be terminated next week once we've concluded a formal investigation and collated all the evidence."

The words 'suspended' and 'terminated' reverberate in my head as I sit and stare at Damon.

"What?" I gasp. "No."

"You brought this on yourself. There's only so long you can break the rules before those rules come back and bite you on the arse."

"This is ..."

"Unfair? No, it's not. We're doing everything by the book."

Book or no book, if he thinks I'm going to roll over without a fight, he's sadly mistaken.

"This is bullshit and you know it. Yes, I spoke to Huxley but it was on a completely unrelated matter — it had absolutely nothing to do with what happened six months ago. And, if you refer to your precious call logs, you'll see I was only on the phone to him for a minute or two."

"Doesn't matter. You were explicitly told not to communicate with him, and you were made fully aware of the consequences."

"No, I'm not having that. This is just the petty excuse you've been looking for to get rid of me: isn't it?"

He leans forward and rests his elbows on the desk.

"As much as I'd love to take credit, this came from above. It seems your fan club in the boardroom has had enough of your behaviour."

His revelation is like a pin prick to my defiance, and I can almost feel myself deflating in the chair.

"I'll give you two minutes to pack up your personal possessions," he continues. "And someone will escort you off the premises."

"But, Damon ... please ..."

"Don't waste your breath. It's out of my hands."

He gets to his feet and nods towards the door. "Let's get this over with."

Still in a daze, I slowly get up and turn to leave.

"Oh, Emma," Damon chirps. "One final thing."

I turn around.

"I hope you don't mind, but I've always wanted to say this."

"Say what?"

He raises his arm and points a finger in my direction. A lazy grin then forms on his face.

"You're fired."

16.

It would be fair to say that being fired is an awful experience.

In my case, the firing was particularly awful for three reasons. Firstly, I had to do the walk of shame across the office, carrying a cardboard box whilst my colleagues watched on. Secondly, I had to make that walk whilst a tearful Gini watched on like an abandoned puppy. And, to cap it all, Damon delegated the job of seeing me off the premises to a smirking Bridget.

As I stand on the stairs outside the office, still holding my box, I remind myself I haven't technically been fired yet. On the scale of delusional silver linings, it's right up there with such greats as *there's plenty more fish in the sea* and *it's the taking part that counts*.

Fucking hell.

Fuck. Fuck. Fucking hell.

I can almost feel a dozen sets of eyes looking down at me from the first floor windows, and I can imagine what they're thinking: there goes poor old Emma Hogan — the last of the dinosaurs.

Head up, shoulders back, I walk away with no idea where I'm going or what I'm to do. I cover thirty yards of pavement when the shame steps aside leaving space for another concern.

After a quick scan of the street, I seek sanctuary in the doorway of a restaurant that won't open for another two hours. I pull out my phone and call Clement's new phone. It rings, and it rings.

"Come on, come on."

I'm about to give up when he finally answers.

"Doll?"

"Where are you?"

"In a cafe near Hyde Park. What's up?"

"I've been fired. Can you come and meet me?"

"Yeah, where?"

"I'm stood outside the Bella Luna restaurant near the office."

"Gimme five minutes."

I expect him to hang up but instead, the line beeps with the pressing of random buttons whilst Clement swears under his breath. Eventually, he finds the correct button to end the call.

There's nothing I can do other than stand and wallow in a pool of negative thoughts. It doesn't take long for several questions to bubble to the surface. What reason did anyone have to check my call logs, and who made the decision? I can't believe Damon has been checking them for the last six months and then suddenly struck lucky. I make scores of phone calls every day — would he really spend hour after hour trawling those records in the vague hope I might suddenly call William Huxley? He dislikes me, but not that much.

Besides, he did say the order to sack me came from above, and that is a grave concern considering events over the last few days.

My phone chimes to signal a text message has arrived. I tap the screen and open it.

The disciplinary issue will go away if you return the notebook and forget Clawthorn. You are in over your head — walk away.

I read it twice: dumbstruck.

The questions I asked myself only moments ago have been answered; only to be replaced with a more worrying series of questions. Assuming the text is from Allen Tamthy, how the hell did he know I've just been disciplined, and how did he get that information so quickly?

There's only one possible answer: someone in the office must have told him the moment I left.

"My God."

The more I think about that, the more questions arrive. Was Tamthy behind the investigation into my call logs? Did the so-called Tallyman call in a few favours of his own?

I read the text for a third time. There's no sender's name but the text ends with an anonymous PO box address. I know from previous experience it's near-impossible to trace who that box might belong to.

"Alright, doll?"

Startled by the sudden boom of Clement's voice, I almost drop my phone.

"Jesus. You scared me."

"Sorry. You okay?"

"Not really."

"Me neither. I had to leave half my breakfast."

I glare up at him. "How awful for you."

"Yeah, it was. Shall we go back to your place? You can tell me what happened on the way."

Without any prompt he reaches down and picks up my cardboard box. I'm beginning to learn Clement has a knack of seamlessly switching from insensitive arsehole to gentleman in an instant.

"Thank you."

As we walk, I recount what happened in Damon's office, and the text message I received barely minutes after I left the building.

"Are you gonna admit it now, doll?"

"Admit what?"

"When I told you the truth about Clawthorn, you thought I was bullshitting."

"No, not exactly."

"Come off it," he scoffs. "You thought this was a game and I was just exaggerating the risk."

"I probably underestimated the threat."

"Yeah, you did."

"But this is so personal, so close to home. I feel ... violated."

"I'm gonna keep saying it — you're not dealing with the boy scouts here. These fuckers have eyes and ears everywhere."

"As I'm learning."

"Still, as threats go, it could have been worse," he suggests.

"Worse? I'm being blackmailed, threatened, and someone at The

Daily Standard is clearly involved. How could it possibly be any worse?"

"Lots of ways to keep someone from snitching. They could have grabbed you off the street, taken you somewhere quiet, and sliced your nipples off with a rusty razor blade."

I don't know if it's possible for boobs to physically shudder, but mine make the effort.

"That's twisted. You've been watching too many Mafia movies, Clement."

"Yeah, that'll be it."

"But I take your point, I suppose. Question is: what do we do next?"

"It's up to you. At least you've got an easy way out, if you want it."

On the face of it, I do — I could easily send the notebook back and return to work next week as if nothing happened. However, I'm now beginning to realise that Clement wasn't exaggerating the risks of investigating the Clawthorn Club. But as that risk increases, so does the potential reward for exposing whoever is involved, including a board member at The Daily Standard.

"If I do send it back, it won't be over, will it? Someone will be constantly watching over me and I'll have to live with the threat of being sacked for some minor indiscretion, and that's assuming I even get my job back."

"I suppose you've got a bit of time on your side if you wanna keep digging around. Even if you send the notebook back today, it won't get there until Monday at the earliest."

With three entire days now at my disposal, and nothing more to lose at this point, perhaps he's right. At the very least it'll stop me dwelling on my impending unemployment.

"You got any plans this weekend, Clement?"

"I stopped making plans a long time ago."

"Great. How do you fancy joining me for some good old-fashion investigative journalism?"

"Will there be alcohol involved at some stage?"

"Almost certainly."

"Count me in."

Just over an hour after we began the outbound journey, we complete the return leg, and arrive back at Kilburn station. We head straight for the flat despite Clement complaining about his unfinished breakfast.

"There's a cafe down the road. I'll treat you to egg and chips once we've decided what we're doing."

"If I make it that far," he grumbles.

In lieu of breakfast, I make him a cup of tea once we're home, and throw in a couple of chocolate digestives for good measure. Seemingly satisfied for the moment, we convene in the lounge.

"You gonna call that Stacey bird, then?"

"Yes, but I need to work out what I'm going to say. It's not fair to drag her into this so I don't want to mention anything about

Clawthorn if I can help it."

"Assuming her old man was a member."

"I've checked. There's not one other person in the Greater London area with the name Nithercott. It has to be him."

"Fair enough. What's your angle, then?"

"His suicide."

"Go on."

"I've been thinking about it, and I reckon Stacey must have considered the same question I did: why would a suicidal man living in the centre of London head fifteen miles out to a motorway bridge and kill himself there? Why not stay at home and down a bottle of pills, or take a five-minute walk to an Underground station and throw yourself in front of a train?"

"You suggesting it weren't suicide?"

"There's one way to check if he had a motive for killing himself."

I reach into my handbag and pull out the notebook. A quick flick through the pages and I locate what might well be Lance Nithercott's tally.

"Zero favours in the 'given' column and two in the 'received' column. Perhaps he was being pressurised to pay his dues and that's why he turned to drink. Stacey said his work dried up which would have meant there was no way to repay his favour."

"It's a theory, doll."

"It's all we've got at the moment."

"Better make that call then."

I finish my coffee and stare at the phone screen for a moment. With no other leads this is a one-shot deal. With that in mind, and knowing how sensitive Stacey was regarding the subject of her father, I'll need to tread carefully.

I call her number and it rings five times before she answers.

"Hello, Emma."

"Oh. Hi, Stacey.

Surprisingly, it appears she saved my number in her address book.

Before I can say another word, Stacey starts gushing about my article, which was apparently published yesterday. Despite her positive feedback, I didn't even want to put my name to it, let alone see it out in the wild.

"I'm so glad it helped, Stacey. And thank you for being so candid during our meeting."

"No, I should be thanking you for keeping your word about my dad. Not many journalists would have been so sensitive."

"Um, yes, that's actually why I'm calling ... about your dad."

"What about him?"

"When we talked, I got the impression you felt there was more to his death than the coroner's report indicated."

"Did you indeed?" she replies, her tone now wary.

"Am I wrong?"

"With respect, Emma, are you heading somewhere with this?"

"I've been thinking about it, and you might be right."

"Based upon what evidence?"

"It's not something I really want to discuss over the phone. Is there any chance I can pop over and see you?"

"I don't know," she sighs.

"Look, it's just a chat, and you have my word: whatever is said, it'll remain between us. I don't have an angle here, Stacey."

A nervous few seconds ensue as all I hear is her breathing.

"Alright, Emma. I can see you at one o'clock but I don't have long."

"Thank you. I'll see you then."

I end the call and turn to Clement. "We're on."

"Nice one, doll. And I've been thinking — while you've got the notebook out, you might wanna check the names against the people in your office. Someone there must have tipped-off Tamthy about you being sacked."

"Possibly," I reply, mildly annoyed I didn't think to do it. "But there must be about thirty people in the newsroom, and probably as many board members and associate directors. That could take a while to check."

"I thought computers did all that shit these days."

Clement is once again ahead of my thinking.

"You know something: you're much smarter than you look."

"And you're much sarkier than you look."

"Thanks."

I dash into the bedroom and retrieve my laptop.

"Okay, I'll just set-up a spreadsheet. Can you read out the names for me?"

I pass him the notebook and, one-by-one, enter each of the surnames into a column, with additional columns for the corresponding tally.

It takes a while, but with the data digitised, all I need to do is find a list of names for everyone associated with The Daily Standard. I open a browser and go straight to the personnel directory on the website. Thankfully, it lists all the staff, directors, and associate directors.

After a bit of cutting, reformatting, and pasting, I'm left with another column in my spreadsheet.

"Okay, I just need to run a formula and it'll highlight any names which appear on both lists."

Clement replies with his now-familiar blank stare.

I hit the enter button.

"Ugh," I groan. "You want the good news or the bad news?"

"Just spit it out, doll. This is boring as fuck."

"Okay. The good news is we have a result. The bad news is that there are three names which appear on both lists: Smith, Grant, and Brown."

"So, whoever is working with Tamthy is one of those three."

"Alas, it's not that simple. There are three men at The Daily Standard with the surname Smith: my immediate boss, Damon, and two directors. There's also a Terence Brown listed as an associate director, and the last name, Grant, is Danny Grant but he's just an intern so I think we can rule him out."

"So we're left with four possibilities? Three Smiths and a Brown?"

"We are."

I return to the spreadsheet and copy the names of the four contenders into a new column. Along with Damon and Terence Brown, we've also got Jeremy Smith, a main boardroom director, and Roger Smith, an associate director.

"You got any inkling which one it might be?" Clement asks.

"To be honest, I don't know anything about the directors but the obvious candidate is my boss, Damon Smith. He's the one who sacked me and would have therefore been in pole position to share the news with Tamthy."

Clement strokes his moustache a few times. "Bit too obvious, don't you reckon?"

"I honestly don't know, and that's the problem. With four candidates we can't be sure."

"Back to plan-A then. We visit this bird and hope she says something worth hearing."

"And if she doesn't?"

"Twenty-five more letters in the alphabet."

There are, but we've only got three days to run through them, and then I've got to make a decision I really don't want to make.

17.

Clement plumped for two eggs, double chips, and four rounds of buttered toast. I went for a ham and tomato sandwich on brown bread.

He finishes his lunch first.

"Your cholesterol levels must be horrific."

"My what?" he frowns.

"You don't know what cholesterol is?"

"Should I?"

"If you don't want to drop dead from a heart attack next week, then yes, you probably should."

"Don't worry about me, doll — I'm immortal."

"That's what my friend, Eric, thought, and I went to his funeral six months ago."

"You wanna get going?" he replies, moving the subject away from his unhealthy lifestyle. Typical man.

"I suppose we'd better, before you have a stroke."

We leave the cafe and head towards the Underground station; Clement pounding the pavements at a pace I struggle to match.

"Are you walking so quickly to prove a point?" I pant.

"Nah, just keen to get there."

The sprint ends on the Bakerloo line platform. Two short train rides and fifteen minutes later, we emerge onto the street outside South Kensington Underground station.

"How far is it?" Clement asks.

"Assuming we walk at a civilised pace, less than ten minutes away."

We set off towards Sydney Street and the walk proves an opportunity to quiz Clement.

"Seeing as you now know so much about me, are you going to open up a little."

"Not sure what you mean."

"I don't exactly know much about you."

"What do you wanna know?"

"Are you single, married? Got any kids?"

"Single. And no kids."

"Any plans to have any?"

"Not now, but I did, once. Think that ship has sailed, doll."

"Not necessarily. People are leaving it a lot later in life to have kids these days. I've got friends in their early forties and they're only just starting a family."

"What about you?"

"Too late for me. I think the alarm on my biological clock has already sounded. It's different for men, though, isn't it? You can keep sowing your seed for another few decades."

"You can if you're Mick Jagger."

"Very true," I chuckle. "And on that subject, what sort of music do you listen to?"

"Anything but the shit on the radio these days."

"It's awful, isn't it? The one positive about never returning to The Daily Standard is I won't have to listen to my colleague's dreadful music in the staffroom again."

"What's wrong with it?"

"They're kids, Clement, and they have no taste. One time I was chatting about music to this young lad, Archie, and I mentioned Paul Young. He didn't have a clue who Paul Young is — can you believe that?"

"Who is he?"

"Archie?"

"No, Paul Young."

I stop dead in my tracks.

"I'm sorry — did you just ask me who Paul Young is? He had five top-ten singles."

"Never heard of the bloke."

"Sod off, Clement," I jeer. "How could you possibly not have heard of Paul Young? He was huge in the eighties."

"Honestly, doll. The name don't mean a thing."

"Okay, what about Howard Jones, or Nik Kershaw. You've heard of them, right?"

"Must have passed me by."

"Christ, did you spend your teenage years living in an Amish community?"

"Something like that."

I roll my eyes and we walk on.

A few minutes later we turn into Sydney Street.

"It's at the end of this road," I confirm.

One aspect of our visit I haven't given a great deal of thought to is how Stacey will feel about including my companion in our conversation.

"Don't take this the wrong way, Clement, but do you think it would be better if you wait outside?"

"Why?"

"We only have one chance to get Stacey talking, and I'm concerned she won't open up if you're there."

"Do you know what you're gonna ask her?"

"I'm just going to play it by ear."

"Alright, I'll hang around outside but don't spend all afternoon in there — I know what you chicks are like when you start rabbiting."

"Oh, I'm a chick now am I? Is that a promotion?"

"Go on," he orders with a glint in his eye. "Piss off."

Not wishing to encourage his disparaging language I bite back a grin. "I won't be long."

As it transpires Stacey opens the door and declares she only has fifteen minutes anyway. I'm ushered through to the kitchen again but there's no offer of a drink or much in the way of small talk as we sit down at the table.

With so little time I need to tread the fine line between sensitive and succinct.

"I know you're busy, Stacey, so I'll get to the point. I've been working on a story and your father's name came up."

"What story?"

"That doesn't matter but I will say it raises questions about his suicide."

"Go on."

"I know this is hard but have you asked yourself why he drove all the way to that motorway bridge?"

"He didn't drive. He sold his car months before as he was always too drunk to drive it."

"Oh, okay. How did he get there then, and more to the point, why would he choose that method to end his life when there were simpler options closer to home?"

"No idea. I asked both the investigating officer and the coroner — they couldn't offer a reasonable explanation."

"Was foul play ever considered?"

"No, there wasn't any evidence to suggest it."

"Not at the time maybe."

Her eyes narrow. "I'm not with you."

"Do you know if your dad was a member of any clubs?"

"He played golf, and I think he was a member of the Freemasons for a few years. Why do you ask?"

"His name was on the members list of a club I'm investigating. For your own protection, it's best I don't go into the details but I know, for sure, the man who runs that club is not adverse to levying threats and breaking the law."

"And you think this man might have had something to do with Dad's suicide?"

"I can't say at the moment, but it would be useful to know if your dad had a connection to any other members."

"And how would I know that?"

"I've got a list of the other members of that club and I was hoping perhaps one or two of the names might ring a bell with you. Perhaps someone who was in regular contact with your father in the months leading up to his death."

"I think you might be clutching at straws here, Emma. Dad was a near-recluse towards the end. The only time he went out was either to the pub or the off licence."

"It'll take two minutes."

"Go on," she sighs.

I retrieve the notebook from my handbag and open it flat on the table to hide the cover. I begin reciting the names.

"It's just a list of surnames?" Stacey interrupts.

"I'm afraid so."

She shakes her head but I press on. Ten pages. Twenty pages. Thirty pages. Not even a hint of recognition at any name.

By the time I reach the midway point I can already sense Stacey's patience is about to break. I speed up.

"Connor."

No reaction.

"Ross."

No reaction.

"Patterson."

No reaction.

"Lang."

The merest flicker of recognition.

"Stacey? Does the name Lang ring any bells?"

"It does," she replies dismissively. "But the Lang I knew never met my dad."

My heart sinks and frustration mounts. "Are you sure?"

"Yes, because I only met him after Dad died — Deputy Commissioner, Thomas Lang, oversaw the investigation into Dad's death."

"Deputy Commissioner?"

"Yes. Why is his rank relevant?"

"Oh, it's just unusual for an officer of that standing to oversee a routine suicide."

"Dad still had a public profile so I guess they just wanted to demonstrate they were taking his death seriously. I think it was just a PR exercise; wheeling out the big guns to make it look like they gave a damn."

As I process Stacey's revelation, a memory barges its way to the front of my mind. The pub in Paddington, and Clement's first disclosure about the true nature of Clawthorn. I'm sure he mentioned the membership included high-ranking police officers.

The buzz takes hold but I try not to let it show on my face. If there is even the slightest chance the man who investigated Lance Nithercott's death is a member of the Clawthorn Club, I can't let Stacey know. She's too headstrong and too emotionally invested, and therefore likely to blow the lead before I get a chance to follow it up.

"Emma?"

"Sorry, Stacey. Ignore me — if this guy never met your dad then he's not our man."

With her frown deepening by the minute I go through the motions of reading out the rest of the names in the notebook. Not one of them sparks her memory.

"So, is that it?" she grumbles as I return the notebook to my handbag.

"Afraid so. I'm sorry to have got your hopes up."

"So am I, Emma," she snaps, getting to her feet. "I'd like you to leave now."

Stacey makes no effort to hide her disappointment as I'm unceremoniously corralled back down the hallway and out the door. I turn to say goodbye but the door is slammed shut before I get the chance. It doesn't look like I'll be writing Stacey Stanwell's autobiography after all.

I turn back to the street as Clement ambles over.

"Eight minutes. I'm impressed, doll."

"I don't think Stacey was so impressed."

"Didn't go well?"

"Not for her perhaps, but I might have something."

"Let's walk."

As we head back up Sydney Street, I relay what I learnt about the man who oversaw Lance Nithercott's suicide.

"I agree, doll. No way would a senior suit get involved in a routine suicide, unless ..."

"Unless perhaps, he wanted to steer the investigation in a certain direction. It's just a theory, but what if Lance Nithercott didn't jump from that bridge, but he was taken there and ... assisted? It would explain why he didn't just end it all at home with a bottle of pills."

"Lots of ifs and maybes."

"I know, but the surname Lang isn't that common, and we know there's no other Nithercott in Greater London. It'd be quite a coincidence wouldn't it? Both men with names in the notebook, and one of them overseeing the apparent suicide of another."

"Yeah, I guess."

"It's worth looking into Lang a bit, don't you think?"

We pause on the corner and I google Deputy Commissioner, Thomas Lang. The first result is a picture of a distinguished-looking man with grey eyes and a thick head of equally grey hair, neatly parted at the side. Clearly an official Met Police photo, he's sporting a black tunic with suitable levels of insignia for an officer of his rank. Below his picture, a Wikipedia entry offers an interesting development in the Deputy Commissioner's career.

"He's now retired."

"I suppose that makes it a bit easier."

"Makes what a bit easier?"

"Interviewing him."

"Oh."

Up until this point we've been on the defensive, but if we're to make any progress we need to switch to an offensive strategy. However, I have an inkling how Clement might enforce that strategy.

"We can't break the law, Clement."

"Who said anything about breaking the law? I'm just sayin' we pay the bloke a visit and have a chat."

"And you think he'll just break down and confess to being involved in Nithercott's suicide, and being part of a corrupt club?"

"Depends."

"On?"

"If he wants to spend his retirement in a wheelchair, or not."

"Yeah, that's what I was afraid you might say."

"You can't fuck around with these people, doll. Fear is the best weapon in situations like this."

"Like this?"

"You wanna expose Clawthorn, you've gotta rip it apart link by link."

"And you think Lang is the weakest link?"

"At the moment, he's the only link."

"I know, but he's not long retired and there won't be any further investigation if we end up being guests of his former colleagues."

"Which is why we can't afford to pussyfoot around — we've gotta scare the shit out of the bloke otherwise he'll just call in his mates."

"I get what you're saying, but ..."

"Tamthy didn't exactly play nice when he sent that dipshit to mug you, did he?"

That much is true. I still have a purple bruise on my lower back to prove it.

"Alright. We'll do it your way, but promise me you won't go overboard. I don't want our only potential link to Clawthorn to end up in the mortuary."

"I don't do promises, but I do know what I'm doing."

I'm glad one of us does.

18.

Finding an individual's address is meat and drink to a journalist, so by the time we reach South Kensington Underground station, I've already established Thomas Lang lives in a village near Hemel Hempstead; twenty-five miles north of London.

Only two questions remain: when and how?

"No time like the present, doll."

"How do we know he'll be in?"

"Dunno how things work these days, but most folks usually just pick up the phone."

"And say what, Clement? Hi, Mr Lang — just checking you're in so we can pop by and rough you up a bit."

"No need for sarcasm."

"Yes, well, in lieu of just heading up there and knocking on his door, sarcasm is all I've got."

"Then it's Hobson's choice. Do you know if he's married?"

"I'll check."

A quick look on Wikipedia provides the answer.

"He divorced four years ago and there's no mention of a partner."

"That's good. Means he probably lives alone."

"Okay, so we're just going to wing it?"

"Guess so. You got a motor?"

"You'd rather go by car?"

"Yeah. If he ain't in, at least we've got somewhere to wait rather than hanging around on the street."

Decision made we descend into the station.

It's just before two o'clock in the afternoon by the time we arrive back at the flat. We head straight to the car and I enter Lang's address into the sat nav.

"It's just over half-an-hour away."

"Thank fuck for that. Not exactly roomy in here, is it?"

"Shall we take your car?"

"Don't have one."

"Quit complaining then."

I reverse out of the parking space while Clement tries to get comfortable.

"Why does every bird drive a tiny motor?"

"It's not our cars, Clement, it's your bulk — what the hell did your mother feed you?"

"Not a lot."

"Maybe it's genetic. Was your dad a big man?"

"I know as much about my old man as you do about yours."

"Oh, I'm sorry."

"Don't be. I got over it a long time ago."

I could push the subject but I know I wouldn't want to answer the questions I'd like to ask Clement. Turning the stereo on ends both the temptation and the silence.

"Fancy some Paul Young?"

"No, ta. Got any Slade?"

"You really are obsessed with the seventies — what gives with that?"

"Nothing."

"Don't you think it's a bit odd for someone your age? Actually, how old are you exactly?"

"Forty-something."

"So, you were born in the seventies, like me. Can't say I remember a great deal about that particular decade, though."

"I do," he sighs. "Like it were yesterday."

"Yeah, but you were just a kid. All I remember is Christmas adverts for toys I'd never own, and the awful tinned meat we seemed to live on."

"Tinned meat?"

"Spam, corned beef, and some awful pork monstrosity in jelly. God, just the thought of it makes me want to gag."

"I used to love those pies in tins. You can still buy them, you know."

"You can still buy Showaddywaddy albums, Clement — doesn't mean you should."

I slow down as two lanes of traffic merge into one. A guy in an Audi tries to force his way into the queue ahead of me. I'm not having it and keep tight to the bumper of the car in front. He reacts by blaring his horn.

Opening the window I yell some motoring advice. "Back off,

arsehole."

The line of cars comes to a halt and the Audi driver takes the opportunity to respond to my advice. He gets out and leans across the roof of his car.

"What the fuck is your problem?"

He's exactly what I expected: in his forties with a ruddy face and thinning hair. And a micro-penis ... probably.

"My problem, mate, is you trying to muscle your way past the queue."

"Stop being such a drama queen," he yells back. "What is it: got the painters in?"

Ironically his comment is a red rag. I get out of the car and slam the door.

"Step over here and say that again," I growl.

His smirk disappears, a fraction of a second before he does, quickly followed by the sound of his door locks clunking shut.

I bend down and glare through the passenger's window. "Pussy!"

Argument settled I get back in the car.

"Feel better?" Clement asks.

"Yes, thank you. I can't stand chauvinistic pricks like that. No offence."

As the queue finally edges forward, I take a second to reflect upon my own statement.

"Why did you stay in the car, Clement?"

"Did you want me to rush to your rescue?"

"Not at all."

"What's your point, then?"

"Most men would have jumped out of the car and started rowing with the other bloke."

"I ain't most men."

"You're not wrong there, but you didn't answer my question."

"You were dealing with that dickhead so what was the point in me getting involved?"

"Because men like you feel compelled to stick up for us helpless woman."

"Men like me?"

"Chauvinists."

"Fuckin' typical," he huffs, folding his arms. "And you're supposed to be a journalist. You wanna try reading a dictionary every now and again."

"Sorry?" I scowl.

"If memory serves, ain't a chauvinist someone who thinks women are less capable, less intelligent, than blokes?"

"Err, I ..."

"Look, doll — you've got more balls than most blokes I know, and you're smarter than most blokes I know. That's why I stayed in the bleedin' car. Does that make me a chauvinist?"

"Well, obviously not, but your language does."

"No, it don't," he snaps. "It's just words. I can't help the way I talk, but it don't mean I'm a caveman."

I've clearly touched a raw nerve and for the first time since we met, Clement appears genuinely incensed. I can understand why.

I give it a moment to let his angst settle, before swallowing some humble pie.

"Sorry, Clement. And thank you."

"For what?"

"Sorry for being a judgemental cow, and thank you for the compliments."

"Don't mention it."

"I mean this in a positive way, but you're much more ... complex, than you first appear."

"You don't know the half of it, doll."

"Hopefully you can fill me in once we've exposed Clawthorn."

"We'll see."

I wouldn't say he was sulking but there's little in the way of conversation for the rest of the journey. For my part, I keep quiet because I'm trying to get my head around the man seated next to me. In the course of my career I've met all manner of people: the kind, the vile, the heroic, the deluded, the compassionate, and the stupid ... plenty of stupid. Even though I've only known Clement a few days, I'm certain I've never met anyone like him before.

By the time we reach our destination, Abbots Langley, I'm no less perplexed.

"We're just a few minutes away," I comment as we pootle through the centre of the village.

"Good. I need to stretch my legs."

The sat nav directs us to take a left, and after a hundred yards along a featureless semi-rural road, a right into a narrow lane. Our destination, Juniper Cottage, is situated at the very end of the lane, apparently.

As we close in on the cottage, I become aware just how sweaty my palms have become over the last few miles. Distracted by Clement I haven't given much thought to the reason we're making this journey. Now we're only seconds away from our destination my hammering heart offers a reminder.

I slow down to a crawl as we cover the final yards of tarmac; an open meadow to our left with a thicket of trees beyond. To the right, Juniper Cottage sits beyond a tall hedge and a five-bar gate. I pull into the turning circle at the very end of the lane and kill the engine.

"Well, we made it," I chirp nervously.

"Not a bad spot, doll. Quiet, no immediate neighbours, and no passing traffic."

"Christ, you sound like a serial killer on a recce."

"Trust me: I don't want anyone dying on us."

Not entirely convinced, I get out of the car. Apart from the sound of a light breeze brushing the greenery I'm met by near silence. The sudden thunk of Clement closing the passenger's door doesn't help my nerves.

He ambles over. "Right, listen, doll. You're gonna knock on the door while l stand to the side. When he opens it, confirm it's him and move to the right. I'll deal with the rest. Got it?"

"What if he's not alone?"

"If someone else opens the door, just say you're lost and looking for directions."

"Yes, but he might answer the door and his girlfriend could be in the kitchen for all we know."

"Let me worry about that."

I follow Clement towards the gate.

Once we clear the hedge we're granted a full view of Juniper Cottage. It's not as twee as the name suggests; a fairly stout, symmetrical box in red brick with a door in the centre and windows either side. More importantly though, the white BMW on the driveway indicates someone is home. Hopefully, that someone is Thomas Lang.

We head up the paved pathway to the front door and Clement steps to one side. The door itself is one of those white plastic affairs with a spy hole in the centre. It might be low-maintenance but it ruins the aesthetic of the Victorian structure.

"Ready?" Clement whispers.

"No," I whisper back, but press the doorbell anyway.

Seconds tick by until I hear footsteps on floorboards. A brief pause before the latch is turned, and the door opens.

A man stands in the doorway and smiles. A distinguished-looking man with grey eyes and a thick head of grey hair; neatly parted at the side. Like the man himself, the tunic has been retired, replaced with a pale-blue sweater.

"Can I help?"

"Mr Lang?" I confirm.

"Yes."

I take an exaggerated step to my right. Puzzled, Thomas Lang's gaze follows me, and that split second of distraction allows Clement to make his move.

It happens in a blur.

The former policeman is knocked off balance as Clement barges straight past him into the hallway. By the time he's steadied himself, it's too late and Clement has gained entry. Once the shock has subsided, the inevitable questions arrive.

"Who the hell are you?" he yells. "What do you want?"

His shouting is likely to attract unwanted attention. Whilst his focus is on Clement I step into the hallway and close the door.

"We just want a word, Mr Lang," I say calmly.

The narrow hallway offers few options for escape. I'm blocking the front door while Clement is stood the other side of Lang, blocking his route back down the hallway.

"Do you know who I am?" he snarls.

"Yeah, we do," Clement replies. "And that's why we're here."

Thomas Lang isn't a small man — around six foot tall and broad shouldered, although he's carrying the excesses of a desk job. Nevertheless, any man who has spent years policing the streets of London can clearly handle themselves. He looks at Clement, and then at me. I'm patently the easier option and he lunges towards the door handle.

He doesn't make it.

Clement grabs a handful of his sweater and drags him backwards. In one fluid movement, he spins Lang around and pins him up against the wall; his forearm pressed up against the older man's windpipe.

"That wasn't clever."

Clement then drops his free hand towards Lang's crutch and grabs him in a place I, as a woman, can only speculate to be highly sensitive.

Lang confirms it by letting out a yelp.

"We're gonna have a quick chat, Tommy boy," Clement exclaims. "You try anything, or lie to me, and I'll rip your knackers off and shove them down your throat. We clear?"

Lang nods as best he can with Clement's meaty forearm wedged under his chin.

"Good. Are you alone?"

"Yes."

"Now, what do you know about the Clawthorn Club?"

"The what?"

Clement turns to me. "Show him, doll."

Presuming he means the notebook I delve into my handbag and pull it out. A quick flick through the pages to Lang's name.

"This ring any bells?" I ask, holding the notebook up so Lang can see the page.

"I ... no."

The veins in Clement's hand spasm as he tightens his grip. Lang responds with a guttural howl.

"Let's try again. What do you know about the Clawthorn Club?"

"I ... I can't ... they'll ruin me."

"Listen, mate — I'll ruin you if you don't start talking."

"We know about Lance Nithercott," I interject.

We don't actually know much about what happened to Lance Nithercott but hopefully Lang doesn't see through my bluff.

"I had no choice. Lance was a liability ... he was pissed all the time."

"Where can we find the Tallyman?" Clement asks, getting back to the point of our visit.

Lang's eyes widen, and not because his testicles are being crushed.

"I don't know ... I swear ... nobody does."

"Alright. Who is he?"

Lang closes his eyes and gulps hard. After a few ragged breaths, he opens his eyes again.

"I'll tell you what ... you want to know, but please ... I can't breathe."

Clement removes his arm, and then the hand clamped on Lang's crotch.

"Sit down," he orders. "You try anything and I'll use this."

I'd forgotten all about Jaydon's knife but Clement pulls it from his pocket and holds it inches from Lang's face.

"Okay, okay," he gasps, before sliding down the wall and pulling his knees to his chest. He makes for a pathetic sight, and it's hard to imagine he was once the second most powerful policeman in London. However, despite the obvious threat Clement poses, I get the feeling Thomas Lang's fear is rooted elsewhere.

I take a couple of steps forward and squat down so I can look him in the eye.

"Why are you so scared?"

"I don't know who you are, or what your game is, but you have no idea what you're dealing with."

"That's why you're going to enlighten us."

"If he finds out I've spoken to you, I'm … it's all over."

"He?"

"This Tallyman character, whoever he is. Other men have talked, in the past, and their lives have been destroyed."

"Like Lance Nithercott?"

He squeezes his eyes closed and slowly nods.

"Come on, Thomas," I urge. "Let's hear it."

He opens his eyes and breathes a heavy sigh. "Okay, what do you know about the Clawthorn Club?"

"Not a lot, so tell us everything."

"I don't know for sure, but I think it shut down nine or ten years ago as all the members were either old men, or dead. But a year or two before I retired, one of my more ambitious colleagues in the Serious Organised Crime Agency got a lead on one of the members and started joining up the dots. I was told to derail his investigation but there was only so much I could do without drawing further attention. Because I failed, I had to repay my debt by tying up a loose end."

"I'm guessing Lance Nithercott was that loose end?"

"I didn't kill him. It was an accident."

"Some bleedin' accident," Clement remarks.

"I just wanted to scare him so he'd stop talking. Lance had a drink problem and as that worsened, he started blabbing about Clawthorn in the pub, and he became a person of interest to my colleagues in SOCA. I was told to shut him up, or my own favours would be revealed in the press."

"Your favours?"

"Three of them, and I wish to God I'd never accepted the first one."

"What was that first favour?"

"Are you mad?" he spits. "I'm certainly not going to tell you."

"Fair enough, but you are going to tell us what happened to Lance Nithercott."

The defiance is short lived as his head bows forward.

"I didn't mean it," he says in barely a whisper.

"Tell us, Thomas."

He looks up, and straight into my eyes. I've interviewed enough people in my career to spot the signs of true remorse, and I would hazard a guess Thomas Lang needs to unburden his guilt.

"I ... I bundled him into the boot of my car one night, and drove to that motorway bridge. The idea was to just dangle him over the edge so he got the message but I ... I messed up. I was holding him over the concrete barrier and he managed to throw a punch ... should have seen it coming but I didn't. I was dazed and lost my grip on his arm for just a second ... by the time I tried to grab him it was too late ... he just fell."

I glance up at Clement. The slightest nod confirms he also believes Thomas Lang's confession.

"What happened with the investigation into the Clawthorn Club, Thomas?"

"I was told they hit a dead end but the file was to remain open. Apparently they had a handful of suspects in mind but evidence was proving hard to come by. My best guess is the Tallyman knew his days were numbered and tried to bury every shred of evidence that the Clawthorn Club ever existed ... except one thing it seems. How did you come by the notebook?"

"That doesn't matter. What matters is finding the man it belongs to."

"Whoever you are, and whatever your motives, I'm sorry, but you're wasting your time. The Tallyman is a ghost."

"He's no ghost, Thomas. He's very much alive, and he's now coming after me."

"In which case, I pity you. Once that man has his claws in you there is no escape."

"We'll see about that. Tell me: what does he look like?"

"Christ knows. I've never met him."

"What? How can you not have met him?"

"The Clawthorn Club worked under a blanket of complete secrecy. If you had a problem, you sent a letter to a PO box and waited for a response. If there was another member in a position to help, the Tallyman would arrange a meeting between the two parties, but he never attended. And no names were ever revealed unless it was absolutely necessary. I did a few favours, and for at least two of those favours I only knew the recipients initials, and neither knew my full name. It was almost impossible to identify other members because the Tallyman wanted to ensure there was no opportunity for potential blackmail. Ironic really, as down the line he was the one doing the blackmailing."

"To be clear: you don't know the names of any other members then?"

To reinforce the need for honesty Clement cracks his knuckles.

"None that are still alive — I swear. Only the Tallyman knew the full names of every member, and to the best of my knowledge, only a handful of people knew his true identity."

I stand up and look at Clement hoping he might have picked up on something we can use to move forward. Our dishevelled former policeman has filled in a few gaps but the Clawthorn canvas is still worryingly blank.

Clement shakes his head. There's only one question remaining I can ask.

"Thomas, does the name Dennis Hogan mean anything to you?"

"Kind of," he sighs, "Only by notoriety."

"Meaning?"

"I don't know much, and what I've heard is mostly anecdotal, but Dennis Hogan was apparently one of the original members of the Clawthorn Club back in the late sixties."

My already rock-bottom opinion of my father reaches new depths. At least his possession of the notebook now makes some sense.

"Carry on."

"Hogan was one of the few people who knew the true identity of the Tallyman — to everyone else, he went by the name of Allen Tamthy, which was just a pseudonym."

"So I've discovered."

"Apparently Dennis Hogan had a major fall out with the Tallyman and ended up in prison when he tried to leave."

"I think you've got your wires crossed. Dennis Hogan left the Clawthorn Club because he was sent to prison for raping and murdering a prostitute."

Thomas Lang looks up at me as if I've failed to grasp the punchline of a joke.

"That's not strictly accurate," he adds "Rumour has it Dennis

Hogan went to prison because the Tallyman framed him."

19.

If Clement were to suddenly punch me in the gut, it would have less impact than Lang's revelation.

"He was set-up?" Clement confirms.

"Apparently, and sentenced to eighteen years. Again, if the rumours are to be believed, Hogan threatened to blow the lid on what was going on, and by that point the Clawthorn Club had enough members with real influence. I presume getting Dennis Hogan sent down also proved a potent example of what would happen if anyone else tried exposing its secrets or breaking the rules. Perhaps you can now understand why I took that trip with Lance Nithercott — it wasn't through choice."

Wide-eyed, I stare across at Clement. For a man who barely knows me, he appears to have quickly developed a knack for reading my body language.

"Let me get this straight: Dennis Hogan had a falling out with this Tallyman bloke and he ends up doing bird for eighteen years?"

"That's what I was told."

I have no interest in anything else Thomas Lang has to say.

"I ... I need to go."

Clement bends down and growls something to Lang — presumably a threat to never mention our visit — but I don't wait to find out.

Escaping the claustrophobic hallway doesn't help. I could run into the middle of the open meadow and the walls would continue to close in on me.

I stagger back across the driveway and out the gate. The bonnet of my car provides a convenient place to sit while I attempt to process what I've just discovered about my father.

All of a sudden, the Dennis Hogan-shaped box which has safely contained all my hatred, all my bitterness, has been ripped open and the contents scattered.

"You alright, doll?"

I look up to find Clement striding over.

"No. I'm not."

He sits down on the bonnet next to me.

"I take it you didn't have the first clue?"

"No."

"What do you wanna do about Lang? I could go back in and rough him up a bit — see if he knows anything else."

"I don't … let's just get out of here."

"Gimme the keys. You're in no fit state to drive."

Insurance, licence, who knows? I don't, and nor do I care. I hand the keys to Clement and fall into the passenger seat.

The driver's seat is rammed back as far as it'll go and Clement clambers in. More adjustments to the seat are made, and then he fixes me with his blue eyes while turning the ignition key.

"You wanna talk, we'll talk. You wanna sit and think, I'll keep shtum."

He yanks the seatbelt across his barrel-like chest and we set off.

Ten minutes in and my mind is so far elsewhere I haven't even thought to set the sat nav. It doesn't appear to matter as Clement navigates our journey in the old-school manner by following the road signs.

We reach the motorway and Clement breaks the silence.

"How you doin', doll?"

"I think my head is fit to burst."

"More bleedin' questions, eh?"

"Too many."

"It ain't too late to knock this on the head. Send the notebook back and you can get on with your life."

"Can I? An hour ago I probably could, but now ... God knows. I'm so confused, Clement."

"In which case, we gotta keep digging."

"Where?"

"Ain't that obvious?"

"Nothing is obvious at the moment."

"It is, doll — your old man was probably one of the last blokes on earth who knew this Tallyman's real identity. We dig into his past and see what turns up."

"That's not much of a plan."

"No, it ain't, but even if it don't help us identify the Tallyman, you might find out what really happened. It's gotta be better than not knowing?"

The only thing I know for sure is I know nothing for sure. If indeed we do have a soul, mine is a vacuum as all I thought to be true has been sucked away. In some twisted way I'd have preferred the bitterness and resentment, rather than this.

"I feel so ... lost, Clement."

He breathes a long sigh. "You're not the only one."

Without warning, he then suddenly tugs the steering wheel to the left and the car veers across two lanes of the motorway. Horns blare and tyres screech as we cut across the chevrons onto a slip road.

"What the fuck was that?" I yell, my chest pounding.

"This is the last services on this stretch. Thought you could do with a cuppa."

"A cuppa? I could do with a bloody Valium after that manoeuvre — you could have killed us."

"Not likely."

In fairness, Clement's erratic driving has succeeded in shifting my emotional state, if only temporarily.

We find a parking space and once the engine is switched off, I confiscate the keys.

"I think I'll drive the rest of the way."

"Suit yourself."

"Why the sudden need for a cup of tea?"

"We need to have a chat — work out what we're gonna do."

"We could have done that in the car."

"Could I have had a piss in the car?"

My puckered face provides an answer.

"Thought not. Let's go."

He extracts himself from the driver's seat. It looks like I'm having a cup of overpriced coffee whether I want one or not.

We wander across to the coffee shop and I order our drinks while Clement goes in search of the toilets. He returns five minutes later looking less strained.

"Christ, you could have floated the Titanic on what I just pissed out," he remarks.

"Thank you for painting that picture — just what I wanted to imagine while drinking a coffee."

He sits down and peers into the paper cup.

"Is that tea?"

"Allegedly."

"'Spose it'll have to do."

Trying to purge the image of Clement urinating, I return to the point of our pit stop.

"What you said in the car — about feeling lost too — why is that?"

"This ain't about me, doll."

"It kinda is, Clement. For some inexplicable reason you've chosen to help me and if I can return the favour in any way, I want to."

"I help you, it helps me. That's the top and bottom of it."

"Perhaps you'd like to be a bit more specific? How does it help you?"

He shakes his head. "What is it with people these days?"

"I'm not with you."

"You know, back in the day, folks just helped one another. Friends, neighbours, sometimes even complete strangers — it was called doing a good deed, and that's how the world worked. Nowadays everyone has an agenda. What's wrong with helping someone out just for the sake of it?"

I think back to the days when I was growing up on the estate. There are times we would have gone hungry if it hadn't been for a neighbour helping out with the odd box of cereal or tin of beans. Every family on that estate lived near the breadline but goodwill was always in plentiful supply — people cared about each other back then.

"The good old days, eh?"

"Yeah, they were."

"Don't take this the wrong way, Clement, but you're … you don't seem comfortable with any part of modern life. Is there a reason for that?"

"I thought we were gonna talk about you?"

"It's called deflection — handy for avoiding conversations I don't want to have."

"But we're gonna have."

Clement's statement hangs long enough I have to respond. "I suppose so."

He takes a sip of tea and grimaces.

"We're gonna do this, right?"

"This?"

"Shift our attention to your old man."

"Given the choice I'd rather rewind the clock back to last week when the name Clawthorn would have been meaningless."

"And you say I'm trapped in the past."

"I wasn't being literal. I'm just … I don't want to rake over the past — nothing good can come of it. Even if my father was set up, he's dead, so what's the point?"

"But you've gotta live with not knowing, and I don't think that's your thing, doll."

"I didn't have you pegged at the perceptive type."

"Yeah, well, when you've been around the block as many times as I have, you get to know what makes people tick."

"And you think you know what makes me tick?"

"Yeah, I reckon."

I sit back and fold my arms. "Go on then — let's hear it."

"You're afraid of the guilt."

"Yeah, right," I scoff. "What do I have to feel guilty about?"

"Spending your whole life hating your old man when maybe he weren't the evil bastard you thought he was. And you can't say sorry to a dead man. There won't be no happy reunion — that's what's fucked your head up."

"Twenty minutes ago I might have agreed with you, but I've had time to think. Even if he was set up, and we've only got hearsay from one man to suggest he was, what happened after he was released?

He chose to stay away because he was a coward. Trust me: I wasn't wrong to hate the man so I don't feel guilty."

"But what if he had paid you a visit, to plead his case?"

"I'd have punched him in the face probably."

"Bit harsh."

"Listen, Clement, " I snap. "My mother thought he was guilty as sin, as did twelve jurors, and a judge. I'm inclined to believe them rather than a rumour from a bent copper."

"And if they were all wrong? Forget this Tallyman for a moment — you've gotta find out what happened cos you owe it to yourself, and your old man. That hate you've been carrying around all your life will eat you up unless you've good reason for it to be there."

"And if I am wrong? What if I discover my father was really innocent?"

"Then at least you know. You're his daughter and until you know who he really was, you'll never know who you are."

"Christ, don't start getting profound on me, Clement. I'm not sure it suits you."

"Don't worry. I won't be making a habit of it."

He takes another sip of tea and fixes me with a stare.

"Well? What we doin'?"

If nothing else, my chat with Clement has succeeded in lifting the fog that clouded my thoughts when we left Juniper Cottage. I'm still not sure I want to know the truth about Dennis Hogan, but the reality is I'm still being blackmailed and there's still a potential story to be unearthed — reasons enough to keep pushing on. Perhaps I'm kidding myself, but for now, they're the easier motives to swallow.

"I guess we keep digging."

"I like you, doll," he smiles. "You're not a quitter."

His comment is too close to sincere and I feel my cheeks flush.

"Um, anyway," I cough. "What do we do next?"

"You said your old man rented a flat out Chiswick way?"

"That's right."

"We should start there, and have a word with the letting agent."

"Yeah, I don't think you'll find him particularly cooperative."

Clements eyebrows arch. "You reckon?"

A smile creeps across my face. "Actually, I think you probably could persuade him to cooperate, and I definitely want to watch you try."

"Shall we head there now?"

"We can't just bowl into his office. Now I've seen your interview technique first hand it's not a good idea having witnesses around."

"Fair point. How do we get the bloke alone then?"

"Give me a minute."

I open the browser on my phone and find the website for the firm of estate agents who employ Miles DuPont. A quick search of their listings and I find a flat in Chiswick being offered with vacant possession. After a quick check of the internal photos, I'm happy the flat is empty and call the number at the top of the page.

"Hi. Can I speak to Miles DuPont please? Tell him it's Emma

Hogan."

I'm put on hold for a few seconds before DuPont answers.

"Hello, Miss Hogan," he says curtly. "I wasn't expecting to hear from you again."

"No, well, I'm not calling with regards to my father's flat."

"Oh, that's certainly good to hear. What can I do for you?"

"I'm actually calling about one of your properties. When I was driving around trying to find the flat on Wednesday, I was quite taken aback by the area. Long story short: I've decided I quite like the idea of living in Chiswick, and the flat you're advertising on Chesterfield Road looks perfect for my needs."

"I didn't realise you were house hunting."

"I wasn't, until Wednesday — well, not actively. I've been living in a rented property for a few years while I decide where I want to lay some roots, and I think I've settled on Chiswick. I've got cash in the bank so I'm ready to buy."

The prospect of an easy commission is all the bait I need.

"In that case," he chirps. "We must organise a viewing for you."

"Great. I don't suppose I could see it this afternoon?"

"The sooner the better with that flat — there's been a lot of interest."

Lying tosser.

"I can be there in an hour if that suits?"

"Perfect. I still have your number on file so I'll text you the full address."

"Thank you, Miles."

"Pleasure is all mine. I look forward to seeing you in an hour."

Not as much as I look forward to you seeing Clement.

I hang up.

"Sorted?"

"Yep. We're meeting him in an empty flat."

"Nice one."

"So, how are we going to play this?"

"You ask the questions, doll, and I'll encourage him to answer."

I down the now-tepid coffee dregs from my cup.

"I like that plan. Let's go."

20.

"What is it with this fucking road?" Clement groans.

"Not a fan of the M25?"

"Why does the speed limit keep changing?"

"Bloody hell, Clement. When was the last time you drove on the M25?"

"Not sure I ever have."

"Seriously? How can you have lived in London all your life and avoided it?"

"I haven't driven for a while."

"Yeah, it shows," I smirk. "They call it a smart motorway and it's supposed to help with traffic flow."

"How the hell does that work? If they just kept it at seventy we'd all get where we're supposed to be a bit bleedin' quicker."

"Ours is not to reason why."

He shakes his head and does nothing but complain about the traffic for the remainder of our journey. In fairness, the congestion in London on a Friday afternoon is enough to test anyone's patience.

We arrive in Chesterfield Road with minutes to spare. There's no sign of Miles DuPont's Mercedes as we pull up outside the flat.

"Nice part of town," Clement remarks.

"Nice, and bloody expensive."

The asking price of the purpose-built flat is just shy of seven figures; the price one pays to live in a pleasant, tree-lined road so close to central London.

We sit for a minute and savour the quiet — only broken by the ticking of the engine as it cools. That quiet is then broken as a white Mercedes revs to a halt behind us. I watch in my rear view mirror as Miles DuPont slithers out.

"Here we go."

I get out of the car and Clement follows me to the front of the building where our prey is already waiting, blissfully unaware of his impending interrogation.

"Nice to see you again, Miles."

He strides over and shakes my hand. His plastic smile quickly fades when he realises I'm not alone.

"Alright, mate," Clement booms, holding out his hand.

Miles hesitantly accepts the handshake. "Pleased to meet you, Mr ..."

"Bastin. Cliff Bastin."

With Clement offering a false name only one of us will be culpable if this little soirée gets out of hand. Miles invites us to follow him and we make our way to the main door of the building.

"The flats were constructed just seven years ago, and there's only five in the building," he comments, while unlocking the door.

"What's the soundproofing like?" Clement asks.

"Oh, it's exceptional. You could hold a rave in the sitting room and your neighbours wouldn't hear a thing."

"Good to know."

We follow Miles up the stairs to the first floor where he unlocks the door to flat three.

"After you."

We step into the featureless hallway.

"It's been rented out for a few years so the decor is a little on the safe side."

He's not wrong.

"Go straight through to the sitting room," he adds.

I lead and Clement follows as we head into a large, empty lounge with a full-height window one end and an archway leading through to a kitchen at the other. The sand-coloured carpet and magnolia walls are achingly dull.

"It's a real blank canvas," Miles coos. "Don't you think?"

Clement closes the door and stands in front of it. The weasely estate agent doesn't appear concerned he's now trapped — he soon will be.

"I need to pick your brains, Miles," I say with a smile.

"Go ahead."

"About my father's tenancy."

"What about it?"

"You would have conducted checks on him, right?"

"Well, yes."

"And what checks did you make?"

"I'm sorry," he frowns. "Am I missing something here? I thought you were interested in purchasing a flat."

"Not really. We just want to know everything you have on file about my father: previous addresses, references, employment history … all of it."

"That information is confidential; we can't just share it willy-nilly."

"Yeah, you can," Clement suggests. "And trust me — you will."

"What is this? Are you threatening me?"

"Pretty much."

Miles reaches for the inside pocket of his jacket, and his mobile phone no doubt.

"If you're thinking of making a call, I wouldn't, mate. I really wouldn't."

Something tells me Miles DuPont doesn't like being told what to do. After a brief pause, he decides to take his chances and dips a hand inside his jacket. The defiant sneer remains in situ for all of two seconds before Clement steps across the room and grabs hold of his arm.

"I warned you."

The arm is then twisted behind his back and Clement grabs Miles by the collar to ensure there is no escape.

"Jesus Christ," he screams. "That hurts … let go!"

"You gonna tell us what we need to know?"

"I can't. It's more than my job is worth."

"Wrong answer."

An inch of vertical movement is all it takes to produce another scream.

Clement looks at me. "Bit of a screamer, this one. If you've got some pliers in the motor, I can always rip his tongue out."

I take a few steps forward so I'm directly facing Miles DuPont.

"I don't wish to worry you, Miles, but I think he means it."

"This is preposterous," he whines. "You can't do this."

"Why not? What are you going to do about it?"

"I'll ... I'll inform the police."

"Without a tongue, that might be difficult."

"Tell you what, doll," Clement interjects. "Go have a look in the kitchen and see if you can find a tin opener — a bit messier than pliers but it'd do the job."

I look Miles in the eye. "Last chance."

His shoulders slump. "Alright, alright."

"Good man," I smile, patting him on the cheek. "Now, what you're going to do next is call your office and ask them to email you everything in my father's file ... and I mean everything. You're then going to forward that email to me. Clear?"

"Yes, clear," he spits.

I look up at Clement. "How long does it take to cut a tongue out?"

"Usually a minute or two."

"And testicles?"

"I can whip those off in seconds."

"Great. Did you hear that, Miles? If you so much as hint about what's going on, there will still be ample time for my friend to get slicey before the police arrive. Understood?"

He nods.

"Good. Make the call."

With his free hand, Miles awkwardly extracts his phone and makes the call. I maintain eye contact for the entire duration; just to ensure he stays on script.

"Five minutes," he confirms, returning the phone to his pocket.

"Well done."

I nod to Clement and he releases Miles from the arm lock.

"You do realise you could have, as Mr Hogan's next of kin, made a formal application for the information we have on file."

"I don't have the time or patience, and besides, this is much more fun don't you think?"

His scowl suggests otherwise.

There is nothing for us to do but wait around. Clement leans up against the door and Miles stares out the window. I've never been so relieved to hear the chime of a mobile phone.

Miles extracts his phone and asks for my email address. He taps away at his screen and seconds later I have an email with a folder attached.

"I think we're done."

Clement has other ideas and suddenly grabs Miles by the lapel of his jacket.

"Gimme your wallet."

"I don't carry cash," Miles bleats.

"Wallet. Now."

The wallet is removed and handed to Clement.

"Ain't cash I'm after. It's your address."

"What? Why?"

"Insurance," Clement replies, studying the estate agent's driving licence. "You tell anyone about our little chat, and I mean anyone, and I'll pop by with my pliers."

"I won't tell anyone … I promise."

Clement throws the wallet on the floor and releases the grip on DuPont's designer jacket.

"For your sake, you better keep that promise."

We leave Miles DuPont scrabbling around on the floor.

Once we return to the car, my immediate priority is to take a look at the information in the email but Clement has other ideas.

"Let's go find a boozer first. I think I've earnt a pint."

"I like your thinking. We'll drop the car back at the flat first."

"Want me to drive? We'll get there quicker."

"I'm already close to a nervous breakdown, Clement. I think I'll drive, if it's all the same."

It takes forty-five minutes to crawl the seven miles across London; a reminder why I rarely take the car. I park up at the back of the flat and we head straight to The Three Horseshoes. I'm not sure which feels more pressing — the need to view my father's tenancy documents or to neck a large glass of wine. Probably the wine if I'm honest.

Clement isn't impressed with my local.

"Can't stand boozers like this — all fur coat and no knickers."

"I've never understood that expression."

"Fancy but fake. I've had a few birds in my time that fall into that category, I can tell you."

"Why am I not surprised."

I dispense with any notion I'll only want one or two glasses, and order a bottle of red wine. Clement predictably requests a pint of lager. We grab a table away from the growing number of office workers who've left their desks early just because it's Friday. I guess, somewhere across town, Gini will be corralling my former colleagues for post-work drinks. For once, I feel a pang of envy I'm not invited, or ever will be now I've been expatriated from the payroll.

"Cheers, doll."

I chink my glass against Clement's while thumbing my phone.

"Right. Let's see what we've got."

I unzip the folder to reveal just three documents — each one, no matter how mundane, a potential insight into a father I didn't know. I open the first document, titled *employment*. There's not a lot to read, but what little there is still takes me by surprise.

"He was head of accounts for something called the NLH Foundation, in Clerkenwell."

"Head of accounts? That might explain how he got mixed up in the Clawthorn Club — someone good at cooking the books would be handy to know."

"Perhaps, but it doesn't explain how he secured such a responsible job. If I ran a business, I don't think I'd want a man who'd spent eighteen years in prison doing my books."

"Depends what sort of business it is."

I google the NLH Foundation. "It's a charity for the homeless."

"Good to see your old man had a sense of humour."

"What do you mean?"

"Don't they say charity begins at home?"

If Clement's observation wasn't so near to the bone, it might be amusing.

My preconceptions about Dennis Hogan are so tainted I never considered the possibility he had a professional career. Part of my coping mechanism was to assume he was suffering a rotten life without us. Coupled with his expensive home in Chiswick, a cosy, white-collar job does not suggest his life was particularly rotten after he left prison.

A large swig of wine helps to ease the bitter taste in my mouth.

"I guess that's the first place for us to try then."

Clement nods in agreement as I open the second document, titled *POI*.

It proves to be a scanned image of a passport — the POI presumably an acronym for proof of identity. His date of birth confirms he was seventy-seven years of age when he died — significantly more life than my poor mother enjoyed.

I pinch the screen to enlarge the photo of my father — a face I've never seen in the flesh. It shows a man with a head of thinning white hair, and eyes sunk into a sallow face etched with lines. Even for a passport photo, his expression is particularly sombre.

"Clement," I sigh, holding the phone up. "Meet Dennis Hogan."

He examines the face of the dead man we've hung our hopes upon. Experience tells me we shouldn't get those hopes up.

"For what it's worth, doll, you don't look much like the bloke."

"That's not exactly a compliment."

I swipe away the photo and open the third document: *references*. It contains a single snippet of information.

"This could be useful. A previous address and the landlord's name."

Clement leans over and squints at the screen. "Nancy Hawkins, Wellington Row, Bethnal Green."

"At least it's in London."

"Gotta be worth a visit."

"Let me just check this Ms Hawkins actually lives at that address first."

I tap through to a website which has proven an invaluable research tool over the years. It confirms Nancy Hawkins is the only resident at the address in Wellington Row, East London. It also confirms her age.

"So, she definitely lives there, and alone."

"Perfect."

"But she's an old woman, Clement. I think it might be better for me to ask the questions this time."

"Don't be too sure about that. They make 'em tough in that neck of the woods."

"I think I can handle a seventy year-old woman, and I have been to Bethnal Green before, you know."

"Used to be a rough old patch, back in the day. The Kray twins grew up round there."

"A bit before our time which is a shame as I bet they had a few stories worth telling."

"They were hard bastards but nothing special, doll. Shall I let you into a little secret?"

"Go on."

"Thing is," he says, leaning forward. "Ronnie Kray was a gayer."

"A gayer?"

"Yeah, you know, a gay bloke."

"*Homosexual* is the word I think you're looking for, Clement, and Ronnie Kray's sexuality is common knowledge."

"Is it?" he frowns.

"Yes. And it seems political correctness has somehow passed you by too."

"Can't keep up with it. One minute you can use a word; next minute some fucker is offended by it."

I have some sympathy. Only last month I was told to remove the term 'whiter than white' from an article in case it caused offence. I've got friends and colleagues spanning the entire spectrum of sexuality, ethnicity, and religious beliefs, and not one of us knows what we can safely say these days. It's a minefield.

"Anyway," I continue, "Gay gangsters or otherwise, we've got a couple of leads worth pursuing. I think we should try the charity first, and then we can head over to Bethnal Green and pay Nancy Hawkins a visit."

"Sounds like a plan, doll."

"It's all we've got so it'll have to be. When do you want to go?"

"Up to you."

I glance at the bottle of wine, and then at my empty glass.

"Let's leave it until tomorrow."

21.

I awoke with a fuzzy head and scratchy throat.

My flatmate proved a bad influence and I ended-up necking two bottles of red wine, and puffing my way through five cigarettes last night. So, despite the chance of a lie-in, I'm up by eight-thirty in search of painkillers.

It was good, though, to spend a few hours basking in a wine-induced haze. I can almost see why Lance Nithercott decided to live his life in a perpetual state of drunkenness; a place to hide away from thoughts of the Clawthorn Club and Allen bloody Tamthy.

I put the kettle on and the rumbling goes some way to drowning out the rumbling from the spare bedroom. For once, I'm disappointed the kettle doesn't take longer to boil. I console myself with an extra strong coffee and plod through to the lounge. The TV provides an equally efficient means to drown out Clement's snoring.

Rather than the TV screen my attention is soon dragged towards the screen of my phone and the photo of Dennis Hogan. A perverse impulse compels me to keep staring at it, as if suddenly everything will become clear. Nothing comes, other than an unsettling conclusion: despite being the reason I came into the world and sharing the same genes, Dennis Hogan could not be more of a stranger.

Today, I hope to change that to some degree, but only for my own selfish reasons.

I finish my coffee and head into the bathroom.

After a long shower, I get dressed and emerge to the sound of cupboard doors opening and closing in the kitchen. If his headache is as bad as mine, I suspect Clement is looking for painkillers.

"They're in the top drawer," I say, poking my head around the kitchen door.

"What are?"

"You're looking for painkillers?"

"Why would I want painkillers?"

"I don't know, Clement — maybe for a hangover? You must have sunk at least eight pints last night."

"I feel right as rain, or I will be once I've had a cuppa."

"What are you looking for then?"

"Teabags."

"Aren't there any in the caddy?"

"Nope, but I found these," he says, holding up a box of green tea.

"If I'm out of regular tea, that's all there is I'm afraid."

"All tastes the same, though, don't it ... black tea, green tea?"

"Erm, try it."

He shrugs his shoulders and plops a teabag into a mug. Once he's filled the cup with boiling water, milk, and three teaspoons of sugar, he gives it a thorough stir and scoops the teabag out.

"I'm gagging for this."

He takes a long sip and then smacks his lips together.

"Fucking 'ell," he blurts, his face contorted as if he'd just sipped seawater. "This is off."

"Off?"

"Yeah, off … tastes like boiled piss."

"It's good for you, Clement," I snigger. "Drink up."

I chuckle my way to the lounge.

Five minutes later he wanders in with a mug of something which probably isn't green tea.

"What's that?"

"Bleedin' coffee," he grumbles.

"I'll pick up some teabags later. Sorry."

My phone rings.

I check the screen and I'm relieved to see it's not another withheld number. I jab the answer icon and mumble a hello.

"Hi, Emma. It's Alex. Alex Palmer."

I was kind of hoping, after Eric's funeral, it would be at least another ten years before I heard from my former colleague again.

"Hi, Alex."

"Sorry to call so early on a Saturday morning, but I've heard on the grapevine thing's aren't so rosy for you at the moment."

"Err, what have you heard, precisely?"

"That you've been … let go by The Daily Standard."

News never travels faster than when those who report it are the subject.

"I've been suspended," I sigh.

"I'm so sorry, Emma. Can I ask: was it for anything serious?"

"In my opinion, no, but you know I like to push the boundaries."

"I do, and that's actually why I'm calling. There's a position available within my company and I think it'd be perfect for you."

"Err, okay. What exactly is this position?"

"I don't know if you're aware but I now work for a telecoms company?"

"I am."

"Great, well, we're looking for a head of PR. The money will be at least double what you can earn as a staff reporter."

Moving from reporting to public relations would be like a gamekeeper turning to poaching. Rather than writing actual news, it's a game of promoting a brand under the pretence of it being news.

"It's so kind of you to think of me, Alex, but I'm not sure I'm cut out for PR."

"Nonsense. You have the contacts, and the insider knowledge — you'd be perfect."

"I don't ..."

"And then there's the perks," he interrupts. "Company car, private health care, thirty days paid leave, share options."

"Um, that sounds ..."

"Why don't we meet up for a drink later and we can chat about it?"

I'm about to decline his offer when the pragmatic side of my brain wakes up. If this whole saga with Clawthorn goes nowhere, I'm jobless, and in deep financial shit. Maybe it would be prudent to cover my bases.

"Just a chat, right?"

"Of course. All I ask is you hear what I've got to say, and you go away and think about it."

The money and the perks do sound appealing — having a drink with Alex, less so. Needs must I guess.

"Okay."

"Great. Where shall we meet?"

"Do you know The Three Horseshoes in Kilburn?"

"No, but I can find it. Shall we say six-thirty?"

"Good for me. I'll see you then."

I end the call and toss my phone on the sofa.

"Who was that?"

"A guy I used to work with. He's got a job opportunity and wants to meet up."

"You don't sound too thrilled."

"It's just all this uncertainty — I can't make any plans until ... well, until I know where we're going with this whole Clawthorn thing."

"Come Monday, we'll know where we are, doll. If we don't turn anything up over the weekend, send the bleedin' notebook back and get on with your life."

He makes it sound so simple, and for him it probably is.

"Yeah, you're right, "I reply, sounding less-than-convincing. "And on that note, finish your coffee and we'll make a move."

He finishes half of it, under duress, and we leave the flat.

The streets of London have an entirely different atmosphere at the weekend. There's no less traffic, but the people seem less stressed about getting wherever they need to be. I wouldn't exactly call it lazy, but laid back, certainly.

As we walk towards the Underground station, I make a quick call to the NLH Foundation to check they're open. Unsurprisingly for a homeless charity it appears they never close. Under the pretence I'm researching a newspaper article, I'm given the name Mandy Burke as a point of contact.

On a relatively quiet Tube train, it takes just twenty minutes to reach Barbican, the nearest station to Clerkenwell. From there, our destination is just a fifteen minute walk, or it would have been.

"I need a cup of tea, doll, and a couple of bacon sarnies wouldn't go amiss either."

I look up at him and frown. "Glad to see my advice sunk in. How you're still alive is a mystery, Clement."

"Ain't it just," he snorts.

We make a short detour to a cafe of my choosing and Clement gets his wish: two rounds of sandwiches with crispy bacon and thick-cut, buttered white bread. Unhealthy or otherwise, I suffer chronic food envy as my plate of poached eggs on wholemeal toast arrives at the table.

"I'll swap you a slice of toast for half a sandwich?"

Clement stops chewing and stares at me.

"What?" I ask.

For a long moment he just looks at me: frozen.

"Nothing," he then murmurs, shaking his head. "Help yourself."

I take a sandwich and thank him. His attention appears elsewhere.

"You okay, Clement?"

"Yeah, it's just … don't matter."

"Come on. What is it?"

He places his half-eaten sandwich down on the plate and wipes his mouth.

"You reminded me of someone, that's all. She did exactly the same thing every time we ate out."

"The same thing?"

"Yeah, ordering something healthy and then nicking stuff off my plate."

"Woman's prerogative, Clement," I smile.

He smiles back but it's followed by a wistful sigh. It seems I've inadvertently triggered a memory he'd rather have kept buried.

"Was she special, this woman?"

"Very."

"Girlfriend?"

He nods.

"No chance of a reconciliation?"

"Not in this life, doll."

I'm about to take a bite of the sandwich but it doesn't reach my mouth.

"Um, you don't mean she's ..."

He nods again.

"Oh, I'm so sorry, Clement. When did it happen?"

"Feels like yesterday, but ... it was a long, long time ago."

I reach across the table and rest my hand on his. "I've heard all the platitudes myself, a million times, so all I'll say is I hope you find peace with it someday."

"Yeah, me too."

Then, he suddenly curls his hand around mine and gently squeezes it. "And cheers for ... you know ... not bending my ear about it."

I return the squeeze. "No problem."

"Now, are you gonna eat that sandwich?"

"This sandwich?" I ask, holding it up.

"Yeah."

"Too bloody right I am."

His grin returns and we put the moment behind us, although it feels good to know there is a heart beating somewhere in that big old chest of his.

Breakfast addressed, we leave the cafe and continue on our way to Rosebery Avenue, and the NHL Foundation. What we find on our arrival is an austere brick building with just a small plaque on the wall next to a set of solid double doors.

"This is it," I remark, pressing the doorbell.

We wait for almost a minute before the door is opened. A thin woman with short-grey hair and a leathery complexion greets us.

"Hi, we're here to see Mandy Burke."

"That'll be me. And you are?"

"I'm Emma Hogan, and this is my colleague, Clement."

"Oh, yes," she chirps. "You rang earlier, about a newspaper article?"

"I did, although I was hoping you might be able to help us on an unrelated matter."

If it transpires Dennis Hogan was as poor an accountant as he was a father, this might prove to be the shortest interview in history.

"It's about my father," I venture. "Dennis Hogan."

To my relief, Mandy's face lights up. "You're Dennis's daughter?"

"I am."

"Any Hogan is welcome here, Emma. Come on in."

We're ushered through a corridor to a pokey office at the rear of the building.

"Please take a seat. Can I get you a tea or coffee?"

"We've just had breakfast so we're good, thanks."

His chance of another cup of tea stolen; Clement scowls.

We both sit behind a crowded desk housing a computer, a pile of folders, and an overflowing in-tray.

"Excuse the mess. The paperwork never ends here."

I return Mandy's smile but her face quickly adopts a more serious expression.

"How have things been, since ... you know?"

I don't know, and my face says as much.

"I mean since your father's funeral," she clarifies.

I consider lying but it's probably best I stick as close to the truth as possible; minus the whole Clawthorn blackmail plot.

"Ahh, well, the thing is, Mandy, I was estranged from my father, and I wasn't even made aware he had passed away."

"Ohh, that explains why I didn't recognise you from the funeral but I just put it down to old age. Sorry, but my memory isn't what it once was."

"Don't apologise. I'm heading that way myself."

Mandy sits back in her chair and glances at Clement. He doesn't notice as he's staring at his feet like a bored schoolboy in class.

"So, the thing is, Mandy, now my father is gone, I'm trying to piece together his life to ... get some closure, I guess."

"I completely understand."

"And I believe he used to work here, as head of accounts?"

"That's not an entirely accurate job description."

"No?"

"No. Dennis Hogan was the founder, and chief benefactor of our Foundation."

I glance across at Clement. He's no longer staring at his feet.

"Oh, wow. I had no idea, Mandy."

"Hardly anyone did. He hated any attention so I guess he gave himself that job title to avoid the limelight. Dennis was one of the most generous, humble, and self-effacing men I've ever met."

Her description is the polar opposite of the man I know to be a rapist and a murderer. I can't help but wonder if we're even talking about the same man.

"Sorry, can I just check something with you?"

"Sure."

I pull out my phone and show Mandy the passport photo. "This is him, right?"

"That's definitely Dennis, although that's not a particularly flattering photo. He was a handsome man, your father, and if you don't mind me saying, you do look alike — I can see it now."

Just to double-check, she then stares at me for an uncomfortable few seconds.

"Um, that's nice to know."

"When did he set it up?" Clement asks. "You know, this place?"

"It'll be twenty-seven years this August. I understand he lost his wife around the time and wanted to channel his grief, I guess. People do that, don't they — take a negative experience and counter it by doing something positive with their life."

Ease a guilty conscience, more like.

"And he funded the whole thing?" Clement adds.

"He did, and continued to make sizable donations over the years. We do receive some state funding, and a number of good people donate regularly, but there is always a need for additional funding because the demand for our support is now at record levels. Despite the pressures, thousands of people have rebuilt their lives as a direct result of the time, work, and cash Dennis poured into the NLH Foundation."

It's a heartfelt monologue about a man any daughter would be proud to call her father. Almost any daughter.

"Did he ever mention me?" I ask, doing my utmost to keep a civil tone.

Her eyes flit left and right as she scrambles for a way to say what I already know.

"He, um, didn't, but don't take that the wrong way. Dennis went to great lengths to separate his personal life from his work."

"Right, and what about family, home life, or friends? Was he in a relationship?"

"I honestly couldn't say, Emma. I worked with him for seventeen years and I can't say I knew any more about his personal life from the first week to the last."

"Did he have an office here?"

"He did. Next door."

"Can we see it?"

"If you like but there's not much to see."

"It'd be nice; just to see where he worked."

"Sure. Come with me."

Mandy leads us back into the corridor and opens the adjacent door. We're greeted by a waft of stagnant, dank air.

"We've got a damp specialist coming in next week," she

comments, waving us in. "There's been a damp problem for years but Dennis was always so busy he kept putting off dealing with it."

With Clement behind me, I step into an office which is probably the same size as Mandy's but feels larger as it's virtually empty.

"I said there wasn't much to see."

She wasn't exaggerating: a desk, an office chair, and a single filing cabinet.

"Has anyone been through the desk drawers?" I ask.

"They have, and I'm afraid all we found were documents relating to the Foundation — not a single personal possession."

I look to the filing cabinet. "What about that?"

"We've had to empty it so the contractors can move it. Again, I had a cursory look through the contents but it's just Foundation paperwork."

Who works in an office for so many years but doesn't have a single memento of their personal life somewhere? From recent experience, I know only too well we all tend to surround ourselves with personal odds and ends, and all that clutter builds up over years in the same job. In my case I had an entire box of crap to carry on my walk of shame. Clearly it isn't a family trait.

"Well," I sigh. "One thing is clear: my father wasn't a material man."

Mandy looks at me inquisitively.

"When I cleared his flat," I add. "His entire worldly goods were contained in just a dozen boxes."

"Everything he owned?"

"Yep."

As she processes that revelation, the three of us just stare into space for a moment before Mandy takes a furtive glance at her watch. I take the hint.

"I appreciate your time, Mandy — it's good to know my father did so much worthwhile work here."

"He did and, if it's any comfort, his legacy will live on through the work of the NLH Foundation."

We shake hands. There's only one question remaining.

"Can I just ask: what do the letters NLH stand for?"

"Never lose hope — a motto Dennis lived by."

As we head out of the damp office, I can't help but think a more appropriate acronym for the Foundation might be ADE — another dead end.

22

Back on the street, I share my frustration with Clement.

"Well, that was a waste of time. Apart from hearing what a saint my father was we learnt the sum total of sod all."

"I wouldn't say that, doll."

"No? Please tell me then: what exactly did we establish?"

The moustache receives a stroke or two.

"He's been funding that charity for years, and I'm guessing that don't come cheap. So, where did he get the money from?"

"I've got no idea. And to be honest, Clement, I've got more pressing questions, like why did he set the charity up in the first place?"

"Maybe your old man was trying to find redemption," he replies, lighting a cigarette. "And trust me, that ain't easy."

"But if he was innocent, as you suggest, don't you think his time and money would have been better invested trying to prove it?"

"Dunno," he shrugs. "Guess we can add that question to the list of things we don't know."

Inadvertently Clement has just yanked a sticking plaster from a still-raw wound.

"I'll tell you what I do know," I snap. "I know he left prison a year before I lost my mother. Where the fuck was the saintly Dennis Hogan then? He's spent the last twenty-seven years helping strangers, yet when it came to helping his own daughter, he couldn't have given less of a fuck. If he was innocent, why didn't he come and see me?"

Clement takes a long drag of his cigarette as I stand and simmer.

"Dunno," he finally replies, puffing a cloud of smoke over my head. "But maybe staying away was the bravest thing the bloke could have done."

"That makes no sense."

"Don't it? What if — 'cos of what happened with Clawthorn — he had no choice but to stay away?"

Throughout my career I've always tried to find balance in my reporting. I've always listened to opposing views and, even when I've not agreed with them, I've tried not to let personal bias taint my work. On this occasion I'm struggling.

"Sorry, but I still think he chose to stay away because he was a coward."

"Fair enough," he shrugs. "But a week ago you thought I was up to no good with a bent politician, yet here we are."

"That's different."

"Is it? I'm just sayin': you need to keep an open mind."

"Fine," I huff. "But once we've proven I'm right, I expect an apology ... and lots of wine."

"Yeah, yeah," he snorts. "Bethnal Green, then?"

"Yes, Bethnal Green."

A truce agreed, we make our way back to Barbican tube station. Seven minutes, two trains, and all that stands between us and our last lead on my father is a half-mile walk.

"What if she ain't in?" Clement asks as we cross the road away from Bethnal Green station.

"I'll pop a business card through her door, I suppose."

We walk on, and ten minutes later we arrive in Wellington Row; an architectural mishmash of a road with quaint Victorian terraced houses on one side and blocks of unsightly council flats on the other. Fortunately, the house we're looking for is situated on the nicer side of the street, about halfway along.

I ring the bell.

As the seconds tick by without a response it looks increasingly like we've had a wasted journey. I'm about to delve into my handbag in search of a business card when I hear the rattle of a security chain on the other side of the door.

It opens.

A woman stands in the doorway. Her lined face and sagging features confirm her age, although judging by her mane of bleached hair and heavy makeup, the woman has no intention of growing old gracefully.

"What can I do for you?" she asks in a heavy East-End accent.

"Would you be Nancy Hawkins?" I reply.

"Depends who's asking, sweetheart. You ain't from the Inland Revenue are you?"

"Err, no."

"That's alright then. Yeah, I'm Nancy Hawkins."

"Oh, great. Apologies for calling by unannounced, but I was hoping to have a chat with you about my father."

"Your father?"

"Yes, Dennis Hogan. I understand you used to be his landlady."

"Good Lord, how is the old devil?"

Shit. She doesn't know.

"That's why I'm here. Could we come in?"

"You got some ID? Can't trust no one these days."

"Yes, of course."

I pluck out my purse and show her my driving licence.

"What about him?" she then asks, nodding towards Clement.

"Don't have any ID, love," he replies with a wink. "But I reckon you can handle me."

"Yeah, I reckon I could, darlin'," she coos back at him. "I like a big man."

From nowhere, a vision of Nancy in a red basque and stockings floats into my head. I shudder as she invites us in.

The inside of the house is much like the owner — chintzy and outdated. We're escorted into what Nancy proudly describes as her parlour, but is just a twelve foot square lounge decorated in a garish flock wallpaper. She then offers us a seat on a sofa which would look more at home on the set of a seventies sit-com.

"So, how is he?" Nancy asks, lowering herself into an armchair.

I'm cast back to the time I had to inform my mother's friends about her death. It didn't get any easier; even by the seventh or eighth time.

"I've got some bad news I'm afraid, Nancy. My father passed away last month."

The colour drains from her face. "No," she gasps. "Not Denny."

Her use of the name Denny is interesting. Clearly she knew him well.

"How'd it happen?"

"It was peaceful. He went in his sleep."

I have no idea if it was peaceful but letting her think otherwise feels unnecessary.

Nancy then turns to Clement. "Be a darlin' and pour me a brandy."

She nods towards a drinks cabinet in the corner and he obliges.

"I hope you don't mind me asking, Nancy, but how well did you know my father?"

"He's been staying here, on and off, for the best part of thirty years. I can't believe he's gone."

Nancy isn't the only one in shock. "Thirty years?"

"More or less. I rent out rooms, you see, like a boarding house. Dennis was one of my first ever guests and we became good … friends."

"Tell me to mind my own business but what exactly do you mean by *friends*?"

Clement hands her a large brandy and retakes his seat next to me. Nancy gulps back half the glass and composes herself before answering my question.

"Up until your mother died — God rest her soul — that's all we were. Then a year or two after he lost her I hoped he might stay here for good, but he made it clear your mother was the love of his life and he'd never feel right being with anyone else."

I catch Clement's eye and I don't need to be telepathic to know what he's thinking.

"You say you hoped he might stay for good, Nancy — what do you mean by that?"

"Dennis never stayed more than a few months before he'd up sticks and be on his way again. Sometimes a whole year would pass and, just when I thought I'd seen the last of him, he'd turn up on the doorstep."

"Did he ever explain why?"

"He was a travelling salesman, so he told me, and his job took him all over the country for months on end."

If it were possible to find an excuse, what I wouldn't give for a ten-minute recess to talk through Nancy's revelations with Clement. As it is, I've got to plough on and hope I ask the most relevant questions from the scores that are now zipping through my mind.

"When did he stay here last, Nancy?"

"Christmas. He said you were abroad and he didn't want to spend it on his own."

"Me?" I gulp. "He specifically mentioned me?"

Her brow furrows. "You were all he ever talked about,

sweetheart. He'd go on about your career and how well you were doing ... sometimes he'd show me newspaper cuttings of reports you'd written, and he always kept a photo of you in his wallet. Mind you, you've changed a bit."

My breakfast makes a half-hearted attempt to escape my stomach. What kind of twisted charade was my father enacting with this woman and, more to the point, why?

"Um, you mentioned my mother, Nancy. He obviously told you about her death?"

"He stayed here a few weeks after it happened and I told him he shouldn't have even been working but he said it helped to keep his mind busy. I'm not gonna lie to you though, sweetheart, he was a right mess for the month he was here. Many was the time I heard him crying in his room, the poor sod."

Yeah, so grief-stricken he couldn't be bothered to attend his own wife's funeral.

"But, over time," she continues. "He eventually got himself together and we ... had one night together. Best night of my life it was."

I fight hard to keep the basque image from reappearing.

"But he wasn't interested in a relationship?"

"Not like I wanted," she sighs. "And if I'm honest, he was too good for me; clever bloke like Denny. He brought me presents, though, every time he stayed. Sometimes flowers — pink roses or daffs — and perfume, and the odd bit of jewellery."

Of everything Nancy has revealed, I'm surprised how much learning about my father's generosity hurts. I never received so much as a birthday card, let alone a present, yet he seemed happy to lavish gifts on his bloody landlady. It would be nothing other than pure spite, but I'm torn between revealing the truth about her beloved Denny, and keeping up the pretence.

"I'm glad he was so nice to you, Nancy."

Coward.

"He was, sweetheart, and who knows, if I'd met him earlier ..."

Her voice trails off as she looks to the heavens.

With our host still in a state of mild shock, there seems precious little point wasting any more time, or emotion, on Dennis Hogan.

"Will you be okay, Nancy? Would you like me to call someone?"

As Clement suggested, they're clearly made of stern stuff in these parts and after wiping away a tear, Nancy pulls herself together.

"Nah, I'll be fine. When you get to my age, you get plenty of practice dealing with death."

"Okay, well, if you're sure, we'll leave you in peace."

"I'm sure."

We all stand and it feels appropriate to give Nancy a hug. In some twisted way I feel sorry for her — she's a fellow victim of my father, and I wonder how many years she wasted, waiting for a liar of a man who would never be hers.

We're shown to the door.

"Take care of yourself, Nancy."

"You too, sweetheart."

With a pained smile, she drops her head and closes the door.

We walk silently back down Wellington Row until we're out of earshot. Clement is the first to break.

"You wanna know what I think?"

"I'm all ears."

"Gotta be honest, doll — I ain't got the first fuckin' clue what your old man was up to."

"That makes two of us. Nothing that poor woman told us made any sense. Particularly all that tripe about him being a grieving widower and proud father."

"Why didn't you tell her then?"

"What would have been the point? She's done nothing wrong."

"'Spose not."

"But I guess we did learn something."

"What's that?"

"My father was either a fantasist, a schizophrenic, or just a worthless piece of shit. Come to think of it — he was probably all three."

"Maybe, but you're still guessing. All of this ... the charity, the bolt hole he's been using all these years ... there's gotta be some kind of explanation."

"Can you think of one?"

"At this moment, nope, but I'm hoping somethin' will come to me."

"Great," I huff. "And what do we do in the meantime?"

"Dunno about you but I'm gonna smoke a fag."

We stop on the corner while Clement lights up. He might still be thinking but I have my own theories.

"The more I think about it the more I reckon my father is a red herring. Pursuing his shady past has just muddied the waters so I think we should re-focus on the names in the notebook."

"I guess you didn't learn what you wanted to learn."

"No, Clement — I learnt exactly what I expected: Dennis Hogan was a waste of space and if his name never crosses my mind again, it'll be too soon."

"Back to yours then?"

"Yep."

The journey to Kilburn doesn't involve much in the way of conversation. Apart from a few half-hearted grunts Clement barely says a word.

"You okay?" I ask as we wander back from the station. "You're very quiet."

"Just thinkin'."

"About anything in particular?"

"This and that."

"Specifically?"

"I don't like problems I can't solve, and this is looking like one of 'em. It's doing my bleedin' my nut in."

"I understand — it seems the more we learn, the less we know. If

I was investigating any other story and kept hitting the same brick walls, I might be inclined to call it a day."

We stop to cross the road and Clement looks down at me. "Do you wanna call it a day?"

There's a hint of lament in his voice; as if this actually matters.

"That really depends on you, Clement, and I'd understand if you want to walk away."

"I dunno, doll. This ain't turned out the way I thought it would, and I'm starting to feel like a spare part."

"For what it's worth, I wouldn't have got this far without you."

"Trouble is, doll, this far ain't anywhere near far enough."

He isn't wrong.

23

Despite his claims not to be suffering a hangover, Clement slumps down on the sofa and closes his eyes. With almost a pained expression he kneads his temples with clenched fists.

"Are you sure you don't have a headache?" I ask.

The slightest shake of the head.

"Can I get you anything?"

"Nah," he mumbles.

With Clement barely responsive, I guess all I can do is take stock of where we are and, more importantly, where we go next.

I grab a notepad and take a seat in the armchair.

What we know is Dennis Hogan, my father, was a member of the Clawthorn Club around the same time as Allen Tamthy — the so-called Tallyman — and is one of only a few people who knew his true identity. Then, in the early seventies — around the time I was born — he tried to leave but was convicted of raping and murdering a prostitute. He was released after eighteen years in prison and pitched-up in Bethnal Green at Nancy's boarding house. Over the following year he came and went; apparently because he was a travelling salesman. And I know he stayed with Nancy just after my mother's death, before he set up the NLH Foundation later that same year.

Taking-up a seemingly insignificant position whilst donating large sums of money, he remained at the NLH Foundation for twenty-seven years and enjoyed his final Christmas with Nancy before he turned up dead in a high-end apartment in Chiswick last month — in possession of a notebook listing the membership of the Clawthorn Club. And throughout all of this, he maintained some delusion of parental pride by having photos of me in his home and his wallet, and by keeping almost every article I've ever written.

We also know the identity of two Clawthorn members: the former Met Deputy Commissioner, Thomas Lang, and the unfortunate Lance Nithercott — the former being culpable for the latter's death. The only other member we're close to identifying is someone associated with The Daily Standard.

Clement was right: not a lot of it makes sense, and we're nowhere near close to unmasking the Tallyman.

There is, however, one final lead to explore.

I retrieve my laptop and open the spreadsheet containing the four names which matched surnames on both the personnel list at The Daily Standard and members of the Clawthorn Club. At the top of that list sits Damon Smith — arsehole, and the man who delivered the news about my pending unemployment. Someone who works at The Daily Standard colluded with the Tallyman to orchestrate my suspension and Damon is by far the likeliest suspect.

However, with no obvious way of proving Damon did anything, the next best option is a process of elimination with the three other names on the list: Terence Brown, Jeremy Smith, and Roger Smith.

I open a web browser and start with Jeremy Smith: the only one of the three who sits on the main board of directors. A little googling tells me all I need to know. It appears his wife has recently been diagnosed with motor neurone disease and Jeremy Smith has taken extended leave to care for her. I think he has bigger issues to contend with. That's one possibility down.

Next up is the associate director, Roger Smith.

More googling and I discover Roger is actually Canadian, and only moved to the UK four years ago after he met his now husband at an awards ceremony in London. If Thomas Lang is to be believed, the Clawthorn Club disbanded whilst Roger Smith was still living in Canada. I think it's safe to say he's not our man.

Two down, two to go, and the odds are stacking up against Damon.

My initial research into Terence Brown prompts a face palm — I've never met the man in person but I've certainly heard of him, although he's better known as Terry Brown. Now semi-retired, Terry has enjoyed a distinguished career in journalism spanning almost five decades, as chief editor for two nationals, and also for one of the leading newspapers in New York. And, if memory serves, I think Eric mentioned him on a few occasions, and always spoke highly of the man.

I'd trust Eric's judgement every time and with that, I'm left with just one suspect on my list — Damon has to be the Tallyman's stooge.

I sit back in the armchair and join Clement in some deep thinking.

It now seems entirely possible Damon instigated my suspension without any such order from above. Of course, he would deny that, but there are two ways I could find out for sure. I could ask Clement to pay him a visit, and watch on as Damon soils himself, or I could go above his head and ask someone on the board.

The first option is so tempting, but it's not without risk. If we push Damon he might well come clean, but he could also report back that I'm on to him. No, it might be better to go above his head and establish my suspension wasn't ordered by the board. At least that way I'll have some solid evidence to use against Damon.

Fortunately, my research has already delivered a suitable candidate to speak to: Terence 'Terry' Brown.

I tap away at the keyboard; digging around my usual sources for a contact number.

"What you doing?" Clement asks, waking from his coma.

"I think I might have established which one of my colleagues was in cahoots with the Tallyman."

"Yeah?"

"Possibly. I've just got to make a call and then we might need to go pay someone a visit."

Clement responds by immediately sitting up, and perking up. "Nice one, doll."

I find a mobile number for Terence Brown and call it. A voice answers with a cheery hello.

"Oh, hi ... Mr Brown?"

"Speaking."

"You don't know me, or at least we've never met, but my name is Emma Hogan."

I'm about to explain who I am but he gets in first. "The same Emma Hogan who works at The Daily Standard?"

"Yes, that would be me."

"Well, in that case, it's lovely to talk to you at long last — I've heard a lot of positive things about you over the years."

"Oh, um, have you?"

"Don't sound so surprised. You're an accomplished journalist, Emma — and Eric Birtles always spoke very highly of you."

It's rare I ever hear praise these days. I'm glad he can't see my flushing cheeks but Clement can, and I turn away.

"Thank you, Mr Brown."

"Please, it's Terry."

"Right. Thank you, Terry."

"I'm sorry we never got the chance to meet at Eric's funeral."

"You were there?"

"Of course. Eric and I went back years and, for a while, we were colleagues in the same newsroom."

"He mentioned your name several times over the years."

"We had some great times, Eric and I. Did he ever tell you about our weekend in East Berlin, just after the wall came down?"

"Err, possibly. Eric had so many tales."

"I bet he did. He was a good man, Emma, and a bloody fine

journalist. The world is a poorer place without him."

"It certainly is, Terry. It certainly is."

It feels appropriate to say nothing and clearly Terry feels the same.

"Did he ever tell you?" he suddenly asks, breaking the reflective silence.

"Sorry? Tell me what?"

"He asked me to put in a good word when you applied for the job at The Daily Standard?"

"Err, no. He didn't."

"He made me promise not to say anything but I guess it doesn't matter now."

"You helped me get the job?"

"I owed Eric, and to be frank with you, Emma, he thought of you as his protégé so it wasn't the greatest of favours considering how much he respected your talents. In my book a recommendation from Eric Birtles was better than any qualification."

It appears I might have inadvertently discovered the board member who has protected me from Damon's wrath over the years.

"It's you, isn't it?" I ask.

"Me?"

"You're the one who's been fighting my corner over the years whenever I've had issues with the management."

"As I said: I owed Eric. And please don't think I was doing it out of charity. I have the utmost respect for your work and I still believe there's a place in modern journalism for people like you."

"People like me?"

"Proper old-school hacks. You know; the kind willing to get their hands dirty from time to time."

"Thank you, Terry — for everything. Unfortunately the reason for my call is because I may have got my hands a little too dirty."

"Oh. How so?"

"I was wondering if you'd heard I've been suspended?"

"I don't have much in the way of day-to-day dealings with what goes on at The Daily Standard, but yes, I had heard a rumour.

"And forgive me for asking, but do you know if it was sanctioned by the board?"

The slightest sigh before I receive an answer. "I believe it was."

Fuck.

"Oh."

"Correct me if I'm wrong, Emma, but I believe you contacted a rather litigious former politician after being told not to?"

"It wasn't quite like that," I huff. "I contacted him six months after I was told, and on a completely unrelated matter."

"I hear you, but ... wait ... is that why you're calling; to see if I can get the suspension reversed? If it is, I can't get involved, I'm afraid."

"It wasn't why I was calling, Terry. I simply wanted to know who made the decision."

"That I can't tell you because I don't know."

"But it was definitely a decision made at board level?"

"Almost certainly, yes. If a member of staff is accused of gross misconduct, the decision to terminate their employment has to be sanctioned by the board, just in case there are any legal issues down the line. You know what newsrooms are like — tempers are lost on a daily basis and things are said in the heat of the moment but we can't have management sacking people every time they fall out with one of their team."

"Okay, fair enough. But what I don't understand, Terry, is why anyone investigated me in the first place."

"Listen, Emma," he sighs. "How or why is incidental. I know it might seem unfair, but legally I don't think you've got a leg to stand on. If you want my advice, I'd hand in my notice before the suspension reaches the termination stage. At least that way you'll protect your reputation."

It's a bitter pill to swallow but I suppose Terry has at least suggested a way to sugar-coat it.

"I appreciate your advice, Terry. I'm actually meeting someone tonight about a job opportunity so maybe I will get the chance to jump before I'm pushed."

"You're welcome, and I hope that meeting goes well."

I'm about to wind up the call when Terry poses a question. "Can I ask, Emma: was it worth it?"

"What?"

"Contacting that William Huxley character. Did it lead anywhere?"

"In a way, but not the way I anticipated."

"So, something good came from it?"

"Maybe. I doubt I'll ever get to publish it at The Daily Standard but I'm either sitting on the story of the century or my career in journalism is about to self-destruct."

"And which is more likely?"

"Good question, but as you know: a story is just a tale without hard evidence. I've got a single piece of evidence which could be explosive but it's not much use without a fuse — that's where I'm struggling. Still, I'm nothing if not determined."

"Well, whatever it is, I wish you luck with it."

"Thank you."

"And if you need a reference, or anything else, please don't hesitate to pick up the phone. Any friend of Eric's is a friend of mine."

"I appreciate it.

We say our goodbyes and I end the call.

"Well?" Clement asks.

"Not what I was hoping to hear. Turns out the man who fired me — our lead suspect — was only acting on orders from above."

"Shit."

"It gets worse. Of the three potential candidates who might have been working with Tamthy, one of them is on an extended leave of absence as his wife is terminally ill, and the second one is a Canadian guy who moved to the UK a few years after the Clawthorn Club disbanded."

"And the third?"

"That was who I was just talking to. And it turns out he was the one fan I had on the board, and a friend of my old mentor."

"So, we ain't got the first clue who tipped the Tallyman off then?"

"Nope."

"Fucks sake," he groans, slumping back on the sofa. "That's it then?"

"I don't know what to say, Clement."

If I had to proffer advice to anyone else in my situation, I'd tell them to resign from The Daily Standard and grab whatever Alex has to offer. I'd tell them to send the notebook back, and to forget all about my father and the bloody Clawthorn Club.

I'd also tell them Clement's frustration is not my problem.

Perhaps I can take my own advice, or nearly all of it.

"Listen," I say, trying to adopt a positive tone. "One thing I've learnt in my career is when to step away, and maybe that's what we need to do here. I can send the notebook back and jack in my job at the paper, but we've still got all the Clawthorn names on my computer so if anything else springs up, we can still pursue it."

"Give up, you mean?"

"It's not giving up. It's stepping away."

"Same thing in my book."

"What else can we do? We've exhausted every lead."

His answer comes in a grunt.

"Tell you what," I continue. "After I've met with Alex tonight, why don't we have a blowout ... my treat? A bit of food and a lot of drink — what do you say?"

"Not in the mood, doll."

"Oh, come on, please. It's my way of thanking you for all you've done."

I get up and reposition myself next to him on the sofa.

"We may not have found the Tallyman," I smile. "But I've found a friend, so it's not all bad."

He looks across and I can't quite decipher his expression.

"So? Dinner and drinks?"

His chest falls as he lets out a resigned sigh.

"You gonna wear that red dress?"

"Can do."

"Yeah, alright then."

He finds a half-smile but it doesn't reach his eyes. For a man who was initially reluctant to pursue the Tallyman, there's an awful lot of sadness, rather than the relief I might have expected.

I shouldn't be surprised. As I'm learning; very little about Clement makes sense.

24.

We arrive at The Three Horseshoes at quarter past six. Clement, having spent the afternoon lounging on the sofa listening to an Arsenal game on the radio, appears to be in a slightly better mood.

With drinks secured I scan the pub for Alex but there's no sign of him yet. The plan is to give him no more than an hour, and then I'll make my excuses so Clement and I can grab some food, and commence our celebrations or commiserations, depending on how you look at it.

"They got a pool table here?" Clement asks.

I nod towards a door. "Through there. Are you going to play on your own?"

"Don't worry, doll. I'll find someone."

"Okay. I'll come find you when I'm done with Alex."

He nods and ambles away.

I lean up against the bar and take a large gulp of wine. Alex Palmer was always a crushing bore and I can't face him completely sober.

My glass is almost empty when the scent of an overpowering aftershave engulfs me. I turn around.

"Hey, Emma."

He leans in and kisses me on the cheek.

My skin crawling, he stands within my personal space, grinning like an idiot. My eyes flick up and down and the view is exactly what

I expected: a slim-fit patterned shirt too tight around the midriff, age-inappropriate jeans, and his round face pink and blotchy from a recent shave. In some way he reminds me of the boys I dated at secondary school — always trying too hard and never quite pulling it off.

"Hi, Alex."

"Can I get you another?" he asks, pointing at my glass.

"Please. Merlot."

He orders my wine and a pint of real ale for himself. I don't quite catch the name but it's probably something ridiculous like Badger's Scrotum.

Drinks acquired, I lead him over to a table where I hope we're not spotted. God forbid anyone should think Alex is my other half.

We sit down and waste ten minutes on banal small talk. Alex then provides a lengthy synopsis of his career since we worked together — in tedious detail — before moving on to his life in general. Unsurprisingly, he's still single but hasn't given up hope on finding Miss Right. If he's any good at picking up signals, I hope he realises I'm Miss No-Fucking-Chance.

"What about you?" he finally asks, drawing breath. "How's life been?"

I could tell him the truth but that will only string out the conversation.

"It's been good. Work has been manic but I like that."

I catch the look in his eye.

"Sorry, work *was* manic," I add.

"What happened, if you don't mind me asking?"

"I'm not bothered because I maintain I did nothing wrong. Six months ago I was told not to contact a potential source. I contacted him this week with a pretty innocuous query and that oversight was deemed enough for me to be suspended."

"Harsh."

"Very."

"But The Daily Standard's loss is my gain."

"Possible gain, Alex."

"Typical, Emma," he chuckles. "Always playing hard to get."

Impossible to get as far as you're concerned, matey.

"Just keeping my options open," I reply with a wry smile.

Alex then launches into a lengthy pitch about the position on offer and why I'd be perfect for the role. In fairness, he does make it sound appealing, and I'm not exactly in a position to be fussy. And, looking at it positively, the higher basic salary would allow me to bring forward my plans to move to the sticks by at least a year.

"I have to admit, Alex, it's tempting."

"How tempting?"

"What's the downside?"

"Apart from working with me, you mean?"

He laughs at his own joke and I feel compelled to laugh along. It is a genuine downside, though.

"The hours can be long," he continues. "And the hierarchy can be demanding, but someone with your experience won't have a problem handling them."

"And I'd get a company car? My own office?"

"Indeed you would."

I sit back in my chair and, for the first time since our conversation began, give some serious consideration to the prospect of ending my journalism career.

"While you digest what we've discussed," Alex chirps, "Let me get you another drink."

He heads off to the bar and joins the growing number of patrons waiting to be served. Saturday evenings can get pretty busy and it appears many have decided to make an early start.

Free from Alex's chatter I half-ponder his job opportunity and half-ponder this week's madness. Perhaps they've coincided with one another for a reason, and it's time to make some changes in my life. I don't necessarily go in for all that fate bollocks but I can't deny the timing doesn't feel serendipitous.

Although I'm not sure how I feel about that, there is one thing I am sure about: I could murder a cigarette. However, with my own packet depleted the other evening, I'll have to ponce one from Clement.

I'm about to get up and head to the pool tables when I spot his unmistakable frame at the far end of the bar next to a fruit machine. He's not alone.

Late thirties, slim, long brunette hair, and wearing impossibly tight jeans, the woman appears engrossed by whatever Clement is talking about. I watch on as she flicks a strand of hair from her face and smiles up at him. Clement then says something and she suddenly bursts out laughing. Loud, shrill, she cackles away and places a hand on his upper arm. It stays there as she edges a little closer to him.

"One Merlot," Alex announces, placing a large glass on the table in front of me.

He retakes his seat and sips his pint. Just beyond his right shoulder I can see the brunette's hand still on Clement's arm.

"You okay?" Alex asks. "You look miles away."

"Eh? Err, yes. I'm fine, thanks."

I snap out of my trance and take a gulp of wine.

"So, Emma. Do you have any questions?"

I look up and face Alex but the urge to check developments beyond his shoulder is overwhelming. I can't help myself and my eyes flick to the left for just a second.

Her hand is now resting flat on his chest.

"Well?" Alex prompts.

"What? Oh, um, no. I think it's all clear."

"Great. And does it sound like a position you'd be interested in?"

Another glance. She's moved closer.

"I ... possibly, Alex. I need to ... to give it some thought."

I reach for my wine glass and try to silence a feeling which has no place being awake.

"I don't wish to pressure you, Emma, but we're looking to advertise the role next week."

"Of course," I reply. "I can give you a definitive answer by Wednesday, if that works?"

"Perfect."

As Alex leans forward and reaches for his pint, I take the opportunity to glance across the bar again. The brunette is now stood inches away from Clement looking up at him like a lovesick teenager.

"Can you excuse me a moment, Alex. I just need to pop to the ladies room."

"No problem."

I grab my bag and march purposefully over to the fruit machine. I get within feet before Clement notices my approach.

"Alright, doll?"

"Who's your friend?"

The brunette turns to me and appraises the threat.

"This is Abbey," Clement confirms.

I hold out my hand. "Nice to meet you, Abbey. I'm Emma."

She cautiously accepts the handshake. "You too."

Despite her smile I get the feeling Abbey isn't pleased to meet me at all. In fairness, it's mutual.

I turn my attention back to Clement. "I'm nearly done with Alex. You hungry?"

"Bleedin' starving."

"Great. Why don't you grab a table and I'll be with you in about five minutes."

Abbey's smile is quickly replaced with a stern glare. "Sorry, are you two an item?"

"We're friends," I confirm. "Good friends."

She looks down her nose at me before turning to Clement. "What's it to be then, big man? Dinner with your mum or some fun with me?"

I answer before Clement gets the chance.

"Tell you what, sweetheart," I growl, jabbing her in the chest with my finger. "Why don't you fuck off and find someone else to play with ... before mummy gets really annoyed."

Her eyes flick in Clement's direction but he just shrugs.

"Whatever," she spits. "Enjoy your cocoa."

Abbey then slopes away while Clement looks bemused.

"Fuck me, doll. I wouldn't wanna cross you on a bad day."

"I was just making a point. I might not be in the first flush of youth but I can still eat bitches like that for breakfast."

"No shit."

"Anyway," I cough, returning to a more genteel tone of voice. "You go grab that table. I won't be long."

Chuckling to himself he shakes his head and does as he's told. I return to Alex.

"Sorry about that."

"No problem."

Within seconds of sitting down my glass is empty.

"Same again?" Alex asks.

"Actually, I need to dash."

"No, you don't," he says dismissively. "Stay for another."

"I really can't. I had a prior arrangement I couldn't get out of."

"Right," he frowns. "That's a shame."

"But we must do this again, properly next time."

He glances at his watch. "We've barely been here an hour. Are you absolutely sure you can't you stay a little longer? Isn't your career is worth more than just an hour?"

"Is it, but my friend is already waiting in the dining area."

"You're staying here?"

"Err, yes."

"Okay," he sighs. "Another time."

I get to my feet.

"I'll give you a call before Wednesday about the job and, depending on how that pans out, we can arrange drinks another time."

"That would be good," he replies, with a feeble smile.

As much as I don't want to spend another second socialising with Alex I do feel bad just abandoning him when he's not even finished his drink.

"Do you want me to ...?"

"It's fine, Emma. You go, honestly."

It takes all my resolve but I lean over and peck him on the cheek.

If we do end up working together, I'd rather keep him onside.

"See you soon, Alex."

I leave him to finish his pint.

Fortunately the dining room is in a partitioned area of the pub so I don't have to sit and stare across at Alex's sad face. Most of the tables are occupied and as I search for Clement, he spots me first and yells across the heads of the other diners. Some of them turn and shoot a frown in Clement's direction but the heads soon snap back to their meals once they identify the source.

I make my way over and sit down opposite him.

"How'd your meeting go?" Clement asks.

"Not bad. He's a bit of a drip but harmless enough. The jobs sounds interesting, though."

"You gonna take it?"

"Possibly. Probably. We'll see."

A waiter delivers plates to the adjacent table and I summon him over before he can escape back to the kitchen.

"Pint of lager and a large Merlot, please."

"And two whisky chasers," Clement adds.

The waiter scuttles away.

"Someone's going for it tonight," I chuckle.

"If all else fails, doll, get wankered."

He then hands me a menu; a less-than-subtle hint he's hungry. I've eaten in The Three Horseshoes more times than I care to remember so I know the menu inside out. I also know what to avoid, and what's just about edible.

"I'll have the linguine."

"That was quick."

"And I'd recommend the mixed grill."

"Thought you said I shouldn't be eating that kinda stuff."

"You shouldn't, but tonight it doesn't matter."

"Not gonna argue."

The waiter returns with our drinks and I place the food order. As he heads off I raise my glass to Clement.

"Cheers, and sorry."

"Sorry for what?"

"Cramping your style with that woman."

"Don't matter. She weren't my type."

"No?"

"Nah."

"Well, anyway, I apologise for breaking up your little tryst."

"No need, doll," he grins. "I know it was only cos you were jealous."

"Yeah," I snort. "That'll be it."

I grab my glass and take a gulp of wine to quell the sudden and unexpected hot flush. I put it down to an early sign of my impending menopause.

"So, Clement," I ask, quickly changing the subject. "What are your plans?"

"Don't have any."

"What were you doing before … this?"

"Been working at a boozer over in Kensal Green. Landlord had a bit of a problem with drug dealers."

"Had?"

"I re-educated them."

"That sounds like dangerous work. Most of the violent crime in the city is down to drugs."

"Nothing I couldn't handle."

"Is that where you live, then: Kensal Green?"

"For now. The landlord let me stay in a flat at the back of the boozer, you know, for services rendered."

"And now those services have been rendered, where will you go?"

"Dunno," he sighs, before taking a long glug of lager.

For such a resourceful man, Clement doesn't appear to have built much of a life for himself. Beyond his transient living arrangements, he's been wearing the same clothes since the day we first met, and nobody appears to care he's eating crap for breakfast, lunch, and dinner. All told, it seems a sad existence.

"There's no hurry, if … you know, you wanted to kip at mine a bit longer."

"Despite the snoring, eh."

"That, and the fact my bathroom is now the subject of a research paper at Porton Down."

"Porton Down?"

"The chemical weapons laboratory."

"Oh, yeah, sorry. I've had dodgy guts."

"Nice. Thanks for sharing that just before we eat."

"Be thankful I didn't order the madras."

"Clearly there is a God."

His smile vanishes in a heartbeat.

"If there is a God," he mutters. "He's got one fucked-up sense of humour."

"I take it you're not a believer?"

"Dunno what I believe any more."

I like to think I'm good at reading people — a useful skill in my job — well, my previous job. In this case Clement's tone suggests he's carrying an unhealthy amount of religion-based bitterness.

"You're not Catholic are you?" I ask.

"No. Why?"

"Doesn't matter."

Our dinner arrives providing Clement with a handy excuse to drop the subject. We begin eating with an uneasy silence but a shot of whisky and an entire abattoir of processed meat helps to lift his mood again.

Once our plates are cleared away we order more drinks and talk, a lot — or at least I do — and Clement listens. I tell him my hopes for the future, and my fears. I tell him all about my childhood, my early career, and my mum.

"Sorry, if I'm boring you. It's been a while since I had dinner with anyone I feel ..."

I leave the sentence hanging.

"Feel what, doll?"

"Forget it," I reply dismissively.

"Go on."

"No. You'll laugh."

"Probably, but tell me anyway."

"Comfortable. You make me feel comfortable, Clement."

He sits back in his chair and appears to drift off as he runs a finger around the rim of his whisky tumbler.

"Sorry," I sigh. "I've made things all weird now, haven't I?"

"Nah."

"I think I have."

He looks up from the tumbler.

"You ain't made it weird, and I get you. It probably don't mean shit, but I feel comfortable too."

His words are an irrelevance. Those eyes of his tell me everything I need to know — the soul-snatching intensity pulling me places I know I shouldn't go.

I'm tipsy. I need to compose myself.

"It means a lot, Clement. Not least because I don't feel such a twat now."

He laughs, and the moment passes.

We return to the much-busier bar area and I'm relieved to see Alex has left. Clement buys another round of drinks and we find a corner away from the masses to continue our journey towards oblivion.

The evening then evolves into a messy routine of drinks, cigarettes, and constant complaining about both the volume and modernity of the music. On Saturday nights the pub employs a DJ who occupies a booth near the dining area. At ten o'clock they clear a space for those drunk enough to dance and, as is often the way, it's not the modern noise that attracts revellers to the dance floor, but the classics.

"I fucking love this tune," I slur, referring to the eighties classic, *Livin' on a Prayer* by Bon Jovi.

I start wailing the chorus into an imaginary microphone.

"Let's go and dance," I yell.

"To this? You gotta be shittin' me."

"It's a classic."

"No, doll, it ain't."

"Alright. Let's go ask the DJ for something else. What do you fancy?"

He thinks for a moment. "You like reggae?"

"Err, yeah. Didn't think it would be your cup of tea though."

"I had a mate who played it all the time. Kinda gets under your skin."

"I'm guessing it wasn't your Irish mate?"

"Nah. Black Brian."

"Why did you call him ... ohh. He was black, right? And his name was Brian?"

"Funnily enough, yeah."

"Right, gotcha. So you want some reggae then?"

"Yeah, I reckon *Double Barrel* by Dave & Ansil Collins — you know it?"

"Err, I think so. It's an insta ... instro ... intro ..."

"Instrumental."

"That's it."

"You're pissed."

"Um, maybe a teeny bit."

"You sure you're up to dancing?"

"Is that a challenge?"

"Come on," he chuckles, grabbing my hand. "Let's see what you're made of."

We head to the booth and Clement shouts his request at the DJ. A thumbs-up is returned, and we stand on the edge of the crowded dancefloor as Bon Jovi wind down.

The track ends and the DJ introduces Clement's request. Clearly a popular choice, the dancefloor remains crowded as we edge closer to the already-swaying masses.

I learn two life lessons within the first twenty seconds. Firstly, it's bloody hard dancing to reggae. I attempt some kind of hip-swaying move but it looks more like I'm trying to reposition a sanitary towel without using my hands. Secondly, I learn whisky and red wine don't mix well.

With my head spinning I resort to slow side-to-side steps. Clement, on the other hand, is going for it.

I take a few steps back and watch on as he appears to lose himself in the music.

"Bloody hell," I whisper under my breath.

Now, I don't know if Dave & Ansil Collins created a dance routine to go with their tune but, if they did, I'd say Clement has nailed it. How a man of his size can move with such ease and fluidity is beyond me, and Clement defies my preconceptions with swagger and style. Such is his captivating interpretation of the music, I'm not the only one to be stood in awe, and the crowd splits to gain a better view of the big man in double denim.

A feeling reaches a part of me I know spells trouble.

The song lasts barely two minutes. As it ends, a cheer goes up and Clement is snagged by several bystanders keen to take a selfie with him. Judging by the length of discussion and Clement's apparent confusion, I'd wager he has no idea what a selfie is. Still, he obliges.

Photos complete and the next song underway, he finally ambles over to me.

"You alright, doll? You look a bit pale."

"I'm ... good."

"Want another drink?"

"I think I've had enough."

"Yeah, I reckon you have," he grins. "Wanna go home?"

"Yes, please."

He offers me his arm which is just as well as the floor appears to be undulating beneath my feet. Clinging to Clement like a drowning man to a lifebuoy we make our way out to the street.

The cool night air does nothing to aid my intoxication.

"Alright, I think ... I'm a little pissed."

"Don't worry. I got you."

I manage to put one foot in front of the other and we move slowly down the street. The walk home usually takes no more than five minutes but, as I have to concentrate on every step, it does take a tad longer. Nevertheless, we reach the end of the street and as we're about to turn the corner onto my road, I misjudge where the pavement ends and the road begins. My balance already compromised I lose grip on Clement's arm and gravity takes over. I'm destined to fall flat on my face until my guardian angel steps in and grabs me around the waist.

"Easy, doll," he cautions, scooping me towards him.

My heart flutters — I put it down to delayed shock. What I can't put down to shock is clinging to the lapels of Clement's waistcoat and gazing up at him.

Beneath the soft glow of the streetlights, I become transfixed by his face, and a scar on his temple I hadn't noticed until now. I raise my hand and gently run my fingertips across his skin.

"How did you get this scar?" I ask softy.

"Playing cricket."

"Really?"

"Nah."

"Did someone do it to you?"

He closes his eyes for a moment and offers a slight nod. When he opens them again they're not the same eyes. I can see it — his vulnerability.

"What happened, Clement? You can tell me."

"Don't matter," he replies, in barely a whisper.

I run my fingertips south and place my open palm on his cheek.

"It was something bad, wasn't it? I can see it in your eyes."

Another nod: slight.

I raise my left hand and mirror the right, cupping his face.

"I think you need someone to look after you. Someone to make everything better."

If I were mindful of the consequences, I wouldn't do it. If I were sober, I wouldn't do it. As it is, I'm neither mindful nor sober, and slowly guide his face towards mine — he doesn't resist.

Our lips near; so close I can feel the warmth of his breath. My head fills with his scent — nothing artificial; the musk of a real man. It is every bit as intoxicating as the Merlot.

I want to savour the moment: the expectancy, the anticipation, the electricity as our lips come together.

Clement places his hand on the back of my head. I melt.

"Excuse me," a gruff voice suddenly barks from behind me. "Sir, madam."

I turn my head; ready to unleash a volley of drunken profanities in the direction of whoever interrupted our moment. The sight of a police uniform immediately stops me in my tracks.

"Sorry to bother you," the officer continues. "Can I have a word?"

Clement lets his hand slip from the back of my head as sobriety and reality crash together.

"Err, sure."

The officer steps towards us and opens his notebook.

"There's been an incident at a premises on the High Road. We're wondering if you'd seen anyone in the area acting suspiciously?"

That word: *incident*. I have to remind myself my journalism career is currently on life support with a terminal prognosis. Even if it wasn't I have more pressing matters to attend to with Clement.

"I'm afraid not. We've been at The Three Horseshoes all evening."

"You haven't seen a man on your way back: late teens to early twenties, tall, thin, goatee beard, and wearing a dark-coloured Adidas hoodie?"

"No."

The officer closes his notebook. Try as I might, I can't help myself.

"What kind of incident?"

"A fire. Possible arson."

"On the High Road?"

"Yes. The fire crews are currently damping down the building but it's gutted."

"That's awful."

"Tell me about it," the officer scoffs. "They did a lovely caramel mocha."

"They?"

"The coffee shop."

"What coffee shop?"

"The Jolly Barista. I'm afraid they won't be serving lattes any time soon."

Bile burns the back of my throat.

"My ... my flat ..."

I gasp hard, repeatedly, grabbing a handful of Clement's waistcoat to steady myself.

"It's ... was ... above that coffee shop."

25.

Clement wouldn't let me see the charred remains of my home; keeping me behind the police cordon some eighty yards away. I screamed, I cried, I pummelled his chest with my clenched fists. In the end, a police officer called over the paramedics and I was hauled into the back of an ambulance. Unsurprisingly they confirmed I was suffering from shock.

"I'm not going to the hospital."

Young, perhaps pretty; the paramedic sits on the stretcher next to me.

"Emma, it's for your own good."

"Forget it. I've got ... things to sort out ... insurance, my ..."

"I'll look after her," a gravelly voice interjects.

I turn my head where the rear doors of the ambulance are wide open, and Clement is stood on guard.

"She needs to be monitored," the paramedic argues. "I really do ..."

"I said I'll look after her."

"Fine. She'll need to sign a disclaimer, though."

I'm handed a clipboard and without reading the form, scrawl my signature at the bottom. On jelly legs, I get up and stagger out of the ambulance.

"You sure you're okay?" Clement asks, taking my arm.

"I'm the absolute opposite of okay, but I'm not going to the hospital."

He leads me to the pavement and the relative sanctuary of a bus shelter, closed in at one end with an illuminated poster advertising home insurance — the irony wasted on me. If nothing else, it provides something stable for me to lean against while the dizziness eases.

Clement remains silent as I try to piece my thoughts together.

"Arson," I eventually mumble. "Why?"

"Nine times out of ten, doll, it's usually an insurance job. A business finds itself in financial trouble and the only way out is to burn the place down."

"But the coffee shop was always busy."

"Could have been another reason — cash businesses are perfect for laundering money. Maybe the owners were washing drug money or something. Could have been a rival dealer putting a stop to their operation."

I shake my head. "I know the owner, Dave, and he isn't the kind to get involved in anything shady."

"Dunno then, but it don't matter at the minute. We need to get you sorted out."

Sorting myself out would usually mean a long soak in the bath with a glass of wine, and then settling down on the sofa to binge-watch a trashy TV show. The reality of my situation suddenly comes crashing down — there is no longer a bath, no longer a sofa, no longer a home.

I've lost everything.

As little as I want it to, my mind begins compiling an inventory of every item I no longer own. There's the practical: all my clothes, my laptop, the kitchen appliances, the TV, all my personal paperwork including my passport and birth certificate. Then the sentimental: photos of my mum, all my jewellery, a signed copy of *Harry Potter* Eric gave me for my fortieth birthday.

Another realisation kicks hard — the sixteen hundred pounds in cash I stuffed in the kitchen drawer. That, and another item related to my father.

"Fucking hell," I groan.

"What?"

"The notebook. I left it on the coffee table in the lounge."

"Shit. But didn't you copy everything to ..."

"Yeah, my laptop. The laptop which is now a pile of smouldering molten plastic."

He shakes his head.

"But saying that, the spreadsheet containing all the Clawthorn members might have saved to my cloud account."

"Your what?"

"Cloud account. It's a data server in the cloud."

"You lost me at *cloud.*"

"Never mind. Basically, it means there might be a copy of the spreadsheet."

"Where?"

"That's the point of a cloud account — I can access my files anywhere on any device."

With Clement still looking bewildered, I delve into my handbag and retrieve my phone. I swipe the screen and I'm greeted with a notification — a text message. In the chaos since we met the police officer I must have missed its arrival.

I tap the icon to open the message.

I warned you. Back off, or you stand to lose far more than your home.

I have to consciously draw air into my lungs, and even then, it comes in shallow, raggedy breaths.

"Doll, what is it?"

If I wasn't suffering shock before, I sure as hell am now. I show the message to Clement.

"It's ... it's from the Tallyman."

He stares at it for a second; deep lines creasing his forehead.

"Don't understand," he says with a frown. "Why'd he wanna torch your drum before he'd given you a chance to send the bleedin' notebook back?"

"I don't know."

The blue lights on the ambulance cut out and it pulls away. In hindsight, maybe I would be better off inside.

A cold shudder arrives; I should have worn a warmer coat than the thin jacket I chose. It is now the only coat I own, and the dress I'm wearing represents the full extent of my wardrobe.

"Let's go, doll."

"Go? Go where?"

"Back to mine."

"But, I need to speak to the police."

"Fuck 'em — do it tomorrow. You need to get in the warm and we need to work out what we're gonna do."

"About what?"

"Everything. Come on."

He puts his arm around my shoulder and guides me away from the bus shelter. We cover a hundred yards of pavement; the stench of acrid smoke easing as we head away from the scene. A cab approaches on the opposite side of the road and Clement waves it down.

I've never felt so relieved to sit down in the back of a cab but, despite the relative warmth, I can't stop shaking. Clement puts his arm around my shoulder and pulls me close. I wish I could forget the last hour and just wallow in blissful ignorance. For the ten minute journey, I try, but the reality that I've lost everything, taunts every thought. By the time we reach our destination, that taunting has sparked a fire — a raging blaze of anger.

Clement pays the driver and coaxes me from the back of the cab. I scan the area which, I suspect, is all the better for being shrouded in near darkness. First impressions of the pub itself are that it's a typical, run-down, backstreet establishment, sited on the end of a row of tatty terraced houses. Its name — The Royal Oak — could not be more inappropriate. There's no trees of any kind in sight, and there's certainly nothing regal about the dilapidated building.

Clement leads me through to a wooden gate at the rear of the pub and into a small courtyard stacked high with aluminium beer barrels. We pass through another gate to a scrubby patch of overgrown lawn with an outbuilding at the rear. No bigger than a modest caravan, I fear the outbuilding is our final destination.

Fifteen feet along a broken pathway and Clement pulls a key from his pocket.

"This is it."

He puts the key in the lock and opens the door. A light is switched on and I'm beckoned in.

If you were to replace words in a dictionary with images, the scene before me would be the perfect depiction of 'depressing'. Whichever way I look, the view is beyond drab. Above me, the ceiling is dotted with patches of mould and a vast spider web of hairline cracks emanate from each corner. Beneath my feet, a stained, threadbare carpet. To my left and right, the walls are lined with faded wallpaper; just about clinging to the damp plaster. Straight ahead, a ramshackle kitchenette has been installed along the back wall; not one of the fitted cupboard doors hang level. The furniture comprises a sofa with exposed foam on the armrests, a coffee table, and the kind of veneered sideboard I haven't seen in any home since the early eighties.

Clement bends down and ignites a gas heater.

"It'll warm up in no time."

He then shows me the rest of his abode: a bedroom just about large enough to house a double bed and a wardrobe, and a shower room with more mould than tiling. We return to the lounge which is now a degree or two warmer than freezing.

"Sorry it ain't much, doll."

It isn't much — on a scale of accommodation it would sit just above a squat. However, it is Clement's home, and with that comes a sense of safety: of sanctuary. I don't think I'd rather be anywhere else right now.

"It's fine, and thank you for looking after me."

Perhaps not used to guests he scratches his head for a few seconds before offering me a seat on the sofa.

"I reckon you need a cup of sweet tea, you know, for the shock."

He steps over to the kitchenette, switches the kettle on, and removes two mugs from an otherwise empty cupboard. A pint of milk is then extracted from an equally empty fridge. The lid is removed and Clement sniffs the contents before deeming it fresh enough for tea.

To my side, the gas heater clicks and hisses as it does its best to warm the dank air — I don't rate its chances. You could frack every square inch of Lancashire and I doubt there would be enough gas for that job.

Clement returns to the sofa with two mugs of steaming tea and sits down next to me.

"Drink up," he orders, handing me one of the mugs. "You'll feel better."

Dubious but grateful, I take the mug and sip from it. Warming, strong, and surprisingly sweet; the tea as much as my host.

"How you feeling now?" he asks.

"I honestly don't know. Scared, angry, bewildered ... but mostly numb."

"It ain't the evening I had planned."

"No, me neither."

We make eye contact long enough to confirm now is not the time to reflect on what might have been. Maybe the ship will remain in port beyond this evening — we'll see.

"Anyway," Clement coughs. "I've been thinking."

"Glad one of us has because my head is a mess."

"Yeah, but mine ain't, and I keep asking myself the same two questions."

"Go on."

"Right, first: how did the Tallyman know you weren't at home this evening?"

"Who said he did?"

"He sent you a message. If you're gonna torch a place when someone's at home, you ain't gonna get in touch with 'em afterwards, on account they're most likely dead."

"I suppose not."

"So, he must have known you weren't at home. How?"

"No idea," I shrug. "Unless he had someone watching the flat."

"That'd be too tricky in your road. What makes more sense is if someone knew you weren't gonna be at home and told him."

"But who would know that, apart from Alex? For all his faults, I can't imagine for one moment he'd have anything to do with the Clawthorn Club — he's too squeaky clean."

"You know the bloke, and I ain't saying it's him. You told someone else."

"Did I?"

"The bloke on the phone this morning."

"Terry Brown? No, that's ridiculous," I scoff. "He was Eric's friend, and Eric was an impeccable judge of character."

"The name 'Brown' was on both lists weren't it?"

"Well, yes."

"And he knew you weren't home?"

"Again, yes."

"So, why is it ridiculous?"

"Because ... I don't know ... gut instinct, I guess."

"There's something else," he continues. "We assumed someone on your paper's payroll was leaking information to the Tallyman. Ain't it possible there was no grass, and the Tallyman himself is on the paper's payroll?"

I almost choke on my tea.

"That's one hell of a leap, Clement. You're saying Terry Brown, the respected journalist, is Allen Tamthy ... the Tallyman?"

"Maybe. How old is he?"

"Not sure exactly. Late sixties, maybe."

"What does he look like?"

I refer to my phone and google Terry Brown's name. A few taps and I find his photo on the Reuters' website.

"This is him."

I hold the phone up so Clement can see the photo. He stares at the screen for a good few seconds before stroking his moustache.

"You said there were two questions," I remind him.

"Yeah, there are."

I sit up. "Let's hear the second then."

"The description that copper gave us, of the bloke seen leggin' it from the scene: did it sound familiar?"

I cast my mind back but much of what the officer said is lost in a haze.

"You'll have to remind me, Clement."

"Late teens to early twenties, tall, thin, goatee beard."

I return a blank stare.

"The dipshit kid who tried to mug you in Paddington. Remember?"

"That description could cover half the teenagers in London."

"Yeah, but half the teenagers in London didn't meet with a bloke who paid them to mug you. And while we're on the subject of descriptions, remember the kid met with a bloke who paid him beforehand?"

"Right."

"And he said the bloke was old, fat, and had a crooked nose."

"Yes."

"Look at that photo again."

He nods towards my phone.

I look at the photo of Terry Brown. It would be true to say he hasn't aged well and is certainly overweight. Tellingly though, his nose has been broken on at least two occasions judging by the odd angle it slopes.

"I see what you're getting at, but it's a bit tenuous. Neither description is specific."

"On their own, maybe not. But this Terry Brown bloke was one of only two people who knew you weren't home tonight, and he has a fucked-up nose like the bloke who paid dipshit to mug you. Lot of coincidences there, doll, don't you reckon?"

"Okay, let's for one minute consider the possibility Terry Brown is the Tallyman. It doesn't explain why he torched my flat."

"Don't it? Think back to what you said to him."

I replay as much of the conversation as I can remember and not a great deal feels relevant, until I recall the part where William Huxley's name came up.

"He asked if it was worth it, contacting Huxley, and I told him it had inadvertently led onto something else."

"Something else?"

"Well, yes — meeting you. If it hadn't been for Huxley, I'd never have met you and I wouldn't have known what that notebook really was, or anything about the Clawthorn Club."

"Putting it like that, doll, this all kinda feels like my fault."

"Don't be silly. I chose not to leave the notebook on the table in that pub. I was warned, but chose to ignore it."

"'Spose so."

"Anyway," I continue. "I'm sure I mentioned a piece of evidence crucial to the story I was investigating."

"And you weren't giving up."

"Precisely. What better way to get rid of the notebook once and for all — whilst also sending me a warning — than burning my fucking flat to the ground."

Perhaps we're forcing the facts to fit the narrative but when you've nothing else, any straw will often do.

"Okay, Clement, I'll concede it's not beyond the realms of possibility."

"Good."

"But."

"But?"

I take a long sip of tea and use the time to collate my thoughts. A number of questions come to mind which I share with Clement.

"Let's assume for one moment that Terry Brown is the Tallyman. How on earth do we prove it? Because we're talking about a man with a stellar reputation. A man with a distinguished career. A man with decades of experience in investigative journalism. He's virtually untouchable, and I can't imagine he won't have meticulously covered his tracks."

"Weak link, doll."

"Sorry?"

"Twice now he's used that kid to do his dirty work. He's the weak link."

"Are you saying we go after Jaydon?"

"Yeah. We find him and have a proper chat."

"I can see two problems with that. Firstly, how on earth do we find him, and secondly, he didn't know anything about the man who paid him."

"He said he met the bloke on the way out of a bookies on Napier Street. Punters tend to stick to the same bookies so we find him that way."

"And then what? Is he likely to know any more than he did last time?"

"Only one way to find out — we find the little fucker and encourage him to get chatty."

It's not much of a plan, and I'm still not convinced Terry Brown is our man. For all the coincidences, he was the one who helped me get the job at The Daily Standard and, over the years, had my back when that job was at risk. He also had history with Eric, and I can't believe for one moment Eric would have knowingly associated himself with any member of a corrupt club, let alone its chief architect.

Thing is: anger is a potent antidote to common sense. Even if there's just a one percent chance Terry Brown is our man, I need to channel my anger somewhere.

"Guess I've got nothing to lose now."

"First thing tomorrow?"

"Are bookies even open on a Sunday?"

"Dunno."

A quick google confirms there is only one bookmaker on Napier Street called Trenchards.

"It seems there really is no rest for the wicked. They open at ten."

"Then we'll be there."

Our plan settled Clement tries to stifle a yawn.

"Tired?"

"Yeah. You?"

"Exhausted."

"I'll take the sofa, doll. You have the bed."

I wish I was still drunk — it would be so much easier to say what I want to say.

"I, um … I don't want to be alone, Clement. Not tonight."

He stands up and offers me his hand. "Come on."

We don't get undressed. We don't say another word. I lay down with my head on Clement's chest; his arm wrapped tightly around me.

As I lie listening to his heartbeat I sense I'm not the only one who doesn't want to be alone.

26.

I awake in an empty bed unsure where I am. I sit up and, one by one, memories of last night slap at my face. A nausea then arrives; partly due to the hangover but mainly due to the realisation everything precious in my life is now gone.

Almost everything.

"Morning, doll."

Clement takes three strides across the bedroom and hands me a mug.

"Sorry. Ain't got any coffee."

I find a smile. "Thank you."

"How you feeling?"

"Shocking."

He slips a hand into his waistcoat pocket and pulls out a packet of painkillers.

"Here. These might help."

The slogan on the packet promises to *stop pain fast*. A bold promise, and my pain runs much deeper than a thick head.

I neck two pills and take a slurp of tea.

"What time is it?"

"Just gone eight."

It occurs to me I have little chance of feeling human without a toothbrush or any means to shower.

"I need to get some things, Clement: toothbrush, hairbrush,

deodorant."

"Write a list. I'll go get them."

"Really?"

"Yeah. Can't have you going out looking like that, doll," he smirks. "You'll scare the neighbours."

I slap him playfully on the leg. "Arsehole."

Still smirking, Clement disappears and returns a minute later with a notepad and pen. I write down a list of basic essentials but I don't think the local convenience store will stock underwear. I'll have to grin and bear it until I get the chance to shop later. I've also got to call the insurance company and speak to the police. This day is going to be a long one — I can feel it already.

Declining my offer to pay Clement takes the list and promises to be back within twenty minutes.

He departs, leaving me sat up in bed with only a hangover, a cup of tea, and a head full of negative thoughts for company.

I need the loo but the bed is warm and the flat isn't. Crossing my legs I continue to sip tea and dwell on the only positive aspect of last night — Clement.

I know so little about him but, having lived in one another's pockets over the last five days, I can't deny certain feelings aren't bubbling beneath the surface. Quite what those feelings are, I'm not sure, but I haven't felt so connected to anyone in a long time. For all his faults, of which there are many, I know there's so much more to him than just inappropriate language, poor diet, and the looming threat of violence. Beneath all of that I've seen glimpses of a kind, if not troubled, soul. I've seen his vulnerable side, his compassionate, caring side, and I honestly think he needs someone like me just as much as I need someone like him.

Maybe, just maybe, something good might come out of all of this.

My bladder screams to be emptied. I put my mug down on the floor and tentatively remove the duvet.

"Shitting hell."

The bathroom, if anything, is even colder. I sit on the loo willing the pee to end before a stalactite forms. I know Clement said he doesn't feel the cold but this is ridiculous. With merciful relief, it ends, and I turn on the hot tap over the sink in the hope of bringing some feeling back to my fingers. As the water runs I look up at a cracked mirror. The view is truly shocking. My hair is pressed to my scalp on one side and a frizzy nest the other, and my face looks like that of a horror movie clown; plastered with day-old, tear-stained makeup.

Clement had a point about scaring the neighbours.

I rearrange my hair but there's little I can do about my face without the items on my shopping list. Until Clement returns I might as well hide beneath the duvet.

I do that until I hear the front door open and heavy boots stomp towards the bedroom. My saviour is back.

"Don't look at me," I yell, as he enters. "I look like shit and need a shower."

"I was only kiddin'. You're ..."

The pause does nothing to boost my self-esteem.

"I'm what, Clement?"

He hands me a carrier bag. "You're the best thing I've woken up to in a long, long time, doll."

There's no hint of a smirk. It appears, unbelievably, he's being entirely sincere.

"I doubt that," I reply in a low voice, taking the carrier bag. "But thank you."

He nods, and steps over to the wardrobe. "Sure I had a clean towel somewhere."

After a bit of rummaging, he produces a dark-blue towel and hands it to me.

"Go sort yourself out and I'll make you a coffee."

"I thought you didn't have any coffee."

"I didn't. I do now."

He disappears again. With a deep breath, I leave the warm bed and scuttle through to the bathroom.

As depressing as the bathroom is, there is at least enough hot water to have a decent shower. Perhaps a tiny, wicked part of me hoped my host might join me but I get the impression he's a bit old-fashioned in that respect.

Feeling vaguely human again I exit the bathroom and wander through to the lounge. It looks no better in daylight.

"How long have you lived here?" I ask Clement, as he hands me a mug of coffee.

"Not sure. Three or four months maybe."

"And before?"

"I've moved around a fair bit. Few months here, few months there."

"When was the last time you lived anywhere approaching a proper home?"

He looks into his cup.

"Clement?"

"Can we just say it was a long time ago and leave it there?"

"Okay, but don't you want to, one day?"

"What I want and what the Gods have in store for me ain't necessarily the same thing, doll."

I move close and place my hand on his arm.

"That's not an answer," I say softly. "Tell me: what do *you* want?"

He lifts his hand and places it on my cheek. "Redemption," he sighs.

"Redemption from what?"

"I wish I knew."

"That doesn't make much sense."

"Welcome to my world."

With that he empties his mug and steps away. I mentally add *exasperating* and *perplexing* to the list of traits I'm not so keen on.

"I'm just gonna have a quick piss," he says flatly. "And then we can get going."

More a statement of fact than a suggestion. He leaves me alone in the middle of the dreary lounge.

"Talk about cold shoulder," I mutter to myself.

Bathroom duties performed, he returns and we step through the front door of his hovel; the spring sun pleasantly warm on my skin compared to the cold, damp environment I've inhabited for the last ten hours.

"You know where the nearest Tube station is?" I ask.

"Yeah, and the nearest cafe. Let's have some breakfast first."

I don't argue, and we walk in silence to a grotty cafe a few streets away. Despite the dismal surroundings the food is surprisingly good. There is no better cure for a hangover than a full-English, and I ravenously tuck into mine, leaving a clean plate.

Although the conversation is stilted, I decide against posing further questions about Clement's past. Besides, as we leave the cafe he appears invigorated by either his full belly or a new-found sense of purpose — possibly both. Whilst his motivations might not be clear, mine are, and I remind myself what I've lost, and who might be responsible, as we stroll to the Tube station.

The journey from Kensal Green to Paddington takes only eleven minutes and, being a Sunday morning, it's far less manic than during the week.

We arrive just before ten and I check the location of Trenchards Bookmakers on my phone.

"It's not far. Less than a mile."

Clement nods, and we set off towards Napier Street.

"What's the plan?" I ask.

"Plan?"

"Yes. If we're able to find out where Jaydon lives, what do you propose we do?"

"Pay him a visit. Get some answers."

"To what questions?"

"Firstly, who ordered him to torch your drum."

"We don't actually know for sure it was him."

"We will, don't worry about that, doll. And when we do, we need to know if he's been paid yet."

"Do we? Why?"

"Cos I'm guessing he did this job for cash, and to get his grubby mitts on that cash he'll have to meet up with our man."

"So, what? We follow him?"

"Don't worry about the details yet. We'll work those out as we go."

I'm not keen on such a sketchy plan but Clement seems happy to improvise so I guess I'll go with it, for now.

We arrive on Napier Street, which happens to skirt the perimeter of a sprawling estate. Three concrete tower blocks dominate the bleak vista.

"How much you wanna bet our friend lives there?" Clement asks, nodding towards the estate.

"I'd say it's a given. Quite the shithole isn't it?"

"You should have seen what was here before."

"Before what?"

"Before they built the estate. Rows and rows of Victorian houses ... slums really. The houses were cramped and falling apart, outside loo, no hot water or heating."

"I'm not sure tower blocks were much of an improvement. Good intentions, badly executed."

The conversation ends as Clement drifts off into his own world.

We pass a row of shops: a hairdressers, a takeaway, and an off licence — all currently closed, and all three premises protected by steel security shutters. We then pass an open area of fenced-off wasteland, possibly earmarked for a development which will never happen, given the lack of investment in areas such as this.

"It's just here," I comment, as we approach another row of shops.

True to its surroundings Trenchards Bookmakers is short on kerb appeal. I follow Clement as he enters.

Inside it's no better. A bank of screens are fixed to the wall on one side with two zombie-like men perched on stools gazing up at them. They show us no interest.

We cross the floor to the counter where a balding, obese man sits behind a Perspex screen. He appears engrossed in something on his phone but eventually looks up and eyes us suspiciously.

There's no greeting; verbal or otherwise. It's left to Clement to start the conversation, and he gets straight to the point.

"We're looking for someone."

"So?" the fat man grunts.

"He's one of your punters."

"Got a lot of punters."

"This one is tall, thin, with a goatee beard. Goes by the name of Jaydon."

The man rubs one of his many chins.

"Yeah, I know Jaydon."

"Where can we find him?"

"Company policy," he smirks. "Can't breach my customer's privacy."

If it weren't for the Perspex screen, I'm pretty sure Clement would reach across and throttle the smug bastard. I wouldn't mind a go myself.

"I have a policy too," Clement replies.

"Yeah, what's that?"

Clement turns around and walks over to the bank of screens. He then reaches up, places his hands on either side of the nearest screen, and with an almighty tug, rips it from the wall; cables and chunks of plaster tumbling to the floor. The two zombies both wake from their respective comas and make a beeline for the door.

I stand shocked, open mouthed, as does our fat friend behind the counter.

Clement returns with his prize and unceremoniously drops it on the floor. It lands with a dull crack.

"That's my policy," he says matter-of-factly. "Now, I'll ask again — where can we find this Jaydon kid?"

The man reaches for his phone. "I'm calling the police."

"Don't much give a fuck, mate. I'll have all six of those off the wall before they get here."

The two men glare at each other but Clement, lacking in patience, shrugs his shoulders and turns away, seemingly intent on removing another screen.

"Wait," the fat man yells.

He then looks at me. "He lives on the estate opposite. Ninety-four Lawrence House, I think."

"Much obliged," Clement taunts.

I mouth an apology to the still-stunned man and grab Clement's arm. I don't let go until we're out the door and out of sight of Trenchards Bookmakers.

"That was a bit much," I chide. "There was no need to wreck his premises."

"There was no need for him to be such an arsehole. Besides, needs must."

My scornful glare is wasted as Clement looks up at the nearest tower block.

"That's it," he says. "Lawrence House."

Refocusing on why we're here my displeasure at Clement's heavy-handed negotiation quickly ebbs away. It's replaced with a mixture of apprehension, anger, and admittedly, a smidgen of nervous excitement. If his theory is correct, we might be tantalisingly close to securing proof of the Tallyman's true identity. That prospect might have come at the expense of both my job and my home, but exposing the Clawthorn Club would make such sacrifices more than worthwhile.

We head towards the stairwell entrance.

The smell on entering the dimly lit stairwell provokes a thousand memories of my time on a similar estate. It's hard to describe the overall stench but hints of damp brickwork, rotting food, and stale urine form solid base notes.

I follow Clement as he strides up the stairs to the first floor. I know only too well the numbering system in these blocks is a mystery known only to the town planners. A quick check of the first flat displaying a number and we confirm ninety-four isn't on this floor.

We return to the stairwell, and the sound of footsteps echoing from above.

"Doll, here," Clement hisses, beckoning me into an alcove which leads to the fire exit.

"What is it?" I whisper.

"Just a theory."

"Care to explain it?"

"Shh."

I roll my eyes and lean up against the wall. The footsteps get louder and come quicker; as if whoever is heading down the stairs is in a hurry. They reach the floor above, and Clement peers around the corner of our nook. With his back to me he raises a hand which I take as a signal to remain silent.

The footsteps are now on the first floor landing.

All of a sudden Clement steps forward and reaches out his arms. As he pulls them back a startled youth is dragged into view — Jaydon.

"The fuck you doin', man?" he squawks, as Clement pulls him into the alcove and pins him up against the wall.

Confused, I look at Clement. "How did you know it was him?"

"I didn't. Just a hunch that fat fucker would call him the moment we left. I think our friend here was tryin' to make his escape before we arrived."

He then turns his attention to Jaydon.

"Remember us, sunshine?"

Clearly he does, and he looks understandably concerned.

"What ... waddya want?" he stammers.

"I wanna know why you torched a coffee shop in Kilburn last night."

"Dunno what you're talkin' about."

Clement shakes his head.

"Listen, dipshit. This is only gonna go one of two ways: you either tell me the truth and we'll leave you in peace, or I'll carry you up to the top floor and we'll see if you can fly. Which is it to be?"

"I'm not admitting nothin'. I ain't no grass."

"Very noble, but in this case you don't have a choice. I ain't messin' around here — I will kill you."

The last four words of Clement's statement are delivered with such icy detachment even I shudder.

Jaydon's eyes dart left and right; everywhere but at Clement.

"He means it," I add, attempting to sound equally as sinister. "And if he doesn't, I fucking will."

His shoulders slump. "You can't tell no one I said anything."

"Just talk," Clement growls, before edging a fraction closer.

"Alright, man ... just ... don't say nothing to no one ... please."

Clement nods.

"Yeah, I started the fire."

His admission causes something inside of me to snap, and before I know it I'm swinging my arm in a wide arc. My fist connects with the side of Jaydon's face; inaccurate and lacking enough venom to do any real damage.

"Fuck, you crazy bitch," he yelps, trying to escape Clement's grasp and retaliate.

"I'm crazy?" I scream, ignoring the pain in my soon-to-be-bruised hand. "You torched my home you low-life cocksucker."

Clement turns to me; his expression somewhere between bemusement and surprise.

"Nice one, doll. Wanna take over?"

"No. I want you to cut his bollocks off with a pair of rusty scissors."

He turns back to Jaydon. "What you might not know, sunshine, is there was a flat above that coffee shop, and it belonged to my friend here."

Jaydon visibly deflates at the revelation.

"And it's true what they say," Clement continues. "Hell hath no fury. I reckon your only chance of getting out of this in one piece is to tell us everything."

Realising there is no good cop in this interview the skinny runt concedes defeat.

"Alright," he huffs. "What do you wanna know?"

"Let's start from the beginning. What happened after you left the alley that evening?"

"Nothin'. I went home and the bloke called me as he said he would."

I take out my phone and show Jaydon the picture of Terry Brown.

"Is this the bloke?"

The face is distinctive enough it doesn't take more than a glance.

"Yeah, that's him."

I catch Clement's eye, and a dose of 'told you so'. Nevertheless, I welcome the sudden rush of exhilaration now Jaydon has confirmed we're honing in on our target.

"And what was said?"

"Told him I couldn't get the bag as some big fucker turned up and did me in."

"How did he react to that?"

"He was pissed, like proper pissed. He said I owed him a favour and he'd let me know when he wanted to call it in. I didn't really give a shit ... got myself some easy cash and I weren't gonna do nothin' else for him."

"But you did."

Jaydon's head drops. Living on an estate is a lot like being a prison inmate — show any signs of weakness and your life will be forever a misery. It appears the kid is about to break that rule.

"My gran," he mumbles.

"What about her?"

"Someone stuck an envelope through my door on Friday morning. It was a photo of my gran's nursing home, and on the back it said she might have an 'unexpected fall' if I didn't do as I was told."

"So?"

"A few hours after the letter arrived, that bloke rang me — said it was his work, and if I didn't do as I was told, he'd carry out his threat."

Clement glances at me. Instinctively, I return a slight nod to confirm I believe Jaydon's story. Targeting his gran was a smart, if not callous, ploy.

"Let me guess," Clement says. "Torching the coffee shop meant your gran stayed safe?"

The kid nods.

"Did he offer to pay you?"

"Yeah. Two hundred quid."

Before Clement can ask another question, Jaydon appears to recall our last meeting, and how his fee was snatched away.

"I ain't got the cash yet," he blurts.

A faint smile forms on Clement's lips. "How you gettin' it?"

"I'm supposed to pick it up later."

"When and where?"

"Why do you wanna know?"

"Simple. Someone is gonna pay for torching my friend's flat so it's either you, or the bloke who paid you — any preference?"

"But what about my gran? If he finds out I told you …"

"Don't worry, sunshine. By the time I've finished with him he won't be in a position to threaten anyone."

Caught between a rock and a hard bastard Jaydon assesses his limited options.

"One o'clock," he eventually sighs.

"Where?"

"There's a pub called The Black Horse on the other side of the estate. It shut down last year but I'm meeting him in the car park."

"Good. All you need to do is turn up, collect your cash, and fuck off."

"And you won't say nothin' about me grassin' him up?"

"You have my word. He won't know it was you, and he sure as hell won't be able to do anything about it, even if he did."

Jaydon nods.

"Right, listen up. We're gonna be on our way, but I've got two bits of advice for you."

"What?"

"Firstly, keep your gob shut. If you give him the nod and tell him we're gonna be at that meet, I'll come for you, and you won't see me until it's too late."

"Alright, and?"

"Do something with your life, dipshit. You reckon that gran of yours would be proud of you gettin' involved in this kind of crap?"

The mention of Jaydon's gran appears to add potency to Clement's advice. The aggressive, spiteful angst replaced by shame.

"Now, fuck off."

Clement steps aside and Jaydon cautiously edges past him without taking his eyes off the big man.

"Remember what I said. You fuck with me and it'll be a first and last."

Jaydon nods before scampering away.

The first part of Clement's plan flawlessly completed he turns to me.

"Seems we've got a lunch appointment, doll."

"Yes, it does."

"And trust me: our friend, the Tallyman, is paying."

27.

With little else to do for ninety minutes, and with no desire to return to Clement's place, we retire to a coffee shop. It does, however, give me a chance to make some phone calls. The police confirm the fire was started deliberately, which I already knew, and they are currently 'pursuing enquiries', which I doubt will lead anywhere. Still, I'm given a crime reference number which I need before I make the next call.

It's funny, but I'm sure when I called the insurance company to get a quote, I was connected in seconds. The claims department clearly don't possess the same sense of urgency when it comes to answering calls and I'm initially sent into a telephonic abyss before I finally get to speak to a human — in Mumbai, judging by his pigeon English.

After a frustrating fifteen minute conversation — all the while watching my battery level sink to critical levels — he confirms I'll be sent a link via email to complete my claim. I am, however, initially relieved to hear I'm covered for the cost of temporary accommodation. That relief is short-lived when I'm told how much they allow.

"Sorted?" Clement asks, as I end the call and toss the phone into my handbag.

"Kind of. I've got the princely sum of fifty quid a night to pay for a hotel."

"Really? You could stay at The Park Lane Hilton for that."

"Yes, I could … if it was 1983."

"How much does a hotel cost then?"

"Put it this way: unless I'm willing to stay in a hotel with less stars than Celebrity Big Brother, I need to rent a room."

He stares at me, puzzled.

"You don't watch much television, do you, Clement?"

"Not really."

"Never mind. I'll book into a hotel tonight and start looking for a room tomorrow."

"Right."

Like a fidgety child he stares out of the window whilst playing with a sachet of sugar.

"You okay?" I ask.

"Yeah, it's just … I was … nah, forget it."

"Come on. Tell me."

His stare switches from outside to the cup on the table. I can almost feel his awkwardness.

"I know it ain't much, doll, but you can stay at mine, you know, until you sort something else out."

I reach across the table and put my hand on his. "That's very sweet."

"But?"

"But nothing — I'm flattered you offered."

"Nah, there's a definite 'but' in your voice."

"Okay, I was just wondering ... what, um, the sleeping arrangements might be?"

He finally looks up and fixes his eyes on mine. "Whatever you want them to be."

"But what do *you* want them to be?"

He starts chuckling to himself.

"What's so funny?"

"What's that word you used ... that's it: deflection."

"I'm not deflecting."

"You answered a question with another question. Bill Huxley told me that's how politicians operate when they're asked a question they can't answer, or don't wanna answer."

"Yes, well, it's just ... this ... I'm not sure what *this* is."

The smile dissolves. "Neither do I, doll, but I sure as hell could do with it."

"Me too. Shall we just see where we go, day by day?"

"That's pretty-much how I live my life so it works for me."

He squeezes my hand and glances up at a clock on the wall.

"Guess we better be going. I wanna recce the pub before either of 'em get there."

Reverting to business mode he gets to his feet. Reluctantly, I follow suit.

The short walk around the perimeter of a sink estate is no place to continue our conversation so I try and make idle chit-chat. Clement is having none of it, though; perhaps because he's focused on what we're about to do, or wondering why he offered to home a cranky, middle-aged liability.

The Black Horse comes into view, and it's a sorry sight. To deter squatters, all the windows have been covered with steel plates, and very little of the brickwork has escaped the local graffiti artists. A weathered sign promises home-cooked food, bar games, live entertainment, and free parking. I guess one of those promises is still valid as a narrow, weed-ridden driveway disappears down the right-hand side of the building.

"Grim," Clement mumbles to himself.

I check my watch — quarter to one.

"What's the plan then?" I ask. "They'll be here in fifteen minutes."

"Ever played hide and seek?"

"Err, a long time ago."

"We're gonna play now. Come on."

I follow Clement down the side of the building; the driveway leading to an open expanse of tarmac enclosed by overgrown Leylandii hedge almost as tall as the pub itself.

"I don't think the gardener has been for a while," I comment.

"Perfect spot for a meeting, though," Clement replies. "It's not overlooked and there's only one way in and out."

We stand for a moment and assess the best place to hide out. White lines are still just about visible on the cracked tarmac, and of the twelve parking spaces, four are taken up by piles of fly-tipped waste, including a sofa and two fridges.

"We could hide behind that sofa," I suggest.

"Nah. We'd be too easy to spot if our man bothers to check, and I'm guessin' he's the kind of bloke who would."

"Where then?"

Clement looks towards the rear of the pub, and an open area enclosed by rickety panel fencing.

"There's probably a beer garden the other side of that fence."

"But no gate."

"We'll just climb over."

"Are you kidding me? It's six feet tall, and I'm wearing a dress and heels."

"So?"

"Getting over it is one thing, but at some point we'll need to climb back over ... quickly. Trust me, Clement, that isn't going to happen."

"'Spose not. Gonna take a closer look."

"We've got twelve minutes," I remind him.

We head over to the fence to assess alternative options.

On closer inspection, an alternative option quickly becomes obvious to Clement. Through neglect, one of the wooden panels has warped, and an inch of daylight is visible where it should sit flush to the fence post. The very tips of five rusty nails are all that hold the panel in place. Those five rusty nails provide minimal resistance when Clement's boot makes contact with the panel, and it departs the post to provide a foot-wide gap.

"After you, doll."

I step through the gap and Clement follows. He pushes the panel back into place and then hammers his elbow into one of the wooden slats.

"What are you doing?" I hiss.

"Not much point standing here if we can't see what's going on."

He then snaps several shards of splintered wood from the slat to create a narrow aperture through which we can view the full width of the car park.

"How long?" he asks.

"Assuming they're on time, seven minutes."

"Perfect."

We take up position and wait. Much to my delight the buzz joins our greeting party.

As it is, we don't have to wait seven minutes as the sound of a can being kicked down the driveway suddenly breaks the silence. Seconds later Jaydon's gangly frame comes into view.

He crosses the car park — all the while looking around but paying no great attention to our vantage point — before taking a seat on the arm of the abandoned sofa.

I check my watch — four minutes.

We watch on as Jaydon takes out his phone and stares at the screen. Long seconds tick by and all I can hear is the Leylandii rustling in the light breeze, and my own heart pounding ten to the dozen.

Two minutes.

To calm my nerves I focus on the possibilities if this goes well. We could be minutes away from identifying the ringmaster of the Clawthorn Club. Minutes away from unmasking the Tallyman, and exposing decades of corruption. Minutes away from a once-in-a-lifetime exposé which would propel my career onto a level few journalists ever reach.

I'm about to check my watch for the umpteenth time when the purr of a car engine echoes from the side of the building. My eyes flick towards Clement but his attention is focused on the car park. I look back through the slit just as a black Mercedes Benz enters view. It swings around in a tight loop and comes to a stop with the driver's window facing our position. Tinted windows keep his identity hidden.

"Get out of the motor," Clement hisses in barely a whisper.

His request isn't heeded but instead, the window slides down. The man behind the wheel, the man we suspect is the Tallyman, is clearly visible. I have to clamp a hand across my mouth to prevent an excited shriek escaping. The driver looks a hell of a lot like Terry Brown.

Jaydon gets up from the sofa and saunters over to the side of the Mercedes. Words are exchanged and Brown hands him an envelope which he stuffs into his jacket pocket. The conversation continues and, judging by Jaydon's animated movement, things appear to be getting heated.

Voices raised and tempers seemingly frayed, suddenly Jaydon delves a hand back into his jacket pocket. At first I fear he's secured another knife, but when he does extract his hand, it's holding an altogether more serious weapon.

He aims the pistol squarely at Terry Brown.

"Fucks sake," Clement groans.

Clearly the kid decided to ignore Clement's advice, and now wants to counter the weakness Brown identified.

"What shall we do?" I whisper.

"Nothing. Just see how it plays out."

"What if he shoots Terry Brown?"

"Saves us a job, I 'spose."

"That's not funny. If he dies, a hundred questions relating to Clawthorn die with him."

Clement turns to me. "Do you wanna go disarm the kid?"

I guess he has a point — doing nothing really is the only option.

Turning back to the car park it appears Jaydon has ordered Terry Brown to get out of the car. Dressed in a pair of tan trousers and a navy blazer the obese journalist is leant up against the side of the car with his hands raised in surrender.

"Should I call the police?" I ask Clement.

"Just give it a minute."

"What if he shoots him?"

"Dunno if that's likely. I reckon the gun ain't real."

"You can tell from this distance?"

"Kinda. If he stopped waving it around I might get a better look."

Real pistol or not Terry Brown looks petrified as Jaydon continues ranting at him. Eventually he settles on aiming the pistol at Brown's chest whilst continuing to hurl abuse.

"What do you think?" I ask. "Is it real?"

"Only one way to find out for sure. Stay here and keep out of sight."

Before I can argue, Clement shoves the fence panel open and steps through the gap. Every fibre of my being wants to drag him back, but his broad strides quickly put thirty feet of tarmac between us.

If his approach was meant to be stealthy, he failed; the windows in the Mercedes reflecting his not-insignificant frame. Jaydon reacts by twisting ninety degrees and taking seven or eight steps back. Now, able to cover both men with the pistol, he waves it left and right between them.

Clement joins Terry Brown by raising his hands in surrender. If he does have a plan, it doesn't appear to be working — perhaps, now he's staring straight down the barrel, he's concluded the initial assessment of the pistol was incorrect.

What the hell do I do?

The obvious, and sensible, answer would be to call the police. Trying to keep my eyes level with the slit I reach down and rummage in my handbag. Touching smooth plastic I extract my phone. The screen lights up just long enough to inform me the battery level is at one percent. The phone then promptly dies.

"Fuck."

Think, Emma. Think.

Another lucky dip ensues as I drop the phone back and rummage for my purse. Across the car park, Jaydon is in conversation with Clement but the gun is still being waved around with far too much casual abandon for my liking.

I pull out the purse and remove my press card. This is a long shot, and possibly the worst idea I've ever had, but as Clement says: needs must.

Holding the card in my hand I step beyond the fence panel and cautiously approach the three men.

I get within fifteen feet, and call out Jaydon's name. He turns a fraction to his right and points the pistol in my direction. Perhaps detecting a potential distraction tactic, he takes another step or two backwards — far enough that if Clement made a move, he'd have time to discharge the pistol at one or both of us.

Contrary to how I actually feel, I attempt to appear calm, and force my face to adopt an empathetic expression.

"Jaydon," I say softly. "You don't want to do this."

"This is my beef," he yells. "You two had no fuckin' right being here."

"Okay. Tell me what you want?"

Judging by his face, it's a question he's rarely asked. If anything his frustration appears to mount.

"I want …" he snaps, pointing the gun at Terry Brown. "I want this prick to know no one threatens my family and gets away with it."

"If you shoot him, Jaydon, you'll spend the next fifteen years in prison and you'll never see your gran again. I know you're angry, but this isn't the way to deal with him. "

He swings the pistol back in my direction.

"Ain't it?"

"No. I have a much better idea."

"What?"

I slowly raise my press card and hold it out so he can see it.

"What the fuck is that?"

"It's my ID card — I'm a journalist."

"So what?"

"We've been trying to identify him," I say, nodding towards Terry Brown. "He's the head of a corrupt organisation and, thanks to you, we've now found him. I promise you, if you let us deal with him, he'll be the one going to prison for a very long time."

Some kind of thought process appears to take place as Jaydon falls silent. I just need to nudge him a little further in the right direction.

"You've met my friend," I add, looking across at Clement. "He's very keen to have a chat with him; if you catch my drift."

Jaydon looks towards Clement who nods confirmation.

"What you gonna do to him?"

"Not sure you wanna know, kid," Clement replies. "But it ain't gonna be quick and it ain't gonna be pretty."

A slight smile forms on Jaydon's face. He steps towards Terry Brown with the pistol still raised.

"Looks like you're in deep shit, mate. I hope you get what's coming to you."

He then takes two steps back and tucks the pistol back in his pocket.

"He's all yours," he grunts, looking at Clement. "But if he threatens my family again, I'll kill all of you."

Point made, pride intact, he lopes away.

Now it's our turn to meter out some threats and, judging by the look on Terry Brown's face, I'm confident we'll soon have some answers.

28.

Before we get down to business, I have one burning question for Clement.

"Was it real; his gun?"

"Yeah, it was."

"Shit. I think we've literally just dodged a bullet."

We both then turn to Terry Brown.

"Nice to meet you at long last, Terry. I think we need to have a little chat."

Taking the lead, Clement steps forward and looms over him. I sidle up next to my partner-in-crime so I can look Brown straight in the eye.

I stare at the sad little man. It's hard to believe he once possessed so much power and influence; that he was the driving force behind a club which has protected so many dark secrets for so many corrupt men for so long.

Now it's time to shine some light on his shady past.

"There are a hundred questions I want to ask you, Terry, but there's one that I need to ask first: why?"

Now there is no pistol on the scene Brown appears to gain confidence and stands upright. He's either brave or stupid, but the expression on his pudgy face looks too close to smug.

"Why what?" he sneers.

"Why you? You've had the type of career the likes of me could only dream about. The best jobs, countless awards, both the respect and envy of your peers — why put all that at risk?"

He shakes his head. "You know nothing, woman."

"Don't I? Perhaps you'd care to explain then."

"I'm saying nothing and, if you don't mind, I think I'm done here."

He turns and reaches for the door handle, but Clement swiftly deals with his impudence; grabbing him by the throat and slamming him up against the Mercedes.

"You're goin' nowhere, pal," he growls.

Brown grabs Clement's arm and attempts to pull it away but it's a contest not worthy of the name. One he has zero chance of winning.

"Let ... go," he rasps.

"You gonna answer our questions?"

"Fuck ... you."

Clement then deploys the same technique which worked so efficiently with Thomas Lang. He grabs a handful of Brown's crotch and squeezes hard. The journalist's face reddens, and he squeals like the pig he is. Too bad for him there's nobody around to hear.

"Say that again," Clement goads. "I dare you."

Brown shakes his head with such fervour his jowls wobble like a jelly on a motorbike. Fear replaces smugness.

"You gonna answer our questions?"

The shaking turns to nodding, or a close approximation to

nodding, what with a hand wrapped around his throat.

With the threat validated, Clement releases him and takes a step back.

"Shall we start again?" I suggest, glaring at Brown. "From the beginning."

He lifts his hand and rubs his neck but, thankfully, not his crotch. I give him a few seconds to find a breath.

"What do you want from me?" he eventually rasps.

"Answers, Terry. Answers."

"And if I refuse?"

"Honestly? It doesn't really matter as the game is up. We know who you are and, very soon, your whole corrupt club and its members will be exposed, whether you answer my questions or not."

"I don't know what you're talking about."

"Oh dear," I sigh, looking up at Clement. "It appears Terry is having problems with his memory. Perhaps you should take over — see if you can give it a little jog."

"Wait," Brown snaps. "You've got it all wrong."

"I don't think so, Terry, or do you prefer to be called the Tallyman?"

His reaction is not what I expected.

"Call yourself a journalist," he sneers. "You really don't have the first clue, do you?"

I swap a frown with Clement.

"I'm not the Tallyman," Brown continues. "So you can do what you like but it won't get you anywhere."

"Bullshit," I snap.

"I don't care if you believe me or not, but it's the truth. Do you honestly think I'd be doing this kind of dirty work if I was the Tallyman?"

"Why are you doing it then? You paid that kid to mug me, and then torch my flat. And it's bloody obvious you were the one who instigated my suspension at The Daily Standard. Why?"

"I'm not denying any of that but, like every other member of the Clawthorn Club, I didn't have a choice."

"With fear of repeating myself — bullshit."

"Believe what you like but I didn't want any part of it. I was told if I didn't deal with you, and your investigation into the Clawthorn Club, my ... past misdemeanours ... would be made public."

"What misdemeanours?"

"Like I'm going to tell you."

"My friend here can be very convincing. Would you like to reconsider before I ask him to get involved again?"

He momentarily glances to the sky and shakes his head.

"I had a gambling addiction," he sighs. "And it got out of control. To the point I stood to lose everything ... until I asked for a favour."

"Let me guess: via the Tallyman?"

"Yes," he scowls. "And that favour got me out of a whole world of trouble. It wasn't exactly legal, though."

"So you're saying you did all of this because you were being threatened?"

"That's exactly what I'm saying. I thought the Clawthorn Club was ancient history, and it was, until you unearthed that damn notebook and posted the photo online."

For the first time I detect a modicum of sincerity in his voice. And with that, a crushing sense of realisation — Terry Brown isn't the Tallyman.

"Who made you do this?"

"*Him*, of course ... the Tallyman."

"And who exactly is the Tallyman?"

It's a question asked more in hope than expectation, and if previous form is anything to go by, he won't know.

His eyes flick towards the ground and he pauses just a fraction too long before answering.

"I don't know."

"You're lying."

"No, I swear. I don't know."

I know he's lying, and I'm pretty sure he knows that — we've both been in the journalism game long enough to spot the tell-tale signs. He straightens up and pleads his innocence again; this time ensuring those tell-tale signs are absent. Too late.

"Let's not mess around here, Terry. If you're not our man then we want to know who is."

"Honestly," he pleads. "I don't know."

"Yes, you do, and I'm going to give you ten seconds to tell me. If you don't, I won't be held responsible for my friend's actions."

Clement dips a hand into his pocket and removes the knife he confiscated from Jaydon. He flicks the blade from the handle and runs his finger along the edge.

"Sharp as fuck," he casually remarks, before looking straight at Terry. "I hope you weren't plannin' on having any more kids."

"Please ..."

"Ten."

"For crying out loud, Emma."

"Nine."

Clement takes a step forward.

"Eight."

"I don't know."

"Seven."

"This is ridiculous."

"Six."

Clement edges a fraction closer.

"Five."

"You're going to regret this. I swear."

"Four."

He scans left and right looking for a means of escape that doesn't exist.

"Three."

"Jesus wept," he groans. "Fine. I'll tell you."

I'm about to press him for the name when his eyes suddenly

widen as he stares over my shoulder. Instinctively, I turn to see what's caught his attention but the muscles in my neck barely get the chance to engage.

An explosive crack rips through the air. Ordinarily I'd put it down to a car exhaust backfiring — if there happened to be another car behind us. I turn my head and there's no car but a tall, skinny youth brandishing a pistol.

"Jaydon," I gasp.

Stood twenty feet away, with the pistol pointing straight towards us, his eyes are glazed and expression vacant. I have a nasty feeling his zombie-like demeanour is fuelled by ketamine, or some other hallucinogenic drug. This is not good.

Jaydon takes a few unsteady steps forward; his head lopping left and right as if he's trying to find focus. He stops maybe fifteen feet away — a distance even the drug-addled youth couldn't miss from.

He finds a humourless grin. "Threaten my gran ... you cunt. You ain't gettin' away with that."

I'm about to try and reason with him when Clement suddenly shoots out an arm in my direction. I receive a shove close to being hit by a truck, and sprawl backwards. Even if I were wearing flats, I'd have struggled to maintain balance — in heels I have no chance. I flounder seven or eight steps before gravity wins and I fall flat on my arse.

From my vantage point on the tarmac I'm afforded a ringside seat of proceedings. It's then I realise why Clement shoved me away

— I'm no longer directly in Jaydon's line of fire. And fire he does: once, twice, three times in quick succession. Unlike the movies, there is no cloud of gun smoke — just a succession of ear-splitting cracks; each so loud my internal organs rattle.

Jaydon then takes two steps forward and fires twice more. Six shots in total; five at near point-blank range.

His arm then drops to his side. I don't know for sure but I seem to recall a pistol only holds six bullets. One would have been enough to accomplish his aim.

My head snaps to the left fearing the absolute worst. There is no word capable of describing the relief of seeing Clement still standing. Whether he's been hit or not I don't know. I scramble to my feet.

Terry Brown is definitely not standing; rather slumped on the floor with his head bowed forward.

I race towards Clement.

"Oh my God," I scream. "Are you okay? Have you been hit?"

He looks down at Terry Brown. "Nah, but he has."

Albeit limited, I have received first aid training although it never covered treating multiple gunshot wounds. I squat down next to Terry and examine the extent of his injuries.

"Terry! Terry! Can you hear me?"

A slight groan but nothing more.

His once pale-blue shirt is now crimson red, and the air thick with the scent of fresh blood.

"He's a goner, doll," Clement says in a low voice. "Leave him."

"No, no," I yell back. "We've got to do something."

I turn my attention back to Terry. The hopelessness of the situation then hits me harder than Clement's shove. I can't be sure how many times he's been hit but, judging by the amount of blood, it must have been at least two or three times. Multiple wounds, all around his chest, and no way to stop the bleeding. Worse still, with a flat phone battery I can't even call for an ambulance.

A thought occurs. I look up at Clement.

"Have you got your phone with you."

"Yeah."

"Then call a fucking ambulance."

He reaches into the inside pocket of his waistcoat while I try to reassure Terry.

"Terry ... can you hear me? We're just calling an ambulance so hang on in there."

On the scale of moronic advice my words surpass stupid. What is he going to do? Look at me and say, *"Yeah, sure. I'll just stop dying for a minute or two."*

His breathing is shallow, raspy, and worryingly faint. A trickle of blood begins to ooze from the corner of his mouth.

I look back up at Clement. He's frowning at the phone with his finger poised.

"What are you doing?" I yell. "Give it here."

I grab the phone and jab the keypad. Just as I'm about to hit the call button, Terry suddenly finds the strength to lift his head a fraction and open his eyes.

I wish he hadn't. So much fear and so little I can do to ease it.

He tries to say something but the words won't come. He swallows and tries again, but all he manages is a baby-like gurgle. Fear becomes frustration as his brow furrows, and his bottom lip bobs up and down.

It suddenly dawns on me that perhaps he's trying to air a dying confession. Could he be about to reveal the identity of the Tallyman?

I lean in so my ear is inches from his mouth, and vice versa.

"What is it, Terry? What are you trying to say?"

Another sound that might be a word — just not one in any English dictionary. I should feel some guilt for caring more about his confession than his impending death but when he does finally slip away, so does our last chance of knowing the Tallyman's true identity.

"I'm sorry. I don't understand."

The same noise, repeated. Frustration mounts.

"Are you trying to say a name?"

He coughs something that sounds a lot like 'bird'.

"Bird?" I repeat.

He makes the same noise but this time it sounds nothing like 'bird'. Clearly I'm on the wrong track.

"Try again, Terry. Take your time."

Considering time is the one thing Terry has very little of, perhaps not the best advice I've ever offered.

I should really call that ambulance.

Withdrawing a couple of feet, I'm about to hit the call button on Clement's phone when Terry suddenly gasps a long, ragged breath — a breath which isn't exhaled.

His eyes continue to stare in my direction but there's no longer any fear. There's no longer any anything.

Clement squats down next to me and puts his hand on my shoulder.

"He's gone, doll."

"No. No ... he can't be."

I'm not so much mourning the death of the man, but our last lead.

"We need to get out of here," Clement adds. "The place will be swarming with Old Bill soon."

With one dead journalist at our feet, and Jaydon having already scarpered, he's probably right. I can't even begin to think how we'd explain our motive for being here.

I stand up and take a final glance at Terry Brown's bullet-ridden corpse. It's hard to find any sympathy, and whatever professional respect I had is now as dead as the man himself. Clearly Clement has little respect either as he delves a hand inside Terry's jacket.

"What are you doing?" I ask.

"Looking for his wallet."

"Jesus Christ. You're robbing a corpse?"

"I don't want his cash. I wanna see if he's got anything which might give us a bleedin' clue where to look next."

"Oh, sorry. See if he's got a phone, too."

He continues to rummage through Terry's pockets and plucks out both a wallet and a mobile phone.

"Right. Let's get out of here," he then orders.

The faint sound of sirens is all the motivation I need.

We walk briskly away from the pub and, rather than head back along the road, we cut through the estate; the maze of alleyways delaying our journey but providing an anonymous passage back to the Tube station.

As we walk a latent sense of shock catches up. It's nowhere near as severe as last night, but the heightened heart rate and prickling anxiety certainly make their presence felt.

I turn to Clement. "I can't believe what just happened."

"I know. Back in the day, gettin' hold of a shooter was bleedin' hard. Now every wannabe gangster has one."

I shake my head.

"I wasn't referring to the fact Jaydon had a pistol. I was referring to the fact you should be heading to the mortuary with Terry Brown."

"Eh?"

"That kid shot five bullets at point-blank range, and God only knows how, but not one of them even grazed you."

"Guess I'm lucky," he shrugs.

"Lucky?" I repeat, incredulous. "It's a bloody miracle you weren't hit."

"They happen, now and again."

I don't share his nonchalant attitude.

"You were a hair's breadth from being shot ... from being killed. How can you be so casual about it?"

"Maybe I've got a death wish."

I stop dead and grab his arm. "Please, don't say that. Not even in jest."

He looks at the pavement, and then at me. "Sorry."

The sincerity in his eyes prompts another thought: if it hadn't been for his quick thinking, I could have shared some of the bullets Terry took.

"You can't die, Clement. Who else would step in and save me when I'm being shot at?"

My smile masks a sobering thought. Perhaps the shock, but I share it without thinking.

"I've lost enough people I care about. I don't want you to join that list.

Just as I expect him to laugh my concerns away he does the opposite. Without saying a word, he wraps his arms around me — it's like being cocooned in a giant, nicotine-scented security blanket.

Time passes, and I have no desire to remove myself from Clement's arms. That decision is then taken off the table as he kisses me gently on the top of my head, and steps back.

"You ain't really lost them, doll," he says softly. "They just ain't here no more."

"Who?"

"The people you cared about."

I gulp hard. "You think?"

"I know."

I've heard a lot of beautiful words over the years but none as sweet as Clement's. I appreciate it's just hollow sentiment, but if I try hard, I could almost believe him.

"Thank you, for saving my life, and for being ... for caring."

"It's what I'm here for — to look out for you."

That too, feels almost believable.

29

After arriving back at Kensal Green I suggest we visit a coffee shop to discuss our next move; if indeed there is a next move.

We secure a table in the corner, away from potential eavesdroppers, and Clement takes his first disapproving slurp of tea.

"Don't like these places," he complains. "The tea always tastes like gnat's piss."

"And the coffee in that cafe this morning tasted like used engine oil. I guess we'll have to find a compromise otherwise this relationship is doomed."

My comment may have been tongue in cheek but Clement's lack of response jars somewhat.

"Anyway," I cough. "Shall we see if Terry's wallet or phone offer us anything to go on?"

He dips a hand into his pocket and removes a black leather wallet and then a mobile phone. As he places them on the table, I reach for the wallet first and open it up.

The right-hand section contains a row of credit cards and Terry's driving licence. Beyond that, a section for bank notes containing sixty pounds in cash. I pull out the notes, hand half to Clement, and tuck the rest in my pocket.

"I think he owes us that," I remark.

On the left-hand side there's a zipped pouch presumably designed for loose change. I undo the zip and find a wad of business cards — no great surprise as you can never have enough contacts in our line of work. I pull them out and place them on the table before returning my attention to the final section of the wallet. That contains a condom and a train ticket purchased a year ago. Considering Terry's physical appearance, I'd speculate the condom has lived in his wallet significantly longer than the train ticket.

"Anything?" Clement asks.

"Nothing."

He reaches over and picks up the pile of business cards. He then flicks through them, sparing a second or two on each, before tossing it onto the table.

"What are you looking for?" I ask.

"Dunno really. Just seeing if any of the names ring a bell."

He drops the last card on the table.

"And do they?"

"Nope."

Clement sits back in his seat and reaches for his cup. Perhaps I'm being overly cautious, but I don't think it would be sensible to leave a murder victim's business cards scattered across the table of a coffee shop. I brush them into a pile so I can return them to the wallet which I'll lose down a drain later.

As I do, I catch a flash of a distinctive, brightly coloured logo on one of the cards. Instantly, it strikes me as familiar — but not as familiar as the name on the card. I pluck it from the table and double-check I'm not mistaken.

"Holy shit," I gasp. "I don't believe it."

"What?"

"The name on this business card — Alex Palmer."

"Who's he?"

"You've got a shocking memory, Clement. Alex is the guy I met at The Three Horseshoes last night — the guy who offered me a job. We used to work together."

"Right. And?"

"It's a bit of a coincidence Terry has his business card don't you think?"

The moustache receives a customary stroke or two as I wait for a reply.

"The only two men who knew you weren't at home last night; they knew each other?" he eventually surmises.

"Exactly. And one of those men admitted he instigated the fire while I was out with the other."

I think back to the conversation with Alex. There was a moment, when I said I was leaving, when he appeared edgy. I put that down to disappointment, but perhaps it was because he knew Jaydon was due to start the fire at a certain time after dark, and he needed me to stay a while longer. He did seem to relax a little after I said I was meeting a friend in the pub for dinner.

"They've gotta be working together," Clement suggests.

"It would be one hell of a coincidence I'll give you that."

"But?" he replies, detecting the hesitancy in my voice.

"Alex is more or less the same age as me so when the Clawthorn Club was in its heyday he'd have been a kid. And all the other members we know of are much older."

"Was his surname in the notebook?"

"I'd check if my battery wasn't dead but I'm fairly sure it wasn't. I'd have remembered a familiar name."

"I don't remember it either."

"So we can assume Alex wasn't a member of the Clawthorn Club. And he sure as hell can't be the Tallyman as he's far too young."

Clement thinks for a moment before sitting forward and resting his elbows on the table.

"Maybe he was just hired help like the kid?"

"But why him? Take it from me, Clement, Alex Palmer is a drip, and I can't believe he'd have the balls to get involved in anything like this."

"But he clearly is as our dead friend had his business card, and the facts don't lie. We need to dig deeper."

The evidence is compelling but not conclusive. Coincidences happen all the time, and many a former colleague has fallen on their sword by presuming such coincidences to be the truth.

"Is there any other connection between them? Think, doll."

I'm already one step ahead — scouring my mind back years to the possible times Alex Palmer and Terry Brown might have crossed paths. Alex, like Terry, was a journalist once and, although I don't think they worked together, it's possible they met. It's not a theory I can prove one way or the other though.

As I cast my mind back further and further memories of my time working with Eric come to the fore. It only serves to remind me how much I miss him, and how I'd give anything for his advice and guidance about now.

And then, to my own astonishment, those same memories of Eric deliver an epiphany.

"Eric's funeral," I blurt. "Terry mentioned he was there when I first spoke to him, and I know for sure Alex was there as he accosted me."

"And did they talk?"

"I ... I honestly don't know. I left the moment the service ended, and I couldn't face the wake."

"So, it's possible they knew each other before this?"

"It's possible, but it doesn't explain why Alex would get involved and, more to the point, why either Terry or the bloody Tallyman would want him involved."

"What does he do for a living?"

"Oh, something ..."

My mind races ahead, leaving my mouth redundant.

"Ohh. Shit."

"What?"

"Alex works for a telecoms company."

"Like phones, you mean?"

"Yes. Specifically mobile phones."

"Like the blokes in that shop you took me to?"

"Oh, no — nothing like that. Alex's company manages software for mobile networks."

Clement's expression is already edging towards bewildered. I fear this might take some explaining.

"It's complicated but, in a nutshell, Alex's company has access to the networks which most mobile phones are connected to. Those networks allow users to make calls, send text messages, and access the Internet."

"Gotcha, I think."

"And someone with that access would be able to track the whereabouts of any mobile phone."

"You might wanna get to the point, doll."

"Remember that night in Paddington when we were in that shithole of a pub?"

"The one with the barmaid with cracking knockers?"

"Yes," I frown. "That one."

"What about it?"

"I received a text message telling me to leave the notebook on the table. Remember?"

"Yeah."

"And we couldn't work out how anyone knew exactly where we were?"

"Right."

"Well, if someone had access to the mobile network data, they'd be able to pinpoint my exact location by tracking my mobile phone."

Finally it appears Clement has cottoned on to the significance of Alex's job.

"Are you saying this Alex bloke can track you wherever you go?"

"I think so, although I'm just putting two and two together. This could be any number but four though."

"It'd explain why they'd want him involved."

"Perhaps, but it's not enough on its own. We need more."

That conclusion leads to two hopes. Firstly, Terry's phone isn't protected by either a password or a fingerprint. And secondly, it contains another link between him and Alex.

I snatch the phone from the table and press the button on the side. The screen immediately lights up.

"Thank Christ for that. No password."

"What are you looking for?" Clement asks.

"Phone records and text messages primarily, but this operating system also has in-built tracking so you can look back and see where you were on any given day. The default setting is usually set to 'on', but if Terry deactivated it, it's not going to help us."

"Are you saying these mobile phones know where you are all the time, and record it?"

"Most of them, yes."

"Fuck. I wouldn't wanna be married in this day and age."

"Good job I wasn't about to propose then, isn't it?"

He answers with an awkward smile.

I open the messaging app — it's completely empty. Clearly Terry deleted all his messages after he'd read or sent them. Hoping for more luck, I then open the call log and check the number on Alex's business card.

"Bingo! Terry called Alex yesterday morning."

"Nice one."

"And, looking at the time, it was only half-an-hour before Alex called me to arrange our meeting for last night."

"That nails it then. They must have been working together."

The evidence is now irrefutable. What isn't so clear cut is who was pulling their strings, and how we identify and track down that person.

I open the contacts app and inwardly groan. Over five hundred names and, unless Terry was a complete idiot, it's unlikely he'd have used the name 'Tallyman' to identify our foe's phone number.

"What you doin'?" Clement asks.

"I was just scouring Terry's contacts but there's too many to check. Any one of them could be our man."

"Anything else you can get from that thing?"

"Hold on."

I open the map app and, from the menu, select the timeline option. Terry's phone is even older than mine and the slight pause while the screen loads feels like an age. Finally, it opens up, and slap bang in the middle of the screen is the last location the phone registered — The Black Horse Public House.

"Get in," I whoop.

"I'm guessing you've got somethin'?"

"The phone has logged Terry's last location so it stands to reason it's been tracking him since he first switched it on."

"And it'll tell us where he's been of late?"

"It will, although I'm not entirely sure what use that will be."

I check back through the data, day by day. I get as far back as Thursday and, frustratingly, it appears Terry spent most of his time at home, in the pub, or flitting between various restaurants. With a deep sigh, I hit the icon for Wednesday and the same routine flashes up on the screen, right up until nine o'clock in the evening.

"Think I've got something."

"Something?"

"Err, yes, although it could just as easily be nothing."

"What is it?"

"On Wednesday evening at nine, Terry drove to an address in Dorset. He stayed there overnight and returned first thing on Thursday."

"From where?"

"His house in Richmond."

"Bit late in the day to schlep all the way from West London to Dorset don't you reckon?"

Beyond Terry's late night dash to the south coast there's something about Wednesday evening that feels relevant. I need to check my own phone, specifically the image gallery, but I won't be doing that until I can charge it.

"Listen, I know it's not great timing but I need to go shopping. I've got to buy some clothes, and a charger for my phone."

"It's alright. You want me to tag along?"

"I can't ask you to do that."

"Might be for the best. I don't think our friend is gonna be too happy when he learns Fat Terry is dead."

"You might be right, and I guess I'll need to get a new sim card too. I don't know how Alex did it, but I don't want him tracking us again — gives me the creeps."

"What's a sim card?"

"It's … don't worry about it. Anyway, I'm pretty sure he can't track us with the phone switched off."

"Let's hope not. Don't want anyone to find out I willingly went clothes shopping with a bird. I've got a reputation to protect."

"You have a reputation?" I reply, with a wry smile.

"Maybe once," he snorts. "Not anymore."

We finish our drinks and leave the coffee shop. From memory the nearest place with any shops is Kensal Town; a short walk away. It's not exactly blessed with retail options but I don't have the time, inclination, or budget to head anywhere better.

One hour, and two hundred quid, later I manage to acquire the wardrobe options of a teenage boy: a couple of pairs of jeans, basic underwear, a few sweaters, a decent coat, socks, and a pair of trainers. It'll have to do for now.

Of perhaps more importance we find a mobile phone shop where I'm able to buy a new sim card and a charger. The only question is where I charge my phone, and that means returning to Clement's flat — possibly the only place more depressing than Kensal Town on a gloomy Sunday afternoon.

"I need to charge my phone, and change out of this bloody dress. Shall we head back to yours?"

"Yeah. Guess so."

It appears Clement is equally unenthusiastic about his home; a subject I decide to explore as we wander back.

"Don't you want to settle down at some point?"

"Settle down?"

"Yes. Live in a nice, comfortable house — maybe one with actual heating and mould-free ceilings."

"Point taken."

"Sorry. I didn't mean to sound sarky. I'm just interested in what you see — you know — for the future."

"Like I've said, doll I don't plan too far ahead."

"But at some point you have to. Surely you don't want to just drift aimlessly for the rest of your days?"

"Don't know how many days I've got."

"None of us do, Clement, which is why it's important to make the most of every one."

With no reply I look up and immediately wish I could read him better. I've no idea if my words are hitting home or he's thinking about his next fry-up.

"Maybe you're right," he eventually sighs.

In an attempt to lighten the mood I nudge him in the ribs with my elbow.

"I'm a woman — of course I'm right. Haven't you learnt that much?"

He smiles down at me. "There ain't enough lifetimes, doll."

It's minor progress and I'm happy to leave the conversation on a positive note. We walk in a comfortable silence, although I do occasionally glance up at Clement, hoping for a hint at what's going on behind those eyes of his. I've learnt precisely nothing by the time we step through the door of his crappy home.

"Do you mind if I get changed?"

"Help yourself. You know the way to the bedroom."

"Which one? The one in the west wing, or the east wing?"

"Keep that up and you'll be kipping on the sofa."

I have no intention of kipping on the sofa.

After a quick attempt to freshen-up in the distinctly unfresh bathroom, I change into jeans and a sweater.

Returning to the lounge, the gas heater is on and the kettle rumbling away. I like coffee as much as the next woman but Clement's appetite for tea is on a different scale.

"I notice you don't have a TV," I remark, taking a seat on the sofa.

"Nothing worth watching these days."

"What do you do for entertainment of an evening?"

"Listen to the radio. Play cards."

"You play cards on your own?"

"Solitaire. It's the only game in town, they reckon."

"My mum loved that song — The Carpenters wasn't it?"

"Preferred the Andy Williams version."

He returns to his hot beverage duties while I scan the room for a power socket. Spotting one in the corner, I get up and plug my phone into the new charger, but not before swapping-out the sim card.

I switch the phone on and once it's awake, I scroll through to my image gallery, looking for one photo in particular.

The result summons the buzz.

"How's this for a coincidence then, Clement? Terry's little excursion to Dorset took place not long after I first took those photos of the notebook and posted them online. Or at least, I thought I posted them."

"Online? That's where everyone can see shit, right?"

"Pretty much. And now I'm now wondering if I did post the photos, and someone managed to delete them."

"So, you show the photos of the notebook to the world, and then within an hour or two, the photos get deleted and this Terry Brown bloke takes a trip down to Dorset."

"Exactly. But who did he go and see, and why?"

"Don't suppose you can tell who he visited?"

"Well I don't think it was Alex. I'm sure he mentioned he lives somewhere south of the river."

"Cos he's been really honest so far, ain't he?"

A sarcastic, but fair, point.

"I'll check."

On this occasion, the land registry records don't provide the name of an individual, but a company.

"The property in Dorset belongs to a company called Sturgeon Holdings."

"Who the fuck are they?"

"No idea."

I open another tab and search the Companies House records. Nothing.

"I've got a nasty feeling, Clement, it's an overseas company."

"Not traceable then?"

"I think they're currently changing the laws, but as it stands there's no way of finding out who owns that company — certainly not with our limited resources."

I return to the sofa as Clement hands me a mug of coffee and sits down.

"What do you wanna do next?" he asks.

"I'm not sure, but I tell you what I don't want to do, and that's anything rash. I think it would be best if we work out a proper strategy rather than attack Alex all guns blazing."

"He's the obvious target, doll. We just need him to talk."

"But what if he doesn't know anything? As you said, he could just be hired help, or blackmailed help for all we know, because I still can't get my head around his involvement."

"If that's what you wanna do."

"I think it would be best. Besides, the last few days have been exhausting and I just want to stop and catch my breath."

"Quiet night in then."

"Would that be so bad?"

"Depends."

"On?"

"If you're gonna order in another takeaway."

I slap his arm. "You've got a one-track mind, and not in a good way."

"Tell you what, though, after we've eaten, I can show you how to play solitaire."

"I'd like that."

"But I 'spose I'd better go get some milk first."

I nod before taking a sip of coffee. "You've run out?"

"Nah, it's just a bit lumpy."

Words, and thankfully my taste buds, fail me.

"Don't worry," he adds. "I poured it through a tea strainer."

"Jesus, Clement — if any man needed a woman in his life, it's you."

"Maybe," he replies, getting to his feet. "Won't be long."

"You're going now? What about your tea?"

He looks into his cup and grimaces. "Think I'll leave it."

Thirty seconds after he's left, I pour my coffee down the sink.

True to his word, Clement returns ten minutes later with milk, and a bottle of wine. He hands it over with an apology.

"Wine ain't my thing so ... sorry if it's shit."

I take the bottle and don't even bother reading the label. It could be Blue Nun for all I care — the thought truly does count in Clement's case.

"No, it's exactly what I drink. Thank you."

"Good. I'm gonna go grab a shower. Do you wanna order in some dinner?"

"Chow mein by any chance?"

"You're learning, doll."

He then disappears off to the bathroom. I retrieve my phone and open the delivery app to order a Chinese. My usual takeaway doesn't cover this area so I take pot luck with the nearest, and I'm informed it'll be an hour's wait.

I'm about to sit back on the sofa when a sound emanating from the bathroom grabs my attention. I stand and listen for a moment.

"No, it can't be."

Someone is singing *Solitaire* — someone who can't possibly be Clement.

Awestruck, I continue to listen. A cliché perhaps, but he actually possesses the voice of an angel — albeit an angel who smokes twenty Marlboro a day.

I remain motionless: just listening. It's then I make a decision which I may live to regret. Whether I regret it within the next sixty seconds, or down the line, remains to be seen.

A dozen steps to the bathroom door. To the soundtrack of Clement's voice and splashing water I strip away my new clothes. There is every chance I'm about to make a complete fool of myself but the need is too great and the desire too strong.

I take a deep breath and glance down at my naked body.

"Good luck, girl," I whisper to myself.

I open the door and step into the bathroom.

30.

Seven o'clock on a Monday morning and not even the shrill alarm on my phone can ruin this bliss. Clement's bedroom is bathed in muted light, and beyond the window the dawn chorus is well underway.

My high-risk strategy paid off. After Clement got over his initial shock — and I got over mine in fairness — I joined him in the shower. We virtually attacked one another and the frenzy continued until the water ran cold. Without even bothering to dry-off we moved through to the bedroom. I already knew Clement was perpetually hungry, but on this occasion his appetite surpassed ravenous. We fucked like animals: primal, raw, insatiable. There was an intensity; a need, like I have never felt before, and there was no doubt in my mind I wasn't alone in that feeling.

Maybe half-an-hour after I first stepped through the bathroom door we lay exhausted. Spent. The hunger sated.

Dinner arrived and we ate it in bed with a glass or two of wine — well, I had the wine — Clement, true to form, supped from a can of lager. He then tried to teach me how to play solitaire but there was only one game I wanted to play, and it sure as hell didn't involve a deck of cards.

Sure enough the cards fell to the carpet as I fell further under Clement's spell. With no need for urgency, and certainly with no thoughts of Clawthorn, Alex Palmer, my lost home, or the tally-fucking-man, we spent the remainder of the evening lost in one another until I fell into a deep, contented slumber.

"Morning, doll. Sleep well?"

Clement stands before me, naked, holding two mugs. He carefully hands me one.

"I slept very well indeed, thank you. You?"

"Yeah, you wore me out," he chuckles.

I take a sip of coffee before placing my mug on the bedside table.

"Did I?" I reply, with a mischievous grin. "So, are you now feeling suitably re-energised?"

He places his mug down next to mine. "Maybe. Why?"

"Hop into bed and I'll tell you."

"You could tell me now."

"I think you'd prefer a practical demonstration."

No further enticement is required. Clement climbs back into bed and we set about creating our own dawn chorus — only louder and filthier.

It could have lasted all morning and it still wouldn't have been long enough. As it is, forty-five minute later we have to face reality again.

We sit up in bed and sip at our near-cold beverages. It doesn't take long for my mind to pose a question — a predictable question now we've crossed the line. I feel compelled to ask it.

"This is a bit awkward but, am I ... is this ... just a one-off?"

"Is that what you want?"

"Christ, no."

"Then it goes where it goes, doll."

"What does that mean?"

After a brief pause, I get my answer. "It means neither of us knows what's around the corner. Let's just take it one day at a time."

"That's not exactly reassuring."

"You want me to make a promise I might not be able to keep?"

"Well, no, but I was hoping you might see some kind of future, you know, for us."

"I do. I mean, I can."

"But?"

He turns to me and strokes my face; the roughness of his hand a stark contrast to the softness of his gaze.

"Let's see where we are once this Clawthorn business is dealt with."

"Okay, but I just need to know: this is more than just a one-night-stand for you?"

"Yeah. Far more."

"That's good enough for me."

Suddenly, I have more motivation than ever to unmask the Tallyman and put the whole saga to bed.

"Oh, and Clement."

"What?"

"One final question. How was last night?"

"Pretty fuckin' spectacular, as it goes."

"Spectacular for ... what was it you said? A bird who's a bit on the old side for your taste, wasn't it?"

"Eh?"

"That's what you said when we first met. Remember?"

"Oh, yeah. Should have known you wouldn't forget."

"Women never forget an insult, Clement. Ever."

I slither out of bed with a wink and head off to the bathroom.

After a far less interesting shower, I get dressed and decide additional caffeine is urgently required. I find Clement on the sofa staring into space.

"Penny for them."

"They ain't worth a penny, doll."

"Just as long as they're not regretful thoughts."

"Nah."

"Tea?"

"Yeah, go on."

I put the kettle on and wash up our mugs. As I wait for it to boil, I turn around to find Clement still away with the fairies.

"Is there something wrong?" I ask.

"Eh?"

"You're miles away."

"Just thinkin', that's all."

"About anything in particular?"

"What would happen if we just walked away from all of this?"

"This?"

"Yeah, the whole Clawthorn thing. Maybe things would turn out okay if we just … I dunno, did nothin'."

"What makes you say that?"

He reflects on my question for a moment before answering with a question of his own. "Do you believe we all have a destiny in life?"

"Not really."

"But imagine if we did. What if I was *supposed* to help you solve this Clawthorn business but I chose not to?"

"I'm not with you, Clement. Who or what could make you do anything you didn't want to do? Everything that's happened has been because we decided to make it happen."

"Did we?"

"Well, yeah. I don't believe the Universe has some pre-determined plan for any of us. We make our own decisions and set our own destiny."

"And what if you're wrong about that? What if we're all here for a specific reason?"

Ordinarily, I'd laugh-off any such suggestion but the look on Clement's face doesn't fill me with mirth. He actually appears deadly serious.

"Okay, that sounds a lot like an excuse to run away, Clement. Is there something you're not telling me?"

An obvious contender for 'something' suddenly parks itself at the front of my mind.

"Wait … please don't tell me you're married."

"No, I ain't married."

"Thank Christ for that."

"But I ... ahh, fuck it. Just forget I said anythin'."

"No, I won't. Come on, tell me."

"Alright," he sighs. "It's just ... I wanna have a life again you know, settle down, do the normal shit normal people do."

"What's so bad about that? It's what I want too — I think it's what everyone wants when it comes down to it."

"Yeah, but I've got this nigglin' voice in my head that just won't shut up."

I perch myself on the sofa next to him.

"That's perfectly normal. Everyone has doubts when they make changes in their life. In time that niggling voice will fall silent — I promise."

He looks up at the ceiling and closes his eyes. For such a strong man, he appears to be suffering from an uncharacteristic bout of self-doubt.

"You don't have commitment issues, do you?" I ask.

He opens his eyes and looks at me.

"Why do you ask that?"

"You don't have a mortgage or even a proper job. You don't appear to own very much, and you're still single. Come to think of it, I've never met anyone who has less commitments than you."

"I had commitments, once."

"What happened?"

"Don't really wanna talk about it."

"Come on — throw me a bone, at least. I just want to be sure I'm not wasting my time here."

"You're not."

"So? What happened?"

"All you need to know is ... one evening my life changed forever. Everything I had, everything I knew, ended that moment."

The kettle comes to a boil and he gets up.

Clearly something awful happened to him and, whatever it was, it must have been traumatic. It almost feels like he's given up on living a normal life; like he's lost and is now just wandering aimlessly looking for someone to guide him. If we're to have a future, I need to tread carefully, and let him open up as and when he's ready.

I stand and sidle up to him.

"Whatever happened," I say softly, taking his hand. "I want you to know it doesn't matter — not to me. And if you don't feel you can talk about it, that's fine by me too."

He replies with a slight nod and a squeeze of my hand.

"And if you really want to drop this whole Clawthorn nonsense, I'm good with that too. Not that I had a choice in the matter but my life is now a blank canvas. I no longer have a job tying me down and, once the insurance company deal with my claim, I can easily sell or rent the flat."

"A blank canvas. Kinda like the sound of that."

"Me too, but as you say: one day at a time."

"Yeah. One day at a time."

"But for now," I add, slapping his backside. "I'll let you make me a coffee."

I kiss him on the cheek and let him get on with my request.

Retrieving my phone from the corner of the lounge, I return to the sofa and switch it on. Unsurprisingly, as I have a new sim card, there are no voicemail or text messages. I check my email.

In amongst the usual crap I'm surprised to see three emails from Gini — all sent yesterday evening. Clearly they can't be work-related but maybe she wanted to meet up for a drink, and to chat through her wedding plans for the umpteenth time.

I open the first email.

It's just a single line stating she's left three voicemail messages and needs to speak to me.

With mild concern, I open the second email.

Virtually the same message but with the word 'urgently' added at the end.

With some trepidation I open the third email.

Again, it's almost the same message but in block capital letters with half-a-dozen exclamation marks at the end. It also lacks any niceties Gini usually adds to her emails — it's more a demand than a request.

"Problem?" Clement asks, handing me a mug.

"Err, I'm not sure. I've got a few worrying messages from a girl in the office.

"Not your problem now."

"I don't think it's anything to do with work. I'd better call her."

"Alright. I'm gonna grab a shower and then I'll nip out and get something for breakfast."

I nod, but I'm only half-listening. My mind is already racing with the possible reasons why Gini is so desperate to contact me. I make the call.

"Hello," she answers within three rings.

"Gini, it's me, Emma."

"Where the hell have you been?" she barks, her voice taut. "I've been trying to get hold of you since six o'clock last night."

"Long story, but I had to change my number and I've only just seen your emails. What's the big panic?"

"It's Danny," she blurts, presumably referring to her fiancé.

"Right. What about Danny?"

"He popped out for some milk yesterday afternoon and ..."

Her voice breaks and it's clear she's trying to keep a grip on her emotions.

"Gini, what is it?"

"A car mounted the pavement and ran him down."

"My God. Is he okay?"

"Severe concussion and he's broken his leg, and his pelvis."

"But he's not ... nothing life threatening?"

"The doctor said it was a miracle he didn't sustain worse injuries than he did."

As shocking as Gini's news is I'm not sure why she needed to share it with me so urgently.

"Um, obviously I'm horrified what happened to poor Danny, but why the urgency to get hold of me? Surely you should be with your fiancé now?"

"Because, Emma, it wasn't an accident."

"Eh? The police have already determined that?"

"No, they haven't. I know it wasn't an accident because I received a phone call at the hospital."

"From who?"

"Someone calling himself Allen Tamthy."

My blood runs cold.

"You know the name, don't you?" Gini continues. "Because he certainly knows you."

"What did he say?" I gulp.

"What happened to Danny was because of your actions ... an eye for an eye, he said."

Clearly the Tallyman found out about Terry Brown's unfortunate passing, but how the hell did he know I was even there? Then I remember — my phone. The battery died not long after we arrived at The Black Horse, but it must have been on long enough for it to be tracked by Alex.

"This is really important, Gini. What else did he say?"

"He said I'd be next unless you keep your nose out of his business once and for all."

The reason Gini's anger is aimed in my direction now makes sense. What doesn't make sense is why the Tallyman targeted my friend, and not me. I can only assume news of Clement's presence has got back to him and he's chosen a softer target to make his point. This is now serious.

"Listen, Gini," I say, as calmly as I can. "It's for the best I don't tell you the specifics because I don't want to put you or Danny at further risk, but what I will tell you is I was investigating a story and it appears I've upset someone enough for them to warn me off. I can't tell you how sorry I am that you and Danny have been dragged into it."

"You're sorry?" she snaps. "I don't want your apologies, Emma — I want your full cooperation."

"My what?"

"I'm not going to let this Allen Tamthy get away with what he's done to my Danny so you're going to tell me everything. I'm going to ensure his face is plastered across the front page so everyone knows what he did."

"No, you're bloody-well not."

"You can't stop me."

"This isn't a game, Gini. That man is dangerous and you need to drop it. Understood?"

"What, like you would?"

Touché.

"I've already hit a brick wall and given up. There's nothing to

381

investigate."

"I don't believe you."

"You should, because I'm your friend, and I'm telling you: nothing good will come of this."

"So, you're not going to help me?"

"Gini, please, just leave it."

"Absolutely not. I'll give it twenty-four hours and if you don't share what you know about this man, I'll find out on my own."

"Gini, please ..."

"Twenty-four hours, Emma, and then I'm going to use every resource The Daily Standard has in order to track that bastard down."

"If you want me to beg ..."

She ends the call.

"Fuck! Fuck! Fuck!"

I throw my phone on the sofa and pad up and down the threadbare carpet. Gini might be young and naive but she's also one of the most dogged reporters on the payroll of The Daily Standard. It seems too much of my influence has rubbed off on her.

Clement wanders in with a towel wrapped around his waist.

"What's wrong? Why all the fucks?"

"We've got a problem."

"We're not out of milk again?"

"This is serious, Clement."

"Gimme a minute."

He leaves the room and returns fully dressed.

"So?"

"Sit down."

I join him on the sofa and relay what Gini told me. He doesn't appear to share my concern.

"What's the big deal? She ain't gonna get anywhere."

"Whether she does or doesn't is irrelevant. The fact she's even digging around will be enough to put her at risk."

"I reckon you're worrying about nothin', doll."

"You don't know Gini and, besides, she isn't thinking straight. This is too personal for her."

"Yeah, but the Tallyman and Clawthorn ain't our problem now, is it?"

I pause a fraction too long before attempting to answer, and Clement picks up on my hesitancy.

"I don't like that look on your face," he says with a scowl.

"I know we discussed walking away, but things have changed."

"Not for me they ain't."

"I think we should do what you first suggested."

"Which was?"

"We pay Alex a visit and drill some answers out of him."

"And, as you suggested, what if he don't have any answers?"

"We have to try."

"No, we don't."

I shuffle closer and take his hand.

"If we don't, and anything happens to Gini, I'll never forgive myself. No matter how remote it might be, there's still a chance to put this to bed, and I have to take it."

"Fucks sake, doll. Can't you just talk her out of it? She can forget about it, we can forget about it, and maybe we'll all live happily bleedin' after."

"How can I stop her, eh? Tell me, because I honestly don't know."

"I dunno. Want me to threaten her?"

"Don't be ridiculous."

"You're the one being ridiculous. This ain't our beef now, so why carry on? If some bird wants to waste her time chasing shadows then let her. You've told her the bloke is dangerous and she chose to ignore you. It's her problem, not ours."

"Fine," I snap, pulling my hand away. "It's not *our* problem now, but it is *mine*, and I'm going to talk to Alex — with or without you."

I snatch up my phone and storm through to the bedroom. A minute passes before a modicum of composure returns. I dial Alex's number.

"Alex Palmer," he answers.

"Hi, Alex. It's Emma."

"Oh, your name didn't come up on my screen."

"No, I lost my phone. This is my new number."

I can almost hear his brain ticking as it dawns on him he can no longer track me.

"Sorry to hear that," he replies.

Yeah, I bet you are.

"Anyway, I've had a think about the job, and I think I'm close to making a decision."

"Oh, really. And are you close to a yes, or a no?"

"More a yes, but I was hoping we could get together later just to iron out a few questions I've got."

"Ah, I'm pretty busy today so just email them over and I'll get back to you soon as I have chance."

"You can't even spare me half hour? I do owe you a drink or two after the other night."

"I'll see. Bear with me."

I hear the clicking of a mouse which goes on for an age.

"I definitely can't do during the day, but I might be able to do late afternoon or early evening."

"Perfect. What time?"

"That, I'm not sure of. I've got to be in Dorset at two and I have no idea how long I'll be there — could be thirty minutes but could be a couple of hours."

One small word containing just six letters but the significance is enough to spike my heart rate. Dorset is a large county, and there are probably scores of reasons why Alex is heading there this afternoon, but seeing as Terry Brown also made a trip to Dorset on Wednesday, it's perhaps more than just coincidence.

I keep quiet for fear of letting on I know anything about the potential significance of his trip.

"Tell you what," he continues. "I'll give you a call when I'm on my way back to London and we can set a time then. How does that sound?"

"I really appreciate it, Alex. Thank you."

I say a goodbye and end the call.

Taking a moment, I sit on the bed and consider the implications of what I've just learnt. A thought occurs, well, more a theory. I run it over and over in my head until I've covered every angle. Finally, I check if Alex's name is on the list of Clawthorn members. As I suspected, it's not, and the final piece of my theory slots into place. It feels sound, but a second opinion is required. Time to swallow my pride.

I find Clement on the sofa where I left him.

"Look, I know you don't want to pursue this, but I've just found out Alex Palmer is heading to Dorset this afternoon."

"So?"

"Bit of a coincidence don't you think? Terry went scurrying down to Dorset on Wednesday evening after I posted that picture online and, now Terry is dead, Alex is making the same journey."

"You don't know it's the same journey."

"No, granted, but there something else I want to run by you."

He breathes a heavy sigh. "Go on."

I sit down next to him. "What if — and this is a long shot — the Tallyman isn't a specific person, but a title."

"I'm not with you."

"Okay, we dismissed the possibility Alex might be the Tallyman because our man was involved in the Clawthorn Club from day one, before Alex was even born, right?"

"Yeah."

"But who's to say at some point, the title of Tallyman wasn't passed to Alex."

"Still not with you."

"You said the Tallyman was like a chairman, and in any organisation when the chairmen leaves, he's replaced. What if the original Tallyman retired, or died even — who would have taken over?"

"You're saying this Alex bloke was his replacement?"

"As I say: it's just a theory. We know Alex is up to his neck in it, yet his name doesn't appear in the notebook. Thinking about that, it stands to reason the Tallyman himself wouldn't give or receive favours because it would undermine his anonymity."

"Kinda makes sense, but you said the bloke was a drip."

"He is, but the more I think about it, the more I'm wondering if that's just a front to avoid suspicion."

"If it is, it worked."

"It did, and up until a few minutes ago there's no way I would have considered Alex to be our man. But now I'm thinking that property in Dorset is his base, and he summoned Terry after I posted my picture."

"So why'd he offer you a job?"

"Maybe it was to keep me in check. Perhaps he thought, if I'm working for him, I'll be too busy to worry about investigating Clawthorn, and he could also keep an eye on me."

It takes but four or five seconds for his hand to reach his moustache. The moment he administers the first stroke I know he's onside.

"Bloody hell," he eventually huffs. "What do you wanna do?"

"I want to go to that address in Dorset; the one Terry Brown visited."

"And do what?"

"Wait, and hope Alex turns up."

"And if he does?"

"Then I think we can safely say we've caught ourselves a Tallyman."

31.

Despite being treated to several rounds of bacon sandwiches at his favourite cafe Clement still doesn't appear too enthused by my plan. I'd have thought, despite the many ifs and buts, he'd want a final stab at unmasking the Tallyman but I'm not convinced his heart is really in it now. I don't blame him — this was never his battle to fight.

"You okay?" I ask, as we walk to the Tube station.

"I'm alright."

I don't believe him. His mood is greyer than the rain-filled clouds hanging above us.

"Listen, if this plan doesn't pan out, I promise I'll make a call to Gini and try to make her see sense. I have to do this, though — please don't hate me for trying to do the right thing."

"I don't hate you, doll. I'm just worried."

"You're worried we're wasting our time?"

"I'm worried we're *not* wasting our time."

"Eh? What do you mean?"

"The job will be done, and ... I don't know where we go from there."

I link my arm in his.

"We'll get on with our lives ... together. That's what you want isn't it?"

"Yeah."

"Well then. What's to worry about?"

He doesn't reply, and I don't want to push my luck by continuing the conversation. The fact he's agreed to help is more than I could, or should, expect.

Our destination is a car rental company in Hammersmith. It's not the nearest, but it is the cheapest. Unfortunately, my own car suffered irreparable damage in the fire as it was so close to the building, so a rental is the only option.

We arrive just before ten and it takes almost half-an-hour to complete the paperwork before I'm given the keys to a shitty Ford Fiesta with more miles on the clock than the average Airbus.

I enter the Dorset address into my phone and it plans our route — a journey of one hundred and twenty miles which will take two and a half hours. Clement isn't impressed.

"Kimmeridge" he grumbles, referring to the village we're heading to. "Never heard of the bleedin' place."

"I know, but it makes sense. I looked at the property online and it's tucked-away in a remote spot, right on the coast and no neighbours within a mile. It's exactly the kind of property you'd own if privacy was important."

"You're convinced it's the Tallyman's lair, ain't you?"

"Not convinced, but I've always trusted my gut and it's telling me Alex Palmer is our man."

The slight roll of his eyes suggests we're not working off the same script.

"You don't think he is?" I ask.

"Dunno."

"I trust your judgement, Clement, so come on — what's your gut telling you?"

"My gut ain't tellin' me anythin', doll. That nigglin' voice in my head is, though."

"And, what's it saying?"

"When I work that out, I'll let you know."

He then settles back and closes his eyes. It seems conversation will be in short supply on this journey.

With Clement either deep in thought or snoozing, I navigate our awful car through the central London traffic towards the motorway. It's a relief when the green road signs finally give way to blue, and I can focus on my own thoughts.

My mind drifts back to the time I worked in the same newsroom as Alex as I try to pinpoint any signs of wayward behaviour. My overriding memory is one of an incompetent journalist who did the industry a favour when he left. It wasn't that Alex was a fool, but he simply didn't have the right tools for the profession. I do remember how frustrated Eric used to get with him. They had numerous fall-outs because Alex hadn't followed his advice, or thought he knew better. Eric was a patient man but even he eventually grew weary of Alex's cavalier approach to the job. I don't think they parted on the best of terms and, in hindsight, I do wonder why Alex even bothered attending Eric's funeral. Maybe he did so to make a point; that he had proven Eric wrong and become the head of an organisation wielding real power and influence. A final chance for Alex to stick his finger up at my old mentor.

As we cross the Hampshire border my thoughts turn to Gini, and her brief encounter with the Tallyman, or Alex, if my theory is correct. I replay our conversation in my head, and offer silent thanks to a God that doesn't exist — unlike my poor mother, at least Danny didn't die at the hands of a hit-and-run driver. Perhaps if Gini knew what I'd suffered she might not have the same appetite for vengeance. Danny's injuries will heal — mine never will. If this trip to Dorset proves futile, maybe that will be my best bet to defuse Gini. I only hope she doesn't receive any further phone calls from a certain Mr Tamthy before I get that chance.

I'm about to overtake a lorry but a distraction occurs; my last thought refuses to leave. It stays firmly put, and plays on my mind long enough for me to consider why it's so reluctant to leave. And then, the reason becomes clear.

"Holy shit."

I nudge Clement's arm.

"Clement! Wake up."

He blinks into consciousness and squints at me. "What?"

"The Tallyman," I blurt. "He called Gini."

"I know. You told me."

"She's heard his voice."

"So what? How does that help us?"

"Directly, it doesn't."

"Triffic. I'm going back to sleep."

"No, you're missing the point. I only ever received emails and text messages from the Tallyman, so why did he call Gini when he never once called me?"

"I dunno."

"I'll tell you why, shall I?"

"You're gonna anyway."

"It's because," I declare, ignoring his indifferent tone. "He couldn't call me because I'd immediately recognise his voice. And that's another reason why I'm convinced it's Alex."

Clement scratches his head. "He never worked with this Gini bird?"

"Nope. It's well over ten years since Alex quit journalism and Gini only started four years ago. They've never met so there's no way she'd have recognised his voice. That explains why he had no issue calling her."

"Alright, it's a fair point."

"It's more than fair. It's highly relevant."

"We'll see. How much longer?"

"About an hour."

"Let me know when we're ten minutes away."

He closes his eyes again and I'm left to continue the conversation in my head. I have to admit I'm a tad disappointed he doesn't share my conviction, but seeing as he didn't want to pursue this lead in the first place, I'm not overly surprised.

I increase my speed a little and focus on the road ahead —
figuratively and literally.

Perhaps I'm joining up the dots to fit my own narrative but, with
every passing mile, I become more convinced Alex Palmer is, or was,
the man who controlled the Clawthorn Club. The only question I
can't answer is how he secured that position. It sure as hell couldn't
have been on the back of his journalism career, and the timing
suggests it must have happened soon after he left our newsroom, as
the Clawthorn Club was disbanded soon after. Perhaps that's why he
was brought in — a younger man with the right skills to eradicate
any digital information pertaining to Clawthorn. It would explain the
lack of any online references to the name.

It's a theory.

After a couple of fraught-filled delays due to heavy traffic, we
finally leave the motorway and continue along an A-road, and then a
B-road, as we close in on our destination.

The county of Dorset happens to be one I'd earmarked as a
potential location for my rural retreat when the time comes. Home to
swathes of glorious countryside, a dramatic coastline, and dozens of
quaint little villages, it's a shame the sombre weather doesn't do it
justice today.

I give Clement another nudge.

"Oi, sleepyhead. We're nearly there."

He stirs in his seat and yawns.

"Remind me never to take you on a road trip," I chuckle. "Nice nap was it?"

"Yeah, sorry. Your fault, though."

"My fault?"

"I'm bleedin' knackered after last night."

"I don't recall you complaining at the time. We'll have to work on your stamina."

For the first time since we left the flat he finds a smile.

"That's better. And just to cheer you up even more, we're only a mile away."

The smile disappears as quickly as it arrived.

"What's the plan then?" he asks.

"I checked the house on Google Street View and …"

"Google what?"

"Oh, it's an online tool. It allows you to virtually view any road or street in the country from a three-hundred-and-sixty-degree perspective."

"None the wiser."

"It's like being able to stand outside a house and look around."

"How the fuck does that work?"

"Do you really want me to explain?"

His frown says it all.

"Anyway," I continue. "The house is situated on a single-track lane so we can't exactly park up outside. It's also got a gated driveway so that's not an option either."

"So how are we supposed to know when mystery dickhead arrives ... if he arrives?"

"I spotted a lay-by about four hundred yards beyond the house. We'll park there."

"That don't answer my question, doll."

"I'm getting to that. There's a wooded area flanking one side of the house. If we walk back up the lane, we can hop over the fence and make our way to the boundary without fear of being spotted."

His frown returns.

"You don't think it's a good idea?" I ask.

"The idea is sound but I ain't a fan of traipsing through the bleedin' countryside."

"It's hardly a traipse. It's a few hundred yards at most."

"Better not be any cows around. Don't trust the shady fuckers."

"You're quite happy to eat them, though."

"When they're dead, yeah."

I shake my head. "I can't believe we're potentially about to expose one of the stories of the century and all you're worried about is a few Friesians."

We reach the final stretch of road before our destination. I turn into the lane and continue in third gear, barely hitting twenty. With open fields to both sides — bordered by a post and rail fence — there's nothing to see but acres of menacing sky, and the odd tree.

As the lane continues the fence is replaced by hedgerow before we hit a sharp bend. Beyond that bend, some two hundred yards away to our left, the roofline of a house pokes above a thicket of leafless trees.

"That's it," I remark, nodding in the general direction of the house.

I speed up a little to avoid looking suspicious as we pass our target. We get to see it close-up for a few seconds, and it looks almost exactly as I remember it from the online imagery. The roadside boundary is formed from a tall, overgrown hedge with a driveway just off-centre, protected by solid wooden gates. Beyond the hedge densely planted trees obscure the view of the house beyond. There's the odd flash of white-painted brickwork as we pass but even at this time of year, Mother Nature has provided an effective barrier to shield the house from the prying eyes of anyone passing. The view to our right isn't much clearer; a wild copse of silver birch and rowan trees hemming the lane in.

I turn back to the left just as the hedgerow ends. There is nothing to see but a continuation of the post-and-rail fence, and the wooded area I identified as our point of access.

Four hundred yards on we reach the lay-by. I pull over, switch the engine off, and take a quick glance at the dashboard clock.

"Twenty minutes," I announce.

"Until?"

"Two o'clock — the time Alex said he had to be somewhere."

"'Spose we'd better make a move then."

We exit the car and make our way back along the lane. Apart

from the rustling of the trees and the occasional cry of a gull, it's eerily quiet.

"Don't like it," he mumbles.

"You don't like what?"

"The ... nothingness."

"I know what you mean. Living in London you get used to being surrounded by noise."

"Not what I meant."

"Eh?"

"Nothin'. Forget it."

We reach the edge of the wooded area and, after a quick and pointless scan to ensure we're not being watched, we clamber over the fence.

"We should head a bit further in," I say in a low voice. "Just in case a car passes and we're spotted."

"Don't reckon there's much chance of that."

"Specifically, Alex's car."

"Right."

It soon becomes clear we're the first humans to walk through the wood in many a year. There's no path so we're forced to tread a virgin trail across the soft, mulchy ground. Thirty yards in I turn around.

"This should do us. Now we just head in a straight line towards the house."

Clement sniffs the air; thick with the scent of the sea, mixed with the stench of damp, rotting vegetation. He shoots a look of disapproval in my direction. Clearly we're a long way from his concrete comfort zone.

I don't wait for him to complain. Turning ninety degrees I begin the final leg of our journey.

Unlike Clement, I'm not concerned about our rural environment, more the pronounced thumping of my heart as we edge ever closer to the house. Somewhere in amongst the nerves and the anticipation I can sense the buzz trying to break through. However, this is now far more than just a potential front page story — too much at stake, too much invested, and all of it too personal. From the reopening of old wounds while investigating my father, through to losing everything in the fire, I'll soon know whether my sacrifices were warranted, or in vain.

I catch a flash of white-painted brickwork through the trees, and stop. Clement draws up next to me as I point at my discovery.

"There's the house," I whisper.

"Can't see shit. We need to get closer."

I nod and we move stealthily onwards, mindful of stepping on a fallen twig and announcing our arrival.

As the trees thin out, we're fortunate the foliage becomes denser, although Clement is forced to stoop as more of the house comes into view. We get within twenty yards and stop again as suitable cover becomes a pressing issue.

I nod towards a sprawling holly bush just off to the left of our position. It's about the same size as a small car and appears to offer both cover, and a reasonable vantage point to watch the front of the house.

Taking the lead I creep over to the bush and squat down.

"What's the time?" Clement whispers, as he squats down beside me.

"One fifty-two."

I shuffle a few feet to my left to gain a better view. From my new position I have clear sight of the flank wall of the house and gravel parking area which occupies much of the space to the front. I can just about see the driveway curving away but the gates beyond are out of view. The house itself, from what I can see, is pretty featureless. I'd guess it was a former farmhouse; built for function rather than architectural merit. The external walls may have been whitewashed to brighten the austere brickwork, but there's no disguising its cheerless appearance, not improved by the backdrop of blackening clouds and spindly trees.

I check my watch again — one fifty-five.

Long seconds tick by and, for the first time since we left London, doubts begin to creep in. I turn to Clement.

"Tell me this isn't as crazy an idea as it currently feels."

"We're hiding behind a bush, in a woods, in the middle of bleedin' nowhere, waiting for a bloke who could be in Bournemouth, or Weymouth, or any other town in Dorset. Ask me again in about twenty minutes."

Put like that it does feel too close to crazy.

"I suppose we'll know soon enough."

I hear the sound of a car somewhere on the lane.

"Listen," I hiss.

It gets louder, peaks, and then ebbs away.

"Sorry. False alarm."

Another check of my watch and the minute hand is now almost vertical. I take solace knowing Alex never was the punctual type.

If the discomfort of squatting down wasn't bad enough, the clouds decide to unburden themselves and fat raindrops begin pattering the ground around us.

"Bleedin' great," Clement grumbles. "We're gonna get soaked."

"Stop moaning."

"Least your coat looks waterproof."

"But my jeans aren't, and these trainers certainly aren't. And besides, you choose to wear that bloody waistcoat every day."

He sulks for a moment before finding something else to complain about.

"I could murder a fag."

"You had one when you got out of the car."

"Yeah, twenty minutes ago."

I'm about to launch into a lengthy, if not hypocritical, sermon about the dangers of smoking when a faint sound catches my attention – the rasp of an exhaust.

"Listen."

It grows louder, throatier, and then drops to almost a burbling rumble. Clearly emanating from the lane the car appears to have stopped outside the house. I continue to listen as the engine is revved twice followed by the sound of tyres crunching slowly over gravel.

A car comes into view — a black Jaguar Coupé. The registration plate confirms it rolled off the production line this year.

"Nice motor," Clement whispers.

The car comes to a stop a dozen steps from the front of the house, and the engine falls silent. With the front end pointing away from us, and the rear window barely a slit, Jeremy Clarkson could be behind the wheel for all I can tell.

Barely daring to breathe, I stare at the car, transfixed, waiting for the driver's door to open.

Tortuous seconds pass until, at last, I hear the clunk of the door mechanism and it slowly opens. First, a leg appears — suit trousers and polished black shoes the attire of choice. For some reason the rest of him doesn't follow. I want to scream at the occupant to get the fuck out but he's taking his time — maybe checking a message on his phone or savouring the opulence of the hand-finished interior a few seconds longer.

My irritation nears boiling point.

And then finally he emerges from the car with his back to us. I don't need him to turn around — I've seen enough to recognise the driver.

32

I just about manage to stop myself from whooping and punching the air. Instead, I grin at Clement like a mad woman and repeatedly mouth the same two words — it's Alex.

My attention is then split between gauging Clement's reaction and watching Alex Palmer plod towards the front door of the house. Within seconds, he disappears from view and a door slams shut. With Alex out of earshot, I can finally speak.

"I fucking knew it was him," I squeak excitedly. "My gut is rarely wrong."

"What do you wanna do now then?"

"Simple — we go and confront him."

"You're just gonna knock on the door and accuse him of being the Tallyman?"

"More or less, yes."

"And what if he denies it, and slams the door in your face?"

"If he does, I have a secret weapon — I have a Clement."

"Meaning?"

"I'm sure you can force the door open and we can then conduct one of your special interviews."

"Yeah, we could, but then what? A confession ain't much good without evidence."

"This house has been visited by both men we know to be involved in the Clawthorn Club. When you consider it's located in the middle of nowhere, and it's registered to an untraceable overseas company, it has to be the most likely place to find evidence."

"Maybe."

"Only one way to find out."

"I ain't sure, doll. You really wanna do this?"

"As opposed to what? Heading back to London and sitting on our hands?"

"No, but ... I dunno. Somethin' don't feel right."

"You need to be more specific."

He squeezes his eyes shut for a few seconds as if trying to dredge his mind for a lost memory. I wait patiently for a reply as droplets of cold rainwater begin trickling beyond my collar triggering an inadvertent shudder.

"I'm getting cold," I chatter. "Can we make a decision?"

He opens his eyes. "Alright," he sighs. "We'll do it your way."

I give him a peck on the cheek before standing upright — much to the relief of my aching back and thighs. I need to act quickly before he changes his mind so I step beyond the hedge and usher Clement to follow.

We leave the cover of the undergrowth and it then becomes clear why the homeowner chose to dump several tons of gravel at the front of the hideaway — it's like walking across a blanket of Cornflakes, and a silent approach is near-impossible.

With stealth no longer an option I decide haste is more important and jog up to the front door. I turn and wait for Clement to catch up but he's in less of a hurry.

And then, behind me, I hear the door open.

I spin around.

"Hello, Emma," Alex says flatly.

I'm immediately struck by his calm demeanour, considering we weren't expected. That, and his odd stance; feet slightly apart and both hands tucked behind his back like a sentry on duty.

I hadn't considered what we might do if Alex casually opened the door and said hello. My muddled brain can't work quickly enough to compute a revised strategy.

As it is Alex makes the first move.

As Clement crunches up behind me, Alex removes his hands from behind his back. With no great sense of urgency he raises his arms out in front of him. In each hand he's holding what looks like a black and yellow power drill. For some inexplicable reason, one of the drills is pointed towards me, and one over my right shoulder in Clement's direction.

I hear the sound of gravel crunching behind me but then, a millisecond later ... pain. So. Much. Pain.

The only muscles I'm able to control are those behind my eyes, and they allow me to view the two wired prongs embedded in my chest. Too late now, but I realise I wasn't being threatened by a power drill, but a Taser.

I collapse to the gravel — I'm not alone. I send a message to my arm, to reach out towards Clement's prone body, but it doesn't arrive. My legs fare no better. Every nerve in my body burns but none of them appear capable of transmitting instructions. I now know what complete paralysis feels like.

Next comes a fear unlike any I've ever felt before — the fear that comes with being completely and utterly helpless. I watch on in horror as Alex kneels down next to Clement, extracts a syringe from his pocket, and jabs it into Clement's arm. My saviour isn't able to save himself — he groans, but then ... nothing.

Alex then pulls out a second syringe and turns to me. I try to speak, but there are no words and even less ability to say them.

"You never did know when to give up," he says, wearily. "Which is why I'm not really surprised you followed me here. Well done, though — I had no idea."

It would be a minor victory but I can't even tell him he's wrong.

He jabs the second syringe into my arm.

"Best you and your boyfriend have a nap while I work out what to do with you."

My head lops to the side and I'm greeted with a panoramic view of a dark sky. It grows darker by the second, until ...

33.

So much of so much.

My mind swims with confused thoughts. What happened? Where am I?

I try to create order but the ... the pain. It arrives from different destinations: my skull, behind my eyes, my shoulders, my chest ... and my wrists. And I'm cold ... so fucking cold.

My mouth is dry but I can taste blood. There's something else, too. Is it a taste, or a smell? I sniff: wood ... damp wood, and a musty odour like old sackcloth.

I dare to open my eyes.

My pupils are dryer than my mouth. I blink several times.

I'm on the floor, on my backside. I hadn't even realised, but now I see my legs stretching out in front of me. I move my head but a splintering pain quickly puts paid to that. The pain of moving my gritty eyes isn't as nauseating, and I look up to find a single window thick with grime and cobwebs. There's nothing to see but a rectangle of patchy shapes in various shades of grey.

I roll my eyes to the left. Walls constructed of wooden slats, and a door with a rusting metal handle. Piecing together what little I know I conclude I'm in some kind of dilapidated wooden structure. A shed possibly?

I roll my eyes to the right. Relief washes over me at the sight of a pair of battered Chelsea boots poking out of bell-bottomed jeans.

"Clement," I wheeze. "Can you hear me?"

No response. I turn my head and grimace at the resulting pain. Closing my eyes I wait for it to ebb away. I open them to a view of Clement, slumped against the slatted wall, clearly out for the count.

I need him conscious but, if I'm to rouse him, I need to get up and cover the six feet of space between us.

Every part of me hurts, and I know the pain is going to get a lot worse if I move. I have no choice — no matter how much it hurts, I need to get up.

My brain tells my arm to move so I can push myself off the floor. The message is sent, and received, but all I get for my efforts is a searing pain in my wrist. I try the other arm and it results in more pain. For some reason I can't move my arms but I'm sure it's not a result of being tasered. I try to cuss, but a jarring realisation steals my breath — my wrists are bound together.

Waves of fear, and pain, and helplessness crash over me in quick succession. Relentless, they pummel my mind to the point no other thoughts can form. No matter how hard I try to resist, the tears brew as the lump dances and my lip bobs.

Squeezing my eyes shut I let my head fall slowly forward as my chest begins to heave.

"Don't ... you ... dare ..."

With no thought to the consequences I open my eyes and simultaneously snap my head to the right. I almost puke it hurts so much, but I don't care.

"Thank God," I blubber.

"Don't bother," Clement rasps. "He ain't listening."

"Are you okay?"

He rolls his head left and right a couple of times wincing in the process.

"Yeah, bleedin' triffic."

Never has his sarcasm sounded sweeter.

"What the fuck happened?" he asks.

"Alex tasered us."

"He did what?"

"We were shot with a Taser — kind of a stun gun that causes temporary paralysis."

"How temporary? Feels like I've been out of it for hours."

"He injected you … he injected us with something. I'd guess a sedative of some kind."

"I ain't feelin' so sedate, doll more like I've been run over by a steamroller."

"You and me both."

"Don't suppose you know where we are?"

"I don't, or how we got here."

"Well, I'm guessin' he slung you over his shoulder but fuck knows how I got here. No way that podgy little tosser carried me."

"To be honest, Clement, that's not really our biggest concern at the moment. Whatever Alex is planning for us I'd rather not be here once he's decided."

"I'm with you there."

He then tries to move and discovers the same issue I encountered.

"My hands are tied."

It's a term I've heard a hundred times; usually uttered by a jobsworth at the local council whenever I dare to make a complaint. This time, it's literal.

"Mine are tied too."

"Fucks sake."

He slumps back against the wooden slats. If his hands weren't tied, I'm almost certain they'd be reaching for the moustache. With nothing to offer myself I give him a moment to think.

He sits forward again.

"I need you to stick your hand in my boot."

"Please don't tell me you've got some kind of foot fetish. Now is not the time, and it certainly isn't the place."

"Nah, but I do have a knife fetish."

"Eh?"

"That dipshit's knife — I tucked it in my boot."

"Did you? Why?"

"Cos I told you I had a bad feeling about this whole caper. You might have been right about that Alex bloke but I was right about something being a bit moody."

"If I could, I'd kiss you, Clement."

"Yeah, let's get the fuck out of here and then you can kiss me all you like."

"Deal. What do you want me to do?"

"Try and shuffle on your arse so your hands are facin' me. I'll twist around and raise my boot so it's close enough for you to get your fingers into it."

"And then what?"

"Grab the knife, flick the blade out, and just hold it still. I'll then back up to you and run these bastard ties across the blade. A couple of cuts and they should be weak enough for me to snap."

I almost find a smile, and begin my shuffle. I've barely lifted my left buttock when a heavy clunk penetrates the wooden door. It sounds an awful lot like a lock being unbolted.

"Move back," Clement hisses. "Company."

I lean back against the slatted wall and attempt to find some composure.

The door creaks open and tepid light leaks in, closely followed by the chubby frame of Alex Palmer. He stands in the doorway and waits for his eyes to adjust to the gloom of our temporary prison.

There are a million things I want to say to him — none of them nice — and I can't help myself.

"What the fuck are you playing at, Alex?"

Now sporting a dark-green wax jacket and Wellington boots, he glares down at me. Sensibly, he keeps his distance.

"I'm not *playing* at anything. Quite the opposite."

"You've got precisely ten seconds to cut these ties and let us go, or ..."

"Or what?" he spits. "I don't think you're in any position to make demands."

It pains me to concede he's right.

"What do you want?"

"That's a good question, Emma. I'll tell you what I *did* want, and that was for you to keep your nose out of matters which didn't concern you. I gave you so many chances to walk away. Christ, I even offered you a job. But, here we are, so now it's no longer a case of what I want."

"What is it then?"

"It's a case of what needs to be done."

He dips a hand into his coat pocket and withdraws what could never be mistaken for a power drill.

"Get up," he orders, pointing a pistol loosely in my direction. It's amazing how you can go through life and never set eyes on a firearm — well, in the UK at least — yet I've now been threatened with a pistol twice in as many days. This really isn't my week.

I turn my head towards Clement hoping he might telepathically offer a solution to our predicament. Judging by the look of concentration on his face and protruding veins in his neck, I'd guess he's preoccupied trying to snap the ties around his wrists.

"I said, get up."

I turn back to Alex.

"Or what? Are you going to shoot me?"

"You don't think I will?"

"I think, Alex, you're a pitiful, pathetic, excuse of a man who doesn't possess the balls he was born with."

He squats down so we share the same eye-line.

"Funny that," he sneers. "Because your little friend, Gini Varma, said something similar on the phone last night. You've created quite the clone of yourself there, Emma."

"This has nothing to do with Gini."

"Like that notebook had nothing to do with you, or your father for that matter."

"Are you going to tell me why he had it?"

"It's not important now. The notebook is gone."

"The final piece of evidence relating to the Clawthorn Club."

"Whatever," he snorts, dismissively.

"Come on, Alex — you might as well tell me now. How did you get involved?"

"That's not how this works, Emma. This isn't a Bond movie so I'm afraid you'll never know."

"I know you're the Tallyman."

No confirmation; just a shake of the head and a smirk.

Switching his attention to Clement, he calls across. "How are you getting on there, Lurch? I wouldn't bother if I were you — those cable ties are virtually indestructible."

"Go fuck yourself."

"No, you're okay, thanks. However, Emma here ..."

Clement's body visibly stiffens, and if looks could kill, Alex Palmer would already be heading to the morgue.

"Don't worry," Alex adds. "I don't do sloppy seconds."

My glare is wasted as he checks his watch.

"As lovely as this chat is we need to go. Get up."

"We're going nowhere."

"Yes, Emma, you are. If you don't, your friend Gini will be joining her fiancé in the hospital, although I suspect she'll be occupying a bed in intensive care."

"You're bluffing."

"Am I? Do you want to take that risk? It just takes one call, and the same man who ran her fiancé down will visit her flat in Shoreditch this evening ... when she's tucked up in bed and all alone."

I know Alex well enough to tell when he's lying, and I don't think he is on this occasion.

"Last chance. Get up."

I move first and struggle like a grounded walrus as I try to get to my feet without using my hands. Clement makes it look a damn sight easier despite having considerably more bulk to shift.

Alex steps backwards through the door, keeping the pistol trained on me. Never has a man looked less suited to brandishing a firearm; like a ten year-old boy playing cowboys and Indians.

"Try anything, Lurch," he warns Clement. "And she'll get the first bullet."

I take the lead and step through the door. Ordinarily, I like a bracing sea breeze — nothing like it to blow away the cobwebs — but, in this instance, the blast of frigid air summons a shudder. It might be approaching dusk but it feels end-of-days dark, with ominous clouds barrelling across the grey sky.

Glancing around I try to get some sense of where we are. There's not a lot to see. Our wooden prison is nothing more than a garden shed, located halfway down a wide lawn, bordered on both sides by a hedge at least a couple of feet taller than me. Looking back up the garden I can see what I presume is the rear of the whitewashed house. At the far end of the garden, some fifty yards away, the lawn abruptly stops and the sky begins.

I turn back to the shed door expecting Clement to stoop through any second. I can't see in, but Alex can, and whatever he can see, clearly it's not a welcome sight.

"Get up," he yells. "Now."

The pistol might be loosely aimed in my direction but Alex's attention is fixed inside the shed. I take a few steps to my right so I can see what's going on. It's possibly the last thing I expected to see.

Clement is back on the floor but this time on his knees with his head bowed forward, as if in prayer. Alex looks as confused as I do.

"I'm warning you," he barks. "Get the hell up."

His order is ignored.

"My heart exults in the Lord," Clement murmurs. "My horn is exalted in the Lord."

Shit. He actually is praying.

"My mouth derides my enemies," he continues. "Because I rejoice in your salvation."

Alex turns to me. "Tell him to get up."

"What? You're the one with the gun — you tell him."

He repeats his order, but Clement keeps his head bowed and continues the prayer.

Alex never was a decisive man, and faced with Clement's refusal to leave the shed, he appears to be caught in two minds. In fairness, so am I. I'm wondering if this isn't a ruse to distract Alex so I can make a run for it. Even if I were able to run the fifty yards to the house, and avoid being shot, where the hell do I go? There are no other houses for at least a mile, and even if Alex was stupid enough to leave my phone in my coat pocket, I can't get at it. No amount of praying is likely to help if that's what Clement expects me to do.

But why else would he choose this moment to pray?

The seconds tick by and the prayer continues. Alex's patience is clearly at breaking point and he orders me to get down on my knees. Slowly, and reluctantly, I comply.

"I'll give you five seconds," he yells at Clement. "Then I shoot her in the head."

The prayer continues.

"Five," Alex snaps.

"There is none holy like the Lord."

"Four."

"For there is none besides you."

"Three."

"There is no rock like our God."

"Two."

Clement looks up and glares at Alex.

"I'm coming," he sighs.

The relief on Alex's face is obvious as he watches Clement slowly get to his feet. Taking a few steps back, he keeps the pistol trained on me as Clement shuffles out of the shed and comes to a halt just outside the door.

"Seems God didn't listen," Alex sneers, his confidence returned having salvaged the situation.

Clement takes a step forward, reducing the space between them to maybe ten feet.

"Maybe. Maybe not," he replies. "But if I were in your shoes, I'd be scared shitless."

"Of God?"

"Nah," Clement replies, taking another step forward. "Of me."

Sensing the big man might be getting too close for comfort Alex swings the pistol towards Clement who responds by looking up to the sky. Instinctively, Alex's eyes follow, and for a second both men are staring up at the dark clouds. One of them blinks first.

Clement's right arm suddenly snaps forward like a whip. There's precious little time for my eyes to catch up let alone for Alex to react. Before either of us can begin to process what just happened, it's too late for one of us.

Alex's right arm drops to his side like a piece of wet string the pistol slipping from his grip. As his face contorts in pain, he looks down and his eyes widen when he realises the full gravity of the situation. Protruding from his jacket — dangerously close to his heart — is a knife handle.

His legs buckle and he collapses to the ground. Even if my hands weren't tied, there is no first aid I could administer to save him. I now realise Clement was only buying time with his prayers; an ideal opportunity to remove the knife from his boot and cut his ties. I should have known, and now it's too late.

Two days. Two men, dead.

This time, however, the man I shared a bed with last night is responsible.

"What the fuck?" I scream at Clement. "Why did you do that?"

"It was him or us, doll," he shrugs, helping me to my feet.

"But ... you didn't have to kill him."

"I didn't kill him. I threw a knife his way and the rest was just bad luck."

He then steps across to Alex's corpse and casually extracts the blade from his chest. A quick wipe on the dead man's jacket before using the murder weapon to cut my hands free.

Ignoring the pain in my arms, I scamper over and squat down to check if, as I fear, Alex really is dead. I try to find a pulse, and listen for breathing, but find neither.

"This isn't what I wanted," I cry.

"People die. Sometimes they deserve it."

I look up at him. "How can you be so cold? He's dead for Christ's sake."

"What do you want me to say? Sorry for throwing a knife at a bloke who was about to shoot us?"

"He wouldn't have shot us."

"You know that do you?"

Whatever Alex was guilty of he didn't deserve to die. Neither, I suppose, did Terry Brown. Yet, both men are dead and, indirectly, some of the blame for their premature deaths rests on my shoulders because I wouldn't back down. From the moment I pulled into that car park at the stables in Surrey, I set off a chain of events which delivered us here. If I'd only driven on by, I'd never have known Clement existed. And if I'd never met Clement, Jaydon would have stolen my handbag and phone, and I'd have been none the wiser about the Clawthorn Club. I wouldn't currently be stood in a windswept garden in Dorset, and Terry Brown and Alex Palmer would both still be alive.

We are both culpable for their deaths, but one of us more than the other.

"What is it with you and death, Clement?"

"Huh?"

"That poor woman at the stables in Surrey — she also died with a knife sticking out of her chest, didn't she?"

"She was a fucking nutjob and died because of it. I didn't kill her."

"Just a coincidence then?"

"They happen."

"They do when you're around apparently."

"What you sayin'?"

The bliss I awoke to this morning now feels tainted. And the man who created that bliss isn't perhaps the man I thought he was.

"You didn't have to kill Alex," I murmur, repeating myself.

"I ain't gonna stand here freezin' my bollocks off if we're just gonna go round in circles. The bloke is dead, and if you want me to be honest, I'm glad, cos it means I ain't going nowhere."

"What?"

"Nothin'."

"Don't ignore my question. What do you mean by that?"

"It don't matter. It's over, and we can get on with our lives."

I wave my hand towards Alex's corpse.

"Do you honestly think we can just move on and pretend nothing happened ... after this?"

"Why not?"

His complete lack of contrition troubles me. It doesn't, however, surprise me — we are from very different worlds. Naively, rather than being concerned about his casual propensity for violence, I romanticised it. I felt safe in his company and savoured the thrill of his devil-may-care attitude. Fuck, I even encouraged him, while ignoring his warnings about what I was getting myself into.

There's as much of Alex's blood on my hands as Clement's.

"This is a nightmare. I wish to God I'd never heard of the fucking Clawthorn Club."

Clement steps towards me but wisely thinks twice about putting an arm around my shoulder.

"Listen, doll," he says. "You've gotta remember who the bad guys are here. I told you, right at the beginning, that we were dealing with some dangerous people. You can't blame yourself for any of this — it was always us or them, and they lost."

"But I ... I didn't think people would die."

He risks putting his hand on my arm.

"You look frozen, and you're probably sufferin' from shock. Let's get you up to the house, and we'll work out what we're gonna do."

I don't want him to be nice to me — there's enough conflict raging in my head as it is. Part of me wants to run back to the car and drive as fast as I can back to London. Another part of me wants to scream at Clement for putting me in this situation.

"We can have a nose around while we're there," he adds. "Weren't that the whole point of comin' down here?"

"I don't know. It feels so ... unimportant now."

"Give it a few days and you won't feel like that."

"Won't I?"

"Nah, you won't. You'll wish you'd taken the chance to find some evidence of what those fuckers did over the years. And if you don't do

421

it doll, someone else will."

A few droplets of icy rain sting my already-raw cheeks. It's encouragement enough to make a decision.

"Okay," I sigh. "But what about Alex?"

Clement looks down at the lifeless body. "Don't think he's goin' anywhere."

34.

As we walk up the lawn towards the house, I weigh up our options.

"Do you think we should call the police?"

"No, I bleedin' don't."

"Why not?"

"I've told you: I don't trust 'em. And there's a dead bloke in the garden which is gonna take some explaining. We'll spend the next six months being interrogated until they find somethin' to pin on us."

"So, what? We just look around the house and then drive back to London?"

"Yeah. If you do find anythin', you can still write your story but nobody needs to know where you got the evidence. Who's gonna know we were even here?"

"Well, no one, but I'm not so sure I want to write the story now."

"Are you shittin' me? That was the whole point of this weren't it?"

"Yes, but that was before ... before people died."

I know journalists aren't necessarily renowned for their high moral values, but the thought of profiting, both financially and career-wise, from the death of two men doesn't sit right.

"And what about all the people who've suffered cos of the Clawthorn Club? What about that Stacey bird — don't she deserve to know the truth about how her old man died?"

"I suppose."

"Doll, listen: we did the right thing, and yeah, a couple of wrong'uns died along the way, but sometimes bad shit happens to bad people — they knew the risks."

"And what about you, Clement? Are you bad?"

"That ain't for me to judge."

"Who then, if not you?"

We reach the end of the lawn and he points to a set of patio doors at the back of the house.

"We'll try gettin' in there," he remarks, leaving my question unanswered.

I don't have the energy to push, and plod wearily after him as he stomps across the patio slabs.

It's no surprise when Clement tugs at the handle and the door slides open. Notwithstanding the homeowner owning a pistol, rural communities tend to be less concerned about opportunistic burglars.

He beckons me in and slides the door shut. The silence and warmth are both welcome, although I'm still not sure how I feel about nosing around a dead man's house. I'd voice my concerns but Clement will only say Alex is unlikely to complain.

We're stood in a modest-sized kitchen fitted with dated pine units. It is unremarkable in every way, and if there is any evidence of the Clawthorn Club in the house, it's unlikely to be amongst the cereal packets and dried pasta. Nevertheless, Clement opens the fridge and has a quick nose before reaching in and extracting a plate containing a sausage roll. One bite and half of the sausage roll is no more.

I glare at him.

"What? I ain't eaten since breakfast."

Ten minutes ago he was extracting a knife from the chest of a dead man, and now he's casually munching on that dead man's evening snack.

"Waste not, want not," he adds, popping the other half into his mouth.

I roll my eyes and nod towards the only door. A thought occurs.

"Shit," I hiss. "What if there's someone else in the house?"

"Like who?"

"I don't know — what about whoever Alex was supposed to meet at two o'clock? And there's no way he could have moved you to the shed without assistance so someone else must have been here at some point."

"Where are they now then? Why aren't they in here trying to stop us nosing around?"

It's a valid question, and one I can't answer.

"Maybe there was someone here and they left. Think about it, doll — why didn't they come outside and help matey deal with us in the shed? It would have been a damn sight less risky if someone else was there to cover his back."

Perhaps he's right. You only have to look at Clement to know what a threat he poses, and even armed it would have been a reckless decision dealing with him alone unless there was no other choice. Ultimately, the point is made by the fact Alex is now dead and we're not.

"I guess so."

"The Tallyman is gone," he adds. "Let's just find what we came here for and be on our way."

"Alright," I concede. "Just be careful."

Clement closes the fridge and beckons me to follow him through the kitchen door.

We enter a hallway with the front door at the far end and three other doors: all shut. My sodden trainers squeak on the parquet flooring as I take a few tentative steps forward. Alex wasn't exactly known for his love of contemporary interior design, but the floral wallpaper and bland prints of rural scenes make the space feel particularly jaded, old-fashioned even.

Clement opens the first door which turns out to be a cloakroom.

We continue up the hallway towards the front door. Reaching the end, we have three options: one of the two doors opposite each other, or the stairs up to the first floor. I suppose there is a fourth option in that we could open the front door and leave, but no matter how dreadful this afternoon has been, I've nudged my own curiosity awake now.

Clement opens the door on my right and a waft of warm air escapes what is clearly the lounge. Again, the furnishings are dated but the open fireplace, thick carpet, and soft lighting from a standard lamp provide a cosy feel. Memories of wintry afternoons spent at my nan's old bungalow flood back.

"Nothing like a real fire," Clement comments. "Don't see 'em so much these days."

The glowing embers suggest Alex was enjoying a roaring fire earlier as we froze to death in the shed. My pity for his untimely demise wanes a touch.

Above the fireplace hangs a painting of a lake surrounded by rolling hills. There are two pillar candles and a brass carriage clock on the mantelpiece, and a couple of generic prints hanging from the walls. It's noticeable there are no photos of family members displayed anywhere.

"There's no other motor outside," Clement remarks.

"Eh?"

I turn around to find him gazing out of the lounge window towards the driveway.

"If there was someone else still here, where's their motor?"

"Okay. Point taken."

Clement then makes for the door while I hang back a few seconds to savour the warm glow of the fire a little longer.

I catch up to him in the hallway just as he's opening the final door.

"This looks more interesting," he says over his shoulder.

I follow him into what was probably a dining room, but is now a study. The same size as the lounge, and decorated in the same drab manner, an oversized desk stretches across the back wall with a filing cabinet and bookcase lined up on the adjacent wall. There's a well-worn armchair in the corner with a reading lamp for days like this where natural light is in short supply.

I flick the main light switch and head straight for the desk where two mobile phones have been discarded — our mobile phones. I can only guess Alex wanted to see what information they held before destroying them. I hand Clement his and slip mine back into my coat pocket.

Turning my attention to the desk itself the first impression is that it's not the kind of desk where any real work is done. There's no in-tray, no files or folders, and no paperwork of any kind — just a basic computer, a desk lamp, and a pot of pens. Something tells me it's only ever used to browse the web and pay the odd bill. I move the mouse and the screen comes alive.

"Shit," I murmur.

"What?"

"It's password protected. There's no way of finding out what's on here without that password."

"Guess we have to go old school then."

Clement approaches the filing cabinet and tugs at the top drawer. It doesn't open.

"Locked."

"Great," I groan. "This day just gets better and better."

"Gimme a minute and I'll have it open. No password required."

He then dips a hand into his pocket and pulls out the knife. If it wasn't so tragic, I'd have to laugh. One minute he's wielding it as a murder weapon the next he's using it as a handy tool to unlock a filing cabinet.

As he fiddles with the lock I turn my attention to the bookcase. The shelves house a broad range of books including many of the classics from the likes of Orwell, Dickens, and Hemingway. There's also numerous biographies — many of which were penned by journalists. It's a crying shame their wisdom never rubbed-off on Alex — we might never have reached this point.

A metallic clunk interrupts my browsing.

"Got it," Clement says.

I return to his side as he slides open the top drawer. It contains several dozen hanging files; each with a plastic tab at the top labelled with just three capital letters. The first file is labelled AJB, the second AMR, and the third BSO. Scanning the rest of the tabs the filing system appears to run alphabetically.

"You thinking what I'm thinking?" Clement asks.

"Only one way to find out."

I extract the first file and open it up. All it contains are three sheets of paper with no more than a few paragraphs of text printed on each sheet. We stand silently and read the first sheet.

"Shit," Clement murmurs.

"Shit indeed."

The same three letters on the tab are repeated throughout the text, and it soon becomes obvious those letters are initials. Whoever AJB is, or was, their first favour is listed in detail, along with the initials of who received it. It seems AJB provided an advanced warning about the annual financial statement of a major bank. That statement included details of significant losses, and the recipient of that information was able to sell their shares in that bank before the bad news became public and the shares plummeted in value. Essentially, AJB was guilty of insider trading.

"This what you were hoping for, doll?"

I move on to the second sheet and quickly digest details of a favour AJB received, and the initials of who granted it.

"It is ... almost."

"Almost?"

"I'm going to guess these files list the specifics of all the favours granted and received by members of the Clawthorn Club. However, there's no mention of anyone's full name."

"So?"

"How many people in the country have the initials AJB?"

"Fuck knows. A lot?"

"Precisely. Whoever devised this system was clever enough to ensure the files were useless from an evidential perspective. AJB might have been doling out financial secrets but there's no conclusive way of knowing AJB's true identity."

"Triffic. We're wasting our time then?"

"I'm afraid ... wait."

"What?"

The realisation, when it suddenly arrives, is so overwhelming I can scarcely catch my breath. Slack-jawed, I look up at Clement but he clearly hasn't made the same connection.

"These files," I gulp. "Are useless, unless …"

I take a moment to let a sudden rush of adrenalin settle.

"Unless you happen to know the surnames of all the members."

Clement's own mouth bobs open as he catches up.

"Fuck," he gasps. "The notebook."

"Exactly. If you know each members initials, *and* their surname, suddenly the information in these files becomes a damn sight more interesting. If we know AJB's surname, for example, and that he was on the board of a major bank, how hard is it to work out his true identity?"

"That's why the notebook was so important — it was the key to identifying who these bent fuckers really are."

"And conversely, the notebook, as we discovered, wasn't much help as it only contained surnames. Together, these files and the notebook are, near as dammit, evidence."

I pluck my phone from my pocket so I can validate my theory by checking the spreadsheet of Clawthorn members. Two words at the top of the screen halt my plan in its tracks: *No Service.*

"Bugger. No connection."

"Eh?"

"We're in the middle of nowhere, Clement. A phone needs to

connect to a mast in order to work, and I'm guessing there isn't a mast for miles."

"What did you wanna check?"

"I wanted to access the spreadsheet of member names so we could cross-reference a few. I'd love to know who AJB is, for example."

"He can wait. What about that Nithercott fella?"

"Of course."

I run my finger across the tabs until I reach the final file, for a certain NDH, whoever he is. Assuming the files continue in alphabetical order, I slam the top drawer shut and pull open the next one down.

Just over halfway, I find the only file that could possibly belong to Lance Nithercott — labelled LGN.

With shaky hands I extract an innocuous buff folder and lay it on top of the drawer. Whatever secrets lie within, they cost Lance Nithercott his life, and Stacey a father.

I open it up to find just a single sheet of paper.

As I scan the text, and with Clement reading over my shoulder, the true extent of Lance Nithercott's involvement with the Clawthorn Club is revealed.

I read it twice, and close the folder.

"That's bleedin' tragic," Clement says in a low voice.

"I know. The poor man."

Stacey mentioned her childhood acting career was put on ice due to ill health. What she didn't mention was the specific detail — a prolonged spell in hospital after she suffered acute kidney failure. It seems the National Health Service had a lack of donors and, in desperation, Lance Nithercott turned to the Clawthorn Club to seek a favour. It involved the illegal procurement of a donor kidney, and the surgical procedure to implant it. Two favours from a corrupt club to save his daughter's life — who wouldn't have accepted such an offer?

With no documents to suggest Lance Nithercott ever repaid those favours, corroborated by the notebook evidence, I can only speculate they never were. Perhaps his artistic principles wouldn't allow him to, or maybe he tried, and failed, to buy his way out of debt. Whatever the reason, the pressure to repay his favours eventually pushed him to alcoholism, and he paid the ultimate price in the end.

I return the folder to the file.

"You see my point now, doll"

I look up at Clement.

"Even after it was supposed to have shut down, someone must have kept on at this Nithercott fella to repay his favours. Your friend outside was behind this bloke's death, and fuck-knows what else. There's a damn sight more blood on his hands than I ever had on mine."

I nod as a slliver of guilt for my earlier thoughts makes its presence felt.

"Maybe" I sigh. "But I still wish he was alive."

"Why?"

"So I could watch the bastard squirm once all of this is revealed."

"You gonna write that story then?"

"Whether I want to or not is irrelevant. I *have* to."

I'm about to start removing all the folders when Clement gently places his hand on my arm.

"It'll be alright, you know."

"What will?"

"You, me, everything. I can feel it."

As I look up into those blue eyes so much of me wants to believe him. I'd love nothing more than to share the rest of my life with the loving, sensitive, caring version of Clement. What I don't want is to spend the rest of my life with a man who can kill another without batting an eyelid. Whether the two can ever be separated I don't know and, at the moment, my emotions are too raw to even think about it.

"We'll see," I reply with a tired smile.

"That'll do for me. For now."

Returning to the job in hand, I grab a handful of folders. Just as I'm about to transfer them to the desk the sudden and slight creak of a hinge pulls my attention. I spin around, and immediately drop the folders to the floor.

Stood in the doorway is a male figure dressed in a maroon sweater and beige cords.

My legs buckle, and only Clement's intervention prevents me from following the folders to the floor. I look at the figure again and squeeze my eyes tightly shut. I open them, and he's still stood in the doorway.

"I'd suggest you put those files back where you found them," he says.

I know who I'm looking at, and I know the voice, but it's impossible I should be seeing or hearing either.

He takes a step forward and the light confirms the impossible.

"No ... it can't ... no ..."

Stood only five feet away is Eric Birtles — my one-time close friend and mentor. The same friend and mentor whose funeral I attended six months ago.

35

As confused as he is, Clement manages to keep me upright. My mind is in an altogether different league of confused turmoil.

I take an unsteady step back and, supporting myself against the filing cabinet, I stare open-mouthed at the man who can't possibly be Eric Birtles.

There are subtle differences from the face I knew so well. This face is tanned, and sports a neatly-trimmed white beard. His ever-present spectacles are also absent, and he's lost at least a stone in weight. Despite those minor differences, and the major issue of Eric being dead, he looks unnervingly similar.

I want to speak but there just aren't the words. The impostor, however, does find a handful.

"Did you hear me, Emma?" he says sternly. "Put the files back."

Frozen on the spot I pant shallow breaths as I try to comprehend the impossible.

"But … you're … you're dead. You drowned … I went to your funeral."

"You went to a funeral," he replies matter-of-factly. "But the corpse currently buried beneath my headstone isn't mine. I think that much should be obvious."

Very little feels obvious and my bewildered expression must say as much. Not only am I staring at a man whose funeral I attended six months ago, but he's chosen the most unlikely time and place to announce his return from the dead.

"Pull yourself together," he chides. "I don't have time for this."

His cold, empty eyes and hard expression are at complete odds with the version of Eric I knew; he was gentle, patient, and kind.

"This?" I repeat. "What is *this*?"

He puffs a weary sigh and shakes his head.

"I'll tell you what it is: none of your damn business. If you hadn't started poking around in that filing cabinet I wouldn't be stood here and you'd be none the wiser regarding my ... situation. Now, I suggest you leave, and forget this unfortunate meeting ever happened."

Incredulity barges shock to one side, and I glare back at him.

"I'm going nowhere ... not until you tell me what's going on here."

"What is going on, Emma, is I witnessed your friend murder Alex Palmer. I recorded the whole sorry incident from the bedroom window and, unless you'd like me to call the police, you'll do as I say."

"I didn't murder him," Clement interjects. "I threw a knife at him because he was pointing a bleedin' gun at us."

"Semantics. He's dead, and you were responsible. If you leave now, the police need never know."

"We ain't goin' nowhere, mate."

Clement takes a step forward. Eric responds with a shake of the head before calmly slipping a hand behind his back. A second later, that same hand returns — holding a pistol which looks remarkably similar to the one Alex was brandishing. He points it at Clement, and the big man stops dead in his tracks.

"I'm not Alex Palmer," Eric then warns. "I have absolutely no qualms about pulling this trigger."

Clement turns to me. "Do you wanna tell me who the hell this bloke is?"

"This, Clement, is Eric Birtles: my old colleague, and I thought, friend. He's back from beyond the grave apparently."

"It's an exclusive club," he mumbles, for some reason. "But what the fuck is he doing here?"

That is a question I'd barely given any thought to, and certainly can't answer.

"If you don't leave without any fuss," Eric says. "I'm going to shoot one of you ... possibly both of you."

We reach an impasse. Clement and I swap glances, and I can tell from the look in his eye there will be fuss.

"Sorry, mate — I don't think we're ready to leave just yet."

To reinforce his point, Clement edges a few feet closer.

It appears Eric is having some difficulty maintaining his confident facade, and doubt creeps into his face. I guess it's one thing to say you're *willing* to shoot another human being, but something very different actually pulling the trigger.

With his control of the situation slipping away Eric then raises the pistol a few inches ... and does indeed find the courage to pull the trigger.

In such a confined space, the blast is deafening and I cower as chunks of plaster explode from the wall behind me; the bullet mercifully passing over Clement's shoulder.

My ears still ringing I'm about to plead with Eric to keep calm. I look across and I'm met with a confused face; his arm, and the pistol, hanging by his side. Perhaps the recoil was worse than he imagined, or maybe he's trying to fathom out how he missed such a large target. Either way, his moment of indecision is Clement's opportunity.

The big man leaps forward and the six feet of carpet between them disappears in an instant. As Eric's eyes widen, he lifts his arm to take another shot. That arm never reaches a horizontal position but, still, the pistol sounds again.

There is no cry of pain and no indication the second bullet hit Clement — quite the opposite. He grabs Eric's wrist and twists it clockwise. The older man yelps, and the pistol falls to the floor. For once, Clement doesn't go completely overboard and hurl Eric across the room. Instead, he grabs a handful of his sweater and pulls him further into the centre of the study.

"Sit down," he orders, pushing Eric backwards.

Whether he fancied sitting or not, my once-dead friend and colleague stumbles back and falls into the armchair. Clement then picks up the pistol and tucks it in his pocket before turning to me.

"What do you wanna do with him, doll?"

Yet another question. I think, this time, I do have an answer.

"I want an explanation."

Eric looks up at me, sour-faced. "Keep me here all night if you must, but I'm not saying anything."

Now I have to contend with my own conscience. Am I hypocritical enough to encourage Clement to use his unorthodox interview technique, or do I just accept Eric isn't willing to talk?

I step towards the armchair.

"I'm sorry, Eric."

"For what?

"For being weak. I don't want this but if you're not willing to explain what the fuck is going on here, there's no other choice."

I look across at Clement. "Make him talk."

"You sure?"

"No, but I guess I can't have the sweet without the sour. Do what you need to do."

He reaches down and pulls the knife from inside his boot. Just the very click of the blade flicking open is enough to make Eric visibly shudder.

"Wait," he gulps. "I'll cut a deal with you."

"Go on."

"I'll tell you everything ... on one condition. You let me go once I've told you, and wait until tomorrow morning before contacting the police, if that's your intention."

"Depends on what you tell me."

"You owe me, Emma."

"Do I?"

"Haven't I always looked out for you? I gave you every break you've had in your career, and guided you every step of the way. You wouldn't even be here now if it wasn't for me. I made you, Emma."

There is no denying I am a better journalist for Eric's mentoring but I think he's giving himself more credit than he's due.

"You're in no position to negotiate, Eric. Your only decision is whether you choose the hard way or the easy way. You will tell me everything, though."

"I'm an old man, and if you set him on me I could die of a heart attack. If that happens, you'll never know the truth."

Clement then offers his opinion. "Does it really matter, doll? I ain't keen on talking to the Old Bill so let him say his piece and fuck off. You've already got all you need to write your story."

"Fine," I huff. "Let's hear it then, Eric. Why did you fake your own death and why the hell are you here?"

He appears to relax a little, and sits upright.

"The reason I'm here is because I was trying to help Alex. He's got himself involved in some kind of corruption scandal and he told me you and your friend were investigating him."

"Why would you help Alex? You didn't exactly get on well when you worked together."

"Because," he sighs. "He's my godson."

"What? Alex is your godson?"

"Was," he says flatly.

"Eh? But I worked with you both for years -- how come neither of you ever mentioned it?

"I took him under my wing after his parents died in a boating accident. He'd just left university and despite his lack of suitable qualifications, I gave him his first break in journalism. I didn't want to be accused of nepotism so we agreed never to tell anyone. Anyway, I don't think you need me to tell you he wasn't cut out for it."

"I'm sorry, Eric, but that doesn't even come close to an explanation. You threatened us with a pistol for crying out loud, and if you already knew Alex was dead, why bother trying to protect him?"

He runs a hand through his wispy hair as his face adopts a strained expression.

"To be frank, Emma, purely selfish reasons. Alex helped orchestrate my apparent death and if you expose him, chances are the world will learn I'm very much alive."

"So, I suppose that brings us nicely on to my next question. Why in God's name did you fake your own death?"

"I had no choice ... and I honestly mean that."

"Let's hear it."

"About ten years ago I helped expose a former drug baron called James Wylie. Because of the evidence I secured, Mr Wylie was convicted of drug trafficking and sent to prison. However, on his release he decided I owed him compensation."

"Compensation?"

"Just over one million pounds, to be precise, for helping to prove his guilt. I had one month to pay or he said he'd kill my wife, and then me."

"Why didn't you just go to the police?"

"Good question. Unfortunately, some of the evidence I acquired wasn't necessarily obtained through legitimate sources — you know how it is. If I'd admitted how I got that evidence, I'd have been looking at a long stretch in prison myself for perverting the course of justice. At my age, it would have almost certainly been for life."

"Why the hell didn't you tell me? I could have helped."

"Shame, I suppose, and I didn't want to put you in harm's way. If Wylie had known how close we were, you would have been at risk too. And besides, Alex had the means and contacts in place to help set up my apparent death, so it just seemed the simplest option. For what it's worth, I am sorry, but it really was the last and only resort."

It's an explanation which, on some level, makes sense. But, whilst I understand his motives for assisting Alex and faking his own death, neither sit right.

"Do you have any idea what Alex got himself involved in … what you've been trying to protect?"

"No, not really. He said it was best I didn't know."

"So, you've never heard of the Clawthorn Club?"

He vigorously shakes his head. I suppose it's not beyond comprehension Alex kept him out of the loop. I guess the less people who knew the truth, the better.

"So, what now?" he asks.

I have most of the answers I sought, although they've come at a price. My friend and mentor is not the man I thought he was, and Alex has taken any remaining answers to the grave. Once we've got the files there's nothing else here for us.

"I can't begin to tell you how appalled I am by what you've done, Eric. If you dropped dead this very second, I wouldn't waste another tear."

"I know, and I can't begin to tell you how sorry I am. I'd have rather you spent a lifetime grieving than discover the truth."

"Yeah, that makes two of us."

He attempts to look remorseful. "It might be best for all concerned if I leave now."

There seems precious little point in prolonging this farce. I look across at Clement to seek clarification we should let Eric leave. He replies with a nod.

I turn back to Eric. "To think: I once loved you like a father. You disgust me, and I never want to see your face again."

Like a cowering dog, he slowly clambers from the chair and shuffles towards the door. He gets within a few feet when Clement places a hand on his shoulder.

"Hold on a sec," he demands.

"What now? I groan.

"He said he recorded what happened in the garden. Don't think I want that going anywhere."

"You're not alone. Hand over the phone, Eric."

"I'll delete the video," he replies dismissively. "You have my word."

"No offence, but your word is no longer of value to me. Hand it over."

Reluctantly, he dips a hand into his pocket and pulls out a chunky mobile phone. But rather than hand it to me, he starts jabbing the screen.

"What are you doing, Eric?"

"As you asked. I'm deleting the video."

"Are you going deaf in your old age? I said I don't trust you so hand it over."

His brief pause is enough to snap Clement's patience. He snatches the phone from Eric's hand and tosses it to me.

"Give that back," he barks.

"What's the problem, Eric? Have you been taking dick pics?"

"Don't be vulgar. There's personal information on there that I'd rather you didn't see."

"Tough."

He makes an attempt to snatch the phone back but, with Clement's hand still locked on his shoulder, it proves a pointless exercise.

Ignoring his ongoing protest, I jab the gallery icon on the home screen and I'm presented with just two files. The first is the video he shot of Alex's demise, but the second file is the one which grabs my attention. I enlarge the image and hold the phone so Eric, and Clement, can see the screen.

Eric suddenly loses his voice while Clement leans in and studies the photo.

"Is that what I think it is, doll?"

"Yes, it's a screen-shot of that tweet I posted — with the pictures of the Clawthorn notebook."

"I ...um ... Alex must have sent it to me by mistake," Eric stammers.

"Oh, really?"

"Yes, yes. I don't even know what a tweet is."

"But when I asked, you claimed you'd never heard of the Clawthorn Club."

"I ... but, I haven't. It's just a stupid photo, and I didn't even pay it any attention."

There is no hiding the panic in his voice. Something tells me Eric knows more than he's willing to admit.

"Let's see what else is on here shall we?"

Eric's tanned face no longer looks tanned — more a ghostly shade of white.

I return to the home screen and tap the icon to open up his text messages. There are plenty of them, but only to three individuals, all identified by initials alone.

"You seem to have sent a lot of messages to a certain AP, TB, and

EH, Eric. I'm guessing AP is Alex Palmer, but perhaps you'd like to tell me who TB and EH are?"

He remains silent so I click one of the messages from TB received Saturday evening. For Clement's sake I read it out.

"I've done what you asked. The flat is now just a pile of ashes as is the notebook. We're quits — I don't want to hear from you ever again."

It takes a second to catch the significance of the words I've just uttered. Open mouthed I turn to Clement.

"TB is Terry Brown."

Before he can respond, I click one of the messages sent to EH. Within a second, I know I'm looking at a message I've read before, and who EH is.

"EH, Eric. That's me, isn't it? The threatening messages I've been receiving were sent from this phone."

He doesn't respond.

"And that makes you ... no ..."

Clement catches up. "Fuck," he gasps, glaring at Eric. "You're the bleedin' Tallyman?"

36.

A long silence fills the air as we both stare at the ashen-faced pensioner. I don't know what Clement is thinking, but my thoughts are dominated by the many ways I'd like to kill Eric. I pace up and down staring at the floor as I try to piece everything together.

The pacing ends with me stood just a few feet in front of him.

"You ... you fucking ... Oh, my God!"

I can't find the words, but I can find the actions. My open hand slaps Eric's face with such force the ensuing sting to my palm provokes a sharp intake of breath. Eric, however, fares far worse and stumbles backwards with a yelp.

"Sit him down," I growl at Clement. "I want answers."

"You ain't the only one," he replies, before obliging.

Clement forces Eric back into the armchair as I draw long breaths and gather my thoughts. Terry Brown's dying words now make sense. When I asked him who the Tallyman was, I thought he said 'bird', but what he was actually trying to say was 'Birtles'. How could I have been so blind? The moment Eric appeared in the doorway I should have made the connection.

"I'm sorry," he pleads. "I truly am."

"Shut the fuck up," I yell. "I don't want to hear another word from you unless it's to answer a question."

I pace the floor again, and return to my own thoughts. One by one, the dots join up but I'm still a long way from seeing the full picture. I need to find some composure so I close my eyes for a few seconds and attempt to regulate my breathing.

"Right," I calmly declare, turning to face Eric. "This is how we're going to proceed. I'm going to ask questions, and you're going to answer them."

He nods.

"And, if I get even the faintest hint you're lying, you should bear in mind one crucial fact."

"What's that?" he murmurs.

"The entire world already thinks Eric Birtles is dead. If you die tonight, no one will be any the wiser."

The gravity of his situation appears to take hold, as he clutches the arms of the chair, his knuckles as white as his face. It's a struggle to even look at him. His guilt makes a mockery of everything I knew. All those years I looked up to him, trusted him, respected him. It was all a lie. The man I've mourned for the last six months is the same man we've been trying to identify — the head of the Clawthorn Club.

I pull the chair from the desk, place it in front of Eric and sit down. With Clement stood to the side of the armchair there is no means of escape.

"So, let's get started, Eric," I begin. "But before we do, I should just check if you prefer being addressed as Eric, or the Tallyman?"

He doesn't answer one way or the other.

"It's a corny moniker, isn't it? Why on earth did you decide on that of all things?"

Still nothing. I look up at Clement and he gets the message.

"Answer her, before I lose my rag."

"Fine," he eventually sighs. "I never much cared for that name, but I suppose it did add a certain mystique to the position. People are scared of the unknown — some children have sleepless nights because of the bogie man, and some adults have sleepless nights because of the Tallyman ... or at least they did."

"Glad we sorted that out. Now, perhaps you can tell me the real reason you faked your own death."

"I had no choice. The police were beginning to believe there was some substance in the rumours about the Clawthorn Club, and our influence within the force was on the wane. One particular detective was getting too close to the truth, and determining my identity. My untimely death and his, um, unfortunate accident curtailed the investigation, but you can only hide the truth for so long, Emma — you of all people should know that."

"The truth?" I sneer. "You wouldn't know the truth if it bit you on the arse."

Wisely, Eric remains silent.

"I'm guessing you were also lying about Alex being your godson?"

"No, I wasn't. If you want proof, I can show you photos of us together when he was just a teenager."

His defensive tone errs on the side of believable.

"So, tell me: how did you drag him into this?"

"His father was a member of the Clawthorn Club and one of only three people who knew my identity. After his parents died, Alex found his father's diaries and, in them, pretty-much the full story of his involvement with the club. Alex confronted me, and I had no choice but to tell him everything. One of the reasons I invested so much time helping his career was to buy his silence, and it was me who helped secure his position within that telecoms company when it became clear he'd never cut it as a journalist."

"Don't tell me: you blackmailed someone in that company?"

"I did what I had to do."

"And did Alex also know you were planning to fake your own death?"

He slowly nods as I recall Alex's words at the funeral that never was. Looking back, he didn't exactly sound grief-stricken but at the time I put it down to their fractious relationship.

"And, correct me if I'm wrong, but I presume it was Alex who told you I posted the photos of the notebook?"

"He did, and he also told me he deleted them."

I thought I was going crazy but it's now clear Alex guessed my Twitter password — not too difficult as I've been using the same basic password since the days we worked together, and he knew it. I can only assume he didn't delete my second tweet as it only showed the cover, or perhaps to avoid raising suspicion. Either way, it's not my current priority.

"I have gone to great lengths to bury every crumb of evidence relating to the Clawthorn Club," he continues. "But then that blasted notebook resurfaced."

"Did you know my father had it?"

"I had an inkling. Alex created a piece of software which would send out a notification whenever the name 'Hogan' appeared on the national death registry database. Once he knew Dennis was dead, he traced his last address but the estate agent wouldn't allow him access. He managed to arrange a viewing but, by the time he got there, you'd taken all of Dennis's possessions."

"It was Alex who paid a visit to my flat when I wasn't there?"

"No, that was Terry Brown."

"Why Terry?"

"Because he was competent in such matters, and Alex wasn't. He told me he'd checked every box and every pocket, but the notebook wasn't there. As far as I was concerned, that was it — I assumed Dennis no longer had the notebook, and it was gone for good."

"Until Alex spotted it on Twitter."

"He did. Fortunately I was already back in the country for a few days, attending to other matters."

"What do you mean, back?"

"I don't live in the UK — that would be far too risky. No, I live ... let's just say somewhere with a more agreeable climate."

That explains his tanned face, although it never featured highly on my list of unanswered questions.

"So, it was you who ordered my flat to be burned to the ground?"

"You were warned, numerous times, to return the notebook. Destroying it was the last resort."

"And let me guess: you were also behind my suspension at The Daily Standard?"

"I had hoped the distraction might deter you from digging around any further. God knows I tried everything to make you realise what you were getting yourself into. I even told Alex to offer you a job but you just kept poking the bear. Why couldn't you just let it lie?"

"It's my job to poke bears."

"And kill them too?" he scowls.

"What?"

"Terry Brown was a good friend and he didn't deserve to die like that."

I glare at him, incredulous.

"Firstly, if Terry Brown was such a good friend, why were you blackmailing him to do your dirty work?"

"Blackmail is a strong word. I simply told Terry he needed to deal with you otherwise we were all at risk of being exposed. Obviously Terry didn't want his prior indiscretions becoming public knowledge."

"Blackmail, threaten ... call it what you like, Eric, but we both know you used knowledge to force others to do your dirty work."

"I simply asked an old friend to do me a favour, and now he's dead."

"That's bullshit, and you can't pin his death on us."

"You were there," he blurts. "And don't deny it — Alex told me."

Not that it matters now, but Eric has just confirmed my suspicions that Alex was tracking my phone.

"Yes, we were there," I confirm. "But it wasn't us. Terry hired some drugged-up youth to mug me, and then torch my flat. When we found that kid, we discovered Terry had been using his elderly grandmother as a bargaining chip. Funnily enough, that youth wasn't impressed and he shot Terry."

He returns a puzzled frown. It seems Eric jumped to an incorrect conclusion when he heard Terry had died.

"Wait ... Gini's fiancé. You had him knocked down because you thought we killed Terry? What was it you said to her: an eye for an eye?"

"Yes, well," he mumbles, shifting awkwardly in his seat. "I'll concede I got that wrong."

"Yes, you did."

"Alex told me you were being assisted by this ... man," he whines, nodding towards Clement. "And I assumed he shot Terry."

"You were wrong, and now I've lost a good friend because of it."

"And I've lost a godson, Emma," he snorts. "In fact, I've lost everything because of the Clawthorn Club, so don't be thinking I've got away with anything."

His expression changes again; despondent, almost remorseful.

"And I've also lost our friendship," he says wistfully. "I always

454

considered you to be the daughter I never had. I think, although he never said anything, Alex was jealous of our relationship."

"And I thought you were the father I never had. Turns out I knew even less about you than I did about my actual father."

"I thought you might unearth a few of his secrets. I have to say I regret what happened with Dennis more than anything. He was a good friend, until ..."

Another realisation drops in and punches me in the stomach.

"Fuck," I gasp. "It was you."

"What?"

"You framed my father."

He sits bolt upright and looks me straight in the eye. "No, Emma. I did not."

"I don't believe you, and I warned you what would happen if you lied."

Breathing heavily I glare at Eric.

"Listen to me," I bellow. "I've had an absolute gutful of this so unless you tell me what happened to my father, I'm going to walk out the door and leave you with Clement and his knife."

"It doesn't matter now."

"It bloody well does," I rage. "I want to know the truth, Eric."

He ponders my request a second too long.

"Fuck this," I spit, turning to Clement. "Do what you want with him. We'll toss his body into the sea when you're done."

I get up and make for the door.

"Please … wait, wait," he stammers. "I'm just thinking of you, Emma. Like the Clawthorn Club itself; some things are best left in the past."

Clement looms over Eric. "Listen, mate: I'm bored, hungry, and I don't wanna hang around this fucking house a minute longer than necessary. Tell her what she wants to know or I'll end it here and now."

Eric's head bows forward a fraction. "Okay," he says in a low voice. "But remember we have a deal. Once you know everything I walk away."

"I don't remember agreeing to that," I reply.

"Do you want to know, or not? Your friend isn't the only one who doesn't want to be here."

"I'm past caring now. Just tell me the bloody truth."

He begins with a sharp intake of breath as I retake my seat. "Dennis and I were members of the original Clawthorn Club, and we jointly decided it needed to go in a new direction. Your father was an ambitious man and he could see the benefit of the favour system, although I don't think it panned out quite how he envisaged."

"The corruption, you mean?"

"That's not quite what I'd call it, but yes. Dennis didn't like how the membership was evolving but, by the time he decided he'd had enough, the club was already well established as a place to find … shall we say … the right people willing to offer creative solutions to problems."

"So, that's when he wanted to leave?"

"It wasn't just our direction of travel — your mother also influenced him."

"In what way?"

"By falling pregnant ... with you. Dennis just wanted to settle down and have a quiet, family life."

"And you couldn't have that," I spit. "So, you framed him, didn't you?"

"I don't know how you arrived at that conclusion but you're wrong."

"I'll tell you how, Eric: it was confirmed by a member of the Clawthorn Club."

I have no idea if he is aware we paid Thomas Lang a visit but his perplexed expression suggests not.

"Thomas Lang," I confirm. "He said the Tallyman framed my father."

"That figures," he retorts, shaking his head. "For a high ranking police officer, Thomas Lang really was an idiot ... always putting two and two together, and coming up with five."

"You're saying he's a liar?"

"Not necessarily a liar — more ill-informed. He of all people shouldn't have listened to the rumours and tittle-tattle. Yes, your father was fitted up but I swear to God it was nothing to do with me. Granted, I didn't discourage the rumours because it helped to keep the other members in check, but you have to believe me, Emma, I had nothing to do with your father's incarceration."

"Who was it then?"

"Could have been anyone. When your father and I originally devised the favour system, it was decided one of us had to remain anonymous to ensure it wasn't compromised or abused, so we tossed a coin. I became the Tallyman and Dennis became the public face of the Clawthorn Club. However, as your father was privy to information a number of very influential people couldn't risk leaking out, his decision to quit didn't go down too well. I suppose any one of them could have framed him to ensure he never got the opportunity to reveal their favours. Not only was he stuck in prison, but who would believe the word of a convicted rapist and murderer?"

How can I believe the word of a man who has already proven himself a consummate liar? Perhaps there is one final question which might ultimately decide whether I'm inclined to believe his version of events, or not.

"How did he even get hold of the notebook and, more to the point, why?"

"Not long after he was released from prison, he broke into this very house and stole it. I assume he also photographed the files which detail all of the member's favours."

"Why?"

"I can only guess he wanted to establish who framed him, and ultimately prove his innocence. In the end he got nowhere, and that's when he decided to systematically blackmail all the members instead.

That, Emma, is the reason why your father spent the latter part of his life hiding in the shadows. My best estimate: he extorted millions of pounds from them over the years. I just wanted to get the notebook back so I could finally lay the Clawthorn Club to rest."

I'm torn. I can't say I believe him, but I can't deny it fits with what I've learnt about my father: the money he invested in the NLH Foundation, his luxury flat in Chiswick, his expensive taste in clothes, and his bolt-hole in Bethnal Green. All of it supports Eric's claim my father spent the latter part of his life extorting money, and hiding from the corrupt individuals he targeted.

"I did warn you, Emma" Eric adds. "Sometimes the truth isn't always what we want it to be."

"Clearly not," I grunt. "It certainly wasn't where you were concerned."

"I can't change anything, and I honestly do regret so much of what's happened."

"Save it, Eric. I've heard enough."

"Fair enough. I think it would be best if I left now."

I look across at Clement and he shrugs.

"What else we gonna do with him?" he asks. "Whatever this arsehole has done he's not our problem, doll. Let's just see him off, grab the folders, and then get the fuck out of here."

"So, he gets to walk away scot-free?"

Clement then glares at Eric. "He'll pay for what he's done. Maybe not today, or tomorrow, but one day he'll have to face the music —

you mark my words."

"Hell and damnation, eh?"

"Something like that."

37.

Clement orders Eric to stand up. Slowly, the old man climbs out of the armchair.

"I need to get Alex's car keys," he says, turning to me.

"Why?"

"I got a taxi here from Bournemouth Airport. If I order a return, it'll take up to an hour to arrive. I'm sure you don't want to sit around any more than I do."

"Fine. Where are they?"

"I assume they're still in his pocket."

He's right, in that I don't want to spend another minute in his company, nor do I want him hanging around while we collate the evidence which will bring his house of cards crashing down. He might be flying off to warmer climes tonight but, by the time my exposé hits the papers, his days of freedom will be numbered.

I extract my phone and hold it up. Before Eric can protest, I take his photo.

"Just for old times' sake," I sneer.

I won't let on it'll be the photo which accompanies my exposé. Whether hell is waiting for him or not, I'm confident he'll be suffering a living hell before long.

Clement orders Eric to walk in front as we exit the study and head back through the house to the patio doors. He strains to slide the door and, as it inches open, a blustery wind howls through the gap.

We step out into a bitterly cold evening; the sky now a shade of slate grey. I'm in no mood to hang around, and neither, it seems, is Eric as he shuffles quickly down the lawn. The pace slows as we approach Alex's corpse and with his shoulders slumped, Eric stops and turns around.

"Do you mind if I take a moment?" he says in a low voice. "Just to say a final goodbye."

I nod, and take a few steps backwards. "One minute."

Eric's old bones creak as he kneels down and leans over Alex's corpse. Knowing the man stood next to me was responsible, however unfortunately, doesn't sit well, and I avert my gaze beyond the sorry sight.

Where the lawn ends, some fifty yards away, a band of dark turquoise abuts the grey sky. I can just about make out the faint light of a ship on the horizon; the captain either brave or foolhardy venturing out in such weather.

"You alright?" Clement asks.

The faint light disappears just before I turn and look up at him. "At this precise moment I'm not sure how I feel. Ask me again in a month."

"We'll still be talking in a month?"

"All things considered ... probably."

"Good, I was kinda hoping ..."

He stops mid-sentence; his mouth and eyes wide open. For a

second I wonder if the stroke I threatened might just have arrived. That theory is given further credence as he staggers back a few steps and collapses to the floor.

Only then do I realise Clement hasn't been felled by a stroke. Poking out of his stomach are two metallic prongs with almost-invisible wires trailing away.

It takes a second to conclude we've been had. Eric was not saying a final goodbye or looking for car keys — he was hoping Alex kept at least one of the Tasers in his coat pocket and had reloaded it. His gamble paid off, and now Clement is convulsing on the floor like a landed fish as thousands of volts surge through his body.

Just as I'm about to turn and confirm my theory, a weight crashes into me. I stumble, and slip on the greasy wet lawn before joining Clement on the ground, albeit five feet away.

I look up just in time to see Eric regain his footing. Without a second glance in my direction, he kneels down and reaches for Clement's pocket.

In any other circumstance, it would be like placing your hand in a bear trap but, with the big man temporarily paralysed, Eric is able to dip his hand into Clement's pocket and remove what he had his sights on all along — the pistol.

I scramble to my feet at the exact same moment Eric stands up. He wastes no time in pointing the pistol at me.

"Move," he orders.

"Where?"

463

He waves the gun towards the end of the garden I was casually observing just a minute ago. "That way."

Panic arrives.

I don't know how long it takes for the effects of the Taser to wear off, but Clement is my only hope of rescue. I need to buy time.

Slowly, I raise my hands in surrender, but stay put.

"Don't fuck with me, Emma," he warns, his voice now frantic. "Move."

He scurries around and stands behind me. To make his point the barrel of the pistol is jabbed between my shoulder blades.

With little other choice, I take a few slow steps forward — the pistol barrel remains in place.

"What do you want, Eric?"

No reply. Perhaps the wind carried my question away. I ask again.

"Shut up," he replies. "Or I'll shoot you here and now."

Silently, we move closer and closer to the end of the lawn; the strip of dark-turquoise sea getting larger with every step. I try to turn my head to see if Clement has moved but Eric nudges me forward by pressing the pistol barrel hard into my back.

The wind grows stronger as the lawn gets shorter and my panic mounts.

Twenty feet.

Fifteen feet.

Ten feet.

Five feet.

By the time we reach the edge of the lawn, and I see what lies beyond, it takes every ounce of resolve to remain upright. A sheer drop of maybe eighty or ninety feet down to an outcrop of rocks at least as wide as the lawn on which I'm currently stood. I stare down in horror as the outcrop is assaulted over and over again by a barrage of frothing waves; each so high the rocks temporarily disappear beneath an explosion of foamy seawater. Either side of the rocks, the sea is a maelstrom of white peaks and dark ridges.

"Turn around," Eric orders.

With no wish to look down on the watery abyss a second longer, I spin on my heels to a sight no less terrifying — Eric has taken a dozen steps back and the pistol is aimed squarely at my chest.

"Jump," he orders.

"What?"

"You heard."

I look over my shoulder, and then back at Eric.

"Are you insane? It would be ... suicidal."

"Well done. That is kind of the point."

"What ...why? You could have just left ... why are you doing this?"

"Because you've left me with no other choice. The truth about Clawthorn simply can't be revealed — I'm sorry, Emma."

"Does it matter now? You'll be ... wherever you go ... and you said ... you can't hide from the truth forever."

"I don't want forever — just long enough for me to enjoy my retirement."

"But ... if you're in hiding, on the other side of the world?"

"Oh, it matters, Emma. Do you have any idea what level of vengeance will be unleashed if you attempt to identify the Clawthorn members? Many of them will not go down without a fight, but if they do go down, they'll do everything possible to take me with them."

"I ... okay, I'll go. I'll leave the files and never mention Clawthorn ever again."

"I'm sorry," he repeats. "The risk is too great, and I know you too well."

"Please, Eric."

"Jump. Now."

My opinion of Eric has already crashed to an unbelievable low, but this is beyond anything I could ever have envisaged. He appears deadly serious — he wants me to leap from this cliff to a certain death.

"What happened to you, Eric?"

"I'm losing patience."

He takes a step forward — I have nowhere to go; another few feet and I'll be making a terminal trip to the rocks below. I glance over his shoulder, and I can just about make out Clement's bulk still lying on the lawn where he fell. In the gloomy light it's impossible to tell if he's conscious or not. I need to buy more time and the only place open is a casino. I've got to take a chance.

"Go on then," I cry. "Shoot me."

"You don't think I will? As you so eloquently stressed in the house, Eric Birtles is dead so it's safe to say I have nothing to lose."

He raises his arm a few inches and fires the pistol. Instinctively, and I suppose, pointlessly, I duck down, but it seems his intention was to fire a warning shot rather than kill me.

"Go on — do it," he urges. "Because dead or alive, you will be heading over that cliff."

I slowly turn my head to the sea. At very least I want him to think I'm considering his insane order. I scan the rocks to confirm what I already know: even if I survived the fall — in itself a near-impossibility — the chances of swimming to safety in such turbulent seas are practically zero. The best I could hope for would be to die on impact; preferable to shattering every bone in my body and then drowning.

"Chop chop, Emma. I haven't got all night."

His casual manner irks.

"Fuck you," I retort. "Let's swap places and we'll see how decisive you are."

"I'm good here, thanks."

I glance over his shoulder and Eric turns to see what I'm looking at.

"He won't be coming to the rescue," he says flatly. "But he will be joining you for a swim."

Some way down the garden I can still make out Clement's frame on the ground. I try and recollect his position the last time I looked. I can't be sure but I think he might have moved slightly. To call it even a glimmer of hope would be a stretch.

Eric turns back to face me. "Ready?"

"To jump off a cliff to my certain death? Funnily enough … no, I'm not."

I have one chance left, and the only way that chance might work is if I can rile Eric the way Alex used to.

"I know why you want me to jump. It's because you're a fucking coward."

"I'm sorry?"

"All this pissing around. You could have shot me, and kicked my body over the edge by now … if you had the balls."

"Actually, Emma, you're wrong. You jump and the authorities will assume it was suicide. However, if your body washes up with a bullet wound in the chest, it'll attract attention I'd rather avoid."

"How very candid."

"But, as we're running out of time, it appears I have little other choice. Even to the very end, Emma, you're proving quite a pain in the backside."

"Well, sorry to disappoint, but I'm not jumping."

He glares back at me and I recognise the same hint of indecision I saw in the house. I need to capitalise.

"Killing someone in cold blood isn't your style though, is it?" I continue. "You prefer to hide in the shadows and let others do your dirty work. People like Terry Brown, Alex Palmer, and Thomas Lang ... and let's not forget Lance Nithercott. Three of those men are dead because you're such a fucking coward."

"Get your facts straight. One of them died because he was a drunken liability who refused to repay his debts and the other two are dead because you couldn't keep your nose out of my business."

"No, Eric. That's the one thing I've come to realise with this whole Clawthorn business — not once have you dared poke your head above the parapet. Fuck, even that stupid Tallyman name was just another way to hide, wasn't it?"

"Shut up."

"Come to think of it: is that why my father didn't want anything to do with Clawthorn? So many dodgy deals and every member taking a risk ... except you, Eric. You were the mysterious Tallyman who knew all those dirty secrets but you didn't put your arse on the line, did you? All ego and no spine — did my father see through your cowardice?"

"I'm warning you."

I've reached the point of no return.

"Touched a nerve, have I? I bet you shat yourself when you realised my father had stolen the notebook, eh? Almost as much as when you discovered I had it."

"You know nothing."

"Aww," I mock. "Did my daddy steal the Tallyman's special notebook? Did you have a good cry about it, Eric?"

Even in the muted light, the veins throbbing in his temple are clearly prominent.

"You know what, Emma," he sneers. "You really are a chip off the old block."

"Meaning?"

"Principled, but gullible. And just like I took away your father's life, I'm going to take yours."

My mocking comes to an abrupt halt.

"What do you mean ... you took away my father's life?"

"Isn't it obvious?" he goads. "It was me who fitted him up for that murder charge."

"What ... why?"

"Because, that self-righteous fool didn't just want to leave the Clawthorn Club — he wanted to shut it down. He threatened to expose our members so I called in a few favours myself, and your father went to prison. And as a happy by-product, your mother disowned him too — for some reason she wasn't best pleased Dennis was in a prostitute's flat in the first place. When you factor in the poor woman was raped before she was murdered, it's no surprise she wanted nothing to do with him."

Eric might not have shot me, yet, but his revelation is every bit as grievous.

"In your mother's defence the evidence against Dennis was overwhelming," he adds, with a sneer. "And the sweetest part, for me, was befriending you. You can only imagine how much that killed

470

Dennis; knowing the man responsible for destroying his life had taken his place."

"I don't believe you ... why would any man tolerate that?"

"What could he do about it? Your mother had already made it clear you didn't want anything to do with him, and I held the only evidence which proved his innocence so he couldn't touch me. He had no choice but to watch from the sidelines as I garnered the affections of his precious daughter. You have to admit: it was a beautiful punishment for stealing the notebook."

"So ... it was all a charade. You befriended me just to get at my father?"

"Initially, yes, but I can't deny I developed a soft spot for you. The problem is, Emma, it wasn't reciprocated ... least not the way I wanted."

"Eh? I don't understand."

"All that nonsense about thinking of you as the daughter I never had — I wanted you to be my lover, not my daughter."

"But ... oh, my God. You're sick."

"Am I? All those hugs and kisses we shared. All those evenings out and weekends away for work. Don't tell me at least some part of you didn't crave more?"

"Fuck ...no ... never in a million years."

"No need to be so dismissive," he barks. "You'd do well to remember it was my feelings that aided your career. Why else do you think I looked out for you? Love, lust ... call it what you will, but I lived in hope my feelings might one day be reciprocated. Hell, I even got Terry to set up a camera in your bedroom when he popped in to look for the notebook. That's how much I missed you."

Every square inch of my skin crawls in response to his admission.

"Unfortunately," Eric continues. "It appears your affections now lie with that Neanderthal on my lawn. So, as much as it pains me, I must now accept you and I will never be ... not least because one of us is about to die."

He takes two steps forward and straightens his arm so the pistol is only five or six feet from my chest.

"This isn't what I wanted," he adds. "But at least you'll meet your maker knowing the truth about your father. And who knows, if you believe in all that religious crap, you and Dennis might even be reunited in the afterlife."

He stares at me, dispassionately. A face I know so well but no longer recognise.

"Last chance, Emma. Three small steps and it'll all be over."

I edge one step back.

"Good girl."

The hopelessness is all-consuming. I now face the last decision I'll ever make — take the jump or take the bullet.

I inch another step backwards.

"That's it," he calmly purrs. "Nearly there."

My body is numb from the cold and my mind numb from the

shock of Eric's revelations. Death would, if nothing else, be a permanent release from both.

I move my left leg back until my foot is only inches from the edge. The wind picks up and howls in my ears; a chorus of whispering voices urging me to follow Eric's instructions. One voice in particular cries the loudest ... a voice deep and gravelly but the words are drowned by the waves crashing behind me. I close my eyes and focus. Is that ...?

My eyes snap open and strain to identify the source of the voice. Beyond Eric's shoulder, the slightest smudge of movement in the gloom. The dark shape staggers left, and then right, and then it stops, stoops, and repeats ... getting closer, larger.

Eric, realising my focus is not where he'd like it, glances back up the garden to see what I can now see — a big man in double denim approaching. Forty feet away, he moves like a drunk; stumbling and faltering every few steps.

Eric swings his arm a full one-eighty degrees and takes aim. The first bullet explodes from the barrel but Clement remains upright — just. Thirty feet, and I can see a tortured face like that of a heavyweight boxer in the twelfth round of an epic fight; every movement a gargantuan effort, but somehow he finds enough strength to stay on his feet.

Clement staggers on — every step closer reducing his chances of dodging another bullet.

Twenty feet and Eric takes aim at a target he surely can't miss.

How many shots has he taken? Two in the house? Two out here?

He waits for the right moment and another shot rips through the air. Clement's left leg struggles to take his weight and he stumbles. There is no cry of pain to suggest he's been hit but now he is so close the final bullet cannot fail to miss. I need to do something ... anything.

I shift my own leaden legs. Three steps, and Eric suddenly twists around — it's my turn to look down the pistol barrel again. One bullet remaining, and barely seconds for Eric to decide who is the biggest threat — the woman who could reveal all about the Clawthorn Club, or the jelly-legged man approaching from behind.

His arm straightens as he makes a decision. At the exact same moment, I make a decision of my own — I will die as I lived; making life difficult for those who deserve it. With no time to consider the consequences, I throw myself to the sodden turf. Eric has already shown himself to be a poor shot so, at the very least, there's a slim chance his last-remaining bullet will hit a limb rather than a vital organ if I make the target as small as possible.

I slide along the grass like a footballer celebrating a goal. As the momentum dissipates, I roll into the foetal position and look up to assess Eric's reaction. He takes two steps to his left in an attempt to improve the angle of his shot; his rotund face pursed with fury, or perhaps panic. No more time, no more options.

I brace for the bullet. The urge to close my eyes is overwhelming but I want him to see my fear, and for that fear to haunt him for the rest of his days.

A blur of blue enters stage left; momentarily pulling my attention away from the pistol. Clement staggers forth and makes a final, desperate lunge towards Eric. There is no finesse, no plan; he simply propels his body forward like a battering ram. The two men collide and the pistol goes off.

As the echo reverberates I await pain which never comes. I'm able to savour a split second of blessed relief before the chaos unfolds in front of me.

Eric stumbles backwards; his arms flailing as he tries to counter the momentum of Clement's shunt. The big man himself is faring no better as he wobbles on legs which still haven't fully recovered from the effects of the Taser. I catch the look of abject horror on Eric's face as his foot slips on the wet grass. On any other patch of grass he'd land flat on his backside but there's no more than a sliver of lawn between his right foot and the cliff edge − any fall will take him beyond that edge.

In desperation he grabs at Clement in the hope of finding an anchor. Clawing fingernails find purchase on the waistcoat lapel as he snatches a handful of denim. For a heartbeat, it appears enough to halt the fall but his still-significant bulk is already pulling him beyond the point of no return. Rather than providing an anchor Clement is dragged on the same trajectory.

The two men, as one, tumble backwards as Eric plants a foot into ground which isn't there. It proves his final effort to stop the inevitable — gravity takes over and drags Eric beyond the cliff edge. As he falls his hand never leaves Clement's waistcoat. The combination of Eric's bulk and desperation condemn Clement to the same fate. They fall from view, and Eric departs with a scream as harrowing as it is brief.

I roll onto my hands and knees, and scramble to the cliff edge. Peering over, the turquoise water is now almost indistinguishable from the dark rocks — a monotone scene of white-tipped waves erupting from a black void. I scan left and right but the scene barely changes. Desperately, I crawl closer to the edge and repeat the scan; every square foot of black sea confirmation of what I already know — they are gone ... they are gone.

TWO WEEKS LATER...

38.

An estate agent who isn't Miles DuPont hands me a set of keys.

"Let me know if there's anything you need," he smiles, with all the sincerity of a Tinder date.

"I'm sure I'll be fine," I reply.

It's a lie. I'm a long way from fine and I don't see when, or how, that will change. I now have a semi-permanent roof over my head but the pokey flat is but a mere shell for an empty soul. Suffering bereavement once is awful enough, but I've had a fortnight to suffer the loss of two men; one who never got the chance to be my father, and one who never got to be ... well, I guess I'll never know.

However, bereavement isn't all I'm struggling to contend with — there's the hatred. It burns with such intensity I struggle to contain it at times. Eric's bloated corpse washed ashore the day after he fell from the cliff and he's being laid to rest next week. His family now have to go through all that grief for a second time, with the added pain and ignominy of knowing the first time was a cruel hoax, orchestrated by the very man they were mourning.

At least they'll be able to pay their final respects, if there's any shred of respect left to pay. I will have no such closure as Clement's body still hasn't been found, and it probably never will be according to the Coastguard.

There's also too much guilt for both the men I've lost.

For as long as I can remember I've been consumed by my hatred of Dennis Hogan. Now there is no reason for that hatred to be there guilt is all that remains. I keep telling myself I had every reason to hate my father — Eric saw to that — but it doesn't change how I feel. He never had the chance to be the father he might have been, nor I the chance to be a daughter to a good man. It is the worst kind of inheritance. And knowing the true reason he filled his home with framed photos and my press cuttings summons far more sadness than pride.

Then there is Clement.

The final hour we spent together was tainted by my own negative thoughts, and I now realise all he wanted to do was protect me. I finally found a man willing to die for me, but the reality is as far away from the romantic notion as you can get. Losing him cuts deep, particularly as I didn't realise what I had, and I'll never know what might have been. I miss him more than I have any right to.

They say you should never have regrets but, in my case, it was only regret, and a savage anger, that prevented me from stepping over the edge of that cliff in Dorset. God knows how long I stood there, sobbing uncontrollably, but eventually I managed to harness my rage and do what I had to do. Despite the sobbing and the shock, I transferred every one of the Clawthorn folders from the house to the boot of the hire car. I then called the police.

As it transpired my shock proved a welcome excuse for the lack of clarity when the first two police officers arrived. I told them about Eric, and how he'd stabbed Alex in a fit of rage, and then tried to force me at gunpoint to jump from the cliff, before Clement intervened. With no other witnesses, and both the gun and the knife at the bottom of the English Channel, all they have to go on is my confused version of events. However, as Eric faked his own death, his desire to keep that a secret is a clear motive so I suspect my statement will be enough.

With everything I've had to cope with, the only way I've retained some semblance of sanity, is by sitting in a hotel room with my new laptop and that pile of folders. One by one, I'm slowly identifying the Clawthorn Club membership and, so far, I have a list of nineteen men whose corrupt behaviour is beyond refute. Their punishment will come; when I'm ready. When I decide to publish my findings, it will be to the highest bidder, and I'm confident it'll prove a blockbuster exposé, considering some of the names involved. Whatever I'm paid, it'll still feel a hollow victory, but I hope some people, particularly Stacey, find the closure they deserve.

Damon decided to postpone my disciplinary hearing until next week but I saved him the bother and tendered my resignation yesterday. Even if they were to decide my conduct isn't worthy of dismissal, there is no way I'm willing to write the Clawthorn story as a staff reporter, and receive nothing more than a pat on the back for my troubles. I'm not sure Gini would welcome my return anyway. Although I've convinced her the Tallyman is dead, and there is nothing more to investigate, I think she still holds me responsible for what happened to her fiancé. Yet another relationship destroyed by

Eric Birtles.

I leave the estate agent's office and return to my rented car that contains everything I own in one suitcase which I'll transfer to my rented home. I have nothing and I have no one — life has never felt so empty.

The pity party continues for the entirety of my journey. I don't like it and I wish I could find some strand of positivity to grasp but I'm sure even the most optimistic of people would struggle to find a silver lining on the dark cloud blotting my horizon.

I park up and get out of the car. I'm about to open the boot when my phone rings. If this is more bad news, I'm likely to get back in the car and return to that fucking cliff in Dorset.

I answer with a curt hello.

"Hi, Emma," a female voice chirps. "It's Mandy Burke."

My silence prods Miss Burke into confirming who the hell she is.

"You know, Mandy, from the NLH Foundation?"

"Oh, right. Yes."

"I'm calling about your father's office."

"Okay. What about it?"

"You may recall I mentioned the damp issue. Well, the contractors made a start on the work this morning, and they removed all the floorboard as the joists need to be replaced."

I have a horrible feeling she's going to tell me the damp is far worse than they expected, and they don't have sufficient funds to remedy it. If she's looking for a donation, she's looking in the wrong place.

"Pardon my bluntness, Mandy, but what has this got to do with me?"

"The workmen found a metal box hidden beneath the floorboards."

"Right. And?"

"There's a large envelope inside with your name written across the front."

I almost drop the phone.

"Really? Have you opened it?"

"No, because written across the flap, it clearly states it is only to be opened by Emma Aisling Hogan."

"Oh."

"And I'm almost certain it's your father's handwriting."

I waste precious seconds trying to guess what might be inside before it dawns on me to go and find out.

"I'll be there in thirty minutes."

I hang up and get back behind the wheel.

Sod's law, the traffic is abysmal but the constant stopping affords me the opportunity to consider why my father stowed away his mystery envelope. It seems he spent a large chunk of his life hiding from those he'd been blackmailing, and perhaps the office at the NLH Foundation was the one place he felt safe. Now I know how he funded the charity, it does explain why he shied away from the spotlight and kept his philanthropy out of the public domain.

Of course this all assumes I can believe what Eric told me. Experience suggests I should be wary.

I arrive on the same street I walked with Clement a few short weeks ago, and park up. What I wouldn't give for him to be with me now.

Putting my heartache to one side, I approach the door and ring the bell. As before, there's a brief wait before Mandy appears. She ushers me in and I follow her through the building to her pokey office.

"How have you been?" she asks.

"It's been a … nightmare, if I'm honest."

Judging by her awkward smile, I suspect she was hoping I'd reply with a standard platitude. Serves her right for asking.

Mandy reaches down and picks up a large brown envelope, carefully placing it on the desk in front of me.

"I'll give you some space," she says, getting to her feet. "I'll be next door when you're done."

True to her word, Mandy then bustles back through the door, closing it on her way.

I turn my attention to the envelope. Perhaps strange, but the first thing I notice is how neatly my name is penned on the front, in uppercase letters. From what little I know about Dennis Hogan he probably used a good-quality fountain pen. I turn the envelope over and, as Mandy stated, the same precise handwriting confirms it is only to be opened by Emma Aisling Hogan.

"I guess that's me, then," I sigh.

I carefully peel away the flap and tip the contents onto the desk. A wad of cash would have been useful rather than the two nondescript envelopes I find.

The first is letter sized, with my first name penned on the front, and the second much thicker. Perhaps it is stuffed with cash. I open it first.

Rather than used bank notes, an elastic band holds together a thin pile of photographs — the top one a black and white shot of a young man in a suit. I sit back in my chair and instinctively turn the photo over. Mum used to write dates and little notes on the back of the photos in our sorry excuse for a family album, and it seems my father did the same. Scrawled on the back in blue pen, it says, 'Dennis 1966'.

It's now clear I'm looking at a picture of my father. There's no denying he was a handsome young man and, even then, he had an eye for a well-tailored suit. The fresh face and broad smile are those of a man yet to truly experience the stresses and strains of life — certainly Dennis Hogan's life.

I switch it to the bottom of the pile and turn my attention to the next photo — the same young man leant up against a car with his arm around a pretty girl who looks equally untroubled by life. She also happens to look uncannily like a twenty-something version of me. I flip it over and it reads: 'Dennis and Susie 1967'.

The next dozen photos are also of my parents; taken over the latter part of the sixties and apparently charting their courtship. In each and every one of them my father's attention appears to be focused on my mother rather than the camera — the kind of dreamy look only someone truly in love would bestow.

I turn my attention to a picture of my mum stood beside a Christmas tree with a glass of something in hand. On the back it reads: 'Susie 1971' and her party dress does little to hide the bump in her tummy.

As I slip the photo to the back of the pile the lump in my throat stubbornly stays put.

The next image doesn't help. I have to clamp my hand over my mouth at the sight of a beaming couple with their new-born baby. I flip it over: 'Our little family 1972'. As tears well, I turn it over again. Unlike all the other photos, my father isn't gazing at my mother, but the tiny bundle she's cradling in her arms. Perhaps it's just my interpretation but that gaze appears to teem with pride and happiness.

In the silence of Mandy's office I can almost hear my heart breaking.

There are three more photos: two of a deliriously happy Susie Hogan holding baby Emma, and the final image which tips me over the edge. My father is seated in an armchair, cradling me in one arm, and gently stroking my cheek. On the back, it confirms my age as four months, and I know the smile on my little face is not a reflex, but prompted by my father's touch. Soon after — possibly within days of this photo being taken — he was stolen away from his little girl on the back of a wicked lie.

With tears streaming down my cheeks, I carefully lay the pile of photos on the desk. Despite the urge to curl up into a ball and sob myself dry, I reach for the final envelope. Trepidatiously, I peel it open and extract two sheets of folded paper. Taking a deep breath, I unfold them and cast my eyes across a handwritten letter. I fear the content will not so much break my heart, but tear it into tiny ribbons. Another deep breath and I begin reading ...

My dearest Emma

If you are reading this, my final hope — that one day we might salvage our relationship — has already passed. All I can now ask is you give me a few minutes of your time. You deserve to know the truth about your father.

I will start by saying whatever you have heard or read about me, it is not who I am. I could write a hundred pages explaining how I got to this point but it would be of no benefit to either of us. All you need to know is that I underestimated someone I considered a friend, and for that one error of judgement, I lost my liberty, the woman I loved, and my precious daughter. That so-called friend was Eric Birtles.

The reasons are long and complicated, and I wouldn't wish to burden you with the details. However, I beg of you — do not trust Eric for he is not what he seems. There is no reason for you to believe me, but you should know Eric and I were friends for over a decade before you were born — if he has never mentioned that fact, you must ask yourself why.

It was, I am afraid to say, Eric who orchestrated my conviction for a crime I did not commit.

If that were not sadistic enough, the evidence was so compelling I lost your mother as a result. I spent eighteen years in prison but, even on my release, the punishment continued as I tried to prove my innocence. I knew the only way I could regain your mother's trust, and indeed yours, would be to overturn my conviction.

Sadly, God took your poor mother before I had the chance. When she left, so too did my resolve.

I cannot put into words how much I wanted to be there for you in the days and weeks afterwards. You would not have known, but I watched her funeral service in the same way I've lived much of my life — hiding in the shadows.

You might question why I have never made contact to plead my case. As much as I wanted to, I feared you might befall the same fate as your mother. Life had made me a deeply suspicious man, and I've always had concerns that what happened to your mother wasn't in some way connected to my actions. Perhaps it was just paranoia, but knowing Eric Birtles has ingratiated himself into your life, and the depths he has plumbed in the past, I just could not take the risk. I chose to stay away to protect you, but know you were never far from my thoughts.

I would stress that while I was not guilty of the crime for which I was convicted, your father is not an innocent man. It pains me to admit it, but I have become consumed by hatred, anger, and a thirst for revenge. With nothing else in my life, vengeance has become my only companion.

I won't shame myself by admitting the details of my crimes but the difference between Eric and I is that my deeds have punished those deserving of punishment, and rewarded the worthy. I have tried to be a good man, and improve the lives of others. If I know anything about you, I know you will follow your instincts and draw your own conclusions.

Together with this letter you will find the photos which have helped preserve all I have of you and your mother — my memories. I treasured those four short months I had you in my life, and I cannot put into words how happy they were. I loved you from the moment I first held you, and I will love you till the moment I draw my last breath. That moment, I fear, will be soon, but know I am immensely proud of the woman you have become. Although I am your father in name alone, I pray one day you might feel inclined to learn more about the man I once was — the man who made you smile.

Whilst I cannot change the past, I hope you will allow me to make a difference to your future. Enclosed in the envelope are my solicitor's details, and all I own is now yours. There is a not-insignificant amount of money which you may do with as you wish — invest it, spend it, give it to charity — whatever you decide, it is a fraction of what I owe you.

All that remains is for me to ask one favour of you. When my time comes, I have secured a plot in the same cemetery as your mother. That plot is opposite her grave, and although it isn't quite where I hoped I would see out eternity, it's close enough. I won't ask for your forgiveness, but I would ask you to stop by one day and say goodbye. I have no right to ask, but perhaps it might help you move forward.

Look after yourself, my angel — Dad.

I want to read the letter again but I can barely see through the tears. A sadness — the like of which I've never felt — threatens to consume me, and I know I'm close to completely losing it. There is just one compulsion holding a total breakdown at bay: an immediate and compelling urge to visit my father's grave.

With shaking hands, I gather the letter and the photos together and return them to the envelope. I get to my feet, and as I search my handbag for a tissue the office door opens.

"Are you okay, Emma?" Mandy asks in a gentle voice.

I bite my lip and nod.

"The envelope. Was it left there by your dad?"

I nod again.

"I miss him," she says. "Ever so much."

Mandy steps across the carpet and pulls me into a hug. My usual instinct would be to flinch, but on this occasion my need for comfort outweighs any social awkwardness. Never has a hug been more welcome.

"He was a good man," she says as we finally break.

"So I've discovered."

"You might be interested to know, the committee have decided to re-name the NLH Foundation."

"Oh, really?"

"Yes, from next month, it will be known as the Dennis Hogan Foundation."

"Wow, that's ... I'm sure he'd be ever so proud ... as am I."

"It's the least we can do," she says, perching on the edge of the desk. "His legacy will live on for generations, we hope. Not least because of the fund he set up which will ensure we can continue our work."

"So, he ensured the charity still has sufficient funding?"

"Oh, yes. He left us several properties in his will, including this one. The rental income from those properties will more than cover our basic needs."

"That's good to know," I sniffle. "I don't suppose he ever told you how he funded his donations?"

"I did ask him once," she smiles. "But he just laughed and said it was his ill-gotten gains. I think he was too modest to tell me the truth."

If only you knew, Mandy. If only you knew.

"It's good to know he had a sense of humour."

"He certainly did, and all our volunteers loved him for it."

I reflect on Mandy's statement for a few seconds. "I don't suppose you're looking for volunteers at the moment?"

"We're always looking for volunteers," she chuckles. "Why? Did you have someone in mind?"

"Me, actually."

"Oh, wow. That would be amazing. And I'm sure Dennis would be so proud you were continuing his good work."

"I'm not sure I'll be quite as influential, but I'm kind of lost at the moment so you'd be doing me a favour ... well, two actually."

"Two?"

"You knew my dad better than anyone. I'd love to know what he was like, as a person, so who better to ask?"

She places her hand on my arm. "It would be an honour."

"Anyway, I'd better get going, and I'm sure you've got enough to be dealing with."

"That's for sure. The place is in a bit of a mess with the builders coming and going."

As I make my way to the door a final question begs to be asked.

"Can I ask, Mandy: why wasn't the damp in my dad's office fixed when he was here?"

"He insisted we leave his office alone, but he made me promise to get it sorted as a priority should anything happen to him."

I guess Mandy was one of the few people Dad could trust, and what better place to hide my envelope than beneath the floorboards of an office nobody knew he worked in.

We depart with another hug and a plan for me to call Mandy in a few days' time. I desperately need a dose of positivity in my life at the moment, and whilst investigating the Clawthorn membership is my priority, it's hard to find much positivity amongst all the lies and corruption. Soon enough, though, that project will be complete and volunteering at the Foundation will help fill the empty days.

I make a quick detour to the adjacent street where I spotted a florist on my drive in.

Armed with a dozen white orchids, I return to the car and take a moment to get my head straight. Ironically, I find myself stood at the edge of another cliff — an emotional one this time. Visiting my dad's grave could tip me over the edge, but I need to do this. As he said in his letter; maybe I do need to close this chapter of my life before I can truly move on.

For the first and, sadly, last time ever, I follow advice offered by my dad, and set off.

39.

My destination — Islington and St Pancras Cemetery — is a thirty minute drive away in North London. Mum grew up in Kentish Town and always said she wanted to be buried in that part of London when the time arrived. That time arrived far too soon but I did my best to honour her wishes. Having never handled funeral arrangements before, I remember, despite my constant haze, being staggered at the cost; particularly as Mum wanted to be buried rather than cremated. I was fortunate she invested in a modest life insurance policy to cover the cost.

Beyond honouring Mum's wishes, the grave also provided a haven where I've been able to relinquish my grief over the ensuing months and years since she passed. I've spent countless hours in the cemetery chatting away to a block of polished granite. Silly, I know, but I'm not sure how I'd have coped at times without those little chats with Mum. It's the bitterest of ironies this will be my first opportunity to chat with both my parents.

In a state of auto-pilot, I drive a little faster than usual and arrive at the cemetery within twenty-five minutes. I park up and, clutching the orchids, make my way through the gates. Just beyond those gates I'm greeted by two century-old oak trees either side of the path. Beneath the trees, a few dozen bright yellow daffodils bob a chirpy reminder spring is now here — a time for new beginnings, they say.

The path snakes on towards the far corner of the cemetery where

Mum's grave is located. I walk on with just the sound of my own footsteps for company. As I get within a dozen yards, I slow my pace and make for Mum's grave.

It's been almost a month since my last visit and the flowers I left on that occasion are a sorry sight. I squat down and replace them with six orchids.

"Sorry it's been a while, Mum," I whisper, getting back to my feet. "Things have been ... actually, I don't know where to begin."

I place my hand atop the cold granite.

"I've found something out ... about Dad."

Pausing for a moment I try to find the right words.

"He, um, was innocent, Mum, and I feel awful ... just terrible. He wanted us to be together, as a family, but that chance was ..."

I choke back the lump in my throat. What I want to say goes against everything I've thought to be true, but there is nothing else I can say.

"If there really is a heaven, it would mean so much to think you're with Dad again, and you're happy. He left me some photos, of you both, and you looked so happy together ... so in love. There were a few other photos too: of me as a baby. They kinda broke my heart but tell Dad he did make me smile again — he'll know what I mean."

I use my coat sleeve to wipe a tear from my cheek.

"Anyway I'd better go say hello to him. I'll be back soon."

I scan the area for a new gravestone and spot a simple wooden cross marking the slight hump of freshly turned earth.

Steeling myself I cross the grass and kneel down. There is a small brass plaque fixed to the front of the cross etched with just a name — Dennis Seamus Hogan.

The guilt I've been carrying for the last two weeks peaks as I recall my conversation with Penny at the second-hand clothes store. I used my dad's headstone as a bargaining tool, and concluded I would rather dance on Dennis Hogan's grave than mark it with a granite tribute. Here now — knelt in front of this token timber cross — I would give anything to take back those words.

"I'm so sorry, Dad," I murmur. "And I promise I'll sort you out with a proper headstone soon."

I carefully lay the remaining orchids in front of the cross. "I'm not sure if you like orchids but Mum did. Actually, she loved flowers of every kind, but I guess you already know that."

It would be madness to expect anything other than silence in reply, but still, it pains me when that's all I get.

"There so much I want to say to you. I wish you could hear me."

Almost on cue, the sun escapes from behind a drifting cloud, warming my back while casting a shadow across the grass. It's a shadow too long to be mine.

I turn my head, and squint at a silhouetted figure on the path.

That figure then speaks. "You'd be amazed what dead men can hear."

Much like when Eric Birtles reappeared in Dorset, reason takes up battle with my senses — the voice is too distinctive to be anyone else, but ... no ... it can't be.

If this is a cruel dream, it feels too real. How can I possibly feel the warmth of the sun on my face, or smell the slight scent of freshly cut orchids?

I slowly stand up whilst focusing on the dull ache in my lower back to determine if this is, as I fear, just a scene being played out in my troubled mind.

The sun slips behind another cloud, and the silhouette is no more.

"Oh ... my God."

My mind erupts into pandemonium as it tries, and fails, to deal with the barrage of emotions.

"I ... how?" I gasp. "I ... I thought ..."

Clement steps onto the grass but I remain frozen on the spot.

"Alright, doll."

Belatedly, my leg muscles engage and I virtually throw myself at Clement. I bury my head in his chest gripping him tightly for fear he'll slip away again.

"Shh. It's okay," he says softly.

Seconds turn to minutes as I cling to my saviour, and joy eventually edges out the fear. I take a step back but keep my hands locked around his waist.

"I thought I'd lost you," I just about manage to whimper.

"Told you, didn't I? Miracles happen sometimes."

"But ... the cliff. How on earth ...?"

"Does it matter?"

"No, I guess ... how did you know I'd be here?"

"Just a hunch you'd wanna come and see your old man's grave at some point, so I've been hanging around here every day for the last two weeks."

"Every day?"

"Yeah."

I fall into his arms again, and wallow in his musky scent. With every breath, the loneliness and the emptiness gradually ebb away. My future no longer looks quite so bleak.

"You okay?" he asks.

"I think so. I'm just hoping this isn't a dream."

"It's no dream, doll."

I look up at him just to be sure he isn't a figment of my imagination. Not trusting my eyes alone I gently place my hand on his face.

"It's really you," I choke. "You've come back to me."

He takes my hand in his, and plants a kiss on my forehead. "I have, and I ain't going nowhere ever again."

As I lose myself in his eyes the world feels an immeasurably brighter place. Ever since that night in Dorset, I've been haunted by a vision of this same face but, the last time I saw it, it certainly wasn't etched with a warm, contented smile. To rid myself of that memory is a blessing in itself.

This face, in this moment, could not be more perfect.

A realisation jars.

I continue to study his perfect face — not a single scratch or bruise. How could anyone fall from a cliff so high, onto jagged rocks, and walk away without so much as a graze? I try to shake off the question but it won't leave peacefully.

Inadvertently, my question prompts another memory — the scene beyond that cliff edge is not one I'm ever likely to forget. Reluctantly, I drag that image from the back of my mind to confirm what I already know.

I take a step back.

"What happened?"

"Eh?"

"That night?"

"Dunno what you mean."

I catch myself just before I quiz him further. I'm being ridiculous — surely all that matters is he's alive?

"I'm being silly. Forget it."

His smile returns as he squeezes my hand. I look down and can't help but check his hand for evidence of the fall. Lots of old scars but not even a broken fingernail.

I should be ecstatic to see Clement again, and I am, but recent events have added a sceptical, suspicious edge to my curious nature. Such is the gnawing doubt I begin to question my own memories. Have they somehow become corrupted by the grief I've suffered of late?

A few seconds thought, and I conclude it's not a hazy memory undermining my reunion with Clement. I've awoken my curiosity and it won't settle until it's been fed.

"Um, how come there's not a mark on you?"

"Must have just got lucky."

Containing my incredulity is not easy, but I bury it beneath a concerned expression.

"Have you been to hospital?"

"Why would I go to the hospital?"

"Well, you fell from a ninety foot cliff onto jagged rocks, and then somehow managed to swim several hundred yards in a stormy sea. And that's before you factor in the temperature of the water — I know you said you don't feel the cold, but you're not immune to hypothermia."

"As I said: must have just been lucky."

"And as I asked: have you been to the hospital?"

"There's nothing wrong with me."

"I know, and that's what I don't understand. Two men fell from a cliff, and one of them died instantly. The other turns up two weeks later without so much as a scratch on him. Would you not be mildly curious how that happened if the roles were reversed?"

"Thought you'd be pleased to see me," he frowns.

"What? No ... of course I am. It's just ..."

"Knew this was a bad idea," he grunts. "I shouldn't have come here."

"Of course you should have. I'm just a bit shocked; that's all."

I try to shake off the tethers which are currently holding me back from what should be a joyous reunion. As much as I try, something doesn't feel right, and Clement can clearly sense my indecision.

"Sorry. I gotta go."

He turns and walks away. Coupled with his lack of an explanation for the supposed miracle his abrupt departure only fuels my suspicion that I'm not in full possession of the facts.

"Wait," I call out. He ignores me.

I gather up all my doubts and scuttle after him; covering a dozen yards of path before I draw level.

"How did you know my dad was buried here?" I ask.

"Just leave it," he replies, without breaking stride.

Frustrated, I throw him another question.

"What happened that evening? I saw Eric drag you over the cliff and I spent ... I don't know ... twenty minutes scouring the sea just in case you somehow survived the fall. But ... you weren't there."

No reply.

"Clement, please. I just want some answers."

He comes to an abrupt halt and looks skyward. His pained expression slowly fades before he looks down at me.

"You really wanna know the truth?"

Whatever his truth is, I can tell from the tone of his voice I probably don't want to hear it any more than he wants to say it. Nevertheless, I nod.

"Come with me," he says, taking my hand.

He leads me further along the path towards the cemetery gates.

"Where are we going?" I ask.

No answer.

Trepidation builds with every step; to the point I can't bear it any longer. I'm about to stand my ground and demand an answer when his pace slows. He comes to a stop, releases my hand, and fixes me with eyes that look almost soulless. Then, the slightest nod towards a neglected gravestone six feet beyond the path.

I stare up at him, confused, before shifting my gaze to the gravestone he now appears fixated upon.

On first inspection there is nothing remarkable about the simple slab of stone. Age-weathered, and covered with a patchwork of mottled moss and lichen, the engraved words are illegible from my position on the path.

"Look closer," Clement orders.

I take half-a-dozen steps across the grass and the name of the poor soul inhabiting the grave comes into focus. There is no surname, but confirmation of the date he died — 9th December 1975.

On no level do I understand what I'm looking at. I now know the headstone is etched with a name I've become ever so familiar with, but confusion still reigns.

"I ... I don't understand," I stammer. "Why are you showing me a grave belonging to someone who shares your name?"

"It ain't someone."

"Sorry?"

"You wanted the truth — that's my grave."

THE END

Before You Go...

I genuinely hope you enjoyed reading Clement's latest adventure. If you did, and have a few minutes spare, I would be eternally grateful if you could leave a (hopefully positive) review on Amazon. A mention on Facebook or Twitter would be equally appreciated. I know it's a pain but it's the only way us indie authors can compete with the big publishing houses.

Stay in Touch...

For more information about me, my books, and to receive updates on my new releases, please visit my website: www.keithapearson.co.uk

If you have any questions or general feedback, you can also reach me, or follow me via...

Facebook: www.facebook.com/pearson.author

Twitter: www.twitter.com/keithapearson

Printed in Great Britain
by Amazon